Also by Bruce Bawer

The Victims' Revolution

The New Quislings (e-book)

Surrender

While Europe Slept

Stealing Jesus

Beyond Queer (editor)

House and Home (with Steve Gunderson and Rob Morris)

Prophets and Professors

A Place at the Table

The Aspect of Eternity

Coast to Coast

The Screenplay's the Thing

Diminishing Fictions

Innocence (chapbook)

The Contemporary Stylist

The Middle Generation

The Alhambra

The
Alhambra

A Novel
by
Bruce Bawer

SWAMP FOX EDITIONS

2017

SWAMP FOX EDITIONS, 2017

Copyright © 2017 by Bruce Bawer

All rights reserved.

ISBN-13: 978-1537471112

ISBN-10: 1537471112

For Michael and Mathias

STEVE DISCH WAS ONLY TWENTY-THREE years old and still a student at UCLA Film School when his first movie came out and made him famous. Well, not really famous. *Sentimental Education* was what they call a "small film." The cast consisted entirely of his friends and fellow students, and Steve himself served as writer, director, cameraman, editor, and lighting and set designer. The costumes were the actors' own clothes, and there was no makeup to speak of, and certainly no special effects. The budget was far too tiny for that – too tiny for almost anything, in fact, except for the telling of a simple story about two characters. Steve told it effectively enough to get *Sentimental Education* into a couple of second-tier film festivals, at one of which it won an "audience favorite" award.

The movie's saga might have ended there, if not for a bit of serendipity. One of those festivals happened to be attended by a veteran novelist who saw *Sentimental Education* and loved it. He loved it so much that he wrote a glowing article about it in a national gay newsmagazine, and then another in the *New Yorker,* no less. This beautiful film about the deep but unspoken and unconsummated love between two male college students, he argued, was one of the best gay movies ever made, and represented a breakthrough in the cinematic treatment of gay men's lives. Steve, in his view, had managed, with his inexpensive camera equipment and his non-professional actors, to capture precisely what love was like for young gay men in "these times" – "these times" being the 1980s – who don't even realize they're gay.

The articles about *Sentimental Education* drew the attention of gay cinephiles around the world. That summer, the film was shown at gay-pride events in two dozen cities. For several months, Steve rode a roller-coaster of media attention. He received bags full of fan mail. He traveled around the U.S. and Europe attending screenings of the film. At some of these events he would give a talk before the screening; at others, he'd be interviewed or answer questions afterwards. Following every screening, audience members would line up to shake his hand and tell him how much they identified with the main character in his movie.

Invariably, at those Q & A's, somebody would ask if the film was autobiographical. Steve always insisted it wasn't. He was lying. Virtually every line of dialogue had come directly out of the diary he'd kept as an undergraduate at the University of California at Davis. It was there that he'd met Daniel Loban, a fellow French major. The two star-crossed lovers in the movie weren't just based on Steve and Daniel; they *were* Steve and Daniel. Every word they said to each other, Steve and Daniel had said to each other. Every look, every gesture, every little detail was drawn from memory. For Steve, indeed, the making of the film had been nothing more or less than a monomaniacal effort to recall and record, with as much precision as possible, his experience with Daniel from the moment they'd first set eyes on each other until the moment, two years later, when Steve had finally confessed his love to Daniel and received an ice-cold reply: *"I'm not gay."* After which Daniel, who had been by far the closest friend he'd ever known, refused to talk to him, returned his letters unopened, and looked away when they passed each other on campus.

For Steve, *Sentimental Education* wasn't just a movie – it was a life-saving mission, the life in question being his own. After Daniel's rejection, Steve had decided that the only way he could survive it and move on would be to recreate their experience together on film. It made no logical sense, but he was a driven man, and in the end it actually worked: he labored obsessively on the film, and once it was in the can, the clouds lifted and he was able to get on with his life. The Steve who traveled around the country talking about his film was chipper, cheery, and, once he'd gotten the hang of the whole process, even glib, as if he'd been doing this sort of thing for years. No one who saw him onstage, fielding questions about *Sentimental Education,* would ever have guessed that only a year earlier, he had been in the slough of despond, barely able to talk to anyone. Nor did he ever admit this – because that would mean admitting that the film was pure autobiography. And he wasn't about to do *that*, because then some enterprising reporter would be able to figure out who Daniel was, and would rope *him* into all this – and the last thing Steve wanted was to drag Daniel into the spotlight, to draw him back into Steve's own life after he had gone to such lengths to exorcise him. And so he told interviewer after interviewer, audience after audience, that the story he'd recounted in *Sentimental Education* was entirely fictional. And after a while, after he'd watched the movie dozens of times in the company of dozens of different audiences, this lie almost felt like the truth.

And then the whole thing was over. The world moved on from *Sentimental Education*, and it was time for Steve to move on, too. He'd managed to make a bit of a name for himself, and had his pick of Hollywood agents. He chose one. He spent months trying to concoct an idea for a second film that some producer would find bankable, but couldn't. So his agent started sending him scripts. The thread running through all of them was an unabashed adherence to formula – a total lack of any consideration for, or understanding of, human feeling.

In short, none of the scripts excited him, though he finally picked one anyway and turned it into a movie. It wasn't a great picture, and Steve accepted much of the blame, because he hadn't really cared about it. The film came and went without a trace, and afterwards, Steve wasn't such a hot commodity any more. Also, he was in debt. So when he was offered a job, he took it. The job was as a writer for *That's Our Abby,* a series on the Disney Channel for kids in their early teens.

FIFTEEN YEARS LATER, STEVE WAS STILL working for Disney. *That's Our Abby* had finished up a successful eight-year run, after which he'd been put on another show with the exact same demographic (and pretty much the exact same premise and characters), *Nikki and Friends.* It did well too. Steve made good money, most of which he just banked because he didn't have expensive tastes. He was perfectly happy with the cheap, one-bedroom rental in Reseda that he'd lived in since film school, he didn't mind driving his old, beat-up 1982 Chevrolet Malibu, and he had no interest in traveling anywhere.

During his years at Disney, his life had become highly routinized. He'd get up at six, drive across the valley to the Disney studios in Burbank, and after work drive to West Hollywood, where he'd grab dinner at some place on Santa Monica and then have a few drinks at one of the bars. Sometimes he'd meet somebody and go home with him. Once in a while it would be somebody he'd been with before, perhaps months or years earlier. He made a few friends this way, guys he'd get together with on the weekends for brunch or a movie. But he never came close to anything that could be called a relationship, let alone a romance.

Then, one morning in the spring of 2000, he couldn't get out of bed. He didn't feel ill, just immobilized. He called in sick and just lay there all day, getting up only to drink water and go to the bathroom. He did the same thing the next day and the next. After staying home for three weeks, during which he lost fifteen pounds, he got up out of bed, went to his computer, and booked a flight to Amsterdam.

II

A YEAR LATER, STEVE LAY IN BED in his furnished studio apartment in Amsterdam, dreaming of L.A. In the dream, variations on which he'd had several times since moving to Amsterdam a few weeks earlier, Steve was driving. That was all – just driving. Speeding down a wide, straight boulevard, past block after block of identical storefronts, gas stations, strip malls. Driving endlessly, alone, in a convertible with its top down, the air as dry as could be, the car never turning or slowing or speeding up, and never reaching a destination.

The alarm went off, a shrill, nasty, metallic sound. He woke to a powerful feeling of damp, the smell of mildew, and the faint spring sunlight streaming in through the window in the top half of the Dutch door that opened onto the garden.

Deur: that was door. *Tuin:* that was garden.

He turned to slam down the button on the top of the taped-up walnut-brown bedside clock radio, circa 1975, that had come with the flat: the time was 11:30 AM.

Klok: that was clock. That was easy. The word for wristwatch wasn't so easy, however. It was *horloge.*

For some reason he couldn't fully fathom, learning Dutch had become an urgent mission for him. It was as if he wanted not only to escape his own country but to escape his own language. Yet it was hard going. He'd majored in French in college, but he was no longer a college kid. It was harder now to get that part of the brain to work at top capacity. Then again, he was enjoying the challenge. Trying to learn Dutch was like trying to seduce a beautiful object of one's affection. The effort made him feel young.

He sat up, leaned forward, and turned the loose, plastic on-off knob on the bright cerulean-blue TV set, likewise circa 1975, that was also part of the original furnishings. It took a few seconds to warm up. He leaned back as a picture emerged. The news was on. There was an anchorwoman, and behind her an image of two male silhouettes and matching wedding rings. Steve couldn't understand every word she was saying, but he could make out enough to get the gist. *Huwelijk:* marriage. *Vandaag:* today. Of course! Somehow he'd forgotten: at midnight today, April first, 2001, the Netherlands had become the first country in the world to legalize same-sex marriage.

Getting up from bed, Steve walked over to the large white kitchen sink, turned on the water – thump, thump, thump – ran some of it into a banged-up old saucepan, turned on the ancient electric stove (which he'd recognized immediately on first looking at the apartment: it was identical to the one in the Anne Frank House), and set the pan down on the front burner. It wobbled. *Well,* he reflected, *here I am in Amsterdam on a historic day. I guess the bars will be busy.*

And then, suddenly, the voice from the TV stopped. Steve walked over to the bedside. The picture was out.

He shook his head. From the back of the kitchen chair beside the bed, he picked up the old pair of jeans he'd been wearing for the last three days and pulled them on. He shambled over to the door – not the one that opened onto the garden, but the one that led to the corridor – threw it open, and walked down the slanted wine-red carpet with its multiple layers of stains and then up a steep, narrow, dusty flight of stairs.

At the landing he hesitated for a second. Was it too early to disturb him? No, how ridiculous. He knocked vigorously.

"*Ja?*" came a weak, raspy voice from behind the door.

"*Het is Steve.*"

"*Wie?*"

"*Het is Steve!*" Steve shouted more loudly. "*Ik heb geen electric!*"

A pause. Steve was about to speak again when Jan replied. "*Een minuut. Ik kom.*"

Slowly, Steve walked back to his apartment, went in, shut the door, and sat on the bed in the semi-darkness. After waiting for two minutes, he stood up, threw on his scratchy emerald-green sweater from college, stepped into his sneakers, turned off the stove, and left.

It was a nice, crisp October morning, chilly but not too chilly. On the sidewalk he turned right, walked to the corner, then turned left onto Weteringshans, which was crowded with people bicycling in both directions and school groups headed for the Rijksmuseum. After ten minutes or so he arrived at Leidseplein, where the bike, tram, and pedestrian traffic were all at peak level. A strolling accordionist played the *Merry Widow Waltz*. A mime in a black full-body leotard performed in front of the McDonalds on the corner, surrounded by tourists. At Hoopman's, the door was open, and customers sat with cups of coffee at some of the outside tables. Steve walked in, took a window table, and met the eye of a young waitress who was standing by the bar. She came over and greeted him in Irish-accented English. He ordered a coffee.

He was halfway through his third cup when a tall, dark-haired young guy walked in. He had on a forest-green jacket and a plum-colored scarf and was carrying a copy of *Gay Krant,* a monthly gay magazine. He looked around, saw Steve, asked a question with his eyes. Steve nodded; the guy smiled. Steve stood up as the guy came over to his table. The guy was a good five inches taller than he was, and about ten years younger. He was handsome, and had a look of immense self-assurance. "Bram?" Steve said.

"Yes," said Bram. "Thank you for meeting me. I'm a big fan of *Sentimental Education*." His English was impeccable and almost unaccented, like that of virtually every person his age or younger in Amsterdam.

"Thanks." They shook hands. Bram slid a black bag off his shoulder and removed his coat, then set both down on a chair and sat in the chair beside it. The waitress was already on her way.

"May I call you Steve?" said Bram.

"Please."

The waitress was standing over them. *"Kaffee, alstublieft,"* Bram said, at once looking up at her and pulling a small tape recorder out of his bag. The waitress nodded and walked away; Bram set the tape recorder down on the table between him and Steve.

"Do you mind this, Steve?" Bram asked, nodding toward it.

"Nope."

"Steve, let's just start with the first question that our readers will be asking. What made you leave L.A. and come to Amsterdam, of all places?"

Why did Bram keep repeating his name? It felt vaguely condescending. "Well, as you may know, Bram," Steve said. "I've been working for the past few years for Disney."

"Right," Bram said flatly.

Steve looked into his eyes. Nothing.

"In California," Steve added.

An understanding but carefully calibrated smile

began to form on Bram's face. "Nice weather," he conceded. "Nicer than *this*."

He jerked his head toward the breezy square outside the window.

"Writing a show for *children*," Steve said.

Bram nodded, with a small charming laugh.

"Spending hours in my car. Driving mile after mile. No matter where I happened to be going, it just took forever."

"There are worse fates."

"I know. But after a while you need a change. Not that I've stopped working for Disney."

"No?"

"No. I got them to let me work from here for the time being. Reduced workload in exchange for a somewhat lower salary. After a year we'll re-evaluate the situation."

"Why haven't you made more films?" Bram obviously wasn't interested in the Disney job.

"I wanted to. It didn't work out." Bram's eyes were drilling into him. Big, green eyes. Silence. He wanted more. Steve went on: "It's a tough business. Even the most powerful people don't get to make the movies they really want to make."

"I know," said Bram. "Everybody knows about that. Even hermits in Tibet know everything about Hollywood. But why Amsterdam?"

"Because it's the opposite of L.A. Intimate. Beautiful. Capitalist, of course, but in a way that seems humane. A way that L.A. isn't. The obscene wealth in that city, and the desperation to show it off, the vulgarity of it all, is beyond belief. And the garbage they're willing to crank out in order to keep shoveling in all that cash, and never risk making something a little better for fear they may earn a little less – it's all just appalling. Also, Amsterdam is *secular*."

"Well, Hollywood isn't exactly run by religious nuts, is it?"

"No, but it caters to them. It feels infinitely superior to them, but it's terrified of them. You wouldn't believe how many innocuous things I've had to take out of scripts because the network was worried about how the religious right might react. That's unimaginable here. There's all these pretty churches, their steeples popping up above the other buildings, but they don't seem threatening, just charming. Reminders of history. Which is another nice thing. There's history at every turn here, while L.A. feels totally historyless, as if it was created out of absolute nothingness two weeks ago. And all those cars! Even since moving here, I dream every night about all that driving. That endless checkerboard of boulevards. Miles and miles of houses and palm trees and strip malls."

"Palm trees aren't *so* bad," Bram said, his

eyebrows rising in a slightly effeminate way, his smile a touch flirtatious.

"Have you been to L.A.?"

"Yes. I liked it."

"Why?"

Bram smiled. "I guess because it was so different from this."

Steve nodded. "Precisely. But it's so *sprawling.* Even after you've lived there forever, there's something – I don't know, scary is too strong a word – but something overwhelming about the sheer scale of it."

"You could say the same thing about America itself."

"Exactly. And I *would* say that about America. That's part of it, too."

"When did you first visit Amsterdam?"

"Just over a year ago."

"And you felt...?"

"I felt *safe* here."

Bram shrugged. "I felt safe in L.A.," he said.

"Well, you're a big boy."

No response. "I also felt safe in New York," Bram added. "I lived there for a couple of years."

"Really?"

"Yes. As a student."

"Where'd you study?"

"NYU. Journalism."

"Cool."

"I loved it. All those tall buildings of concrete and steel. It feels like a fortress of civilization. So much wealth. So much power. You look at those towers and you think: what force could ever take these down? You know what I mean?"

"Absolutely. But of course in New York you also have this sense of just how big and crazy and intimidating the world is. In Amsterdam it's the opposite: when you're here you can get lulled so easily into feeling that the world is this calm and gentle place. Orderly. Beautiful. Just the right size. With just the right combination of old and new. Canals, cobblestones, bicycles. People who all seem to get along somehow, to make the most of their corner of the world, and even make it feel almost like a corner of heaven. I mean, just think: as of today, for the first time in human history, a country has legalized gay marriage. And it's no coincidence that it's *this* country."

"When do you think America will legalize it?"

"I can't imagine. The religious right is just too powerful. Fucking idiots."

"You're not feeling too patriotic these days."

"No, I'm not. You're so lucky in this country, not having a religious right. And I'm lucky too. To be here. Away from *them*."

Bram smiled. Steve was delighted to see that it

was a sweet smile, a genuine smile. "Well," Bram said, "*I'm glad you're here.*" Their eyes met.

THREE HOURS LATER, STEVE LEFT Bram's tiny flat on Bloemstraat in the Jordaan and made his way slowly toward Rozengracht.

It had been a fun interlude, if a bit unsettling. Bram, who at Hoppman had seemed rather smug and supercilious, had proven to be surprisingly tender and vulnerable. When it was over, Bram had wanted to cuddle, and when Steve stood up instead and said politely that he had to go, Bram asked, plaintively, almost pleadingly, when they might get together again. He already seemed to be seeing this brief encounter as the beginning of something. Steve hadn't been prepared for that. One thing he'd liked about Amsterdam from the beginning was that these Dutch guys were even more matter-of-fact about sexual encounters than L.A. guys were. They weren't into romance or love talk. They just wanted to have sex and maybe become friends – no, not even friends, really. Drinking buddies.

Turning at Rozengracht, Steve walked slowly toward the city center. At Nieuwezijds Voorburgwal, he went into Gall & Gall, across from the Royal Palace, where he bought two bottles of the usual sauvignon blanc for five guilders – just two dollars fifty – apiece. Then he headed down to Koningsplein, a small square dominated by a big three-story bookstore, and turned on to Reguliers-dwarsstraat, Amsterdam's principal "gay street." It was Sunday afternoon, and several of the bars had happy hours, although he could never remember exactly which places had happy hours at exactly which times. He started to pass April, the biggest and most popular gay bar in town, because it didn't look busy enough in there to be happy hour, but then decided to look in anyway, on the off chance that Jordy might be there.

Jordy, who was in his early twenties and was studying to be a clothes designer, had been Steve's first friend in Amsterdam. Frisky, effeminate, full of energy, he was the perfect Dutch *vriendje,* who at the end of an evening of beers and gossip about Amsterdam's fashion scene would offer Steve a roll in the hay as casually as he might offer a cigarette. Steve hadn't seen Jordy in a few days and missed his company. But when he made a quick circuit of the bar, which proved to be busier than it had looked from outside, he saw no sign of him.

Heading back out onto the street, Steve felt a tap on his shoulder. He turned – and looked up. It was Joop, all six-foot-seven of him, looking as movie-star gorgeous as ever. As always, he was dressed casually but neatly, in an indigo polo shirt and slim-fit jeans. "You walked right by me," Joop said. "I was at the bar with a friend. Come join us." Steve did so. Even before he'd slid onto the stool, Joop had ordered him a *biertje.*

Joop's friend was a heavy-set, bespectacled older guy with a salt-and-pepper beard and a mole on his cheek. He wore a gray beret, and a brown sport coat over a maroon turtleneck. With a solemn expression on his face, he grunted out his name: "Huub." His voice was gravelly, his manner gruff. He scratched his chin.

"Steve."

"British? American?" For some reason, they always said "British" first.

"American."

From the look on Huub's face, it seemed to be the wrong answer. That was often the case. It was fine to be British or Irish, a plus to be a Canadian or Australian or New Zealander, but being American was a definite no-no. America was a superpower, a warmonger, full of loud, illiberal bigots who strode around the world as if they owned it. Steve looked away from Huub, picked up his beer, and took a sip of it. Piled up in front of Huub on the bar, he saw, were four old morocco-bound books.

"Mooie boeken," said Steve.

Huub snorted, presumably at his bad pronunciation, and replied, in stuffy, Oxbridge-accented English, "I own an antiquarian bookstore in Den Haag. That's The Hague to you." He reached into his jacket and, with a self-regarding flourish, handed Steve his business card. Steve looked at it, then pocketed it.

"I always thought it would be fun to run a bookstore," he said. This was obviously a stupid thing to say.

Ignoring Steve, Huub turned to Joop and asked him in Dutch what he'd done the night before. "*Niets,*" Joop replied. Nothing. He'd just stayed at home and listened to music. Joop then switched to English. "Do you know who this is?" he asked Huub, nodding toward Steve. "Do you know the name Steve Disch?"

"No." Huub scratched his chin again.

"You never heard of a film called *Sentimental Education?*"

"Well, of course I know the novel by Flaubert. Is it an adaptation?"

"No," Joop said.

"The title is a reference to Flaubert," said Steve. "But there's no direct connection."

"A *reference* to Flaubert," Huub said. "Interesting choice of words. Would you say it is an homage?"

"If you like."

"It's a love story," Joop said. "About two boys in college. Who love each other but are both too scared about being gay to ever say or do anything about their love for each other."

"When is this set?" Huub growled, looking at Joop as if Steve himself weren't there.

Joop looked at Steve. "About fifteen years ago," Steve said.

Huub nodded. "Not long ago. But at the same time, quite long ago."

"Yes."

"In just the last two decades," Huub said slowly, "the world has changed so much. So much! And so fast. It's impossible to explain to younger gay people nowadays. How you could be desperately in love and yet feel blocked from acting upon your feelings. Or speaking them out loud to the one you loved. Or even, perhaps, from acknowledging them to yourself."

"That's what the film's about," Steve said.

"I assume – " Huub paused to cough into his hand. "I assume it's autobiographical."

Steve had always lied, and lied smoothly, when asked this question. Now, suddenly, maybe because of Joop's presence, he couldn't bring himself to lie. But even before he could put a sentence together, Huub responded to his hesitation.

"That's a yes. What was his name?"

"Daniel," said Steve. It felt funny. It sounded funny. He hadn't spoken the name in years.

Huub nodded. "Not Dan. Or Danny."

Steve smiled. "Never. Always Daniel."

"And you never said 'I love you' to each other."

"No."

"But you're sure it was mutual."

"Yes."

Huub took this in, then picked up his beer. Steve and Joop did the same.

In his head, Steve continued talking to Huub: *Yes, I know that and more, much more. I know that Daniel saw me across a classroom on the very first day of college and decided then and there to make me his best friend. He proceeded to court me, whether he consciously viewed it that way or not, in the same way that any straight boy courts a girl, and he won me. There was nothing remotely physical about it - no talk of being in love, or of being gay. We were best friends - friends to the exclusion of everyone else; friends living together in our own world, so close, after those first few weeks, that when one of us walked into a room, the other one knew just from looking into his eyes where he'd just been and whom he'd been talking to. Friends who, on occasion, shared a bed, saying good night with a long, lingering stare, and then rolling over to face away from each other. Friends who, one evening, stood side by side at a sink in a dormitory bathroom, our heads touching as we stared into each other's eyes in the mirror, both silent until Daniel whispered: "Our eyes are exactly the same color."*

"So what ever happened to him?" Huub asked.

"To Daniel?"

"Yes."

"He went on to a very glamorous job working for the government."

"What do you mean, glamorous?"

"I mean the kind of job you can't talk about."

Huub scrunched up his face. "If you can't talk about it, how can there be any glamour attached to it?"

"Good question. Perhaps *glamorous* isn't the *mot juste.*"

"Is he with another guy?"

"No. He got married – to a woman. And he became a father. He lives in Europe now."

"Have you ever been in contact with him?"

"No."

"And are you still in love with him?"

"No." This Steve said firmly and without hesitation.

For the first time, Huub stared closely into Steve's eyes.

"I believe you," he finally said. "But what about this one?" He jerked his head toward Joop. "There's something between you two, I can see it." His tone was matter-of-fact, throwaway, Dutch.

"Well," Steve said haltingly, looking at Joop. "Joop and I – we – "

"We're good friends," Joop said.

Huub looked at Steve and then at Joop, as if studying the title pages of two old vellum folios of undetermined provenance. Then he finished off his beer, picked up his books, and stood up. "Well," he said, scratching his chin one last time. "All I can say is *carpe diem*. And *tot ziens*." As he walked out, Steve noticed he had a limp.

"So," he said to Joop. "How do you know him?"

"Just from here. He's always offering to pay me for sex."

"Did you ever take him up on it?"

Joop made a face. "What do you take me for?"

Steve shrugged. "If he paid me in nice old books like those ones he had with him, I might have to think about it."

Joop grinned and shook his head. "Do you want another beer?"

"Yes." Joop gestured to the bartender. Steve and Joop sat there in silence and waited for their beers. Joop didn't speak until after they'd gotten them and taken a slug.

"So," he said. "Here you are. Living in Amsterdam."

Steve shrugged. "I told you."

"And I didn't believe you."

"Who would? It doesn't make any sense. My moving here."

"I should have known you well enough to understand you meant it."

"I meant everything," Steve said.

"I realize that now," Joop said. "So did I."

"I know."

"So. What kind of glamorous job?"

"What?"

"Your beloved from college. What kind of glamorous job does he do for the government?"

"Believe it or not, he's in the CIA."

"And you said he lives in Europe?"

"In Prague."

"So he's a spy?"

"I guess so."

"How do you know?"

"What do you mean?"

"How do you know for sure that he's in the CIA? Isn't that the sort of thing they're supposed to keep to themselves?"

"Never mind. I know."

"But how? Did he tell you?"

"No. We had a professor who was an old CIA man. Before he became an academic, he ran a cultural foundation that was a CIA front. He told us about it. I wasn't sure at the time if it was true or not, because he was a big drunk who liked to brag about how many women he'd slept with – "

"Some professor."

"I know. He was a scandal, but they couldn't fire him. Tenure."

"So he told you about this CIA front."

"Yes. And years later, after he died, I ran

across a reference to it in some magazine – the *Atlantic*, I think, or maybe *Harpers*. Someplace like that. Everything he'd said about the foundation was right there in the article. Anyway, I know he recruited Daniel. I just know it. It makes sense. I know from following Daniel's moves online that after college he went to the Harvard School of Government and then entered the Foreign Service and was sent to the U.S. Embassy in Prague. After a few years he left the Foreign Service and took a job at some international corporation I never heard of."

"Also in Prague?"

"Yes. But both jobs have been covers."

"How can you know that?"

"I know it. I know him. But enough about him. And me. What's new with you?"

Joop brought him up to date. He'd changed jobs – last year he'd been working at McDonalds; now he was a security guard at a store on Kalverstraat. Steve told Joop where he was living now.

"Maybe you could give me the phone number?" Joop said.

"Of course," Steve said. He asked the bartender for a pen and a piece of paper, and wrote it down, along with the address, then handed it to Joop.

"Thank you," Joop said, pocketing it carefully.

"You're welcome," Steve said.

Ten minutes later, having said he needed to catch up with work, Steve was back out on the street, walking home.

He didn't know how to feel about seeing Joop again. It had been bound to happen. He probably should have phoned Joop weeks ago, as soon as he'd settled in. He'd told himself so at the time. But he didn't want to give Joop the wrong idea. For Joop was the one person who'd ever said to him those three terrifying words that he himself had said to Daniel all those years ago: "I love you."

THREE DAYS LATER, STEVE WAS HAVING his morning coffee when the phone rang. It was his friend Henk, a professor of gay studies at the University of Amsterdam. Steve had met Henk years ago, when Henk had a sabbatical year at UCLA. It was not long after *Sentimental Education* came out, and Henk had written a nice review of it for some Dutch academic journal. Steve had looked Henk up during his first visit to Amsterdam, and had met him for drinks regularly ever since. There had never been anything remotely sexual between them: there seemed to be a quiet understanding on both their parts that they weren't each other's type. Probably, Steve had reflected more than once, they were too much the *same* type. In any case, aside from having a certain European-academic dryness, Henk was a good guy to have a drink with. They'd met most recently a few weeks earlier, after Steve had moved into his apartment. Much of their conversation that day had been about how awful the apartment was.

"Are you still looking for a new place?" Henk asked now.

"I can't say I'm actively looking," Steve replied, "but if you know about something I'd definitely be interested."

"Well, it's like this. I've just run into an old friend. He wants to sublet his place for six months. It's kind of urgent: he had somebody lined up, but the guy just pulled out and Rob – that's my friend's name, Rob – is leaving this week."

Henk read out a phone number, and Steve called it immediately after hanging up. Rob spoke excellent, mellifluous British English, of a kind rarely heard these days except in old English movies; in fact he sounded like a character in a Noël Coward play. "Lovely to hear from you," he said. "I'm a great admirer of *Sentimental Education.* It would be grand if you could come up some time before lunch." He gave Steve his address. It was on a canal called the Krom Boomsloot, which sent Steve both to his dictionary (it meant "crooked tree ditch") and to his Amsterdam map. The Krom Boomsloot, he discovered, was a canal just east of the Red Light District and off the beaten tourist path. Although he'd spent much of his time in Amsterdam wandering the streets and discovering neighborhoods, he'd never seen it before.

Two hours later, he walked there. The canal proved to be delightful. It was, indeed, crooked, and, unlike most of the canals in Amsterdam, it was narrow enough for the branches of trees on both sides to hang over it and give it a cozy, sheltered feeling. It was also a short canal, and the streets leading onto it were narrow, so that it felt like a place apart. It looked, in fact, almost like a stage – the setting for an operetta.

Steve found Rob's address. The house had three stories, each with two high windows facing the canal. Next to it was a similar building, only with a large-windowed storefront facing the street. The word *GYM* was stenciled on the window; inside Steve could see a row of workout machines.

He walked up two steps to the front door of Rob's building. Beside it were three bells in a vertical row. He pressed Rob's. Buzzed in, he found himself at the foot of a long, narrow stairway, perhaps the steepest he'd seen in the Netherlands. At the top, two stories up, Rob waved to him with a smile.

"Up here!" he shouted.

Steve started climbing. Halfway up, there was a small landing and, to his left, an apartment door which, as he approached, opened slightly. An elderly woman in a faded periwinkle robe peered at him through the crack with nervous eyes and didn't respond to his smile. At the top, Rob's friendly grin instantly put him at ease. Rob was sixtyish, small, and slightly built, and wore a finely tailored gray suit, vest, and tie. Taking Steve by the arm as if they were old chums, he led him into the flat.

"Well," he said, making a theatrical gesture with his arm, "this is it!"

Steve looked around. He was in awe: though tiny, it was glorious, with a comfortable-looking maroon couch, a matching pair of upholstered chairs, a scarlet Oriental carpet, and – best of all – those two high windows overlooking the canal.

They had a very brief chat. Rob explained the reason for the sublet: he spent six months of every year in Japan, where he had a boyfriend. He showed Steve a picture of a bony little man – stark naked, full frontal. *Only in the Netherlands,* Steve thought, not for the first time. Rob also said he had a boarder, Kees, a student who lived in a small room upstairs, and who came into the apartment every day to use the toilet and shower. Steve nodded.

Once again: *Only in the Netherlands.*

"There are two other flats in the building," Rob told Steve. "On the ground floor we have the wife and children of the landlord, who seems to live elsewhere."

"Are they divorced?"

"God, no. They're Muslims. Filthy Muslims."

Steve's head jerked back slightly at this blunt expression of bigotry. Had he heard correctly? Had a cultivated-seeming gay man in Amsterdam, the world capital of tolerance, actually said such an ugly thing?

"He bought the building a couple of years ago," Rob said. "He lives somewhere else, presumably with another wife. A younger one. Without kids, I'd wager."

"But you said he wasn't divorced?"

Rob looked at him as if he were slow. "No, he's not divorced. He's *Muslim.* They can have as many wives as they want."

"Oh. I thought that was something from the olden days, or at least not something they brought to Europe. Surely polygamy isn't allowed here?"

"I don't know how long you've lived in the Netherlands, but one thing we're good at is making laws and then turning away discreetly when people break them – especially people from some other culture to which we're expected to bow in respect. Anyway, he doesn't know I'm subletting to you, but I have the legal right to rent out for six months of the year. If you ever see him, just nod hello."

"Okay."

"And just under us is Yeti. She's an old widow. She's lived here for even longer than I have. She's an intelligent and educated woman, and used to be quite vibrant and outgoing, but after her husband's death, which happened five or six years ago, she became – how to put it? Timid. A recluse. You might almost call her a hermit. Be nice to her."

"Of course."

"That's it for now. Can you drop by again at around nine this evening?" Steve nodded. "Good. We'll have a glass of wine and you can meet my ex-boyfriend, Niek, to whom you'll be paying the rent."

On the way home Steve picked up *De Volkskrant* at a corner tobacconist's. He spent the next couple of hours sitting on his bed and reading it, or trying to, making constant use of his two-volume Dutch dictionary. He quit at shortly before eight and followed a rambling route back to Rob's flat. It was a perfectly beautiful evening. He didn't remember ever feeling so content. When he arrived at the house on Krom Boomsloot, he found Rob sipping red wine with Niek, who was about Steve's own age and height.

Unshaven, tousle-haired, and dressed in a food-stained Boston Red Sox jersey and jeans that looked as if he'd slept in them for a week, Niek could hardly have seemed more different from Rob, whose Old World bonhomie and crisp, natty attire made Steve feel as if he was at a formal (but very friendly) dinner party. Rob, handing him a beautiful cut glass half filled with wine, told Steve, "Niek and I broke up ten years ago, but we're still best friends."

"Well, that's civilized," Steve said as he sat down

on one of the chairs. Rob and Niek were both sitting on the couch.

"No, it's just Dutch," said Niek.

"Same thing," said Rob.

"In any case, we're definitely not Americans," said Niek.

"What do you mean?" Steve asked.

"You know what I mean," Niek said. "You people are so puritanical. Just like your Pilgrim ancestors."

"Well, you may be trying to offend me, but you're not. I'm the first one to criticize American Puritanism. I was going on about it just today, in fact."

"But doesn't it bother you that we have gay marriage now, and your country doesn't? The land of the free?"

"Why do you think I'm here?"

"*Touché,*" said Rob.

"But of course you have your own share of stiff-necked Calvinist ancestors, don't you?" said Steve. "And, horrible though it may be, don't we deserve *any* points for liberating you from the Nazis?"

"Well, actually that was mostly the Canadians," said Niek.

"Really? Tell it to all those American soldiers buried on Dutch soil."

"In any case, America didn't go to war with the Germans and Japanese because they wanted to conquer evil. They did it because the Germans and Japanese had cut off almost every market on the globe from American capitalists."

"If we're going to talk about evil," said Steve, "remind me which European country sent the largest percentage of its Jews – "

"Now, now," Rob said with a broad gesture involving both his arms. "Let's not go there."

Steve moved in two days later. Toting his stuff up the two long, steep flights of stairs left him hyperventilating and dripping with sweat. But when he was done, he felt a sense of triumph: finally he was living in the kind of place he'd dreamed of when he'd first imagined moving to Amsterdam.

For a few days, life was bliss. Waking up every morning to that ridiculously beautiful view, Steve felt like one of those characters in a Merchant Ivory or Woody Allen film who just happen to live in the most gorgeously situated apartment in all of London or Venice or Rome. After spending an hour or so sipping coffee at a small table by the window, all the while looking out at the canal and thinking, *Yes, this is my life, believe it or not,* he went out and walked around Amsterdam, looking at the people and the buildings, throwing bread to the ducks in the canals, enjoying the cool, bracing breezes and the sudden thundershowers, and trying to figure out what to do with what was left of his life.

He also met Kees. On the first morning after he moved in, he heard a footfall on the stairs leading down from the attic, then a two-knock knock. *"Kom binnen!"* Steve said, and the door opened. A chubby, bearded guy in a once-white tattered robe shambled in, barefoot, looking half awake. He shuffled over to Steve.

"Hi, I'm Kees," he said in a near-mumble, raising his hand in a funny little wave. His Dutch accent was strong and unfamiliar; he certainly didn't sound like a native Amsterdammer. "I guess Rob told you about me?" He nodded as he talked.

"Yes, hi, Kees. Good to meet you."

"Good to meet you too. I'm going to shower now."

"Sure."

Then, one evening, the front-door buzzer sounded. Steve figured it was Niek dropping by to pick up Rob's mail – he'd said that he'd be doing this regularly – so Steve pressed the button to buzz him in. Opening the apartment door, Steve looked down to see two men coming up the stairs. They looked menacing – like hit men in an action movie. Steve ducked back into the apartment and locked the door.

The clomp-clomp of footsteps stopped. Someone knocked – loudly, aggressively. *"Wie is het?"* Steve shouted through the door. A voice came back loudly, in English: "I leef downstairs. I want to talk *met* Rob."

"Rob isn't here."

Steve heard the two men conversing on the other side of the door. Then the same man said: "So I want to talk *met* you."

"What do you want to talk about?"

"Open up the door. I want to talk *met* you."

"Who are you?"

"I live downstairs."

"What do you want to talk about?"

"Open up the door."

"I'm sorry, I don't know you. Tell me what you want to talk about."

"I want to talk *met* you face to face."

"I can't open the door unless I know who you are. Surely you understand that."

"No, I don't."

"Well, I can't open the door. Do you know the guy upstairs?"

"What?"

"Kennen jullie de kerel die boven woont?"

Now another, deeper voice spoke. A booming voice. "You combine English and Dutch. Is that what you do? Do you speak Dutch or not?"

"Een beetje."

"What? I don't know what you are saying."

"I'm sorry, I'm trying my best."

"Open up the door. We want to talk to Rob."

"He's not here. Do you have a message for him?"

"How many people are living in there with you?"

"Nobody."

"That's not true, I hear one other person in there with you."

"No, it's just me."

Steve heard Kees coming down from the attic. Kees began speaking with the visitors. Since he apparently considered it safe, Steve opened the door and stepped out. On the landing, dressed in a pale blue button-down shirt and ash-gray trousers, stood a stern little man in his forties who looked Indian; on the stairs, a step below him, was a big, husky, red-faced, red-bearded Dutchman of about fifty who was wearing a yellow and black plaid shirt and worn jeans and looked like a lumberjack.

Plainly the Indian-looking man was the one who had spoken first through the door, but now it was the lumberjack who was conversing with Kees – in Dutch, of course. Their exchange was intense and intermittently heated, and they both talked so fast that Steve could follow only bits of it.

Huurcontract: lease. *Huisbaas:* landlord. *Huurder:* tenant. *Wet:* law. *Advocaat:* lawyer.

Part of it was plainly about him. At one point the bearded man pointed a fat, red, stubby finger at him, saying something to Kees. Steve thought he heard the word *slimme*, which means "clever," "bad," "sly," "sneaky." Through it all, the Indian man stood there silently, like a military officer happily watching an underling – his "muscle" – do his dirty work.

After several minutes of this, the lumberjack seemed to be saying goodbye and extended his hand smilingly for Steve to shake – a typically Dutch way, as Steve knew by now, to end even an encounter as unpleasant as this. Steve had no idea what had been going on, but since Kees had just shaken the man's hand, he did, too. But then the lumberjack and Kees resumed talking, or arguing, as intensely as before. Finally Kees told the intruders that he wanted to explain the situation to Steve.

"It's like this," Kees said to Steve in English. "There were, um, complaints about noise from this flat since half a year ago."

"Okay." Steve turned to the little Indian man. "Of course you realize I just moved in here."

The Indian man didn't change his surly expression. "Every time you close the downstairs door," he said, as if making an accusation of murder, "it makes a big, big noise in the ground-floor flat!"

The lumberjack chimed in, speaking in Dutch with an irrational intensity. He had some kind of regional accent that made it especially hard for Steve to follow him, but Steve understood what point the man was making: immediately after moving in here, the man insisted, Steve should have introduced himself to all of the

37

neighbors, so they might know who belonged here and who didn't.

The Indian guy asked Kees, in Dutch, if Steve had a phone; Kees replied, also in Dutch, that Rob's phone had been disconnected. The man turned to Steve and asked, brusquely, in English: "No cell phone?"

"No," Steve said.

"Bullshit."

"Sorry, but it's true," Steve said. What he omitted to say was that he'd already had his own landline put in. "I'm trying to live simply and cheaply. Who are you, anyway?"

The Indian guy ignored his question. Kees scribbled down his own number and offered to go upstairs and get Niek's number, too.

"Don't bother, Kees," Steve said. "I'll get it." He went back into the flat, took his phone off the hook (lest it ring and thus give away his possession of a working phone), and picked up a piece of paper with Niek's number on it. He took it back out onto the landing and read it to the Indian man, who then asked for his name. Steve went inside and got another piece of paper and a pen and returned to the landing, where he wrote *Steve*.

"Family name, too!" the Indian guy spat out.

Steve gave him a sharp look. "Who the hell are you to talk to me like that? Do you want me to call the police?"

Suddenly the big red-faced man stepped up onto the landing and got right in Steve's face, so close that Steve could see the busted capillaries in his swollen nose. "You say you don't have a phone," the man shouted, "but you're going to call the police?"

"Just write your last name," Kees said to Steve, his eyes pleading. Steve did so. The big man grabbed the paper out of his hand and the two visitors left. Steve went back into the apartment, waving to Kees to join him.

"I need a drink," Steve said. "You?"

Kees nodded.

Steve made two screwdrivers while Kees explained to him that the dark-skinned little man was named Ahmed. "He's from Morocco. He owns the building."

"What about the other one?"

"He didn't say his name. He said he was from the *gemeente.*"

"The city," Steve said, handing Kees his drink.

"Thank you," Kees said. "Yes. The city. The city government. I'll make some phone calls and see if I can find out about him. He doesn't seem like a real city official. Maybe he's just on some community – um – "

"Community board?"

"Yes. Can I call Niek?"

"Good idea."

Kees phoned Niek. He rolled his eyes. "No answer.

Should I try the big guy's number?" Steve nodded. Kees did so. He shook his head. "No answer there either." He hung up.

"Sit down," Steve said. He was in one of the chairs; Kees sat on the couch. "So what's the deal with this Ahmed?" Steve asked.

Kees shrugged. "He bought this building three years ago. He's been trying ever since to get us out of here. Rob, me, Yeti – all three of us. We've been here for a long time and we don't pay enough rent to make him happy. He's gone to court to try to have us removed, but he keeps getting – um – "

"It keeps getting thrown out of court."

"Yes. Believe it or not, he even tried to commit Yeti to a mental hospital so he could take her home."

"Jesus."

"His wife and children and mother-in-law live on the ground floor," Kees said. "But Ahmed seems to live somewhere else. I don't know where. He's a pretty shady – is that the right word?"

"Sounds like it."

"Yes, a shady guy. He's friends with the owner of the *sportshal* next door, who's quite simply a gangster."

"*Sportshal*? You mean that little gym?"

"Yes," Kees said. "The man who runs it is a convicted thief. He has this group of men who hang out there and do robberies together."

"You're kidding."

"No."

"This probably sounds stupid to you," said Steve, "but I'm really shocked by the thought that even Amsterdam has mobsters."

"Well," said Kees, "I don't mean anything by this, but these are Muslims."

Steve looked at Kees, remembering Rob's remark about Ahmed.

"Rob," Kees said, as if reading his mind, "calls Ahmed the dirty foreigner."

Steve shrugged. "Well," he said, "I guess to Ahmed, *I'm* the dirty foreigner."

The next day there was a knock at the door. Steve opened it. It was an elderly woman. Not Yeti. She smiled and introduced herself, in Dutch, as Yeti's friend. She said that she was sorry to complain, but that Yeti said he was making noise walking on the floor.

Steve apologized and promised he'd do his best to be quieter.

THAT NIGHT AT ABOUT TWELVE, Steve left Gaiety, a bar on the Amstel, holding his change in his hand – a couple of ten-guilder notes. He crossed the narrow street and stopped for a moment to take in the view – the water, and, across it, every light ablaze, looking more like a cruise ship than like a building, the Hotel de l'Europe. Beyond the hotel, on either side, the water receded into the distance, spanned by small bridges, lined by low-lying, warmly lit buildings. It was a sight he'd often paused at this spot to take in, as if it were a work of art.

Suddenly he felt something sharp poking him in the back. He turned reflexively to see a wiry, dark-skinned youth – Arabic? Turkish? Persian? – wielding a long knife. More frightening even than the blade was the boy's ice-cold expression. Shoving his face into Steve's, he growled out a demand in broken English for the money in Steve's hand.

Without even thinking about what was wise to do in this situation, Steve said, instinctively, "No," and started to step away from him. Instantly, the mugger was right up against Steve, the side of his blade pressed to Steve's throat.

"Money, faggot!" the boy hissed. He was wearing a lime-green hoodie and jeans; his eyes were large and brown, and under other circumstances Steve might have found them beautiful.

"Okay, okay," Steve said. The boy moved back a half-step, took the cash out of Steve's now-open palm, and ran off, turning at the Halvemaansteeg, right in front of the attractive brick building that housed De Kleine Komedie, a cabaret theater, to race toward Rembrandt-plein.

Shaking, Steve walked quickly the other way, up the Amstel to Muntplein. He crossed the square, dominated by the Munttoren – a low tower that, centuries earlier, he knew, had been part of the wall surrounding Amsterdam, and for a brief time in the seventeenth century had been used as a mint. He then walked down Vijzelstraat, turned onto Reguliersdwarsstraat, and made his way to Exit, a late-night gay club. He went inside. It was packed, and very noisy. He climbed two flights of stairs – it was always quieter upstairs – and sat at the bar.

A short blond bartender came over. "Gin and tonic?" he asked, plainly remembering what Steve had ordered last time he'd been here. Steve responded with a jerky, nervous nod. For a second or two the bartender looked at him with curiosity, but then went off to make the drink.

Only after Steve had pounded back that one, ordered another, and started relaxing a bit did it occur to him that he should have reported the incident at once. By this point, it already seemed too late – his assailant was probably on the other side of town already. What, in any case, could he have told the police? The encounter had been over in seconds. And though the mugger's face had been only a few centimeters away from his own, Steve probably wouldn't recognize him now if they passed on the street.

At three, Steve left Exit and took a taxi back to

Krom Boomslott, where he lay awake in bed, exhausted but unable to sleep. He thought about the mugger. And he thought about Ahmed. The "filthy Muslim." What was going on?

Suddenly it was if he wasn't in Amsterdam anymore.

After nearly an hour he gave up trying to sleep. Switching on the bedside lamp, he sat up in bed and started poking through Ron's bedside bookshelves, which were crowded with beautiful books, mostly works of art and history in Dutch, English, French, and German. After paging through a couple of them, he pulled out a big royal-blue volume that looked like a photo album or scrapbook. Opening it, he saw that it was a notebook filled with neat handwriting in two languages, German on the verso pages and Portuguese on the recto.

Steve didn't know Portuguese, but he'd majored in French and taken both Spanish and German. Examining the first few lines of the two texts, he realized that they were identical in content. He read a few pages, shifting from one language to the other whenever he was stumped by a word or by the handwriting. It soon became clear that this was a journal, written on his Amsterdam deathbed by a young man from Fortaleza, Brazil. In the very first sentences, he explained that he was keeping this record because he wanted his memory to be preserved after his death, which, he had been told, was imminent.

Steve read several pages. The young man recounted his move to the Netherlands, with his parents, at the age of twelve. The family settled in Amersfoort, where his father found work in a factory. He loved his parents deeply, and they loved him – right up until the day he told them he was gay. His mother wept, his father beat him, and they both ordered him out of their home.

He was sixteen.

Steve closed the book, unsure if he should be reading this or not. Was he sticking his nose into things that were none of his business, or was he letting a young man live again, if only in his, Steve's, mind, and for just a few minutes, in precisely the way the young man had apparently intended?

Steve was sliding the book back onto the shelf when something kept it from going all the way in. He took the book out again and reached in to see what was in the way. His hand grasped something cold, hard, metallic. He pulled it out. A handgun. Or was the proper term a pistol? It occurred to Steve that he didn't even know the difference. He'd never had anything to do with guns, never even held one. Holding it was unnerving. And even more unnerving was the question that instantly popped into his head. Namely, why did Rob keep a gun by his bed? Was he that worried about Ahmed?

After turning the gun over in his hand for a few seconds – feeling its weight, putting his finger on the trigger with the gentlest possible motion – Steve returned it delicately to its place behind the books, then, with equal delicacy, put the dead boy's journal back where it belonged.

A COUPLE OF DAYS LATER he was awakened by the front door buzzer. Ahmed? He pushed the button, then opened the apartment door and looked downstairs. The building door opened. It was the FedEx man.

"*Een pakje,*" he called up, smiling.

"*Ik kom,*" Steve replied, and ran downstairs.

The FedEx man was just a boy – blond, clean-cut. The package was from the Disney office – an outline of a sequence of fifteen episodes he had to turn into scripts within the next two months.

The next day was sunny and mild. At lunchtime Steve went to the Spui, where he picked up the London *Times* at the Athenaeum Boekhandel before going into the Café Luxembourg, where he read it at a window table over a cup of coffee and a club sandwich. Then he went back home.

He'd barely sat down to work at his computer when the phone rang.

It was Niek. "Ahmed is really trying to have you removed," he said.

"Well, I can't say I'm surprised."

"I've made some calls to try to find out who that man was that Ahmed brought with him."

"Did you find anything out?"

"No. I'm going to have to speak to Rob's lawyer."

"Are you concerned about this?"

"No. It's a free country. Rob has a legal right to sublet his own apartment. Ahmed can't do anything. He's just being a nuisance."

"I can't believe this guy."

"He's a monster. He tried to put Yeti in a mental hospital just to get her flat."

"I know."

"You do?"

"Yes, Kees told me."

"Horrible, right?"

"Of course."

"You're not even human anymore when you do something like that."

"No, you're not."

"Oh, and one other thing," he added. "I got a call this morning from Yeti's friend. She said that you're making a lot of noise walking around the apartment."

"Yes, she came upstairs to complain the other day. I told her I'd do my best."

"You spoke to her?"

"Yes."

"But she only speaks Dutch."

"I know. We spoke in Dutch."

"You speak Dutch?"

"Yes. Not fluently, but enough to have that conversation."

"Really?"

"Look, whatever you people like to think, Dutch is not nuclear physics, and Americans are not all monolingual cretins. I was a French major. I can speak more languages than you can. Do you want to give me a test?"

"Sorry, sorry."

"Look, Niek, I walk around here in my socks. I try to walk softly. I've lived in apartments all my life and never had to deal with this sort of nonsense. What do you think, I'm deliberately trying to walk heavily? You think I want all this trouble? I probably don't even walk across this room more than five times a day. And I'm not goose-stepping. I'm an American, not a Nazi. Although I know you have trouble telling the difference."

"I'm sorry. You're right."

"What kind of a woman are we dealing with here, anyway? Yeti's friend, I mean. She seemed reasonable enough when I talked with her."

"Oh, she's okay. They're both okay. It's just that Yeti sees ghosts. I don't mean literally. It's a Dutch expression. Do you have that expression in English?"

"I don't know. I don't care."

"All I'm saying is that she's very nervous about your being there. It would help a lot if you introduced yourself to her. She speaks English."

"You know, Niek, I'm pretty much done with meeting people in this building. I'm pretty much done with all this bullshit. I just moved in here. I don't appreciate having to deal with all of Rob's crap."

There was a pause. Then Niek said, "I understand. This really isn't fair to you. I can see that."

There was another pause. "Look, I have a proposal."

"Yes?"

"Why don't you leave Rob's place and move into my flat on Bellamyplein? I can move in with my girlfriend."

"Girlfriend?"

"Yes."

"Do you mean an actual girlfriend, or just a friend who happens to be a girl?"

"I mean girlfriend."

"I thought you were gay."

A pause. "Look, as an American – "

"Yeah, I know. As an American I wouldn't be able to understand it. Cut. Print. Go on."

"What?"

"Never mind. So what's the deal with this girlfriend?"

"I already basically live with her anyway. I haven't slept in my own place in a year. I just go there during the day."

"Okay."

"The alternative is just to leave things as they are and wait to see what Ahmed's next move will be. And there will be a next move."

"I see. Mind if I think about it for a day or so?"

"Sure."

"Okay. Bye."

Steve hung up.

Depressed, he decided to go out for a walk. After a couple of blocks he thought it might be advisable to take a look at Niek's neighborhood. The problem was that he had only a vague idea of where Bellamyplein was. He walked to the Dam, then turned onto Raadhuisstraat, which cut across the major canals, led into the Jordaan, and became Rozengracht. After a few minutes he turned onto a narrower street, headed north. He then turned west onto Westerstraat and, crossing a canal, Lijnbaansgracht, came out of the Jordaan at a square called Marnixplein. Feeling that he'd gone too far north, he crossed another canal, the Singelgracht, and then headed south along Hendrikstraat. He was now in a residential area, some distance from tourist Amsterdam.

He asked one passerby, then another, for directions. Even the locals didn't appear to be certain where Bellamyplein was. But he was pretty sure he was getting closer.

Block by block, the neighborhood grew shabbier. There was graffiti, garbage on the street. There were dirty storefronts with signs in Arabic. He passed a small business whose sign identified it as a travel agency and "telecenter." In its window were large, crudely handwritten posters listing how much it cost to phone Morocco and Turkey and to fly to the Turkish cities of Istanbul, Ankara, Antalya, Izmir, and Dalaman. He passed a group of men who looked like Arabs or Turks or Persians and who were standing on the sidewalk holding a loud, angry-sounding conversation in some Middle Eastern tongue. As he walked by, they all turned, every one of them, and gave him unfriendly, suspicious looks. One of them said something to him. He didn't understand the words, but he could guess at the sentiment. Further down the street, he passed a woman in an Islamic head covering who was pushing a baby carriage and was flanked by two toddlers. Half a block later, he passed another woman, also covered; this one was pregnant and pushing a child in a stroller.

Steve had spent quite a bit of time in Amsterdam, but he'd never seen, or even heard tell of, a neighborhood like this.

Finally he found Bellamyplein. It turned out to be a triangle, two sides of which were lined with the dirty façades of three- and four-story houses and the third side of which faced a grimy, brick-walled foundry or factory featuring a row of garages and a front gate that looked like the entrance to a Victorian madhouse or debtor's prison. On closer inspection he noticed that tram tracks led into each of the garages, and when he peered inside through the soot-covered windows of the garage doors, he could see – faintly – tram cars.

Inside the triangle, meanwhile, was a sad little park – a forlorn stretch of salmon-pink concrete, with patches of grass and benches around its edges. Along one side of the park were two rusty, graffiti-covered, eight-foot-high, steel-gray metal cubes whose function he couldn't imagine; along another side was a row of wide, waist-high green metal dumpsters.

Steve couldn't remember Niek's street address, so he walked along the house fronts, reading the names beside the buzzers. He finally found Niek's. It was next door to a pet-food store on the corner of a street called Agatha Denkenstraat. On the ground floor of Niek's building was a storefront establishment with a huge red Turkish flag flying over the door. A sign, in English, identified it as a "neighborhood center." There was no front window, just a brick wall, and a door with a square window in it that was only a few inches across.

Steve walked over and look in. About twenty feet from the door, at the far end of an otherwise empty room, a dozen or so swarthy men, all with beards, were clustered around a table. One of them noticed Steve and said something to his friends. They all turned to look at him and, in unison, scowled.

Down the street there was a café. It looked cozy. Walking back to Krom Boomsloot, he clung to the idea of that café.

When he'd returned to Rob's apartment and was sitting by the window eating takeout from KFC, he called Niek and told him about his walk. In an effort to put the best possible face on his impression of Niek's neighborhood, he mentioned the café.

"It looked pleasant," he said.

"I would recommend that perhaps you should avoid that café," Niek replied. "There have been two knifings there lately."

Niek added that burglars had broken into his apartment twice in the past year, most recently two months earlier. "They stole my gold medal from the Gay Games."

"You won a gold medal at the Gay Games? In what?"

"Bridge."

"Wow. I didn't know you were such a jock. So guys with girlfriends are allowed to compete in the Gay Games?"

Niek hung up.

THE NEXT DAY WAS A SATURDAY. Steve got a lot of work done. In the evening he dropped into Gaiety and chatted over a beer with Piet, the bartender, an easygoing, chipmunk-cheeked guy who enjoyed a laugh. The only other person in the café, several stools away, was a small, dark young man with a surly expression and a two-day beard. Shooting him a flirtatious smile, Piet invited him in English to come over and sit next to Steve so they could all chat. The young man joined them but didn't chat. He sat there looking sullenly down at his drink and responding to Piet's and Steve's questions with clipped one-word answers. His name? Roberto. Where was he from? Bologna. How old was he? Twenty-two. (But he looked older.)

Why, Steve asked Roberto, was he here? Roberto shrugged. His answer, given in English far worse than that of any Dutchman Steve had ever met (Jan, the monolingual concierge, didn't count), was long but partly vague and partly just plain incomprehensible. Roberto sneered at Piet's intermittent flirtations, and continually seemed about to get up and go. When Piet invited Roberto to come home with him after work, Roberto shook his head no, firmly. Yet he stayed till closing time, then accompanied Steve to Mix Café down the block, which was open two hours later than Gaiety, and where Piet said he'd join them in a few minutes. After Piet turned up, the three of them moved on to yet another café further down the Amstel. Ten minutes later, Roberto left with Piet.

THE FOLLOWING MORNING STEVE WOKE at about ten o'clock. He was having coffee at his place by the window when the front doorbell buzzed. Ahmed? He pushed the button by the buzzer, opened the apartment door, looked downstairs. A young guy in uniform was standing in the street doorway holding two envelopes. Mail? On a Sunday? He yelled up to Steve. *"Ik heb drie tekenbriefen!"*

"Ik kom!"

Steve had never heard the word *tekenbriefen*. But he knew *teken* was "signature" and *briefen* was "letters."

Ergo, registered mail. But *three* pieces?

He pulled on his jeans and went downstairs, barefoot and barechested. It was cold out. The comely young delivery man held out a clipboard and handed him a pen. Steve signed, and the young man gave him a big smile and three envelopes.

"Vielen dank," Steve said as he looked through them. They were addressed to himself, to Kees, and to Niek.

On the way back upstairs, he ripped open the envelope with his name on it and scanned the letter quickly. It was from a lawyer representing Ahmed. To Steve's surprise, he could understand almost every word.

It recounted Ahmed's visit, charged that Ahmed had received complaints from his other tenant about Steve's making noise, and claimed that Steve had told him that Rob had moved out and that Steve was now living in the apartment with Kees. The letter went on to demand that Steve and Kees leave within fourteen days. Otherwise, Ahmed would have them removed.

Also enclosed in the envelope addressed to Steve was a copy of a separate letter to Rob, which told him that within fourteen days he was to remove Steve and Kees from the apartment, write a letter to Ahmed explaining their presence in his flat, and resume residency in it himself or risk the consequences.

Steve walked up past Rob's apartment to the top floor and knocked on Kees's door. "*Wer ist?*" Kees said sleepily through the closed door.

"Steve."

"Oh. One minute."

Odd: Kees had spoken in German.

Kees opened the door, shirtless, in his white briefs, and invited Steve in. Steve walked into a tiny, dark, low-ceilinged room, ice-cold, barely larger than a closet, with a bed, a rug, a big, comfy, musty chair, and books flowing from a low set of shelves onto the floor. Steve handed Kees the letters. Kees read them, shaking the sleep out of his head. "Can we go downstairs?" he mumbled. "It's warmer there."

"Sure."

They went down to Rob's apartment. Steve poured Kees an orange juice while Kees phoned Niek at work. No answer. He left a message. They sat down and talked. Kees gave him a word-for-word translation of the letters, just in case he'd missed or misunderstood something. It turned out he hadn't missed anything, though one thing he learned from the letters was that Dutch had a special word for a "noise nuisance": *geluidsoverlast.*

A few minutes later Niek called back. Kees read the letters to him, then put Steve on the phone. "Well," Niek said with wry humor, "it happened sooner than we thought."

"Yes."

"I will pick up the letters and take them to the lawyer," he said, "and we will talk later."

"Okay."

Hearing Yeti's friend being buzzed in, Kees went downstairs and talked to both women. He came back and told Steve that according to Yeti, she hadn't initiated a noise complaint to Ahmed; Ahmed had come to her and asked her about noise. Kees added that, in any case, she no longer considered Steve to be a *geluidsoverlast.*

Steve was about to say that he didn't care what Yeti did or didn't consider him to be when Kees added: "I'm sorry. I have to go upstairs and get to work."

"What are you working on?"

"My dissertation."

"What's it about?"

"The Nazis," he said. "I'm working on a degree in art history."

"Nazi art?"

"Not exactly. Did you ever hear of the 'Degenerate Art' exhibition?"

"I read about it once."

"Really?"

"Yes. It was a show of art works that the Nazis saw as degenerate. Right?"

"*Juist!* It was in 1937. It consisted of art that they considered representative of everything they wanted to stamp out. I thought it was weird – well, first of all, I thought it was weird that they'd put together an exhibition of art they hated."

"Right."

"But also, I thought it was interesting that some of the artists included in it were represented at exactly the same time in another show of Nazi-approved art."

"Really?"

"Yes."

"That's fascinating."

"Isn't it? So I decided to look into it. And the more I looked into it, the more interested I became in the Nazi mindset generally – how they came to think as they did, not just about art but about everything. Where had their ideas come from?"

"Isn't the answer to that question already pretty well established?"

"Yes and no. Nazism was peculiar because it combined pagan religion with science. Yes, it was discredited science, science done by eugenicists who considered Aryans a superior race. But how did these two strains come together, the pagan religion and the discredited science? That's what I want to figure out."

"And nobody's done this before?"

"Not really. Not to my satisfaction."

"What do you want to do that they haven't done?"

"I want to get inside the Nazi mind. I want to understand how seemingly normal people came to buy into such a crazy mix of religion and science."

"And your professors approve of this? It doesn't make them – well, uncomfortable?"

"Funny you should ask, because some of them think the whole thing is a horrible idea. They say it's inappropriate to try to understand how the Nazis thought or why people were drawn to Nazism. They say Nazism can't be understood."

"Right," Steve replied. "As if it just materialized out of thin air."

"They're used to treating the Holocaust as a unique historical event."

"Right."

"You shouldn't try to analyze and understand it, like everything else in human history; you should just step back and stare at it in horror."

"Well, that's silly."

"*I* think so."

"I do too."

"You do?"

"Yes."

"We're supposed to look at what happened under the Nazis and say 'never again' – but how can we say 'never again' when we refuse even to ask how and why it all happened? If we're serious about wanting to prevent it from happening again, we need to understand what it is inside of us, inside the human animal, the *homo sapiens,* that's drawn to that kind of evil. You know?"

"Sure. I totally agree."

"I mean, if some people are uncomfortable with what I'm doing, it's because they need to believe that the Nazis were unique in their evil, different from the rest of us in some essential way."

"They don't want to confront the uncomfortable reality," Steve said, "that the Nazis were us."

"*Precies!*" said Kees. "There's evil all over, every-where, every day, only on a smaller scale. And of course in the last century alone, other than Nazism, there have been so many other monstrous evils in the world, also based on monstrous ideologies. Stalin. Mao. Pol Pot. And of course what's happening in this city and other cities."

"What do you mean?"

Kees looked uncomfortable. "You know."

"No, I don't know."

"Really?"

"Yes."

"Well, I mean – well, Islam."

"What about Islam? What are you talking about?"

Now Kees looked surprised. "How long have you lived in Amsterdam?"

"Just a few weeks."

"Well, you'll see. What am I saying? Of course you've already seen."

"Seen what?"

Kees shrugged as if it were a stupid question. "Ahmed," he said.

"Ahmed? I know he's a creep, but what does that have to do with religion?"

"You need to read up on Islam."

"But is it any worse than Christianity?"

"Read up on it," Kees said. "I'm not criticizing Muslims as people. I'm criticizing Islam as an ideology. An ideology like Nazism."

"Really? You would go that far?"

"I've studied it a lot. And Christianity too. Did you know my father was a priest?"

"A Roman Catholic priest?"

"Yes. Before he married my mother, of course. Long before. As a young man, he was a *missionaris* in Pakistan. He built schools and hospitals. He had a friend who was a Muslim clergyman."

"Would you compare *him* to a Nazi?"

"No, not at all. He was a very good man. But he wasn't a very good Muslim – just as my father wasn't a very good Catholic. They were just very good men. Which is why one day they both decided to switch services. My father did the Muslim service and his friend did the Catholic service."

"And they both got in trouble."

Kees grinned. "Yes, exactly. But the worst happened when his best Muslim friend died. My father went to his superior, who said to him that his friend was in hell. That was when he quit the priesthood."

"So Christianity isn't so great either."

"Well, of course not. No human institution is. But Islam is different."

"How can you say that?"

Kees looked at him. "One piece of advice. Get a Koran. Read it."

"Okay."

They sat there in silence for a moment.

"Do you know how I came to live here?" Kees asked.

"No."

"After Niek and Rob broke up ten years ago, Rob met a Brazilian boy who was dying of AIDS. His parents were very pious Catholics. And they had thrown him out of the house for being gay. Rob gave the boy the upstairs room – " Kees nodded toward his own little flat. " – and the boy spent his last months there."

"Lordy," said Steve.

Shit, there it was again. *Lordy* was a word that had never passed his lips until he'd met Daniel. It had been a staple of Daniel's vocabulary. And within a few weeks, it had become a part of Steve's, too. And so it had remained to this day.

"Rob is a very good man," Kees said, "though he wouldn't want you to know that. Anyway, after the boy died, a friend of his, who was also a friend of my mother and who knew that I was looking for a flat, told me about the vacancy. Back then I was living with my mother in Breukelen."

"Where's that?"

"It's a little town of about fifteen thousand people between here and Utrecht. That's where the name of Brooklyn came from. Brooklyn in New York, you know?" Steve nodded. "So I called Rob and two days later I was living here. That was eight years ago."

63

Finally Kees excused himself and went back upstairs.

After he left, Steve stood at the window. It was a bright, beautiful day. The sky was a blue-white wash, the clouds white as freshly fallen snow. The water in the canal sparkled silver and gold, and the façades of the brick buildings across the canal looked as if they were being viewed through a lens lightly tinted with orange.

THE NEXT DAY STEVE MOVED to Bellamyplein. When he first walked in from the street, the ground-floor landing smelled like raw sewage and the stairs were pitch dark. Niek's flat was on what the Dutch called the first floor – in other words, the floor above the ground floor. Steve knocked at the door and heard Niek shout, "Come in!"

The door was unlocked. Steve let himself in.

The room he entered was dimly lit, shabbily furnished, with a sagging couch and a wooden floor covered with scratches. Niek, dressed in the same Red Sox jersey and jeans he'd worn the night they met, was sprawled on the couch drinking a Heineken from the bottle while a woman of about his age paced back and forth among a dozen or so bags and boxes stuffed with clothes and other items. She was conducting a cellphone conversation – obviously business-related – in intense, rapid-fire Dutch. This, Steve surmised, was Niek's girlfriend, Miep. She was dark-haired and generously proportioned, and was wearing an emerald-colored sheath dress that was as neat and conservative as Niek's clothes were wrinkled and messy.

Hanging up, she immediately switched her attention to Steve. "Lousy situation, huh?" she asked good-humoredly in excellent American-accented English, her voice loud and firm. She exchanged a few pleasantries with Steve, making it clear between the lines that she was in charge of the situation. The more she spoke, the more Niek seemed to fade into the background. This was, Steve gathered, the dynamic of her and Niek's relationship. From the outset, she talked to Steve as if he was a good friend, or at least somebody deserving of a degree of respect, and seemed almost apologetic for Niek, whom she plainly considered unworthy of respect.

At the same time, she seemed to be very happy that Niek was moving in with her.

"You won't have to worry about neighbors or the landlord here," she said to Steve. "Nobody lives on the ground floor, and the people upstairs will be in Greece for months. Mykonos."

Steve whistled. "Mykonos. Not bad."

Miep turned to Niek as if to a servant. "Show him around," she ordered. He nodded obediently and pushed himself up off the couch, then led Steve over to the washer and dryer, which were ancient-looking and tucked away in a dark tiled closet off the flat's main corridor. To Steve's alarm, the shower was also located in this same closet, separated from the washer and dryer by nothing more than a five-inch-high ridge on the floor. The shower tiling was filthy and cracked; rusty pipes and exposed electrical wires ran along the shower wall. Could such an arrangement be permissible under Dutch fire codes?

Niek picked up a container of fabric softener and showed it to Steve. "It's good for the environment," Niek said. "But I would prefer that you don't use the dryer, because it takes too much electricity, which *isn't* good for the environment."

"You're big on the environment, huh?"

"Well, Miep is. Did you know she's represented the Netherlands at two international environmental conferences?"

"No, I hadn't heard."

"Yes, and she was on a panel with Hillary Clinton at that big women's conference in Beijing."

Funny, thought Steve, *how they all hate America so much, but interacting with famous Americans, even for them, is the ultimate badge of honor.*

After Steve had carried all his own stuff up to the flat, he helped Niek carry his dozen or so bags and boxes down to Miep's tangerine-colored Mercedes. When Niek and Miep finally drove off, Miep was grinning broadly and waving, while Niek was slumping in his seat with a wan smile. Steve went back upstairs to check out his new digs.

It was Huidekoperstraat all over again, only worse. The bedroom floor was covered with a filthy coffee-colored rug; the mattress, when he tried it, proved to be thin and lumpy and uncomfortable; the urine-hued linoleum kitchen floor was missing large pieces through which he could see wooden slats that were black with dirt. Off the kitchen and bedroom was a dark, splintery wooden terrace that was sagging and waterlogged and half-covered with bright green mold. On top of a low shelf at one end of it was a foot-high pile of some gray-brown chunky substance that looked like the putrefied carcass of some poor creature but that he realized, after studying it for a moment, was an old beehive. Next to it was something that was unequivocally the remains of an animal – a dead pigeon, partly decayed, its feathers still intact.

Steve went to the other end of the apartment, the living room, and looked out the window. It overlooked the square, on which a woman in a head covering was pushing baby carriage while two small children walked alongside her.

He went back outside, took the tram downtown, and had a few beers at Gaiety. He returned to Bellamyplein on the last tram, well after midnight. At least the tram stop wasn't far – just three short blocks away on De Clercqstraat.

Bellamyplein was silent, deserted. He let himself into the smelly building, felt his way up the dark stairs, struggled to find the lock with his key, then let himself in and closed the door. A lamp he had lit earlier was still on. He took his shoes off and padded across the living room into the bedroom, where he threw off his clothes and got into bed. The springs squeaked, and squeaked again as he rolled onto his side and shifted around, trying to get comfortable. Finally there was silence. He lay there for a while reviewing the events of the day and trying not to be bothered too much about the sour smell of the pillow and the fact that the mattress springs were poking into his flesh. He was about to drift off to sleep when he heard a voice.

A male voice. And a rather loud one, at that.

No, it wasn't coming from outside. The next-door neighbors? But no, there were no next-door neighbors: in this building there was only one flat per floor. And the people upstairs were in Greece. Mykonos. That left downstairs. The "neighborhood center."

The word flowed back into his mind: *geluidsoverlast*. On Krom Boomsloot, his footfall was a *geluidsoverlast* for Yeti. Now he was living in a place where a bunch of guys hanging around a "neighborhood center" were going to be a *geluidsoverlast* for him.

Terrific.

Lying there, he listened. The man was speaking a

language Steve didn't know. Arabic? Or one of those languages. Urdu? Pashto? He sounded angry. Another man replied, apparently in the same tongue. The conversation went on, then died down. Steve heard a door slam. Then silence.

H IS ALARM WOKE HIM AT TEN. Feeling unusually energetic, he got dressed and went out. It was a perfect spring day, bright and mild. He walked to the Spui and bought the London *Times* at the Athenaeum Nieuwscentrum, then read it while sipping coffee at a sidewalk table at Café Dante – a classic Dutch café, high-ceilinged and elegant, with a long bar running along the left wall.

He strolled around for a couple of hours, had lunch at a waterside table at Café de Jaren. He then returned to the apartment on Bellamyplein, read, napped, woke up at sundown, and walked to Gaiety. He found Piet tending bar and Roberto sitting there talking to him. Steve sat next to Roberto and said hello. To his surprise, Roberto gave him a big, friendly grin, as if they were old buddies.

"I'm waiting for Piet's break," Roberto told him.

Piet put on a CD of the song "No Matter What," a current hit by a group called Boyzone, and sang to Roberto in his heavy Dutch accent: "I know this love's

forever, / That's all that matters now, no matter what."
When the song was over, Piet leaned in close to Steve:
"Guess what Roberto did last night? He wanted to have a
bathe, so he put that thing in the thing to make the water
stay in the thing – what do you call that in English?"

"The tub?"

"No, the thing you put in the thing."

"I don't know. No, wait. Stopper. Or plug."

"Precies. So then he forgot about it and came to
bed, and when I woke up my apartment was flooded!" Piet
grinned with delight.

S TEVE LEFT SHORTLY BEFORE MIDNIGHT, and as he
climbed into bed in the apartment on Bellamyplein
he was so exhausted that he almost fell asleep
instantly.

But then, once again, he heard a voice.

It was so loud that he wondered: was there a hole
in the floor? The man was speaking the same language
Steve had heard the night before. He went on and on,
delivering what sounded like a speech – a harangue. Steve
was surprised not to hear anybody reply. Finally the man
stopped talking. There was silence for a moment. Then
another man spoke. In Dutch. Steve made out one word:
Nederlands. He wanted the other man to speak Dutch.

There was some mumbling. More than one voice.
Steve couldn't make any sense of it, or even tell what

language it was in. Then the same man who'd spoken in Dutch said, "OK. English. Please. English."

What Steve heard next made his whole body tremble.

III.

THE VOICES FINALLY WENT QUIET after about an hour. It took Steve another couple of hours to calm down and nod off. He slept fitfully. When he woke up just a few minutes after nine o'clock, his mind flooded instantly with the memory of those voices. At first he lay there frozen, listening for them. Nothing. After about ten minutes he crept nervously out of bed, padded into the kitchen as quietly as he could, and made himself a cup of instant coffee, which he took back into the bedroom.

He set the cup down on the dusty bedside table and crouched down to look under the bed. He couldn't see anything, other than huge clumps of dust. He got back on his feet and stood there silently for a few minutes on the thick coffee-colored rug, feeling scared and foolish. Then, screwing up his nerve, he leaned over and pulled the bed as gently as possible away from the wall. Nothing. Just rug, all the way to the wall.

He pushed the bed back. He stood there, breathing heavily, and drank some coffee. Then he put the cup back down and pulled the bed out again. He lay on it, belly down, facing the wall, and reached down to grab the edge of the rug. He yanked at it. It didn't give in the slightest: it was solidly attached to the floor.

He got up, went back into the kitchen, and opened the top drawer next to the sink. Just forks and knives and spoons. He opened the second drawer. It contained a mishmash of cooking implements – a spatula, a ladle, a whisk, and so on.

At first the third drawer resisted his efforts to budge it – it was as if no one had gone into it in years – but when he finally succeeded in getting it open, it proved to be full of tools. He found a screwdriver, a hammer, and a wrench, took them back to the bedroom, and tossed them on the bed. Leaning back across the mattress, he grabbed the hammer and slipped its claw under the edge of the rug. He tugged at the hammer, to absolutely no effect, then tugged harder. Staple by staple, click by click, the rug started to come up. He put down the hammer, picked up the wrench, grabbed the loose part of the rug, and pulled as hard as he could. The angle was tough, but after a moment the whole thing came loose, raising a cloud of dust and grit that made him cough – and exposing a severely worn wooden floor in which a big chunk of one of the slats was missing, creating a space about two inches across.

Steve got up, closed the bedroom door, and pulled shut the chocolate-colored curtains. Leaning back across the bed, he looked down at the hole.

And saw light.

He caught his breath. Then he put the rug back in place, stood up, and pushed the bed back against the wall.

Throwing on a jacket, he stuffed his laptop and the Disney script outline into his shoulder bag and shoved Niek's keys into his pocket before heading out.

It was a bright, chilly morning. He took the

number 14 tram from DeClercqstraat to Dam Square, then walked up Spuistraat to the Spui. He checked his watch. It was just a couple of minutes after eleven.

When he got to Café Dante, he went inside. A couple of waitresses moved between the kitchen and the area behind the bar, setting things up. There was nobody else in sight; Steve appeared to be the first customer of the day. He took a table by the window and looked out at the Spui, this old square in the heart of Amsterdam. Tourists and shoppers wandered across the pavement; bicycles streamed past. Students clambered up the steps of one of the University of Amsterdam's stately old buildings, whose high windows looked out onto the Spui.

Time passed. A tram clanged by, and another, and another. Neither of the waitresses was in a hurry to take his order.

Finally, one of them walked over. She was young and made no effort at friendliness.

"*Koffie, alstublieft,*" Steve said.

"Anything to eat?" she asked in English.

"Not yet, thanks."

He pulled out the script outline and started reading through it.

> *In the school library, Emma breaks up with Joshua because she has a crush on the new quarterback, Logan. Later, in the lunchroom, Seth and Garrett discuss ways to meet girls. After school Emma meets Ryan at the mall to talk about her breakup with*

Joshua. Kaitlyn and Olivia overhear their conver-
sation, and that evening at the bowling alley they tell
Aidan what they heard. The next day in Spanish class,
Logan asks Jasmine out, but she tells him she's already
started dating Owen. Meanwhile Hannah and Jasmine
plan to hold a party at Hannah's house while her
parents are out....

Steve looked up from the page and glanced out the window at the square, the people.

He had sat in this café many times before and looked out at the same square. He thought he'd known this place. He thought he'd loved it. But now he felt as if he'd never really known it at all.

He thought about the voices. The voices coming up through that hole in Niek's floor.

Now what do I do? he wondered.

After a few minutes, the waitress brought his coffee and set it down without a word or a glance. He put in the sugar and the brown creamer, stirred the coffee, and took a sip. Coffee in the Netherlands was always delicious, and this cup was no exception. On the saucer, next to the cup, was a little packaged cookie. Steve pocketed it for later, to throw to birds.

During his years in L.A., Steve had met people of all kinds. But as far as he knew, he'd never encountered a Muslim. He'd read a lot of history, but his knowledge of Islam was pretty scanty. He'd certainly never given the religion much thought.

He remembered that he'd once read a book about Sufism, an Islamic mystical tradition, but he didn't know why he'd read it and couldn't recall anything in particular about the contents. There had also been a good deal about Islam in a James Michener novel, *The Source*, that he'd read and enjoyed in his teens.

What else? He scoured his memory banks. Let's see. *Lawrence of Arabia*. Omar Khayyam. Omar Sharif. *Casablanca*, although that hardly counted, given that the characters seemed to come from pretty much everyplace except Casablanca itself. Bob Hope and Bing Crosby in *The Road to Morocco*, although of course now his list was getting ridiculous.

Okay, he thought. *What to do? What to do?*

He reassured himself with the thought that he didn't need to come up with something right away. *Take time to think*, he told himself. *Think. Think.*

On the wall facing the bar was a rack of the day's newspapers, all neatly arranged – and, as yet, unread. Almost idly, he went over and took down a copy of *Trouw*. He carried it back to his table, glanced over the headlines on the front page, then leafed through the rest of the paper. At first he did so quickly, casually. Then, at around page ten, he went back to the first page and started over again, carefully checking every headline on every page and reading the first sentence or two of each story.

He didn't understand every word, but, as always, he was able to make out enough to get the gist. There were reports about government power shifts and economic policies, about highway accidents and soccer games, and on and on and on. But nothing about...things like this.

He folded up the copy of *Trouw,* returned it to the rack, then took down *De Volkskrant* and went through the same meticulous process. Then he returned *De Volkskrant* and took down *NRC Handelsblad* and went through it, too, page by page, column by column. He did so with a mounting sense of urgency.

Where was it? he wondered. Where was the one news story, just one, that might reflect the reality of landlords like Ahmed, of muggers like that boy on the Amstel, of men like those whose voices had come up last night through the floor of Niek's bedroom?

But no. There was nothing.

Three young Dutchwomen walked into the café, chatting merrily, and after surveying the room selected a table some distance away from Steve's. The same waitress who'd waited on him went over to them almost at once and gave them a big smile. Regulars, probably. After taking their order, she swung by Steve.

"Another coffee?" she asked. "Anything to eat?"

Suddenly he felt restless. "No thanks," he replied. She nodded and went into the kitchen. Steve didn't know what to do, but he knew he needed to do something, not just sit there. He finished his coffee, shoved the script summary back into his shoulder bag, left a ten-guilder note on the table, and walked out onto the Spui. He waited while a tram passed on its way to Centraal Station, then crossed the Nieuwezijds Voorburgwal and went into the American Book Center. He walked up the curving stairs and looked around. He'd been in this store a few times, but he'd never before looked for a religion section. After poking around for a while he concluded that there wasn't one.

Okay, that left the library.

He walked up to Prinsengracht. The library was a clunky modern building surrounded by beautiful seventeenth-century houses. He climbed the steps and went in. The room he entered was largish, brightly lit, and lined with shelves; library users, mostly schoolchildren, were reading and writing at several closely packed tables, and the three librarians sitting at the big, curved counter looked busy. He crossed the room and, after consulting a directory on the wall, walked up a couple of flights of stairs. On the second floor he made his way through the stacks and found the religion section. Christianity. Catholicism. Protestantism. Most of the books were in English.

Islam.

Aha.

He knelt down and read the spines. There were volumes on Islamic theology, Islamic history, Islamic culture. Finally he found a book – a single chartreuse-covered book – about Islam in Europe.

He pulled it off the shelf. It was in English, the product of a small British publisher. He walked around, found an unoccupied table, sat down, and read the first few pages. The author, a man named Watson who was identified in the front matter as an Oxford graduate and a *Guardian* columnist, stated in his very first sentence that he wasn't a Muslim himself. His book, he explained, was in part a study of recent history – the mass immigration of Muslims into the cities of Europe during the last quarter century or so – and in part an argument. The argument was straightforward: that Islam, contrary to the claims of some critics, did not in any way represent a threat to Europe, even though, as Watson readily admitted, the number of Muslims in Europe was growing rapidly. Those who suggested that these developments *were* a threat, he maintained, were nothing but bigots and fearmongers. Far, indeed, from being a threat, he insisted, Islam represented "a rich, new source of spiritual nourishment for a continent that has become far too secularized."

Steve looked through Watson's book for the names of people who'd raised concerns about the rise of Islam in Europe. After a couple of minutes he discovered that Watson singled out one individual for special vilification – a Dutch politician named Jeroen Schrama. Originally a professor of sociology, Schrama had entered politics in the mid nineties precisely because he worried about where Islamic immigration was leading. Since then he'd gained a considerable following – a fact Watson described as "disturbing." He called Schrama a "fascist" and a "racist." A few sentences later, however, Watson mentioned in passing that Schrama was gay – with a Moroccan ex-boyfriend, no less – and he quoted a statement in which Schrama decried Islam's brutal oppression of women and gays and condemned this oppression as a threat to the proud Dutch heritage of liberty.

So which was it, then? Was Schrama a fascist? Or was he an anti-fascist?

Curiously, while citing Schrama's criticism of the treatment of women and gays under Islam, Watson didn't seem to have any response to it. He left the impression that what was offensive was not Islam's oppression of gays and woman but, rather, Schrama's concern about it. Watson also seemed to imply that he, Watson, was morally superior to the likes of Schrama because he was prepared to overlook that oppression in the name of respect for Islamic belief and tradition.

Steve returned Watson's book to the Islam section, then went downstairs and outside, where he walked along the canal to Leidsestraat. Why, he wondered, hadn't he ever heard of Schrama? After all, he'd immersed himself in Dutch culture, history, and language. No, he hadn't put as much emphasis on following the Dutch news day-to-day, but he *had* looked at Dutch newspapers enough to get a sense – or so he thought – of what the big issues were and who the important public figures were. But he'd never run across anything about Islam in the Netherlands – or about Schrama. Could it be that the editors of the major Dutch media had – well – an agenda not unlike Watson's?

And what about his friends in Amsterdam, who'd never talked to him about any of this?

He thought of Henk, his friend at the university. What did Henk know about all this? At Leidsestraat Steve made a left and headed back toward the Spui. At Koningsplein he continued on down Heiligeweg toward Kalverstraat and made the first left turn on to Handboogstraat, a narrow, cobbled pedestrian street that opened on to the Spui. Halfway down the block he walked up a half-flight of iron steps and pressed a buzzer next to Henk's name.

After a moment, a voice came through the speaker. "Hallo?"

"Hi Henk. It's Steve Disch."

"Oh, Steve!"

"Sorry to bother you, but I just want to talk if you have a couple of minutes."

"Sure," Henk said, and buzzed him up.

Inside, Steve climbed a set of steep, narrow stairs to a door that Henk opened just as Steve reached it. "Hi, hi," Henk said heartily, and gave him a hug. "Come on in."

Henk was about Steve's height and about his age. His flat was charming. There were no canal views, but the location couldn't have been finer and the main room, though small, was very sweet, with a high ceiling and walls covered with books. There was a graceful old rolltop desk cluttered with papers, two beautiful old chairs by the window, which looked out across the Handboogstraat at a couple of other elegant old buildings about ten feet away.

"Would you like coffee?" Henk asked. "Or perhaps it's not too early for a beer?"

"I'll have something if you do," Steve said. "I don't want to keep you too long...." He gestured toward Henk's desk.

"I wasn't doing anything important," Henk said. "Just reading some mail. I don't teach on Tuesdays."

Henk walked out and came back after a moment with a couple of three-deciliter beers. He handed one to Steve, and raised his glass.

"To gay marriage in the Netherlands," he said.

"To gay marriage," Steve said.

They drank. The beer was cold and bracing. Steve swallowed.

"You, as much as anyone else, deserve congratulations," Steve said.

"A lot of people do."

"I'm sure."

"Some of whom are no longer with us."

"It's a wonderful thing. I never imagined – I mean, when I was in college – "

Henk smiled. "Me too. It's been a long struggle." He sipped some beer. "But I have to say that we're lucky to have such a sensible system here. It isn't emotional and crazy and...*hysterical*...like in the States."

"No."

"Nobody was whipping up the people into antigay prejudice and telling them that God hates fags. We presented arguments based on logic and principle, and the politicians debated the issue in a civilized way, and over time the fair and sensible view won out. And here we are. The first country in the world, ever, with gay marriage. Think of it! I'm sorry, please, sit."

Steve sat down in one of the chairs and Henk took the other. They put their beers down on a small antique table between them.

"So tell me, how's it going?" Henk asked. "How's life on the Krom Boomsloot? You did move there, right? Rob told me before he left that you guys had made an arrangement."

"Well, actually that didn't work out in the end," Steve said. "But thank you anyway for introducing me to Rob. He was very nice."

"Yes, he's a good man. He was a good source for my book about gay life in postwar Amsterdam. He used to know everybody. You don't happen to own a copy of that, do you?"

"No, I'm afraid not. I'll look it up."

"No need. I have a million extra copies. Drink some of your beer." Henk got up, left the room again, and after a moment came back with a slim pink paperback. "Here, you can work on your Dutch," he said, handing it to Steve.

"Thank you, Henk." Steve looked at the book, then set it down next to his beer.

"So you're still living on – what was it, Huidekoperstraat?"

"No. Actually, now I'm on Bellamyplein."

"Oh! Bellamyplein."

"I guess you're familiar with it."

"Of course."

"It's a...well, an interesting neighborhood."

"It certainly is," Henk said. "That building that still has tram tracks leading into it? That used to be the main place where they stored and repaired trams. An interesting history."

"An interesting present, too."

"Yes, it's more and more diverse these days. It's actually a lot like an immigrant neighborhood in New York. Very dynamic and colorful. So I suppose maybe as an American you feel more at home there than in sleepy Huidekoperstraat or on the quaint old Krom Boomsloot!" Henk laughed.

Steve sipped some more beer.

"You're right," Steve said, "it's very different from the Amsterdam I thought I knew when I moved here. But it's not really diverse in the sense that...well, I guess it's kind of like Chinatown or Little Italy. You know, so many people being from the same part of the world, with the same culture."

"Yes."

"In fact, there's actually a Turkish flag hanging in front of the building I'm living in."

Henk's expression shifted slightly. Discomfort? "Yes, we do see that sort of thing now." He picked up his beer and took a long, drawn-out slug.

"And not just in Amsterdam, right?"

84

"No, in all the big cities. Here and in Belgium, too. There are even more people from the Muslim countries in Rotterdam than in Amsterdam."

"Really?"

"Yes. A lot more, actually."

"Wow."

"And very many in Antwerp."

"Around Bellamyplein there are lots of women in those...those head coverings. Whatever they're called."

"Hijab," Henk said.

"Right, hijab. Which represents submission, right?"

"Yes."

"I've even seen little girls wearing them."

Henk nodded. "I have, too." His tone was noncommittal.

"So what do you make of all this?"

"What do you mean?"

"I mean is this a good thing? These ideas coming here?"

Henk shrugged, and took a lengthy pause. "Well," he finally said, "it's their culture."

"But what about your culture? What about the liberal Netherlands? And gay rights? Doesn't this represent a threat to everything you believe in? And have worked for?"

Henk drank some beer and then looked into Steve's eyes for several seconds. "You wouldn't happen to be interviewing me for an article or something, would you?" he asked.

"Lordy no," Steve said. "Of course not."

"Private?"

"Totally private."

"Okay," Henk said. "Well, speaking entirely off the record, I can't say I haven't thought about this subject more and more. But it's very hard to talk about it, especially with people at the university. You can almost say it's *verboden* to talk about it."

"Really?"

"I'm afraid so. The reigning idea is that it's racist even to contemplate it critically. After all, we're talking about people who are poor and downtrodden, people who have been cruelly oppressed, people who have maybe been victims of Western colonialism and imperialism. People who we may owe something to. A new life. Possibilities of the kind that we enjoy here."

"But those little girls in...in hijabs. What kind of possibilities do those hijabs symbolize?"

"I know," Henk said. "It's a tough one."

"I feel sorry for people who have been oppressed," Steve said. "But when you see little girls in hijab, it looks as though they've brought the oppression with them."

Henk nodded ruefully. Then, noticing that Steve's beer was empty, he asked alertly: "Would you like another?"

"I don't want to keep you."

"Please. I'm glad you're here. I'll get you another." He picked up Steve's glass as he rose to his feet. While he went out, Steve picked up the pink book and paged through it.

Henk came back with another beer and handed it to Steve.

"Thanks." Steve sipped some beer, swallowed it. "Speaking of all this," Steve said, "I was mugged the other day. By a young Muslim guy."

Henk was genuinely perturbed. "Oh, I'm so sorry," he said. "Were you hurt?"

"No. I was lucky. But it was weird. In my whole life in L.A., I was never mugged. Not once. I used to go out drinking in Santa Monica and Venice, and sometimes after the bars closed at two A.M. I would walk up and down the beach, all alone, half drunk. Anybody who knows that part of town could tell you that that was a reckless thing to do. But nothing ever happened. And yet it happened to me here in Amsterdam, just the other day. In the last city on earth where I ever would have expected such a thing."

"Where exactly was this?"

"On the Amstel. Right outside Gaiety."

"Shit. Maybe your guard was down?"

"Oh, it was. Definitely. It was late at night and there was nobody around and I was holding money in my hand where anybody could see it. I would never do that in L.A.."

Henk nodded.

"He called me 'faggot,'" Steve added.

Henk took this in, wincing in sympathy. Steve sipped some more beer, and Henk did too.

"The thing we have to hope," Henk finally said, "is that these people who come here from these places will change over time, with our influence. Those little girls in hijab are living in the freest city in the world. That mugger is living in the gayest city in the world. It has to have an impact on them as they grow up. Don't you think so? We have to hope, that's really what it comes down to. We have to hope."

They sat there in silence for a moment.

"But that's not what your life has ever been about," Steve finally said. "You've never just sat and hoped. You fought."

Henk nodded wordlessly. He had some more beer, then put his glass down. When he spoke, his voice was low.

"I don't know how to fight this," he said simply.

After another long pause Steve cleared his throat. "What do you know," he asked, "about Jeroen Schrama?"

A fond smile crept across Henk's face. "He's actually an old friend of mine," Henk said. "We were students together. We were very involved together in some of the early gay-rights stuff." He smiled. "I wanted to sleep with him – he was very beautiful – but I wasn't his type. But he was nice about it. He's immensely charming. And smart. He's from a rich old family in The Hague, you know. They even have a castle – an actual castle, a *Schloss* – in Beieren...Bayern...um..."

"Bavaria."

"Yes, Bavaria."

"How do you feel about what he's doing these days? Do you consider him a fascist or a racist or anything like that?"

"Of course not, that's all a bunch of nonsense. He stands for everything I stand for. He believes passionately in freedom. He's a very good man, and a lot braver than I am. A hundred times braver! He knew when he started speaking out that he would lose his academic career and most of his friends. Do you know much about his career?"

"I'm ashamed to say I never even heard his name before today."

"Well, until he started writing about Islam and immigration he was a respected sociologist at the university in Rotterdam. He quit his job to be a full-time politician, and joined one of the non-socialist political parties. But he got too hot even for them, and they kicked him out like a leper. He had to start his own party. And he's so brilliant at putting into words the – how to say it? – the liberal values of the Dutch electorate, and their frustrations with the unliberalism of Islam – you can say that, no? Unliberalism?"

"Illiberalism. Illiberality."

" – he's so wonderful at that, that in the last election, to the shock of absolutely everyone in the political and media establishment, all of whom despise him, he won a seat in the Tweede Kamer. You know what the Tweede Kamer is, no?"

"The Dutch legislature."

"The lower house, actually. But in this country the lower house is the more powerful house. It's the one that really matters."

"Like the Commons in Britain."

"Sort of."

"So Schrama lost a lot of friends...but also made a lot of friends."

"Millions of them. A constantly growing number. It's possible he'll be our next Prime Minister."

"Really?"

"Yes. More than just possible."

"A gay prime minister?"

"It would be appropriate, no? First country with gay marriage, first country with a gay Prime Minister."

"Wow."

"But what it will be like if that happens, I can't begin to imagine. He is so universally hated by the elite, not just the politicians and media but also the corporate bosses, that his election would be this giant 'fuck you' to them from the voters."

Steve and Henk sat there in thought for a few moments, and sipped some more beer. "There's something else," Steve eventually said. "I don't know if I should mention it or not."

"What's that?"

"Where I'm living. It's just above a – well, the sign calls it a community center. It's the place with the Turkish flag."

"Yes."

"I'm just above it, on the first floor. I can hear them talking below me. Through the floor."

"And?"

"I don't know. Last night I heard them say some things. They seemed to be...they seemed to be planning something."

"How could you tell? What language were they speaking?"

"Well, first they were speaking some language I don't know. Arabic or whatever."

"Maybe Turkish, given the flag."

"Of course. How stupid of me. Yes, probably Turkish."

"But then there was a person there who couldn't speak that language. He was speaking Dutch. But it sounded as if some of the others couldn't understand Dutch."

"That is more than likely."

"So they all started speaking English."

"Yes, many of these people who have lived here for years can't speak any Dutch, but they can communicate with the – you know, the social agencies and police and so forth – in broken English."

"Yes, that's what they were speaking. Broken English. Very broken. Anyway, they were planning something."

"What kind of thing?"

"Something...something violent."

"Are you sure?"

After a moment: "Yes."

"How could you be sure? How could you hear so well from upstairs?"

"I wondered that too. So I looked this morning. Under the bed there's a hole in the floor. Where the wood has worn away. Just...worn away."

Hank shot Steve what Steve interpreted as a skeptical look.

"If you don't believe me, come on over. I'll show you."

"Oh, certainly I believe you," Henk reassured him. "Remember, I know this city inside out. You yourself have been around enough to see all the houses with the steel beams leaning against them so they won't topple over. This whole city is nothing but a bunch of crumbling old wood. Standing in polluted water. On long algae-covered wooden beams. That are stuck dozens of meters into the soft, marshy land far below. And all of it getting more rotten every day." He paused and then added: "Not that it keeps me from loving every square meter of it."

He smiled. Steve smiled back.

"I know you love it too," Henk said.

"I do."

Suddenly Henk stood up. "One more," he said, nodding toward their beer glasses, both of which were almost empty now. He picked them up and disappeared again into the kitchen.

He returned a moment later with two fresh beers.

Handing Steve his glass, Henk drank from his own as he crossed the room. "So they were really planning something violent?"

"Yes."

"What?"

"Some kind of attack. It wasn't clear where. Or when."

"Have you told anybody else?"

"No."

"Why didn't you go to the police first thing this morning?"

"I don't know. The whole thing just kind of stunned me. I needed to...think. I guess maybe I needed to have this talk." Steve gestured, indicating Henk and himself. "I guess I've been so discombobulated by this apartment problem – "

"What problem?"

"Never mind, that's not really important now. It's just that I've only been in this flat a few days, and I'm emotionally exhausted from the drama – "

"Drama? Does it have anything to do with Rob? Because he – "

"No, not Rob. His landlord."

"What kind of trouble could you have with his landlord?"

"Oh, it was just impossible."

"Really? That's curious. In this country, people can be very stubborn, but there's *always* a way to work things out."

"The landlord's name is Ahmed. He wanted to use the sublet situation as an excuse to evict Rob."

That silenced Henk. Finally he said, simply, "Oh."

"But there's no need to go into that. It's just that after moving to Bellamyplein, I didn't want to be plunged into the middle of another mess and didn't want to have to move yet again. But that's not logical. It's silly, selfish thinking."

"Yes, it is," Henk agreed with typical Dutch bluntness.

"But then again, what exactly *do* I have to offer the police? A few overheard sentences, with no details whatsoever. If the police went over there, these guys could just tell them I misunderstood what I was hearing. And they'd be off the hook, and I'd have to move because they'd know I'd ratted them out."

"Even so," Henk said, "you have to go to the police. That's all there is to it. If you have to move, you have to move. We'll find some other place for you. That's not what matters."

Steve picked up his beer and finished the whole glass off before speaking again. "You're right," he said. "Of course you're right. I'll go right now."

"Do you want me to come with you?"

"No, thank you, Henk. That's kind of you, but it's not necessary. I can handle it."

Steve got up, prepared to go. "Wait one second," Henk said.

He got up, left the room, and came back with another slim book. He placed it in Steve's hands. The cover was simple – black words on a white background: *De Islamisering van Nederland.* The author was Jeroen Schrama.

"I'm sorry, but this one is only a loan, not a gift," Henk said. "I don't have another copy. But I think you will find it useful reading."

T HE CLOSEST POLICE STATION Steve was aware of was on Lijnbaansgracht, down the block from Leidseplein and across the street from Melkweg, a large modern building outside of which he was always seeing teenagers lining up for rock concerts. Leaving Henk's apartment, he headed up Leidsestraat. It was late afternoon now, and the street was crowded not only with the usual tourists but also with locals heading home from work. Bicycles swarmed in both directions.

At Leidseplein he made a right in front of the Stadsschouwburg, a handsome old brick theater, and walked down the narrow Lijnbaansgracht. The police station was on the right, up a half-dozen steps. Steve climbed them, opened the door, and walked in. A middle-aged woman officer sat there, her elbow resting on her desk, and her head resting on her hand, her bony fingers spread out across her cheek.

"*Goedemiddag,*" she said, sitting up straight and looking him right in the eye.

"Good afternoon," he replied in English. "Do you mind if I speak English?"

"That's fine," she said crisply. Already her expression was impatient.

This wouldn't be an easy exchange, Steve saw. One thing he'd learned back in L.A., where he'd read every history of the Netherlands he could get his hands on, was that Dutch women, for many centuries, enjoyed rights that women elsewhere in Europe, no matter what their social class, could barely imagine. But in order to secure and preserve those rights, and to exercise them safely and successfully, they learned to exude a strength and independence – and, above all, what some men might call a sexlessness – that set them dramatically apart from their counterparts in, say, France or Germany or Italy. To this day, many Dutch women, especially those who sat behind desks in positions of power, continued to possess those same daunting traits. Steve had already run across a few examples of the type – most recently, Miep. Was this another? As she stared coolly at him, taking his measure, asserting her authority, she certainly seemed to fit the stereotype.

"I think," Steve told her, trying to match her self-assurance with his own, "there's something I need to report."

"You *think* there's something? Or there *is* something?" Her tone was no-nonsense, her voice that of a veteran cop interrogating a suspect.

"There is something," Steve said.

"What kind of something?"

"Well, it's something I overheard that I think maybe the police should know about."

"Something you *overheard?*" She made it sound ridiculous.

"Yes. It may be nothing, but I thought I should come here anyway."

"So what is it then?"

"Well, I'm living in a flat in Bellamyplein –"

"Are you a Dutch citizen?" Her eyes hadn't moved from his.

"No. American."

"United States?"

"Yes."

"Because you know of course that American can mean anyone in North or South America."

"Okay."

"Do you have a Dutch residence permit?"

"No. I'm here on a tourist visa."

"You have a tourist visa but you are living in an apartment? Do you own it?"

"No, I'm just staying in it. It belongs to a friend."

"Are you renting it?"

"Yes."

"Do you realize that it is illegal for foreigners who are here on tourist visas to rent apartments?"

"No, I didn't."

"Well, it is. It is illegal."

"That's interesting, given that there are several

97

big companies in this city that do nothing but rent apartments to foreigners who are here on tourist visas." As he spoke, she sat there stock still, looking as if she were posing for a portrait. "And as far as I can see," he said, "they operate totally openly. I mean, it's no secret what they're doing." He mentioned the name of the company from which he'd leased the apartment on Huidekoper-straat.

"Just because they do it does not mean that it is legal. Did you rent the apartment from that firm?"

"You mean the one I'm in now?"

"Yes."

"No. As I said, I'm just renting it from a friend."

"And you are here on a brief vacation? A week or two?"

"No, I'm here for longer."

"How long have you been here so far?"

"A little over a month."

"Do you know that you cannot stay more than three months on a tourist visa?"

"Yes, I know. I've been planning to apply for a longer-term visa."

"Well, you shouldn't plan, you should do it."

"I'll do it. That's no problem."

"Do you have a job in the Netherlands?"

"No. I have a job in California."

"You have a job in California?"

"Yes."

"Then why aren't you in California?"

"I'm doing the job from here."

"Well, in that case, if you plan to stay more than six months, you will have to pay Dutch income taxes, do you know that?"

That was one thing Steve had actually never thought of.

"Okay," he said.

"How long *do* you plan to stay?"

"I don't know. Maybe a year. Or maybe I'll want to stay here permanently, if possible."

"All right, you say that you overheard something?"

The policewoman's sudden switch back to the subject at hand threw him. He took a breath. "Yes. I was sleeping last night and I heard voices from downstairs. A place that calls itself a community center. It has a Turkish flag flying outside. There were people down there talking."

"Talking about what?"

"About plans. Plans to commit...some kind of terrorist attack."

She exhibited no discernible reaction to this. "And how could you understand them? What language were they speaking?"

"They were speaking English."

"They were planning a terrorist attack in English?"

She made *this* sound ridiculous, too.

"Well, first they were talking in what I guess was

99

Turkish. But one guy there was speaking Dutch, and they didn't understand each other, so they all went into English."

"And what did they say in English?" Steve couldn't be sure, but her tone struck him as sarcastic.

"They talked about planting explosives at some place and blowing it up."

"Which place?"

"I don't know."

"When?"

"I don't know."

"And you don't know who these terrorist plotters are, either? Their names?"

"No."

"But you do know that they are Turks. Or something like that," she said dryly.

"I guess so," Steve replied. "I don't know. Maybe not the Dutch-speaking guy. Who knows?"

The policewoman sat there silently for a few seconds. She looked down at her papers, then up at Steve again. "How can you hear something so clearly through a floor?"

"There's a hole in the floor."

"There's a hole in the floor," she echoed him. "Did you put it there?"

"No, of course not."

"There is no 'of course' about it. How do I know you did not put the hole in the floor?"

"Well, I didn't."

"Still, even if there is a hole in this floor, do you not think that perhaps you misunderstood what you heard?"

"No, I don't think I did."

"Perhaps they were speaking British English and you didn't understand it very well because you are an American, who speaks American, not actual English."

"I have no trouble understanding British English."

"They are two very different languages." This, Steve had discovered, was a favorite Dutch conceit.

"No, they aren't."

"So let me summarize what you are telling me. At this very moment you are living in this country illegally, and working here illegally, and renting an apartment illegally, and you want to make trouble for people whose status in this country is most likely entirely legal."

"I'm only trying to do what's right."

"It is the Netherlands that is trying to do what's right. These people – and what we are talking about here, of course, is people from the Muslim world – they have been subjected to enough...enough..." She reached for a word, then finally said: "...*vooroordeel.*"

"Prejudice."

Her eyebrows shot up just a bit. "Yes, prejudice. So you understand some Dutch."

"*Ja. Een beetje.*"

"Well, if you want to live here, then try to understand not just our language but our values. And one of our values is our belief in helping the poor and weak people of the world. You in the United States may be proud of your power and your wealth, but here in this little country of ours we do not need to be rich and to have everything and get fat while other people are starving. We believe in sharing from what we have. Maybe you should go back to Bellamyplein and think about that."

STEVE WALKED BACK DOWN the steps outside the police station, more or less numb. His steps took him back to Leidseplein, and then down Leidsestraat. He turned onto Reguliersdwarstraat and went into April. It was happy hour. The place was packed. He surveyed the crowd. No Joop, no Jordy. Nobody he knew. He went back outside, continued down the street, crossed Muntplein, and walked down along the Amstel to Gaiety. Peering in through the windowed door, he saw one customer, alone at a table – the wizened old man who was always at Gaiety at this hour, reading newspapers. Piet was on duty. Steve went in and sat at the bar.

"Hoi!" Piet greeted him cheerily as he reflexively grabbed a glass and started tapping Steve a beer. "That Roberto," he said.

"What about him?"

"He's one confused guy." Piet put the beer in front of Steve.

"What do you mean?"

"Just confused," said Piet. "He's going back to Italy tomorrow, you know."

"Oh."

"He wanted to spend today with me, but I was busy. And tonight he wanted to have dinner with me, but I'm going to Haarlem to have dinner with a friend."

Piet went to the men's room. Steve noticed something new on the wall behind the bar: a thousand-lira note, signed "Love, Roberto."

When Piet came back out Steve said, "Hey, Piet."

"Yeah?" Piet started wiping down the bar with a cloth.

"You know I just moved to a new place."

"Oh yeah?"

"Yeah. In the Oud West."

"Oh!" He made a face.

"Not your favorite part of town?"

"A shit part of town. Watch your step."

"Also, I never told you. I got mugged the other night. Right outside here. A guy with a knife."

"Fuck. Did he hurt you?"

"No, I gave him my money and he ran away."

"A *Marokkaan*?"

"I don't know."

"Well, he wasn't Dutch or American or English or anything like that, was he?"

"No, he looked north African or whatever."

"Yeah. No surprise. It's always them. Scum!" Piet looked up at the clock. "Fuck, almost time to go Haarlem. Where the hell is Willem?" Willem was the old man who owned Gaiety and who alternated bar shifts with Piet.

Steve was just finishing his beer when Willem showed up. Steve greeted him, said goodbye to Piet, and went back out. He walked around the corner to the Febo automat on Reguliersbreestraat, the wide street connecting Muntplein with Rembrandtplein, and "ate from the wall" – shoving coins in the slots next to a couple of chicken sandwiches and then scarfing them down as he walked down toward Rembrandtplein.

He turned onto the narrow pedestrian street, Halve Maansteeg – Half Moon Alley – and peeked into a couple of the bars. They were crowded – it was happy hour there, too.

No Joop, no Jordy.

Steve continued on down to the Amstel and turned left and walked along the river and glanced into Gaiety as he passed. There were only two people inside: Willem, who was behind the bar reading a newspaper, and Roberto, who was sitting at the bar looking sullen.

Steve hesitated for a moment, then went in.

When he sat next to Roberto, Roberto hardly acknowledged his presence. Willem gave him a friendly nod, put down his paper, and drew him a beer. He put it down in front of Steve, who picked it up and sipped it.

Finally Roberto spoke. "You know Piet is in Haarlem."

"Yes, I know."

"His friends are more important to him than me."

"Well, maybe he had an important engagement he couldn't cancel."

"Piet doesn't take anything seriously. Especially me and my feelings. He's just a joker."

Willem, who was fussing with bottles behind the bar, overheard. Turning, he wagged a gnarled, arthritic finger at Roberto. "Never become serious with a bartender!" he admonished him.

FINISHING UP HIS BEER AT GAIETY, Steve told Roberto that he had to go back home and get some work done. "I'm leaving tomorrow morning," Roberto said with mournful self-pity.

"I'm sorry to hear that," Steve told him. "Have a good trip. I enjoyed meeting you."

"I enjoyed meeting you too," Roberto said.

"Maybe you'll come back again soon?"

Roberto shook his head. "I don't think I will ever come back to Amsterdam. It is so beautiful, it breaks my heart."

Steve left and walked up the Amstel. It was dark now. Across the water, the Hotel de l'Europe was ablaze in lights. He told himself that he should, in fact, head back to Bellamyplein and do some work. But at Muntplein, instead of grabbing the tram home, he headed up the Singel.

A couple of minutes later he was in April. It was still crowded. He squeezed his way up to the bar and raised his voice over the hubbub to order a beer. He was waiting for it when he felt a tap on his shoulder. He turned around – and looked up.

Joop.

IV

S O WHERE IS THIS HOLE?" Steve and Joop were in the apartment on Bellamyplein. They'd bought two cheap bottles of chardonnay at Gall & Gall before getting on the tram. Now Joop was standing next to a side table in the living room, opening one of the bottles with a corkscrew Steve had found in the kitchen.

"Shh."

"This is actually a nice apartment," Joop said, lowering his voice.

"Well, it *could* be nice," Steve replied. "It's just filthy and full of old crap. And there *is* that hole in the floor."

"Even so, by Amsterdam standards, it's got a lot to offer. This isn't L.A., after all, with swimming pools all over the place." Joop poured two glasses of wine, then put the bottle down. They picked up the glasses. "*Proost*," Joop said, lifting his.

"*Proost.*"

They sipped.

"So where," Joop said again, "is this hole?"

"I told you. Under the bed."

"Let me see."

"I can't."

"Are you kidding?"

"No. It's too late already. They might be down there. I don't want them to hear us moving the bed."

"Okay."

"You can see it in the morning."

"Okay."

"Not that there's anything to see. It's just a hole in a piece of wood."

Joop had offered to stay until morning. They'd made it clear: no sex. Just a chaste sleepover, so he could listen with Steve for voices, and help him make out anything that might be said downstairs in Dutch. And provide moral support.

That was all.

"So you think they might be there now?" Joop said. "Maybe we should go in and listen."

"Okay."

Steve led Joop across the dark dining room into the bedroom. They were both in their stocking feet, having left their shoes just inside the apartment door, Dutch style. They stood in the bedroom in silence, heads cocked. Joop was wearing a white dress shirt, a forest-green sweater vest, and jeans. In that small space, standing so close to Steve, he looked even taller than usual.

Their eyes met.

"Do you hear anything?" Joop whispered.

Steve shook his head. "You?"

Joop shook his head, then led Steve back into the living room, where they sat on the couch.

"So how come all the time I was salivating over this country," Steve said, "you never told me about all this Islam stuff?"

Joop shrugged. "What should I have said?"

"You could've at least mentioned that it existed."

"Why ruin your fun? I never believed you would actually move here. You know how many summer tourists, especially Americans, talk about moving here? It's an old joke in this town. And if I *had* believed you'd really move here, I never would have thought you'd end up in Bellamyplein. Not you. Not Mr. Disney."

"Oh god, don't call me that."

"Most Americans who do live in Amsterdam – these people with fancy corporation jobs – they never see these parts of the city. Even if they stay here for years. And of course tourists don't see them either."

"What about Jeroen Schrama?"

"Huh?"

"Jeroen Schrama. You know the name?"

"Of course."

"What do you think of him?"

"I don't know. On the news they talk about him as if he's the Devil."

"But what do *you* think?"

"I don't know."

"Honest?"

"Of course."

"Don't gay people here talk about him?"

"Nobody I know. You know how it is in the Netherlands. Unless you're very, very close to somebody, you don't talk with them about certain things. Not like you Americans."

"But you have close gay friends. They never talk about Schrama? Or about the whole Islam thing?"

"Well, if they have enough beers, and it gets late, maybe they lean in close to you and they say something about how one of their neighbors or their grandmother got mugged by a *Marokkaans*. Maybe they'll say a *verdomd Marokkaans* - a damned *Marokaans*. And maybe if they're angry enough or drunk enough, they'll say something about the fucking Muslims. And maybe they'll say that Schrama has a point. But they're almost scared to say it."

"Really?"

"Yes. And more than that, you're almost scared to hear it. You feel like - I don't know, like you're talking about something you shouldn't be talking about."

"But this is a free country."

"Yeah, it's a free country. But it's also a very small country. People like to get along. They *have* to get along. So we have a strong tendency for, what's the word, *overeenstemming.*"

Steve reached for his van Dale Dutch-English dictionary, a dark-blue hardcover. "What's that word again?" Joop repeated it, and Steve looked it up. "Consensus," Steve said.

"Right. Consensus. We all feel more comfortable with consensus."

"And Schrama goes against the consensus."

"Yes, to put it mildly. Nobody in this country has gone against the consensus so much in my lifetime, I think."

Suddenly they both heard it. The front door downstairs, slamming shut.

In silence, their eyes met. Then Joop stood up, snapped Steve's glass out of his hand, and moved with cat-like steps over to the table, where he refilled both of their glasses. He looked at Steve as he did so.

"There's time," Joop said softly. "We can have another glass in here."

Steve nodded.

Joop brought the glasses over and handed one to Steve. "I did know about the importance of consensus here," Steve said, trying to keep his voice down. "Every book about how to deal with Dutch business people talks about it. But they make it sound positive. How everybody's opinion counts, from the CEO to the guy in the mail room."

"Right."

"And you try not to make a decision until you can come up with something that everybody can agree on. Yes, as a result it takes longer for businesses to make decisions, but it also ensures that everybody walks away happy. But the kind of consensus you're describing is something kind of different. People like Schrama come along and disrupt – I don't know – the harmony, or the illusion of harmony, by saying that the emperor has no clothes, and they're...pushed away. Demonized."

"Well, in politics it's different I guess than in business," said Joop. "*Overeenstemming* got to be important here because we had a lot of groups with very strong and different opinions. Calvinists, Catholics, Lutherans, Mennonites, Quakers, Jews, atheists, everything. We saw other countries going to war over these kinds of differences. We didn't want that. We're not warriors. We're practical-minded people. Commercial people. We wanted to get rich together, not kill each other, like the rest of Europe. So we arrived at this system."

"*Overeenstemming.*"

"Yes. Every group not only gets a hearing, a vote, but gets respected and gets what they want and need. It's how we got gay marriage. The gays came along and said, well, we're not happy with the way things are. We feel we need this. And so instead of saying fuck you, fuck off, you're a small minority, who cares what you think you want or need, the people in the Tweede Kamer say, okay, we need to do something to make this group happy, because we're all part of the same society and we all need to be able to live together and work together so we can prosper together and be happy together. So they talk and talk and the people who are against gay marriage raise their concerns, and the gays address them, and after they talk enough – and of course you know Dutch people love to talk – "

Steve smiled.

" – there's this growing feeling of mutual trust and respect and understanding, and so they all eventually finally come to an agreement, and so, well, we become the first country in the history of the whole world, ever, to get gay marriage."

111

Joop smiled, plainly touched with national pride. He sipped a bit of his wine.

"But with Schrama?"

"With Schrama it's different. He's not a group. In fact he's *against* a group. The Mohammedans – sorry, the Muslims – they've become an official group here, just like the Calvinists and the Catholics and the others. And that's the most unacceptable thing in this country, the most *verboden* thing: to be against any of the accepted groups. The first principle, the basic principle – "

"The foundational principle."

"Yes. Is that every group accepts and respects all the others. That's the only way to work together and live together productively in such a small country. In America you can have the Jews in New York, the Mexicans in Texas, the gays in San Francisco, the Mormons in Utah – Utah, right?"

"Yes, Utah."

" – and they can all hate each other as much as they want, because none of them ever has to see any of the others, because it's such a big country. And it works. But here we're all on the same tram together every morning. So to keep the country from falling apart, we have to have this – this *overeenstemming*. And Schrama needs to be made *persona non grata.*"

"Except more and more Dutch voters are supporting him."

"That's right. And so we're in a – a *dilemma*, isn't that the same word in English?"

"Yes, dilemma."

"A growing dilemma. The people in the Tweede Kamer won't talk to him. But now he's in the Tweede Kamer, so they *have* to talk to him. They try to keep him out of their committees and whatever as much as possible...but if he gets enough support from the voters to form a government – what then?" Joop shook his head and sipped some wine. He looked toward the bedroom. "Should we go listen?" he asked.

Steve nodded.

Joop picked up the bottle of wine, gave him a look to ask if he should bring it. Steve nodded again. They walked softly into the bedroom and gently set the bottle and glasses on the floor beside the bed. Then they stood there for a moment, listening.

Nothing.

"Well, I am going to sit," Joop whispered.

To Steve's surprise, Joop began to remove his clothes, as slowly and methodically – as reverently, almost – as a verger in a sacristy. First the sweater vest, then the shirt, finally the pants. He folded everything neatly and piled it up on a chair. Steve followed suit, to the best of his ability. They sat down on the edge of the bed in their underpants and for a few minutes just sipped their wine in silence. Then, suddenly, there was the sound of somebody walking below them. Not just walking. Clomping around. Heavy shoes. Boots. Then scraping sounds, as if chairs were being moved.

But no voices. Yet.

Joop, holding his wineglass in one hand, gestured with the other. A pen. Steve nodded, stole into the living room, and came back with a pen and paper. Steve put them on the bed between himself and Joop. Joop didn't touch them.

They sat there for another few minutes, sipping wine. Finally Joop picked up the pen and wrote: *Boring.* Steve nodded and took the pen. *At least we have wine,* he wrote. Joop smiled and gestured for Steve to give him the pen. *This is the dullest time I've ever spent in bed with anybody.*

They both laughed soundlessly.

Time passed. They polished off the wine and Joop padded into the living room to open the other bottle. He came back with it, refilled their glasses, and they drank in silence. When they were halfway through the second bottle, Joop wrote: *Tired. I need to lie down.* Steve tapped his chest as if to say: *Me too.* So they both lay down, Joop closer to the wall, the two of them facing away from each other. Soon Steve cold hear Joop snoring lightly. But still there were no voices from downstairs. And then Steve fell asleep, too.

THE MORNING WAS GRAY AND DRIZZLY. Steve left the apartment with Joop and they took the tram together to Dam Square, where they parted ways in the middle of a crowd in front of the Royal Palace. Joop headed down Kalverstraat to the clothing store where he worked as a security guard; Steve walked across the Dam and plunged into Damstraat, a narrow, grungy, traffic-ridden street that was lined with pubs, gambling joints, used bookstores, cheap eateries, and tiny souvenir shops, most of them housed in dilapidated buildings.

Even at this early hour, the street was packed with tourists. It crossed several dirty-looking canals, the same ones that ran through the Red Light District, which lay just slightly to the north, to Steve's left; and every time it crossed a canal, it changed its name – first to Oude Doelenstraat, then Oude Hoogstraat, then Nieuwe Hoogstraat. Each time, it became just a bit seedier. Posted at every streetcorner were one or two scruffy-looking guys who hissed the word "coke" or "hash" or "marijuana" – or, oddly enough, "business" – into Steve's ear just as he passed them. This meant, of course, that they were selling drugs.

At the end of his walk was the Krom Boomsloot. Steve walked up along the canal to Rob's house, reached into his pocket, and took out the key that he'd forgotten to return to Niek after moving out – and that Niek had forgotten to ask him for.

Steve unlocked the door as quietly as he could, slipped his shoes off at the bottom of the steps, and tried to climb them as silently as possible. He passed Yeti's door expecting it to open, but it didn't. He reached the top and paused for a second in silence. He'd already decided that if Niek or Kees turned out to be inside, he'd explain that he had come back because he couldn't find something – his passport? his Amex card? – and thought he might have left it in Rob's flat.

Steve turned the key in the apartment door and let himself in, then closed the door quietly behind him.

It was as beautiful as ever, this place where he'd had his tantalizingly brief taste of a picture-postcard Dutch life. He looked around, taking it all in, allowing the strangeness of this return to wash over him, then walked into the bedroom, steeling himself against the possibility that Niek was snoozing in the bed. Thankfully, he wasn't. Steve walked around the bed and sat on it, facing the bookshelves. Pulling out the Brazilian boy's diary, he reached into the gap this left on the shelf.

Yes, it was there. He pulled it out and shoved it into the front of his pants. He put his hand back into the space on the shelf and felt around behind the books. Nothing else there. He removed a few more books and explored further. No. He put the books back, and tried the same thing on the shelves above and below. He finally satisfied himself that Rob hadn't hidden anything else behind any of the books.

Where else? He looked through the drawers of the bedside table, the dresser, the desk. Nothing. He wandered around the apartment, looking for other possible hiding places. He scoured the kitchen and bathroom cabinets, the spaces under the sinks. And that was about it. He couldn't think of anyplace else to look.

After about a half hour, he opened the apartment door and padded slowly down the stairs, zipping up his jacket and making sure it covered the bulge and butt of the gun. This time, as he approached Yeti's door, he heard her lock turning. The moment he set foot on her landing, her door opened: obviously she had this business down to a science. She stood there, clutching the door, staring into Steve's eyes from only inches away with something just this side of terror.

"*Het is OK,*" Steve reassured her. "*Ik vergat iets in het appartement.*"

Her expression didn't change. It felt strangely liberating not to have to care. Steve continued down the stairs, put his shoes back on, and opened the street door. Before leaving, he looked back up. She was still standing there, watching him, neither smiling nor scowling, just staring at him in the way he imagined she stared at her TV all day.

"*Tot ziens!*" he said to her, and left.

It was still drizzling. His jacket zipped up only halfway, Steve made his way back to the Nieuwe Hoogstraat and headed toward the Dam. At the far end of the bridge that crossed the Kloveniersburgwal, one of the shady drug merchants sidled up to him.

"Business?"

The guy was scrawny and relatively young, with a drawn, sallow face and watery eyes. He wore a black zip-up jacket with a big rip in it and a pair of black jeans. He looked as if he'd done his own share of drugs over the years.

Steve stopped for a moment. "Do you know where I can buy bullets?"

The drug dealer's eyes widened. "What?"

"Bullets. *Patronen.*"

The guy shook his head nervously, and slid away from him.

Steve continued down the street. At Oudezijds Achterburgwal he encountered another dealer. "Hash?" the guy said. This one was smaller, sturdily built, in his forties, with sharp green eyes, a three-day beard, and a green-red-and-black-striped ski cap.

"*Patronen,*" Steve replied bluntly.

"*Patronen?*"

"*Patronen. Waar kan ik patronen kopen?* Where can I buy bullets? For a pistol?"

The dealer's eyes darted this way and that. "Are you kidding, mate?" he asked in a thick Irish brogue.

"No."

"What kind of pistol, then?"

Steve hesitated. "I don't know."

"Well, if you don't know what kind of pistol, I don't know what kind of bullets."

"Okay, one second."

This time Steve was the one whose eyes darted around. He unzipped his jacket, waited for a tourist family – dad, mom, and three daughters – to pass, then, for a split second, pulled the handgun halfway out of his pants.

"One more time, please," the dealer said.

"What?"

"I think I know what you got there, but you were so fast I can't be sure."

"You really know guns?"

"Yes, you lucked out."

They both looked around again. Steve waited while some more people walked by, then showed him the gun again. As he zipped his jacket back up, the dealer nodded. "I can fix you up. Meet me here tomorrow at this time."

"Tomorrow? Can we make it later today?"

The dealer looked at his watch. "Okay," he said. "Five o'clock."

Steve nodded, but the guy was already heading down the canal. Continuing along the street, Steve looked frantically around, worried that some cop had witnessed the whole thing, or that somebody had been standing at a window at just the right moment to glimpse the gun.

From the Dam, he rode the tram back to the stop on De Clercqstraat. In the apartment on Bellamyplein, he went straight to the bedroom, took out the gun, and put it under the pillow. He then walked into the living room, opened one of his suitcases, took out the dress shirt, tie, suit jacket, and trousers that he hadn't worn once since moving here, and changed into them. After he'd done so, he zipped open a compartment in another suitcase, removed his navy-blue passport and battered old Disney ID badge, and slipped them into the inside pocket of the jacket. He was about to leave but then had another thought, which sent him to yet another suitcase. He opened it, rummaged around, grabbed one of the three VHS tapes of *Sentimental Education* that he'd brought with him from Los Angeles, and squeezed it into his jacket's hip pocket.

He headed out again immediately. This time he took the tram all the way to Centraal Station, which, as always, was crowded with a roughly fifty-fifty admixture of Dutchmen in a hurry and confused-looking tourists with luggage. He waited in line at one of the big, banged-up, canary-yellow ticket machines, punched in his travel information, fed a few coins into the slot, waited while the gears ground noisily, and grabbed his ticket when it dropped into the basket. Checking out the overhead departures board, he walked through the main concourse to the magazine shop, where he bought copies of *De Volkskrant* and *NRC Handelsblad* from the same indifferent, fat old man in suspenders from whom he remembered buying his very first *strippenkaart* for the tram.

The train was already standing at platform fifteen. Steve scrambled up the stairs and boarded it. It was jam-packed with travelers and their suitcases. Steve stood near the door and started looking through *NRC Handelsblad*. Fifteen minutes or so later the train arrived at the airport. Almost all of Steve's fellow passengers clattered out clumsily, dragging their suitcases and talking animately among themselves. When the train pulled out, the only people left in the car were Steve and a couple of guys in their twenties who were sitting together some distance from him. Steve slipped into a seat and continued perusing his newspaper. After a minute or two he put down *NRC Handelsblad* and picked up *De Volkskrant*.

He looked outside. The train was chugging along past farmland. In the distance was a perfect tidy row of identical trees. Next thing he knew the train was stopping at Leiden, where the two young guys got off and an elderly woman in a knitted cerise sweater got on, making her way slowly to a seat. Ten minutes or so later, shortly after Steve had finished looking through *De Volkskrant,* the train reached The Hague. Leaving the newspapers on the seat, Steve stepped off the train, headed for the station exit, and walked past a sea of parked bicycles to the street, where he turned left.

It was drizzling here, too. Herengracht was quiet: Steve passed a couple of somber-looking young women with shopping bags, then an old man with a limp walking his old black-and-white mutt, who also had a limp. After four or five blocks suddenly there it was, looming ahead on his right – the Dutch Parliament. It was a striking modern edifice, with a façade of smooth gray stone and huge glass windows. He crossed the street and went inside. The lobby was massive, high-ceilinged. Nattily dressed, alert-looking men and women walked this way and that, alone and in pairs. There was a front desk, and standing behind it, looking as if they didn't have much to do, were two sleek young men in spiffy outfits that looked like flight-attendant uniforms. Beyond them was a bank of elevators, plus a wide staircase leading up to a mezzanine. Steve didn't see any sign of extraordinary security measures. He decided to just walk past these guys. One of them looked over at him as he passed, just the slightest hint of uncertainty in his eyes. Steve gave him a preoccupied nod. He nodded back, apparently reassured.

The thing, Steve told himself, was to keep moving at just the right pace – briskly but not too briskly – and not look lost or befuddled. The elevator seemed the best idea. He went straight to it and pushed the up button. The doors opened instantly. It was empty. He stepped in. Which floor? He picked five. The doors closed, and the elevator rose smoothly and silently. At the fifth floor the doors opened and he stepped out into an area with some blond-wood chairs, a glasstop coffee table covered with newspapers, and a vaseful of white tulips. There was a corridor, so he walked down it. After a few steps, he encountered another door, which he opened. Another corridor. He headed down it, too. After he'd gone another few steps, a door opened and a slim young man in a white shirt and tie but no jacket came out, his arms full of papers. He looked a bit harried. An intern? "Excuse me," Steve said to him in English.

"Yes?"

"I'm so sorry to disturb you," Steve said, in what he hoped was coming off as an insouciant tone, "but I seem to have gotten myself hopelessly turned around. Would you happen to know where Mr. Schrama's offices are?"

"Oh yes, of course," the intern said, entirely unsuspicious. His English was distinctly British-accented. "You're on the wrong floor. You need to go up to six. The woman at the desk will help you."

"Thank you so much."

Steve went back the way he'd come and took the elevator up one floor. Sure enough, there was a woman behind a desk. She was all business – fortyish, with tightly coiffed hair, a tight-fitting dark gray vest and pale gray blouse. Steve walked over, and she greeted him with a professional smile.

"Hi," Steve said, giving her a big smile back. "May I speak English?"

"Certainly," she said. She was every bit as polite and deferential as the policewoman in Amsterdam had been rude and brusque. Maybe, he thought, he should have worn his suit there, too.

"My name is Steve Disch," he said. "I'm a producer from Hollywood. I'm planning to make a documentary about the Netherlands and would like to talk to Mr. Schrama about the possibility of his appearing in it."

There it was, that look. Even in the seats of European power, the word "Hollywood" made an impression.

"Mr. Schrama, you say?" she asked.

"Yes, Mr. Schrama."

"And – sorry, once again – your name is?"

"Steve Disch."

She looked down at a piece of paper on her desk, scanned it, then looked back up at him. "Do you have an appointment?"

"I'm afraid not."

"You really should have an appointment."

123

"I know. It's – well, it's an unusual situation. Things are moving fast on this project, and I happened to be in town today, and I'm very anxious to ensure Mr. Schrama's participation in it."

Steve reached into his jacket pocket and took out his passport and Disney ID. "Anyway, here's my passport if you want to see it," he said, setting them both down on the table. "Oh, sorry, I didn't mean to hand you that," he said as she inspected the badge.

She seemed hesitant.

"You can tell him," Steve added, "that I'm a friend of Henk Steen."

She nodded reflectively, visibly in doubt. After a few seconds she made up her mind. "Let me see if he is available," she said, snapping up her phone receiver and punching in a number. After a couple of seconds she started speaking. Steve heard her say his name, the words *"Amerikaans producent,"* and the words *"vriend van Henk Steen."* She paused to listen for a few more seconds, then said *"Ja, jazeker"* and hung up. She lifted her hand and pointed down a corridor. "It is that way. His name is next to the door." He had already started down the corridor when she called his name. He turned. "Your passport and ID," she said, pushing them across the desk.

"Thank you," Steve said, walking back to pocket them.

In the corridor, he passed one door, then another. Next to each was a small plaque bearing the name of a member of Parliament in gold-serifed letters. At the third door, the plaque read *Jeroen Schrama.* Steve opened the door.

Another desk, another woman. This one was young and animated, with a blonde ponytail and a magenta dress. She was already smiling. "So you want to talk to Mr. Schrama?" she said in a friendly tone. Behind her, a very tall, cute, almost alarmingly skinny young man was xeroxing some papers. He was wearing dark blue trousers and a white dress shirt with a narrow red tie, no jacket. He barely looked old enough to be in college.

"Yes, if possible," Steve said.

The young man looked over at him. Their eyes met. Steve detected just a hint of arrogance, of amused smugness, in the young man's eyes. Then Steve recognized him. He was a fixture at April, where he routinely turned up for Saturday-evening happy hour, invariably wearing a sleeveless black t-shirt, ultra-slim-fit black jeans, and a single large hoop earring.

"He's about to leave for a lunch appointment," the young woman said, "but he can give you a few minutes."

"That would be great."

"Go right in, he's in there," she said with a wave toward a door. The wave, and her tone, were casual; it was as if she and Steve were old chums.

Steve walked to Schrama's door, opened it.

Not until he saw the man sitting there behind his desk – surrounded by messy piles of books and papers, a visible reminder that he'd been a professor before becoming a politician – did it occur to Steve that he hadn't even known what Schama looked like. He was a man of fifty or so – intelligent-looking, with a proud Dutch nose and a playful gleam in his eye. He was wearing a beautifully tailored gray suit, and had a wealthy man's air of ease and self-confidence.

As Steve approached his desk, Schrama stood up. He was six-four or so. He extended his hand, and they shook.

"Have a seat, please," Schrama offered amiably, his English more Dutch-accented than Steve had expected. Behind him was a large window that afforded a spectacular view of The Hague.

"Thank you," Steve said as they both sat down. "And thanks for agreeing to see me."

"I'm sorry I don't have more time," Schrama said. "Maybe we can arrange something on another day."

"That would be good," Steve said.

"So you are a friend of Henk Steen?"

"Yes, I've known him for a few years now."

"I've known him forever."

"I know. He told me. He's very fond of you."

Schrama was obviously pleased by this. "That feeling is mutual," he said. "So! You are a film producer? From California?"

"I am, yes."

"And why should you be interested in a member of the Parliament of our little country?"

"I'm interested in the Netherlands generally. I'm

living here for a while. I want to make a documentary about it. And so – "

"And so you naturally want to include the troublemaker in the Dutch Parliament?" There was a glimmer of amusement in his eye.

"Well," Steve replied, "I wouldn't put it that way."

"Then you will be the first!" Schrama said, laughing heartily. "But why the Netherlands, of all countries?"

"Because I revere your heritage of liberty. Because there would be no America without the Netherlands. Because this country has been at the forefront of freedom for centuries. And now, with gay marriage – "

"Are you gay?"

Steve reached into the side pocket of his jacket, took out the VHS tape, and placed it on Schrama's desk. Schrama's eyes lit up. "Oh, I remember this film! Did you have something to do with it?"

"I wrote and directed it."

"Is that so? Well, I'm sorry for not recognizing your name. I remember liking it very much."

"Thank you."

"I seem to recall a specific scene. Perhaps I'm misremembering. But wasn't there a scene where the two college boys are driving across the country, and they stop at a hotel – "

"A motel. In a very small town in Nevada."

"Yes, of course, a motel. And they decide to swim

in the motel pool, so they change into their bathing costumes together in the motel room, and there is such a strong feeling of awkwardness and curiosity between them – "

"Yes, exactly."

"And they go out to the pool, and swim a little back and forth, and then they stand at one end of the pool together, and there is this – I don't have the words for it – and here I am a writer – "

"I don't have the words for it either. That's why it's easier to be a filmmaker than a writer. You don't have to figure it out and find the right words. You just show it."

"But then again, when it's something that matters so much, isn't one still driven to try to find the words? To try to understand what one is experiencing and articulate it, not just feel it?

"I suppose so. Yes."

"The water wasn't an incidental part of that scene," Schrama said. "It wouldn't have been the same if they'd been changing into football uniforms, and then gone out and kicked a ball around on a field. The water mattered."

"Yes, it did."

"And why?"

Schrama looked at him as if he expected an answer.

Steve smiled. "You tell me."

"Because it's primal. Somewhere inside each of us is the intuitive awareness that we're descended from species that crawled out of the sea, that each of us was incubated in a watery womb, that we're mostly water ourselves. And of course we Dutch people are especially drawn to water because it's such a big part of our lives – we have canals right outside our windows, our ancestors grew rich sending trading ships out onto the sea, and they protected the country from storms and tempests by becoming experts in building dikes. Water was, and is, a friend and a foe."

"I never thought about it that way. But I suppose that's part of what attracted me to this country."

"Have you ever been to a *naaktzwemmen?*"

"Yes. And to the nude beaches at Zandvoort and Scheveningen."

"Scheveningen," said Schrama, correcting Steve's pronunciation. "Do you know, by the way, the role that Scheveningen, the word itself, not the beach, played during the war?"

"No."

"If someone who claimed to be Dutch was suspected of being a German spy, he was asked to say Scheveningen. Because only a Dutchman can pronounce it properly." Schrama smiled. "I have to say I've always been fond of public pools and baths, of *naaktzwemmen* and *naaktstrenden.* You know enough Dutch...?"

"Yes."

"The attraction isn't erotic."

"No, it isn't."

"It's that when you go there you're stripped of

the uniform that identifies your position in society. You're thrust into what I think of as the ultimate democratic experience. Not that all bodies are equal. But in such situations all bodies are not only disrobed but, curiously, disarmed. People are always peaceable in those situations. Always. It's striking. Have you ever noticed that?"

"Yes."

"Of course you have. It's all there in your film. And so now, in any event, you want to make a documentary about the Dutch heritage of liberty?"

"Yes," I say. "And about the threats to it."

"By which you mean...?" From the look that suddenly crossed Schrama's face, Steve suddenly realized that the man was used to seeing *himself* identified as the major threat to Dutch liberty.

"By which I mean," Steve said, "the kind of thing I've seen in the Oud West in Amsterdam."

"The Oud West."

"Yes. That's where I'm living now."

"I see," Schrama said, meeting Steve's eyes thoughtfully.

At that moment someone knocked on the door. Steve turned. The young woman peeked in and told Schrama that Herr Bloem had arrived.

Schrama jumped to his feet. "I'm sorry about this," he told Steve, pushing the VHS across the desk to him.

"No, please keep that," Steve told him.

"Oh. Thank you. I look forward to watching it

again. But in the meantime we will have to make another date. Very soon. I promise."

"But there's just one more thing I need to tell you about," Steve said.

"I look forward to hearing about it," said Schrama. "Please leave your contact information with Sanne!"

And before Steve could say another word, Schrama was out the door, moving fast, and as elegantly as a dancer.

At just after six that evening Steve walked into April. Happy hour was in high gear – inane dance music was thumping away, and the bartenders were pouring drinks as fast as they could. Steve scanned the faces. There were several guys who were easily closer to seven feet than six, but none of them was Joop.

Steve squeezed through the crowd to the bar, where he ordered a beer. The bartender handed him two tall ones – two for the price of one, that was the happy-hour drill at April – and he carried the glasses toward the door, where he set one of them down on a high shelf and started in on the other. The place seemed impossibly packed already, but the customers kept pouring in. After a couple of minutes, Joop entered. He saw Steve immediately. Steve handed him the second beer.

"I'm sorry about last night," Steve said, almost shouting so Joop could hear him over the noise.

"That's okay. I can come back tonight if you want."

"Really?"

"Sure, why not?"

Steve realized that he still wasn't used to Joop – how laid-back he was, how undemanding. Steve thought about the night he'd first seen him. It had been right across the street from here, at Exit, the late-night dance club. Steve had been there that night with Jordy, and when he'd first seen Joop across the crowded room, he'd assumed that Joop was the sort of person who'd give him short shrift – throw him a sneer, look down at him as if he were some presumptuous bug. At that time Steve was still used to the gay bars in West Hollywood, where it was next to impossible to find anybody who looked remotely like Joop who didn't ooze narcissism and condescension.

But he wasn't in L.A. anymore. When Jordy noticed that Steve was interested in Joop, he simply took Steve by the arm, walked him over to Joop, and told them to introduce themselves to each other. Joop grinned. They talked. Joop turned out to be shy. Shy! Him!

Ten minutes later, they were dancing together, each of them more awkward and self-conscious than the other. They had dinner the next night, and the night after that. Even after they'd slept together, Steve couldn't shake the thought that Joop was playing some kind of elaborate, cruel joke on him. He was just that handsome.

Eventually Steve came to understand that Joop truly didn't think of himself as anything special – which was, after all, typically Dutch. Yet even by Dutch standards Joop had proved to be surprisingly unpretentious and low-maintenance, just as happy to grab a chicken sandwich from the wall at Febo's as to share a *rijsttafel* for two at the city's priciest Indonesian restaurant. It shouldn't be so surprising, then, that he was perfectly prepared to spend another dull evening sitting quietly with Steve in that flat on Bellamyplein, sipping white wine and listening for voices.

"You don't have anything better to do?" Steve asked.

"I'm feeding a friend's cat, in the Jordaan. But I already took care of that just now. So why are you so dressed up?"

"You like it?"

"It looks uncomfortable."

"It is. But I didn't have time to change. I went to Den Haag."

"What?" Joop bent down to hear Steve.

"I say, I went to Den Haag. I met Jeroen Schrama."

"You're kidding!"

"No."

"You mean you ran into him?"

"No, I went to his office."

"At the Tweede Kamer?"

Steve nodded.

"How could you get in to see him?"

"So you're impressed?"

"Yes, that's pretty amazing! But why?"

"What else can I do about those people downstairs? I have to do *something*. I mean, if the cops won't listen, I figure he might. It's worth a shot."

"Oh, you really *are* an American!"

"What do you mean?"

"Those stupid movies aren't exaggerating. You all want to save the world."

"Look who's talking. You're the one who offered to sit up another night with me."

"I'm just keeping you company." Joop grinned. "So what did Schrama say?"

"Nothing yet. I'd barely started talking and he had to go to lunch."

"Fuck."

"But he says he'll meet me again. Soon. Maybe by then I'll have something more substantial to tell him."

They had a couple more beers, then went down the street to Rosa's Cantina. Steve talked Joop into letting him order a pitcher of margaritas. When they left two hours later, they were both tipsy.

"Are you sure you want to waste another evening with me in that shithole?" Steve asked.

"Yes," Joop said. "But first, Gall & Gall."

WHEN THEY GOT TO BELLAMYPLEIN, the "community center" was dark. Steve unlocked the street door and they walked upstairs. Steve tripped on a step. Half drunk.

"Are you okay?" Joop asked.

"Yes."

Steve unlocked the door, then shut it behind them.

"Show me the hole," Joop said.

"I'll bet you say that to all the guys."

Joop laughed.

"Well," Steve shrugged, "it's late, but it looked dark downstairs, so why not?"

Joop put down the bag from Gall & Gall and followed Steve into the bedroom. Steve pulled the bed away from the wall, lay prone on the mattress, yanked the rug up. Joop leaned over the bed and took a good look. "Hmm," Joop said.

Steve started to move the rug back to cover it. Joop stopped him.

"Leave it," Joop said. "We'll hear better. If there's anything to hear."

"OK," Steve said.

He started to push the bed back into place, then decided to let it stay where it was. "Let's just remember to keep it dark in here." Steve stumbled over to the window, pulled the curtains shut. As they left the room he turned off the lights and shut the door.

Then, suddenly remembering, he opened the door again, went to the bed, reached under the pillow, and grabbed the gun.

When he walked out of the bedroom with it, holding it by the barrel, Joop gasped. "Holy shit!"

"Shh!"

"Is that for real?"

"No, it's made of chocolate. Delicious Dutch chocolate."

"Where the fuck – "

"Shh!"

"But where – "

"It's Rob's. I took it from his apartment."

"But – "

"Don't worry, I'll give it back. He doesn't need it right now. He's in Japan."

"That's not what I'm worried about. Do you know how to use one of those things?"

"What's to know? You point and pull the trigger, right?"

"Have you ever shot a gun?"

"No, but hey, as you like to say, I'm an American. A born cowboy."

"Right, a Hollywood cowboy. Like Reagan."

"Don't knock Reagan. He brought down the Iron Curtain." Steve, who'd never liked Reagan, was surprised to hear himself saying that.

"Can I look at it?"

"Oh, you say that to all the guys."

"Come on."

Steve handed him the gun.

"Jesus," Steve said.

"What?"

"From the look on your face, somebody'd think you were holding a live grenade."

"Sorry. I've never held a gun." With the utmost of

care, Joop pointed it toward the wall and turned it over in his hands. "Is it loaded?" he asked.

"No. But I have bullets." Steve reached into his jacket pocket and removed the cartridges that he'd picked up from the pusher on Oudezijds Achterburgwal, whose prices had turned out to be surprisingly reasonable. "Here, help me load it." Steve walked over to the couch and sat down; Joop followed and sat beside him. Together they tried to figure out how to load the gun. "Here." "No, here." "This way." "No, like this." They were so sloshed that they both dropped cartridges on the floor, and both said "Shh!", and both laughed.

Once the gun was finally locked and loaded, Steve set it down on the couch between them. They looked at each other.

"I don't approve of guns," said Joop, "but I think I maybe approve of this one."

They'd had more than enough to drink already, but Joop was visibly shaken up by the presence of the pistol, so Steve didn't protest when he opened a bottle of wine and poured out two glasses.

"Maybe we should just go in there," Joop said, gesturing toward the bedroom, after they'd taken a couple of sips. "It's already pretty late."

"OK."

They took their glasses. Joop picked up the bottle with his free hand, while Steve picked up the gun, holding it by the barrel. As they approached the bedroom, Steve said softly: "Remember! No light!"

"I know, I know."

Steve opened the door; they went in; Steve shut the door quietly. In the dark, Steve heard Joop place the bottle and his wineglass on the floor. Steve put his own glass on the floor, too, and set the gun down next to it. Steve reach out for Joop, touched his shoulder, pulled Joop's ear down to his lips.

"I put the gun on the floor, right here," Steve said. He ran his hand down Joop's smooth, sinewy arm to his long, thin fingers, and pulled his hand down to touch the gun grip. Joop then moved his hand up Steve's body, pulled Steve's ear to his mouth. "OK. I'll get in bed first."

They stripped down in the total darkness. Their bodies touched as they piled their clothes on the chair. Steve heard the springs squeak as Joop got into bed. Then Steve climbed in next to Joop. He reached out. His fingers touched Joop's back, only a couple of inches away. He remembered one night last year when they had been lying together in the dark like this, and Joop had suddenly put all his cards on the table. *Ik hou van je,"* he had said – *I love you.* Steve had lain there, stunned, frozen, mute. Unable to put together a reply.

He had never replied. The silence, and the awkwardness, had just deepened. They had lain there, side by side, each alone in his own mind, until sleep had finally intervened.

Now, lying beside Joop again on Bellamyplein, Steve felt strangely safe – so safe that he drifted off.

Driving. A quick dream of driving. Himself and Joop, in a convertible, on the open road...

And then, suddenly, he was awake again, stirred back into consciousness by the feeling of Joop's body moving away from his.

He felt as if he'd been asleep for only a second, yet it took a moment for him to remember where he was, whom he was with, and why. He realized that Joop, who was closer to the wall, was leaning over the side of the bed, the wall side, looking downward. Steve could actually see him, dimly. Joop's body moved back toward him. The springs squeaked. Steve could make out his profile. Joop found Steve's ear with his mouth. "Light," Joop whispered.

"What?"

"It's light downstairs."

Yes, of course it was, Steve suddenly realized: how else would he be able to see Joop? He felt an adrenaline rush. What had happened? Had they missed somebody coming in downstairs while they were in the living room? But how could that be? Had they been so drunk – and talking so loudly – that they missed it? Or had somebody come in while he was asleep?

How long *had* he been asleep?

Steve lifted his head and upper body, resting his weight on his left elbow, and moved to bend over Joop. Steve couldn't believe how loudly the springs squeaked. He put out his right hand to steady himself and found himself touching Joop's bony posterior: he wasn't wearing underpants. Steve shifted his hand to rest his palm on the mattress and lean over Joop. All the while, the springs kept squeaking.

Sure enough. Light.

Steve lay back down. The springs finally fell silent. Steve's face was buried in Joop's hair, and his right arm lay across Joop's flat belly. Steve could feel his own heart beating, and could hear Joop's breathing. In, out. In, out. Steve turned his head slightly, and saw the light beam from downstairs shining on the ceiling.

He had never imagined it would be that bright.

Minutes passed.

The downstairs front door slammed shut. A footfall. And then...a voice.

Steve felt Joop tense up.

Another voice. And before Steve knew it, the door slammed again, and there was a third voice. Speaking – what? The same language as before. Turkish? A reply. An exchange. A conversation.

The voices were loud. Were they arguing, or did it just sound that way?

After several more minutes, the door slammed yet again. Loud footsteps, and a loud, authoritative voice.

Speaking Dutch.

Joop took a heavy breath.

And then, as before, they all switched into English.

With his right hand, Steve reached for Joop's right hand. He clutched it tightly, and Joop tightened his own fingers over Steve's.

The men got right down to business. No formalities. No niceties. Steve couldn't make out every word, but he could follow most of it. The challenge was putting it all together, figuring out the larger meaning, making sense of it.

The men devoted much of their time to a highly technical discussion about explosives. They talked about flights between Amsterdam and Munich and about the Munich tram and subway systems. They also mentioned the Alhambra. And at a point when it seemed as if the conversation was petering out, one of them said a person's name in passing. And then they talked a little more, and another one of them said the same name, clearly and firmly, and with more than a little emotion in his voice.

Schrama.

Then there was silence.

And, then, the sound of chairs scraping, men walking across the floor, and, finally, the front door slamming shut.

Steve and Joop lay there quietly for another couple of minutes, listening to each other's breath. Then Steve whispered into Joop's ear: "Let's get up."

"Wait," Joop whispered back. He leaned over. Steve heard him fussing – moving the rug, covering the light from downstairs. The room went dark. "Okay," Joop finally whispered.

Steve swung his legs out and set his feet down on the floor. And instantly he panicked. Because the soles of his feet were damp.

"Oh, shit," he said softly.

"What?"

"You covered the hole?"

"Yes."

Steve stood up, walked over to the door, turned on the bedroom light. The wine bottle had been knocked over – obviously by Steve, kicking at it in his sleep.

As Joop stood up, Steve pointed at it. Joop's eyes met his. Joop started to speak, but Steve gestured with his hand for Joop to stay silent. Steve opened the bedroom door and led him into the living room.

"Do you think any of the wine went into the hole?" Steve asked when they got there, trying not to be hysterical. He suddenly felt terribly vulnerable, and the fact that they were both stark naked only made it worse.

Joop shook his head. "No," he said – trying, Steve thought, to sound more certain than he felt. "The rug must've absorbed the wine."

"But it was a lot of wine."

"It's a thick rug. It's one of those old thick rugs from the 1970s. Also, it must be so full of dirt and dust – "

Steve went back into the bedroom to survey the situation. He leant over and touched the rug next to the lip of the bottle. It was absolutely soaked. He picked up the gun. At least *it* was dry.

He walked back into the living room, gun in hand. Joop was standing at the side table, opening another bottle of wine.

"Don't stop me," he said. "On this kind of night, a man needs a drink."

"Believe me, I have no plans to stop you."

There was silence. It lasted perhaps three seconds. Then, between one instant and the next, everything changed. Suddenly there came the sound of the door downstairs being smashed open, and then, immediately after, a sound like that of cattle stampeding madly up the steps.

Joop and Steve exchanged a look. As if by instinct, Joop picked up the bottle he was opening and smashed it against the side table, turning it into a weapon. Steve readied the gun.

A half-second later, the apartment door crashed open and two bearded men rushed into the room. Since Joop, standing at the side table, wasn't visible from the doorway, they both charged directly at Steve, brandishing long knives, the wide blades flashing with the reflected yellow light of the living-room lamps.

With a presence of mind that shocked him, Steve raised the pistol to waist height and squeezed off one shot, then another. The sound was deafening, the strong recoil a surprise. One of the men, the taller and heavier of the two, who was wearing a black leather jacket and jeans, went down, clutching his chest, his face slamming against the wooden floor.

The other man, who was wearing a thick, dark-red sweater and brown corduroys, kept charging. He was about to thrust his blade into Steve's gut when Joop, who was at least a foot taller than he was, leapt on him, taking him down, both their faces plunging toward the floor only inches from Steve's feet. Just as they were about to hit the floor, Joop, with a strength that surprised Steve, plunged the broken wine bottle deep into the front of the man's neck and pulled it efficiently across his throat.

In the space of a half-second, both Joop and the man struck the floor and blood began gushing out of the man's aorta in a mighty torrent. As Joop rose to his feet, Steve pumped additional bullets into both of the strangers' heads, then rushed to the apartment door, Joop at his side.

They looked down the stairs. Nothing. The absolute silence and stillness, after that sudden burst of noise and activity, felt eerie.

They looked back at the two men on the floor. They were motionless. Blood pooled on the scratched-up wood, soaking the smaller man's sweater. Steve caught himself thinking, absurdly, that it was good the man had chosen dark red, because the blood didn't show as much.

Joop looked at Steve. "How many were there downstairs?"

"I thought four."

"I thought four, too. So what – what – "

"We can talk later. First let's get out of here."

"Yes."

They rushed into the bedroom. Joop dressed swiftly while Steve stood guard with the gun, then he passed the gun to Joop and threw on his own clothes. He took the gun from Joop, shoved it into his pocket, and they both pulled on their jackets.

"One second," Steve said as Joop hurried ahead of him across the dining room and toward the front door. Jumping over the bodies, Steve went to the living room couch, grabbed his laptop, shoved it into his shoulder bag, and pulled the shoulder bag handle over his head. Then he pulled the gun out of his pocket and started reloading it – this time as fast as hell, and with the precision of a cold-sober professional. While he was doing this, Joop stepped over the body of the man with the slit throat and knelt down quickly between the two corpses, careful to avoid getting any of their blood on him, and started checking their pants pockets.

"Shouldn't we call the cops?" Joop asked. He held up a set of keys from a pocket of the man in the sweater. He dug into another pocket.

"No cops."

"Why?" Joop held up a wallet.

"First we get the fuck out of here. Before any more of these guys come up those stairs. Then we can talk about the fucking cops."

"But we're disturbing a crime scene."

"I don't give a damn. That could be us lying there."

"Okay. You're right. I'm not thinking straight." He held up another set of keys, and another wallet.

"Neither am I." Steve finished loading the gun and poured the remaining cartridges into his jacket pocket. Joop stood up, shoved his booty into his own pockets. Steve rushed over to him at the apartment door.

"What if they're waiting for us outside?" Steve asked.

"Well, you're the one with the gun."

"Good point."

They ran downstairs. Joop swung open the outside door while Steve aimed the gun, ready for any surprises. Nobody was there. They ran out onto the sidewalk. The "community center" door was closed, the light inside still on. At the windows of apartments on the west side of the square, Steve could see faces peering out. The shots had rung out like claps of thunder. How many of the neighbors had already called the cops?

"Let's move it," Steve said.

As they ran up Agatha Dekenstraat toward De Clercqstraat, Steve shoved the gun into the front of his pants. It was late: no traffic, no pedestrians. All the shops were dark, as were the apartments above them. When they reached De Clercqstraat, a busier thoroughfare, Joop stopped. A car sped by, and another. "Walk slow," said Joop.

"Are you sure?"

"Slow!"

They turned right, heading toward the *centrum*. Steve expected to see or hear a police car any second, but they made it across the Bilderdijk canal without incident. On the other side, Joop said, "This way." Steve nodded. They turned right again, and walked along the quiet

Bilderdijkkade. They'd made it almost a full block before a police car, siren wailing, sped along De Clercqstraat, behind them, toward Bellamyplein. Joop and Steve exchanged a look.

"Over here," Joop said when they reached a small square, Kwakersplein. Joop led Steve across it to Bilderdijkstraat. There was a bit of traffic here, too. Suddenly a cab appeared in the dark. Joop waved it down, and it pulled over. Steve ran around to the other side of it and they both clambered in. "Muntplein," said Joop to the driver, a stout, middle-aged Dutchman.

As they headed toward Muntplein, Joop turned to Steve and started talking in Dutch – his tone light, his content entirely frivolous. Empty chitchat about made-up people, as if they'd just left a party and were gossiping drunkenly about the other people who'd been there. The traffic was light, and they were at Muntplein in five minutes. Joop handed the driver some cash and they got out.

"Now what?" Steve said as they stood across the street from Munttoren. It was late, but even so twenty or so people were on the square, walking through it in pairs or groups or waiting for a light to change.

Joop watched the cab they'd just gotten out of as it headed up the Damrak in the direction of Centraal Station. Then he hailed another cab that was racing toward them up the Vijzelstraat. It pulled over, they got in, and Joop gave the driver an address on Elandsstraat. Steve didn't recognize the address, although he knew that

Elandsstraat was somewhere in the Jordaan, west of here – in other words, in the direction from which they'd just come. The driver – dark, bearded, presumably a Muslim – nodded and took off at top speed.

It was a very short trip, with no traffic and no lights against them. By the time they'd reached their destination, Joop had already given the driver a couple of bills. They jumped out; the cab took off. "Come on," Joop said, leading Steve at a gallop down Elandsstraat.

At Lijnbaansgracht, Joop turned left, with Steve hot on his heels. They'd run just a few steps along the canal when Joop made another left, this time onto a very narrow, unpretty street – barely an alleyway, really – called Lijnbaansstraat. Here the buildings were relatively new – built no earlier than the 1960s, Steve guessed – and their façades, some covered in graffiti, looked like the back walls of factories. Joop stopped at a banged-up black metal doorway, fished a key out of his pocket, and unlocked the door.

"Who –"

"Shh."

Wordlessly, Joop led him up two flights of narrow stairs to the building's top floor. He unlocked a door, gestured for Steve to enter, followed him in, and locked the door behind them. Joop flipped on a light. They were in a tiny, immaculate eat-in kitchen. Through an archway was a small, tidy living room. There was another door, only partly open. From beyond it came a sound. Steve steeled himself.

A jet-black cat pranced into the room and jumped up on the kitchen counter to say hello. Joop and Steve petted him.

"Meet Bart," Joop said.

"Hi, Bart." Bart purred.

Steve looked at Joop. Their eyes met. Without another word, Joop put his arms around Steve. Instantly, Steve reciprocated.

"Holy shit," Joop said.

"Holy shit," Steve agreed. And for a long moment they just stood there in silence and clung tightly to each other.

V

STEVE CAME BACK FROM THE BATHROOM to find Joop making coffee. Or trying to. His hand shook as he poured the powder, causing it to scatter on the kitchen counter and floor.

Steve drummed his fingers on the counter, his brain firing on a hundred cylinders at once.

"First of all," Joop said, "not that this is the most important thing in the world, but is my name anywhere in that apartment?"

"No. I promise. I got everything." Steve gestured toward his shoulder bag.

"You sure?"

"Yes."

"And is there anybody you know who might suspect that you're with me?"

"Only Jordy," Steve said.

"But even Jordy doesn't know my last name," Joop said. "Does he?"

"Not that I know of. But, I mean, if they identified him as a friend of mine, and he told them about you, and gave your first name and a physical description, somebody at April or wherever would be able to ID you, don't you think?"

"I guess so." Struggling not to shake, Joop tamped down the powder with a spoon. "Still, we're probably okay in, what do you call it, the short term," he said. "At least for a few hours. I mean, there's no reason to expect the cops to be knocking at this door in the next ten minutes. Right?"

"I don't know. Whose apartment is this?"

"My friend Arjan. We grew up together."

"You're feeding Bart for him?" At the sound of his name, Bart, who'd been snoozing on the floor, looked up.

"Yes."

"Who else knows you're feeding his cat?"

"Nobody. I only told you." He turned on the coffeemaker.

"Okay. No problem there. But then there's the matter of the cab driver. He could tell the police where he dropped us off."

The coffeemaker burped and gurgled.

"I know. But he picked us up at Muntplein and drove us back in this same direction. I'm hoping they won't connect what happened on Bellamyplein with a cab that took on two passengers at Muntplein and drove them to the Jordaan. As far as him leading them to us, I would've given him an address farther away than this, but I didn't want us to be out on the street any longer than necessary."

"I understood that. I would've made the same call. But we're awfully close to where he dropped us off. Do any of Arjan's neighbors – I mean, are you around here a lot? If somebody in a two-block radius of here were shown a picture of you, do you think any of them would know to send the cops here?"

Joop shook his head. "No."

Steve walked across the room, stood at the window for a minute or so, looking out, then walked back. The coffee was ready. Joop poured a cup and handed it to Steve.

"Thanks," Steve said. He took a sip. It was the worst coffee he'd ever had in the Netherlands, though by any other measure it was decent enough.

"By the way," Joop said. "You're a pretty good runner."

"I was always a good runner. In school, it was the only sport I was any good at. I couldn't throw or catch or hit a softball, but I could run faster than anybody else. Everybody was pretty shocked, actually. That a fag could beat them all in a race."

Joop smiled. "I stunk at football, but I was the best at volleyball."

They stood there in silence for a while, sipping their coffee.

Suddenly Steve remembered. "The wallets," he said.

"Shit!" They both put down their cups. Joop fast-walked over to the coatrack by the door, where both their jackets were hanging, and pulled the two dead men's wallets out of the pockets. He came back to the counter with them and tossed one to Steve.

It was thick and black and looked both cheap and brand-new. Steve opened it up. It was stuffed with thousand-guilder notes – forty or fifty of them, the equivalent of twenty or twenty-five thousand dollars.

Steve looked through the various pockets in the wallet. Nothing, not even a form of ID.

He looked up at Joop and held the wallet open so he could see. Joop looked up for a moment.

"Wow," he said, then resumed poking through the other wallet, which was brown and thin and badly worn. He finally plucked out a single folded piece of paper and tossed the wallet on the counter. He unfolded the paper, looked at it, and held it out to Steve. Steve put down the black wallet and took the piece of paper from Joop. Three words were written on it:

Die Hirtenflöte – Fabien.

"Does this mean anything to you?" Steve asked.

Joop shrugged. "Well, *hirt* is a sheep herder."

"A shepherd."

"Right. And *flöte* means flute."

"So...a shepherd's flute."

"Yes. And Fabien is just a name."

"I wonder what this means, then?" Steve put the piece of paper down on the counter.

"No idea."

They sat there in silence.

"Look," Steve finally said, "I'm kind of still in shock here – "

"Me too."

"About the police..."

"Yes?"

"What do you think? Do we go to them?"

"I don't know. Give me a minute. I can't think straight."

"Me neither. But it's not like we'd be in real trouble. It *was* a pure case of self-defense." Joop started to speak, but Steve interrupted him. "In fact, there's no reason to involve you at all. I can go to the cops myself and say I was there alone."

"Nonsense. Twenty people who live on Bellamyplein must've seen the two of us come out of that house. Besides, one of those bastards not only has a bullet in his skull but a throat cut from one end to the other with a wine bottle. That's pretty neat work for one guy."

"I'm sorry. You're right."

"Anyway," Joop said, "it's not getting in trouble with the police that I'm worried about."

"What do you mean?"

"One second. Drink your coffee." Joop poured a cup for himself and tasted it. "Oh God, what awful coffee." He dumped it unceremoniously into the sink.

Steve looked at the wall clock. It was almost six A.M. "Do you have to go to work today?"

"No. Day off."

"Thank goodness."

"Yes. A small blessing."

"But about the police..."

"Okay, let me be honest," Joop said. "I just don't trust them."

"You don't?"

"Don't get me wrong. I don't mean I think they're

corrupt. Nothing like that. I think they're totally honest and they mean totally well. But I also think that when it comes to this kind of thing, they may not understand what they're dealing with. No, fuck that. They *don't* understand. Not at all. No question about it. They're clueless. They're naive. They're fools. I don't need to tell *you* that. You're the one who went to the police station and tried to explain to that woman about those bastards. The way she reacted? They're all like that. Every one of them." He opened the fridge, took out a bottle of Heineken, screwed off the top, and took a slug. "You want one?" he asked.

"Not right now, thanks."

Joop drank some more. "For both of us," he said, "the most important thing right now, the only thing, has to be protecting ourselves. Full stop. And I know the police would want to protect us. But they've never had to protect anybody from...from *this.*"

"You're right. They'd be in way over their depth."

"Yes, that's exactly the right expression. In over their depth. As I say, they'd want to protect us. But even more important for them, a thousand times more important than protecting us, would be to not offend the Mohammedan community. That's how things work here. That's how people think here. Especially the people in power. And if that's more important to them than our safety..."

"Then we're sunk."

"We're fucked."

Steve walked over to the sink and poured his

coffee out, too. "Who am I kidding?" he said. "I need a beer." He went to the fridge, opened it, took out a bottle. "But I'm also thinking about this. We killed two of them. What about the others? Presumably they're not going to show up at that so-called community center again anytime soon. But that doesn't mean they're going to drop their plans. You don't deter a terrorist cell, let alone destroy it, let alone put the kibosh on a whole terrorist organization, by eliminating a couple of its members. They still have their – their goals. Their objectives. Their agenda. They're still out to do what they've been plotting to do. Aren't they? So shouldn't we somehow get word to somebody about that? About what we know?"

"It makes sense," Joop said. "But I don't know. I just don't know."

"I don't either."

"If we phone the cops, they could trace the call. Right?"

"Right." Steve opened his beer and took a sip. "But there must be a way."

They stood there in silence for a minute or so. Joop looked at the wall clock. "Are you tired?" he asked.

"Exhausted. I'm sure you are, too. But I'm so keyed up, I can't imagine being able to sleep."

"Me either. But you want to try anyway?"

"Okay. Maybe that's what we both need the most right now."

"Yes. I think it's a good idea." They put down their beers.

156

Joop led Steve into the bedroom. It was every bit as orderly as the kitchen. The window looked out onto a brick wall just eight or ten feet away, across the narrow street. The bed was neatly made, and the sheets looked clean and inviting. Joop undressed, piling his items of clothing one by one on the floor. Steve did the same. "One second," Joop said, and disappeared into the bathroom. He returned with a glass of water and two pills. He handed Steve one: a Valium. They popped them, washed them down, then climbed into bed together and turned to face each other. Joop put his arm around Steve.

"I'm so sorry to have gotten you into this, Joop," Steve said.

Joop shrugged. "I'm sorry my country isn't everything you dreamed it was."

"I was a fool."

"It's okay to be a fool."

Steve closed his eyes. The fact that they had just killed two people still wasn't real to him. Neither was the fact that their own lives were in danger. Steve was far more stressed out than he'd ever been in his life. But he was also thoroughly exhausted, and after a couple of minutes he slipped into unconsciousness and plunged into a dream.

In the dream, he was driving with Joop. In a convertible. Joop was at the steering wheel; Steve was riding shotgun. Shotgun. In fact Steve was holding a shotgun, resting the barrel on his car door. They were in America, tearing down some Interstate highway, crossing what looked like the Nevada or Utah desert at thirty or forty miles an hour over the speed limit, the hot summer air whipping at their faces. There were no other cars in sight – no other people, for that matter, no buildings or power lines; just the burning sun, the broad desert, and the distant, treeless mountains. They drove at breakneck speed for what seemed an eternity, alone together in the world. They were young, and alone together, and safe in the good old safe USA.

Steve awoke with a name on his lips.

"Daniel," he said.

He looked at the window. It was light out. Bart, having heard Steve's voice, came trotting into the room. He stopped at the foot of the bed and meowed.

"Hmm?" Joop stirred.

"I'm sorry, go back to sleep." Steve sat up.

"No, what is it?" Joop started to sit up, too.

"Daniel."

"Who?"

"My friend Daniel. You know, the one from college. The one in *Sentimental Education*."

What about him?"

"He's CIA. Remember?"

"Well, you told me he was. But are you sure?" Bart jumped onto the bed and trotted closer to them.

"Yes," Steve said, scratching Bart under the chin.

"Really?"

"Absolutely."

"And so?"

"He can help."

"Would he want to?"

"It's his job, isn't it? We're talking about terrorism here."

"But even so, exactly how could he help us?"

"I don't know."

"Great."

"But *he* would know how he could help us. This is what he does. It's his job."

"Okay. Do you know how to reach him?"

"No. But I can figure it out. I need to go online."

Joop got out of bed. "I'll make us some breakfast. You figure it out."

Steve got out of bed, too, and followed him into the kitchen. So did Bart. While Joop poured water into a saucepan and set it on the stove to boil, Steve dug his laptop out of his shoulder bag. "Where can I plug this in?" he asked.

Joop unplugged the kitchen phone from the wall socket. "Here."

Steve plugged the laptop in. It took several minutes for him to get online and hook up to AOL. Meanwhile Joop took a few eggs out of the refrigerator. When Steve was finally connected, he went to the Yahoo search engine. He typed in Daniel's name. After a few seconds, the results appeared onscreen.

There were eight hits. All but one were for a small-town politician in Ohio who happened to have the same name as him.

The very last hit on the list was the one Steve wanted.

He'd seen the page before: it was the website of Albrecht International Dynosystems, the corporation for which Daniel now supposedly worked, running the Prague office. On the page there was a list of the firm's offices around the world and the names of the people in charge of them. There were e-mail addresses for several of those offices. But no phone numbers.

Steve wrote down the name of the company and logged off.

"Any luck?" Joop was opening a can of cat food.

"I need a phone number in the Czech Republic."

"Okay." Joop spooned the entire canful of cat food into a red plastic bowl and put it on the floor, where Bart lunged at it ravenously. "Poor Bart," he said. "We're only here because I promised to take care of him. And here I forgot to feed him before we went to bed. One second." He went into the bedroom and came back a moment later with his cell phone. He handed it to Steve. "Okay, go for it."

"What's the number for international information?"

Joop gestured for him to hand back the phone. "I'll do it," he said, taking it. "So what do I ask for?"

"Albrecht International Dynosystems."

"Who international what?"

Steve repeated the name.

"Dynosystems? What does that mean?"

"They use modern science to bring dinosaurs back to life. Who the hell knows."

"In Prague?"

Steve nodded.

Joop punched in a three-digit number. After a few seconds he asked for the number of Daniel's company. *"In Praag. In Tsjechië,"* he said. Another few seconds passed. Then: *"Ja."* He passed the phone to Steve. "She's connecting you."

"No," Steve said, frantically canceling the call.

"What's wrong?"

"Call him on the house phone."

"Why?"

"I just realized. I don't want him to be able to trace the call to you."

"It's okay. The phone isn't registered in my name. Or in any name."

"You sure?"

"I'm sure. There's no way to trace it to me."

"Okay, I'm sorry. Can you do it again?" Steve handed the phone back to him, and Joop went through the whole rigmarole a second time. He handed the phone to Steve, who held it to his ear and listened. One ring, two. Click. "Albrecht International Dynosystems." A woman's voice. No-nonsense, with an upper-class British accent.

"Good morning," Steve said. "May I please speak to Daniel Loban?"

"And who may I say is calling?"

"My name is Steve Disch."

"Is Dr. Loban expecting your call?"

Doctor? As far as Steve knew, Daniel didn't have a doctorate in anything.

"No. But please tell him that it's me, and that it's urgent."

"Yes, sir. Would you mind repeating your name?"

"Steve Disch. Dr. Steve Disch."

While Steve was waiting, he looked over at Joop. Joop dropped four eggs into the pot of water, which was now boiling, then took clear plastic containers of cheese, ham, and salami out of the refrigerator and placed them on the counter. He looked at Steve. "Coffee?"

"No, thanks."

"Was it that bad?"

"Yes."

"You're right. It was. Coke?" He held up a can of soda. Steve nodded. Joop handed it to him. The woman who'd answered the phone came back on the line.

"Hello?" she said.

"Yes?"

"I'm sorry," she said, "but Dr. Loban can't speak to you."

"But – "

"Again, I'm sorry. Good day."

Click. Agape, Steve handed the receiver back to Joop.

"Oh well," Joop said flatly, hanging it up.

"I can't believe that," Steve said.

"Why did you expect anything else?"

"Because. We were – we were so close."

"But you weren't really boyfriends."

"No."

"Also, you went on to make a movie about your friendship with him. Maybe he didn't care for that."

"It's not like I used his real name."

"I know, but still. Think of it. You're openly gay. Maybe that makes him uneasy, even now."

Steve pondered this.

Joop added: "He *is* an American, after all."

Steve shrugged. "Well, kind of. I mean, he *was* born and raised in America. But he always described himself as Russian."

"Russian? Why?"

"Because his dad was Russian. Is. Whatever. I don't know if he's still alive or not."

"Did you ever meet him? The father, i mean?"

"Yeah. I spent a couple of nights at their house in Bakersfield."

"Where's that?"

"California. The Central Valley."

"Okay. And what about the dad, then?"

"He was very old school. You know what I mean? A Central European professor from Central Casting. Who ended up in the Central Valley."

"No, I don't know what you mean."

"Strict. Severe. The kind of guy who, if his son ever came out to him, would tear him to bits."

"Charming."

"And Daniel worshipped him. All he ever wanted was to impress him, live up to him, be made to feel worthy."

"What a horrible burden."

"That's why he ended up in Eastern Europe. And also why he couldn't deal with being gay. Because he knew his father would never be able to deal with it. So he pushed it away as hard as he could."

"Well, doesn't that explain perfectly why he pushed you away just now?"

Steve looked at Joop, for what felt like a very long time. "Shit," he finally said, his voice hollow. "Of course. How fucking blindingly obvious."

"Okay then," Joop said after only a moment, putting it all behind them. "Breakfast time."

Steve wasn't in any mood to eat, but Joop shoved a stool under him, slid a plate onto the counter in front of him, and lined up the containers of food. It was a typical Dutch breakfast: hard-boiled eggs, cold cuts, rolls, jars of jam and Nutella. Steve started eating, and realized immediately that he was famished. Meanwhile Joop switched on the TV and found a news program.

Steve looked at the clock. It was a couple of minutes after ten.

On the TV, a young reporter whose face seemed a mere footnote to his impressive head of blond hair was standing in front of the UN building in New York and talking about U.S.-China relations. When his story was over, he threw back to the in-studio anchorman, a

164

distinguished-looking middle-aged man who segued into what he called, in a solemn voice and with a solemn expression on his face, "last night's incident at Bellamyplein." The program cut to a pretty young woman reporter who was standing outside Niek's building.

"Holy shit," said Steve, staring at the screen.

"Well, this cuts out the possibility that the whole thing was a bad dream," Joop said.

Late last night, the reporter said, calls from neighbors had drawn Amsterdam police to a first-floor walk-up apartment on Bellamyplein in the Oud West, where two dead men were found in the living room. Both had been shot several times at point-blank range; one of them had also been all but decapitated.

Two photographs flashed onscreen. The "victims."

Steve and Joop looked at each other. Steve felt himself trembling.

Both men, the reporter said, were naturalized Dutch citizens of Turkish origin – family men and regular mosque-goers who had lived in the Netherlands for some twenty years and who were "highly respected members of the community."

From their pictures, the news program cut to a video, taped earlier in the morning, of the same reporter shoving a mike in the face of the hijab-clad wife of one of the two "victims," who, standing at her front door on Schimmelstraat, a few blocks from the scene of the crime, clutched a baby to her chest as she wept hysterically.

Then, suddenly, Steve's passport photo flashed on screen.

"Jesus," Steve said. "I actually look like a murderer."

"It's not your best picture," Joop agreed.

The reporter described the suspect: an American homosexual who had been living mysteriously in Amsterdam for several months without a job or a residency permit. He had already resided at two, perhaps three, different addresses in the city, and, according to information received within the past hour from judicial authorities, was a defendant in a recently filed lawsuit involving *"verstorend"* behavior at his previous residence.

"Verstorend," Steve said. "What's that?"

"Troublemaking. No...like, making a disturbance. Or disruption."

"Disruptive."

"Yes. Shh!"

The reporter said that witnesses had seen two suspects fleeing the scene, but that it was too dark for them to be able to say more than that the second suspect was also a white male.

The news program then showed the reporter interviewing a policeman in front of the house on Bellamyplein. The cop described the murder scene as gory and violent, "like something out of an American film." He made a remark about the "American gun culture" and suggested that this crime represented the introduction of that culture into the peaceful Netherlands.

This exchange was followed by an interview with a professor at the University of Amsterdam, who was shown at his office desk. The professor was about sixty, slim, with a trim white beard, and his desk was cluttered with papers and piles of books. Behind him was a large window looking out on the Spui.

"Nice office," Joop said.

"Looks like he's right around the corner from Henk."

The professor, with an angry edge to his voice, suggested that this "heartless double murder," as he described it, was the result of the kind of anti-Muslim bigotry spread by the likes of Jeroen Schrama. "It only serves to remind us," he said, "that, Schrama's racist lies to the contrary, it is not Muslims who have brought violence to the Netherlands but Americans who spread violence all over the world."

The report ended with the reporter, in close-up, stating that the suspects had been seen fleeing down Agatha Dekenstraat, toward De Clercqstraat, but that the police had no information as to their current whereabouts.

And that was the end of the report. Joop turned off the TV.

"Well," Steve said, "at least they didn't finger you."

"Yet."

"And they haven't talked to that cab driver."

"Yet."

"But weirdly, they also haven't addressed the

question: why were those two guys in that apartment to begin with? They haven't even mentioned that the guys had knives. There's no hint that this was an act of self-defense."

Joop shrugged. "Maybe somebody went into the apartment after we left and removed the knives?"

"Could be. Or maybe, for some reason, the police aren't sharing that information with the media?"

"Hmm."

"Joop," Steve said after a few moments' silence, "I think maybe the best thing for you is for me to get out of here."

"But how? Where can you go?"

"I don't know."

"You can't fly anywhere. They check passports."

"I could take a train."

"Your picture's been on the news. It's probably in every newspaper in the country today. I'm sure the cops at all the railroad stations are on the lookout for you." He chewed and swallowed a forkful of ham. "Of course, you could drive. I'd rent a car for you. Or else I could drive you."

"No, no, no. That would defeat my purpose in leaving here. The whole problem is that by being here in this apartment, I'm leading the cops to you."

Suddenly Joop's cell phone rang. Steve and Joop looked at each other.

After a moment's uncertainty, Joop accepted the call. Instead of answering the phone by saying his last name, in accordance with standard Dutch practice, Joop simply said, "Ja?"

There was a pause. Steve heard a voice on the other end. Joop's eyes widened. "Yes," he said in English. "He's right here."

Joop handed Steve the receiver. "I'm sorry," said the voice on the phone. Steve would have recognized it anywhere. Daniel. "I had to get a secure line. Now tell me. What's wrong? What's urgent?"

"It's me and my friend...Bart."

Joop gave Steve a startled look. Bart glanced up at Steve from his food.

"We've been through this, um, rather remarkable experience," Steve told Daniel. As briefly as possible, he summed up the main points: the voices, the killing. Their escape from the scene. Then Steve started to tell Daniel about the news report he and Joop had just watched – including the fact that it hadn't mentioned their assailants' knives.

Daniel interrupted him. "Save all that for later," he snapped. "First tell me what you and Bart heard them say. What they're planning. Don't leave out any detail, however inconsequential it may seem."

"Okay." Steve told him everything he could remember. Joop pitched in with additional details, which Steve passed on to Daniel. When Steve couldn't come up with anything more, he said to Daniel, "I'm sorry, when I listen to myself it all sounds so vague and feeble. I wish I could give you more."

169

"Don't worry. Where are you now?"

Steve explained the cat-feeding situation, but without giving Daniel the address. "Of course," Steve said, "we could've just turned ourselves into the police and explained what happened. But, um, Bart and I both feel that the police here – "

"Say no more. You probably did the right thing. For now, just stay away from the police. If you can."

Joop waved his hand to get Steve's attention. "One second," Steve said to Daniel. "What is it?" he asked Joop.

"The Alhambra."

"That's right," Steve said to Daniel. "I forgot. They mentioned the Alhambra."

"The Alhambra? You mean as in the palace in Spain?"

"Yes."

"What did you hear them say about it?"

"I don't know." Steve turned to Joop. "We didn't hear them say anything in particular *about* the Alhambra, did we?"

"No."

"Nothing in particular," Steve told Daniel. "Sorry."

"The Alhambra," Daniel repeated.

"I know, it makes no sense."

"Look," Daniel said. His tone was crisp, business-like. "Two things you and Bart should know."

"One second," Steve said. "Let...let Bart listen in."

"Sure." Steve waved Joop over, and held the phone so that both of them could hear Daniel speak.

"Well, first of all," Daniel said, "you and Bart don't need to worry in the long run about ending up in the slammer or whatever. We'll take care of that. But, second, and let me emphasize this, we can't take care of it now. If word gets out that your name's been cleared, the other members of this group will put two and two together and conclude that we're on to them. We don't want that. They can't be sure how much you guys heard. We're going to bet that *they're* betting you didn't really hear enough to get a bead on the specifics of their plan."

"In other words," Steve said, "you're betting that they're going to go through with it."

"Yes."

"But how sure can you be of that?"

"Not sure at all," Daniel said. "But as long as you're officially on the lam, and as long as the Dutch police and the Dutch media continue to talk about you and Bart as murderers and these two dead guys as victims, we're betting that they're going to assume you didn't hear enough to feel confident enough to come out of hiding and take your information to the police. You got that?"

"Yes. So what should Bart and I do now?"

"Stay put."

"That's it?"

"Yes, stay put. Period. Wait it out. Don't go outside. Not *you,* anyway. Let Bart go out and buy groce-

171

ries and do whatever else needs to be done. I'll be in touch. Our first order of business here will be to get the word about the facts of this matter to Dutch Intelligence – or, at least, to friends in Dutch Intelligence who can be trusted not to blab to the police. For the time being, we want the police to remain in the dark. Knowing what I know about them, I suspect that if you lay low, they won't be able to track you down. But, hey, if they do, no sweat, we'll handle it. Are you following me?"

"Sure."

"But – " Joop was speaking.

"One second," Steve told Daniel, and put his hand over the mouthpiece.

"What?" Steve asked Joop.

"This isn't my flat, remember? We can't stay here forever."

"When does Arjan get back?"

"In a week. He's in Thailand."

Steve nodded, and took his hand off the mouthpiece. "Sorry about that, Daniel."

"Any problem?" Daniel asked.

"No."

"OK, good. Look, if you need to get in touch with me for any reason, I'll give you a phone number now. Ready?"

"One second." Steve looked up at Joop and mimed writing with a pen. Joop ran into the bedroom and came back a moment later with a ballpoint and a small pad of paper with a Heineken logo at the top – the kind they kept behind the bar at pubs in Amsterdam so that customers could trade contact information. Daniel recited a phone number and Steve wrote it down. Daniel then told him to read it back. Steve did so.

"Okay, then," said Daniel. "Take care. We'll talk."

And he hung up.

Steve handed Joop the phone. "Well, that's a relief," Steve said. "We're off the hook."

"It's good to have friends in high places," Joop said.

"Yeah."

"The power of America."

"'We'll take care of that.'"

"Yes. Like he was talking about picking up a couple of cinema tickets for us."

"I know."

"I can't imagine what it feels like to be an American and to have that kind of power on your side."

"We take it for granted."

"Yes, you do."

Steve walked across the room to a window. Like the one in the bedroom, it faced a brick wall. Steve looked down at the narrow street below.

"It's good for us your friend became a CIA guy and not a – a rubbish collector," Joop said.

"Or a Hollywood hack."

"Or a dumb security guard."

Steve turned around and smiled. "He sounds exactly the same. His voice."

"He sounds very – what's the word? *Autoritair.*"

Steve chuckled. "He was always like that. He turned a lot of the other students off. Most of them thought he was an arrogant asshole. Or else they just found him preposterous. What they didn't see was that he was doing it with a twinkle in his eye. Like a private joke."

"Well, it's not a joke anymore."

"No, I guess not. He sure sounded like the real thing, didn't he?"

"Yes, he did."

"I guess he's already gotten to work on this."

"Maybe he's talking to Schrama right now."

"Yeah."

"Or the AIVD."

"What's the AIVD?"

"You don't know? The *Algemene Inlichtingen- en Veiligheidsdienst?* It's like the Dutch FBI. And then there's the MIVD, the *Militaire Inlichtingen- en Veiligheidsdienst,* which is like the CIA."

"I didn't know that. But then I guess there's a hell of a lot I don't know about this sort of stuff."

"Well, same here."

Steve sipped some of his Coke. "Funny."

"What? What's funny?"

"Just how life works out. All those years ago, Daniel and I went pretty much everywhere together every day. We took the same classes, read the same books. I always knew what he was doing, he always knew what I was doing. Our lives were totally intertwined. And now?

Now his life is a total mystery to me. I can't even begin to imagine what somebody in a job like that does when he gets to work in the morning."

"He probably has a nice cup of coffee," Joop said.

"You know what I mean."

"Of course I do. But that's the way life is. Everybody's life is a *vraagteken* – a question point – "

"Question mark."

" – a question mark to everybody else. You look at his life, and it's so mysterious to you. If he gave any thought to it, he would probably say the same thing about your life. Only I get the impression he's not sitting around trying to figure out what it's like living in your skin or anybody else's."

"Well, unless he's changed completely, you're certainly right there."

Joop suggested that they go into the living room. Steve followed him in. Joop put on some music while Steve sat on the couch. Steve listened to the first few bars. "Mozart?" he asked.

"Haydn." Joop sat down beside him.

"Arjan has good taste," Steve said.

"He plays the flute. He's in the Royal Concertgebouw Orchestra."

"Really?"

"Yeah."

"I didn't know you knew anybody like that."

"What do you mean?"

"You know. Some hot shot with a fancy job."

"I know *you*, don't I?"

"True."

Suddenly Steve broke into a laugh.

"What's funny?" Joop said.

"Haydn. That's what we're doing. Hidin'."

"Ha. Yes. 'Waiting it out.'"

"'Waiting it out.'" Bart trotted into the room and jumped up on the couch between them. Steve scratched his head.

"A week, huh?" he said.

Joop nodded.

"And what do we do after that?" Steve asked. "This could go on for months. Or more."

"Relax. We'll take it day by day."

"'Wait it out.'"

"Right. When Arjan comes back, he can drive us to my place. In the middle of the night, so nobody sees you."

"Hmm."

They sat there for a while and listened to the music.

"And that brings *Arjan* into it, too," Steve finally said. "It doesn't feel right."

"What doesn't feel right?"

"All of this. Even staying here for a week...for one thing, it's not fair to you."

Joop looked at him.

"Believe it or not, I actually *like* being here with you."

"Believe it or not, I actually like being here with you, too. But not under these circumstances. I feel I should be doing something."

"I know. That's how we got to be in this pickle to begin with. Because you felt you should be doing something."

Steve laughed.

"What?" Joop said.

"'Be in this pickle.' Where did you get that from?"

"What do you mean?"

"That expression. Being in a pickle. Where'd you pick that up?"

"Oh, I'm sorry. It's a Dutch expression. It means being in the middle of, like, a big mess."

"Really? You mean you can say that in Dutch too?"

"Sure. You can say it in English?"

"Yeah."

"I didn't know that. I just translated it in my head without thinking about it. That's funny."

"Come to think of it, I guess maybe English took it from Dutch," Steve said.

"Yes, back in the old days you guys took words from us. Now it's the other way around."

"Yep."

They sat there and listened to Haydn. They took turns scratching Bart, who was in heaven.

"Look," Joop finally said, "i know it's early in the day, but..."

"Please. I'd love one."

Joop went into the kitchen, and quickly returned with two beers. He handed one to Steve. They opened them and started drinking. Then Joop spoke up, in a darker tone than before: "I'm sorry, but – "

"But what?"

"I have one question."

"What's that?"

Joop hesitated. Then: "How can we be sure that Daniel can be trusted?"

"Trusted?"

"Yes. He told you that they'll fix things for us if the cops pick us up. But how can you be sure of that? Aren't these guys from Bellamyplein, and whoever they're working with, a thousand times bigger a priority for Daniel than we are? Come to think of it, wouldn't it make everything easier for Daniel and his friends if they just bumped us both off?"

"You mean if *Daniel* had us bumped off?"

"Yes."

"Are you kidding?"

"No. Think about it: wouldn't it keep things simpler for them to just remove us as a – what do you say – a factor in this equation? They know we've already told them everything we know. They have no more use for us. So why should they want to keep us alive? Just because you and Daniel had this weird thing going on back when you were students? Face it, from this point on, we can only be trouble for them. An inconvenience."

"You've seen too many movies," Steve said.

"American movies."

"Yes, but in America we know they're just movies. The evil CIA. The secret CIA inside the CIA. And the super-duper-secret CIA inside that. Made-up nonsense. Over here, you people all seem to think they're documentaries. Especially since you've already got this poisonous view of America that's been pumped into you ever since your first day of school and the first day you saw the news on Dutch TV. Hasn't it ever occurred to any of you that it just doesn't add up? On the one hand, you all think Americans are so amazingly and brilliantly and miraculously devious, with riddles inside of secrets inside of mysteries, assassination conspiracies and hidden UFOs and all that. And yet on the other hand you think we're a bunch of imbeciles who can't tie our shoes without help."

"Whatever. But it's also true that your view of things is totally colored by your affection for this guy. For Daniel."

"I don't have any affection for him anymore."

"Yeah, right."

"I don't."

"Fine. But if you trust him so completely, why did you tell him that my name is Bart?"

"I don't know. In the moment it just seemed wiser not to give anyone any information that they didn't need to know." Steve took a sip of his beer. "Okay. Let's say, for argument's sake, that you just might be right about the CIA wanting to bump us off. Well, in that case, all the more reason for me to hit the road instead of being a sitting duck. And for you to go home instead of sitting here. So let's say we do what you suggested?"

"What's that?"

"You rent a car."

"No. We need to stay put. 'Wait it out.' You heard the boss. Hey, there's another word you stole from the Dutch language: *boss.*"

"No, you stay put. At *your* place, not here. But I can't. I need to go."

"But where? Where are you gonna go?"

"Where else? Munich."

"Munich?"

"Yes."

"Are you kidding?"

"No."

"But what can you hope to accomplish in Munich?"

"I don't know. Maybe I can figure something out that they won't be able to."

Joop gave him a funny look. "What are you doing? Competing with Daniel?"

"What makes you think that?" Then: "Yes, maybe. A little." Steve looked at him. "I didn't realize you knew me so well."

"Remember, he's a professional at this. You're not."

"Yes, but by the same token he's just a person, like anyone else."

"That's not what you were saying before. You were talking about what a mystery his life is and all that."

"We're talking about two different things here. Yes, he and his people have high-tech equipment, an international network of contacts, and so on, all of which is imposing. And of course they have their power, which can seem unlimited, and which is all the more impressive for being so – so clandestine. You know, clandestine?"

"Yes, *clandestien.*"

"Same word in Dutch?"

"Yes."

"But when you're trying to figure out a situation like this, what it all comes down to is a single human mind taking in the known facts and trying to make something of them. Right? It's about deduction, about intuition. And that's something I can do as well as any of them. I mean, it's not as if they're all such a bunch of friggin' geniuses. And I'm not a total idiot."

Joop mulled over this assertion. "No," he finally said. "Not a total one, I guess."

"Schrama," Steve said.

"What about him?"

"Schrama and Munich. I wonder what the connection is."

Steve plugged his laptop back into the phone socket, went online, and tried a Yahoo search: *Schrama* plus *Munich*. No, nothing.

He tried *Munchen* instead of *Munich*. Nope. He tried *Munchen* and *immigration*.

"What's German for immigration?" Steve asked Joop.

"*Einwanderung.*"

He typed *Munchen* and *Einwanderung*. Nope.

"What are you looking for?"

"I'm not sure."

He typed *Munchen* and *Islam*. Nothing. Joop watched over Steve's shoulder. Steve added the word *Konferenz*. No.

"Instead of *Konferenz*," said Joop, "try *Tagung*." Steve did so. Nothing.

"Change it to *conference*. In English."

Steve did so. Pay dirt.

There it was on the screen right in front of them: *First Annual International Conference on the Islamization of Europe*. They both stood there and stared at it for a moment.

"Shit," said Joop.

Steve clicked on the link. "It's next Tuesday," Steve said.

"Next Tuesday?"

"Yes."

"What's today? Thursday?"

"Yes." Steve read aloud the beginning of a description of the event. "*Members of Parliament from all over Europe are expected to attend the continent's first....*"

"Click on that," said Joop, pointing to the words

Tentative list of participants. Steve did so. After a moment, another page appeared. It contained a list of forty or fifty names, each followed by a title. There were mayors of small towns here and there in Western Europe, city councilmen from a few of the larger European cities, and a couple of members of the French and British parliaments.

"There he is," Joop said. "There's his name."

Sure enough. *Jeroen Schrama, Tweede Kamer, Den Haag, Netherlands.*

"But where exactly is this thing taking place?"

"Scroll down."

Steve did so. Nothing.

"Go back to the main page."

Steve clicked on the back arrow, then scrolled down again.

There it was.

"*At the present time,*" he read aloud, "*the location of this event is not being made public. Interested parties are kindly invited to contact the organizers.* There's a phone number with the German country code."

"I guess they're scared of terrorism," Joop said.

Steve picked up the pen that Joop had brought in from the bedroom and scribbled the number down on the piece of paper he'd found in the brown wallet.

"How can you be sure that's what this is about?" Joop asked. "How can you even know whether Schrama's really planning to be there?"

"Of course he is. His name is right there."

"That doesn't mean anything. You could end up going to Munich for no reason."

"Okay, there's one way to find out. Can you phone the Tweede Kamer for me?"

Shrugging, Joop took out his cell phone and called directory information. He asked for the number of the Tweede Kamer, thanked the operator, then hung up and punched it in.

He handed Steve the phone.

"Tweede Kamer," a woman's voice said.

"Jeroen Schrama, please."

"And who is calling?"

Steve hung up. "No, I can't do it this way," he said. "I'm sorry, can you call that number again?" Steve handed Joop the phone.

"Boy, do you know how to run up a guy's phone bill."

"Sorry."

"Just kidding." Joop punched *redial* and started to hand the phone back to Steve.

"No, you talk to her. Ask for Sanne in Schrama's office."

"Sanne?"

"Yes."

Joop did so. He nodded at Steve to indicate that he'd been put through. Steve reached out for the phone. Joop handed it to him.

A female voice answered. "Jeroen Schramas kantoor."

"Sanne?" Steve said.

"Ja?"

"It's Steve Disch. I was there yesterday, remember?"

"Oh," Sanne said.

Steve could tell from that one syllable that she'd seen the news.

"I know what you've heard," Steve said, "but they're not telling the whole truth. Those guys were terrorists and they were trying to kill me. This is why I came to see Herr Schrama yesterday. Please let me talk to him. I know things that he needs to know. Please. It's a matter of life or death."

For a moment Sanne was silent. Then she spoke. "Hold on."

Steve thought he could hear in her voice a readiness to help him. But who could tell?

After being away from the phone for a minute or so, she came back on.

"Hello?"

He could hear it clearly: the professionalism had reasserted itself.

"Yes?"

"Mr. Schrama says that he'll be glad to talk to you, but first you have to turn yourself in to the authorities. He urges you to do that. He says that if you're innocent, you'll be okay."

"Please ask him just one thing for me," Steve said.

"I'm sorry," Sanne replied, "but I can't say any more to you until you turn yourself in."

"Munich," Steve said. "One word. Munich." But she'd already hung up.

Steve turned to Joop. "We've got to get word to him. Not to go to Munich."

"Are you sure?"

"What do you mean?"

"I don't know. If they don't get to him in München, they'll get to him somewhere else, no? This way, at least we have some clue about the where and the when. And if you really trust Daniel and his friends to do a good job, or if you think you might get to the bottom of it yourself, maybe it's best to leave it alone. Or am I missing something?"

Steve thought long and hard.

"No," he finally said. "I don't think you're missing anything. Unless, of course, *I'm* missing something."

"Then München it is?"

"München it is."

VI

I T WAS EARLY MORNING. Steve was headed down the E35, the four-lane divided highway that links Amsterdam in the north to Rome in the south, on the far side of the Swiss Alps. The sky was clear and the traffic light.

He'd already driven through Utrecht and skirted Arnhem. To his relief and surprise, he hadn't had any trouble making sense of the European traffic signs. They'd always been Greek to him, but Joop had given him an intensive three-hour course, complete with homemade illustrations.

He *was* having some trouble with the manual transmission. Never in his life had he driven anything but an automatic, and after picking up the car a couple of hours earlier at the rental agency – which didn't have a single automatic-transmission car on the lot – Joop had had to give him an impromptu lesson in when to shift gears and how to do it without stalling out. So far he'd done better than he'd expected to, although he wasn't about to win any awards for smooth driving. Already the car had jerked disconcer-tingly a couple of times when he'd tried to shift gears going up or down a hill.

Now the German border was only a few minutes ahead.

As he approached it, he tensed up a little. He knew that in today's European Union, driving from one country into another was no bigger a deal than crossing a street; borders had become all but invisible. But not entirely. There were still such things as border patrols, which were usually on the lookout for cars whose trunks might contain, say, an extra bottle or two of booze on which the driver didn't plan to pay duty. And, needless to say, on the lookout for fugitives.

Like Steve.

Steve was suddenly very aware of the gun in his pants pocket.

And aware, too, that he had killed. Killed: it didn't seem real. He ran the scene – the men bursting into the apartment, the gun firing, Joop slitting a throat – over and over again in his mind. It had all happened so fast. It seemed more like something he had observed than something he had done.

He tried to push the thought away.

A large blue exit sign loomed up ahead. It was in German and English, but not in Dutch. *Grenzstation*, it read. *Zoll/Douane. Bank/Change.* He drove on for another mile or so without seeing an explicit *Welcome to Germany* sign. Nonetheless, he gathered he was now in Germany. Otherwise nothing had changed. The highway continued to be lined on both sides by solid walls of trees. Funny, he reflected. Every hamlet you drive through in the U.S. has big signs announcing that you're entering it and leaving it. But the Federal Republic of Germany? Nothing.

So he'd crossed the border without incident.

He looked in the mirror for any sign of police. The road behind him was empty.

During the next couple of hours he drove past

Duisberg, then Düsseldorf, then Cologne. The traffic grew heavier, but not by much. Just after passing Bonn, he glanced at the radio. When he'd started driving, he hadn't wanted to listen to it, for fear of being distracted, but now he switched it on and hunted for a congenial station.

He found some classical music. It sounded like Schubert. He thought about Joop and the Haydn. And about Arjan. Steve didn't know anything about Arjan except that he was in the Royal Concertgebouw Orchestra. Joop said they'd been friends since childhood. Was Arjan gay? His apartment had provided a couple of possible clues – the cat, the tidiness. But nothing definitive.

Were Arjan and Joop an item?

Steve left the music on. When the piece ended, the announcer said that it was indeed Schubert. Steve experienced a nanosecond of irrational cheer: if he could get *that* right, he found himself thinking, maybe he could get this whole business right, too.

The Schubert was followed by another classical piece. Steve recognized it from the first note: Brahms's Third Symphony. Daniel, who'd played French horn in the college orchestra, had loved it. Steve reached over reflexively to change stations. But then he stopped, and decided to listen.

The first movement was majestic, stirring; the second was just fine. But it was the third movement that clinched it. As always, it struck Steve as impossibly magnificent – grand, rich, lush, complex, and yet, in its most sweeping melodic moments, sweetly simple and pure, and possessed of some profound, comforting wisdom about life and death that couldn't be put into ordinary human language and didn't need to be. It was as if God himself were whispering gentle words into one's ear, communicating some sublime revelation, making some divine promise, in a tongue you'd never heard but somehow realized you'd always known.

Haydn. Schubert. Brahms. For him, that had always been Europe. Music, art, literature of the highest order. Civilization at its pinnacle. Humankind at its most accomplished.

As opposed, for example, to *Nikki and Friends.*

Back in L.A., it had all seemed so simple. But now Europe was turning out to be something very different from what he had thought it was.

He drove straight through Limburg, and by the time the symphony was over, he was almost in Frankfurt. He looked at the fuel gauge. It was getting low. Time to start keeping his eyes open for a gas station. After ten minutes he started panicking. Where the hell were all the gas stations? Was this, of all things, going to be his downfall? But then he saw a sign indicating that there was gas up ahead. He moved into the right lane, slowed gradually, and a couple of minutes later took the turnoff, shifting gears clumsily as he did so.

He slowed even more, turned, pulled up next to a bright-red pump under a metal sign with a giant number two on it, and stopped the car.

Now came the perilous part. Stepping out into the

warm afternoon, he walked over to the gas station and went inside. Behind a counter sat a sturdy, grim-faced woman of sixty or so in a pale blue uniform. She wore a pair of glasses on a chain around her neck and a blue plastic nametag: *Agneta*. The sun beat down through the big window, making it uncomfortably hot inside. Agneta seemed untroubled. Steve told her the number of the pump – *zwei* – and how much he wanted to spend on gas. He studied her face for any sign of suspicion. Nope. He took out his wallet and pulled out Joop's Mastercard. "Okay?" he asked. She nodded unsmilingly and took the card, all but yanking it out of his hand. *I guess this is my "welcome to Germany,"* he thought.

He looked around at the shelves of candy and gum, the fridge full of soft drinks, and, right at his hip, a rack of newspapers. While Agneta swiped his card through the machine, he stepped back, crouched down, and surveyed as quickly as he could the visible front-page headlines. *Frankfurter Allgemeine. Allgemeine Zeitung. Wiesbadener Tagblatt. Bild.* No, nothing there. Not above-the-fold, anyway. Agneta handed him the credit-card gizmo, and he punched in Joop's passcode. Agneta looked at it, waited for it to beep. It didn't. She looked puzzled, but mostly irritated. Finally she made a sound of exasperation and handed it back to him.

"*Noch einmal,*" she sighed. Steve punched in Joop's code again. Had he misremembered it? Or had the account been blocked? But no, this time it went through; he must've entered it incorrectly the first time. After a moment the machine beeped, and a small receipt printed out, which Agneta ripped off indelicately and slapped down in front of him, along with a pen. He picked up the pen and did his best imitation of a *handtekening*, the Dutch equivalent of a signature, which typically looks less like a name than like the product of somebody testing a pen.

Back outside the gas station, Steve flipped open the fuel door, twisted off the gas cap, and put it on the roof. Clumsily, he took the gas-pump valve out of its socket, stuck it in the car's filler neck, and pumped away, his eyes on the register as the number of liters and the price sped upwards. So focused was he on the register that he didn't notice the person coming up behind him until he felt a tap on the shoulder. Steve swung around with an adrenaline rush to see a hulking middle-aged man in overalls and cap. The overalls, and the man's cheeks, were black with grease. On the cap was an Esso logo. *"Ihre Karte,"* he said. With his right hand, also black with grease, he held out Joop's Mastercard.

"Danke schön!" Steve said, unable to hide just how rattled he was. Steve smiled; the man didn't. He just lumbered away.

Steve finished pumping the gas, feeling utterly shaken. If he'd driven off without that card...then what? There were so many little details, all so easy to forget, any one of which could doom his mission.

Not that he was at all sure what, exactly, his mission was.

Back on the road, he switched the radio off. No

more distractions! He spent a good ten minutes cursing his absentmindedness, then decided it was a better idea to forgive himself and try to calm down. After a while he put the radio back on. Chopin.

By mid afternoon he was closing in on Nuremberg. The sky had clouded over and the temperature had dropped, and the traffic had gotten a bit heavier. He tried to hold to a steady speed, but now and then had to slow down and shift gears when a car entered the highway in front of him moving at a slightly lower speed than he was. And then he felt obliged to drive faster again when he felt a queue of cars on his tail eager to race. His gear-shifting was klutzy but, he felt, serviceable.

Nuremberg. The trials. *Triumph of the Will.* Ever since the first time he'd come to Europe, Steve had been intensely aware of the weight of history around him – aware, in Amsterdam for instance, that every time he stepped outside he was retracing the steps of Rembrandt, van Gogh, Spinoza. And here he was only a half hour or so out of Munich. Mozart. Wagner. The Beer Hall Putsch.

He was congratulating himself on having made it all this way without a problem when he noticed, in his rear-view mirror, a green car behind him. On its hood, written in large white letters, was a single word.

Politzei.

He froze. Was this it? Were they on to him? But how? There was no way. He and Joop had watched the news before going to bed last night, and then again after waking up this morning. Both times, the TV news people

193

had covered the killings at Bellamyplein, but all they'd really had to say was that there was nothing new to report. He and Joop had spent the night at Arjan's apartment, but Joop had promised he'd head straight home as soon as Steve left and would spend the rest of the day there. There was no good reason, then, to believe that the police had caught up with Joop – and thus with Steve.

I just have to make sure, Steve told himself, *not to behave suspiciously.*

For the next several miles, he drove along with the police car right behind him. A sign announced an upcoming exit: route 73, which in one direction led to Erlingen and in the other to Nuremberg. Steve was so unsettled by the presence of the cops on his tail that when the turnoff for Nuremberg appeared – it was a big cloverleaf – he took it.

And so did the police car.

He felt his heartbeat quicken. What the hell was going on? Was this just a coincidence? Or were they following him? But if they were on to him, why not just pull him over already and be done with it?

Now he was on another limited-access highway. He wasn't yet in Nuremberg, but after a couple of minutes it became clear – more and more buildings, more and more cars – that he was on its outskirts. Eventually, the cops still on his tail, he found himself approaching a point at which there was a crossing and traffic lights: the *Autobahn* had turned into an ordinary city street. The light up ahead was red. Steve could see that the traffic on the cross street was heavy, and that it was all flowing from left to right. So it was a one-way. Reaching the crossing, he stopped. So did the police car. Steve looked in his mirror. He could see two silhouettes, both apparently male – one in the driver's seat, the other beside him.

The signage was confusing, but his impression was that downtown Nuremberg was to his left, and that the cross-traffic he was looking at now, in mid-afternoon, was the beginning of the Friday rush hour – people heading out to the suburbs after a day's work. When the light changed, he continued down the highway. After only half a minute or so he came to another crossing with traffic lights. Sure enough, there was a tiny sign reading "*Centrum*," pointing to the left. He had a green light, and he took the turn.

So did the police.

Now he was sure they were after him. But what kind of game were they playing? Did they know who he was, or were they just tormenting a randomly selected victim in a rented Dutch car?

One fact of which he'd become aware, through the occasional offhand comment, was that a great many Dutch people still had chilly feelings toward their German neighbors – EU brotherhood or no EU brotherhood. The Dutch still vividly remembered the war, the Occupation, and the various acts of evil in which they – or, rather, their grandparents and great-grandparents – had been forced to be complicit. What about the Germans? Was the feeling mutual? Was that what was going on here? Just some kind of xenophobic game?

After a moment, the road he was on split in two, with yet another *"Centrum"* sign, this one pointing to the right. Steve followed it, the cops staying behind him. Now he was on a two-lane, one-way street, with sturdy old two- and three-story apartment houses to his left and, to his right, a cobblestone-covered shoulder three or four lanes wide and, beyond it, at least a couple of train tracks, running parallel to the street he was on.

He kept driving. After a few blocks, the street he was on came to an end at a right-angle intersection with another two-lane street. A small blue sign reading *"Hauptbahnhof"* pointed to the left. He followed it. The cops stayed behind him. A couple more blocks, and then there was another blue *"Hauptbahnhof"* sign, this one pointing to the right. Steve took the turn, onto a boulevard. So did the cops. To his left now, stretching along the roadside, was an old stone structure that looked like the outer wall of a fortress; on his right was a jumble of low buildings, some of them older and distinguished-looking, apparently apartment houses, others newer and tackier, with seedy-looking shops at street level. After a few blocks, there appeared on his right a handsome old brick edifice that reminded him of the Stadsschouwburg on Leidseplein in Amsterdam.

He drove another couple of blocks. Then suddenly, in front of an ugly modern building with the word *"Hotel"* spelled out over its entrance in garish electric-blue letters, he saw three or four parking spots in a row. Making his decision in an instant, he turned off the road, slid into the space, switched off the ignition, grabbed his shoulder bag, and leapt out of the car, all in what felt like one smooth move. He ran into the hotel, looking behind him as he pushed through the revolving doors. The police car drove past, apparently continuing on its way. In the lobby, he paused for an instant. Had he overreacted? Were they really not after him? Should he go back to the car and continue his journey? He pushed his way outside again through the revolving doors, and saw that, a couple of vehicle lengths ahead of his own rent-a-car, the police cruiser had stopped in the right traffic lane, and one of the officers – the one who'd been sitting in the shotgun seat – was climbing out, his back to Steve. Realizing that the cop had seen him enter the hotel, Steve rushed down the sidewalk, away from him, and turned the corner – whereupon he started running as fast as he could down the narrow side street that ran along the right side of the hotel. Reaching an intersection, he made a left and kept running. Ahead of him, at the end of the block, loomed a monumental stone building with the letters "DB" over its elegant entrance: the train station.

Steve ran inside. It was one of those grand old European railroad terminals, and at the moment it was pretty crowded. Instead of going to a ticket window, he found a ticket machine. It wasn't very different from its counterparts in Amsterdam, so he wasn't entirely at sea. After a moment, he figured out how to select his destination, Munich, after which he slid in Joop's credit card and punched in the passcode. The machine made a grinding sound and the ticket dropped into a metal trough. He fished it out and looked up and around in search of the departures board. He saw it and ran over to read it. The next train to Munich was leaving from track six in eleven minutes. Steve looked around to locate the gate, then realized there were two things he had to do first.

One of them was to take out money *now*, before the cops tracked down the rented car and blocked Joop's bank card. Steve looked around, saw a stout old man using an ATM by the main station entrance, and rushed over to it. The elderly gent was taking his time, punching in numbers slowly and meticulously. He was wearing a dirty white coat that was too heavy for the weather and a crumpled brown hat that looked a hundred years old. Steve looked up at a wall clock. A minute passed. Another. And another. While carrying out his transaction, the man kept clearing his throat in a particularly disgusting way.

Eight minutes to the train. Finally the old man tucked his bank card and money carefully into his wallet, put the wallet in his pocket, and moved away from the machine at a tortoise's pace. Steve stepped up to it, almost pushing him aside, and shoved in Joop's card. After tapping in the passcode, he asked for 5000 Deutschmarks. A message appeared on the screen telling him that he couldn't withdraw such a large sum. He tried again: 3000.

A few long seconds went by, and then he heard

the crisp sound of bills being dealt out mechanically. There was a welcome whirr, and the money slid out. He grabbed it, yanked out Joop's card, and wove quickly through the crowded station toward the gate for track six.

Hurrying down the stairs, he found the train, sleek and shiny, standing there, waiting. He stepped onboard. It was almost full. It had that railway equivalent of a new-car smell. He made his way up the aisle toward the front of the train until he found a W.C. It was unoccupied. He opened the door. It was antiseptic, spotless. He stepped inside, slid the door shut, locked it, and took the piss that he suddenly realized he'd been needing to take for the better part of an hour. After flushing the toilet, he shut the seat cover, sat on it, took Joop's cell phone out of his pocket, and dialed Joop's home number.

Joop picked up after a single ring, and said "Visser." His last name.

"Joop?"

"Where are you?"

"Nuremberg. On a train about to leave for Munich."

"Nuremberg? What happened?"

"Not much time to talk right now. But I've compromised you. There were cops on my tail and I had to ditch the rental car. I'm sorry."

"Cops? Are you OK?"

"Yes."

"Don't worry, then," he said. "It's fine. Do you have the gun?"

"Yes."

"Good. What are you going to do?"

"Take this train to Munich. It's only a half-hour trip."

"Okay. Meanwhile I'll go back to Arjan's, just in case the cops come looking for me here. I'll go right now and stay there. It'll give us a week, anyway."

"I guess that's the best idea."

"Let me go now, before it's too late."

"Right."

Steve hung up, took a deep breath, and did some thinking.

First of all, he'd fucked things up for Joop, that was for sure. So much for trying to keep him out of trouble. That didn't last long. Did this mean Joop's picture would be all over the news, too? Or would the Dutch police decide that for some reason it was better not to broadcast his name and image? Steve found himself hoping fervently that this would be the case. He was, he realized, far more worried about Joop than about himself. Joop had, after all, been nothing but good to him, and he, in return, had brought nothing into Joop's life but trouble.

Steve's thoughts then turned to himself. Both his time and his funds, he realized, were now strictly limited. He didn't know if his picture had been widely disseminated in the German media prior to this, but he assumed it would be now.

The train lurched to a start. Almost at once, there was a knock on the W.C. door. Steve froze up. *Okay,* he thought, *if this is it, this is it.* He unlocked the door and slid it open. A bald, middle-aged man in a business suit stood there, looking down at the floor. As Steve stepped out of the W.C. and out of the man's way, he noticed a walnut-sized growth on the side of the man's neck. The man went in and shut the door.

Steve looked up and down the length of the car. Nearly every seat was occupied. And there didn't seem to be any seats at all that weren't next to somebody. What to do? On the one hand, wouldn't he be drawing too much attention to himself if he stood all the way to Munich? But on the other, did he want to get forced into a conversation with some German who'd quickly be able to identify him as an American?

He gave the question a moment's thought. He reflected that while Germans were quick to pick up on unconventional behavior, they weren't all that eager to start conversations with strangers. So it was probably safer, he concluded, for him to sit down. It all depended on whom he sat down next to.

He walked up the aisle and surveyed his choices. An elderly woman in a gray shawl who looked anxious and kept scratching the back of her veiny, rice-papery hand? No. A skinny, thin-lipped college-age guy with a goatee and wire rims who was reading a newspaper, an intent expression on his face? No. An older, heavyset, plainly dog-tired man in a rumpled caramel-colored suit who

201

seemed to be struggling to stay awake while he stared glassily at an article in *Capital*, a business weekly? Well, okay. Steve slipped into the seat next to the man, putting his shoulder bag on his lap; the man exhibited absolutely no reaction to Steve's presence.

Good.

One way to help ward off any unwelcome conversation, it occurred to Steve, would be to have his nose in some reading matter. He dug into his shoulder bag and took out Henk's copy of Schrama's book. He opened it wide, so that his seatmate wouldn't be able to see the title. He plunged in, not very hopefully: he could read articles in Dutch newspapers well enough to get the gist of them, but the prose in Dutch-language books was almost always a bridge too far – just difficult enough to cross the line from comprehension to incomprehension. The fact that Schrama had originally been an academic only contributed to his sense that this was going to be a futile effort.

But he was wrong: Schrama's prose proved to be surprisingly easy to follow. Yes, every now and then a sentence went over Steve's head. But for the most part it was amazingly lucid. Schrama wasn't serving up abstruse theories or trying to impress with jargon: his facts were straightforward, his manner direct, urgent, even stirring.

> *Our forefathers here in the Netherlands spent centuries building up this country and its culture – a free and prosperous culture remarkable for its high*

level of intellectual and artistic accomplishment, its unique degree of tolerance, its decency of character, its remarkable technical expertise and mercantile proficiency. Over the generations we have triumphed magnificently time and again – over the ever-present threat of poverty, over nature herself in the form of the ravaging sea, and, not least, with the help of good friends and allies, over evil itself in the form of cruel and barbaric enemies.

Today, as a result of our forefathers' efforts, we stand as a proud model of what a civilization can and should be. But even as we stand here as grateful stewards of our splendid inheritance, we face an enemy that seeks to bring this edifice crashing down to the ground, and to bring it down, moreover, in the name of a strange and alien god – a god who is neither loving nor just; a god who is brutal and monstrous; a god who teaches his followers to hate everything that we are and stand for and believe in; a god who demands that they crush our precious freedom and force us into submission – submission, of course, being their faith's very name...

Steve was so engrossed in Schrama's book that after reading a few pages he looked up with surprise to find that the train was already pulling into Munich – and that the man sitting next to him had dozed off, his magazine lying open on his lap. Steve tossed the Schrama book into his shoulder bag, stood up, and went to the door. When the train stopped, he was the first one off. Rushing down the platform into the station proper, which was even larger, grander, and busier than the one in Nuremberg, Steve took Joop's phone out of his pocket and dialed Arjan's apartment. It rang once, twice. After ten rings without an answer, he hung up. He tried Joop's place. No answer there, either.

Shit.

Okay, he told himself, *calm down. Eat something.* He realized that he was, in fact, starving.

Stuffing the phone back into his pocket, he took a look around the station concourse and saw a Burger King next to the street entrance. He walked over and went in. There were several long lines at the counter; every table was taken. Walking back into the train station, he scanned the busy concourse again. On the opposite side was a small, upscale-looking grocery; over its entrance, a sign read *Vin et fromage.* Steve made his way over through the crowd and into the store, which proved to have an extensive, appetizing-looking selection of sausages, cheeses, cold cuts, breads, crackers, juices, sodas, wines, and beer. Steve picked up a shiny metal shopping basket, into which he tossed a package apiece of Swiss cheese and Westphalia ham, two rolls, and a can of Coke. His hand, he noticed, was trembling. He went to the cashier, a bright-eyed young woman in a pale blue uniform who said, *"Noch etwas?"*

"Nee, dank je," he replied, the Dutch words emerging from his mouth automatically. Before pausing to

think, he switched languages: *"Non, merci."* The cashier smiled, in a not unfriendly way, at his confusion. This time he actually stopped to think for a half-second and got it right: *"Nein, danke schön."* Nodding, she placed each item carefully in a plastic sack as she rang it up, then handed the sack to him, smiling again and meeting his gaze as she said in ringing Dutch (obviously having come to the wrong conclusion about his nationality): *"Alstublieft!"*

Steve carried the sack through the concourse and outside, where, in addition to all the commuters and travelers rushing in and out of the station, there were sizable groups of dark-skinned young men – Turks? Arabs? – loitering just beyond the entrance. Two tram tracks ran past the front of the station, and there were platforms with benches. On both platforms, dozens of people were standing and waiting. The benches, however, were almost empty. Apparently, these Bavarians were too hardy – or too proud? – to sit, even after a long work week. He walked over, crossed the tracks, and sat down on a bench, his shoulder bag between his legs, the sack of groceries on his lap. He took out Joop's cell phone again, and tried Arjan's number. He let it ring twenty times. No answer. He tried Joop's apartment. Twenty more rings. Nothing.

He stuffed the phone back into his pocket and reached into the sack, his hand trembling. He pulled out one of the rolls and started nibbling on it.

A tram clattered up and stopped at his platform. Dozens of people poured out, dozens got on. While he was examining the faces in the crowd, somebody slipped in beside him on the bench. He glanced over. The guy was young and Mediterranean-looking, scrawny and wide-eyed. He reminded Steve a bit of the boy who'd mugged him outside Gaiety. The guy leaned in toward him. *"Haben Sie Geld?"* he said in a surprisingly raspy voice. His teeth were rotten, and his breath stunk. He twitched in a way that made his cheek almost touch his shoulder.

"*Nein*," Steve said, with a nervous smile. Picking up both his shoulder bag and the sack of groceries, Steve stood up and walked off down the platform. The tram pulled out. Ahead of him, a pigeon was poking its beak at an empty ketchup packet. Steve tore off a bit of bread and dropped it in front of the bird, which dived at it as a couple of other pigeons swooped down out of nowhere. Steve gave them all some bread. The more bread he passed out, the more pigeons appeared. He ended up giving away all his bread – and drawing irritated looks from other people on the platform. Germans didn't do things like this. Too disorderly; too messy. As he stood there watching the pigeons eat, a tram pulled in, headed in the opposite direction from the last one.

Where to go?

That was the question facing him as he stood there surrounded by feasting pigeons and by Germans heading home from work. The question immediately turned into another one: where would Jeroen Schrama go? If Schrama were in this city, where, of all the possible places to go, would he go? That, he suddenly (and belatedly) realized, was the operative question here: *Where would Jeroen Schrama go?*

The area around the train station, he noticed, was growing more crowded by the minute. He walked away from it and stopped for a red light at Bayerstraße, a relatively narrow but, at the moment, very busy street that ran along what Steve decided must be the station's south side. At the corner, he was surrounded by several people, including two slim young guys in business suits who set off his gaydar big time. When the light changed, they all crossed the street, which also involved crossing a maze of tram tracks. On the opposite side of Bayerstraße the two gay guys kept keep walking straight ahead, and Steve moved closer to them. "Excuse me," he said in English. Without stopping, they glanced over at him, their expressions vaguely haughty. "Sorry to bother you. Would you guys happen to know where I might find a gay bar?"

They stopped walking, and Steve stopped too. The one closer to him, who was slightly balding and somewhat older than the other one, said in a flat, expressionless voice, and with only a hint of a German accent, "You're lucky, the gay district isn't far from here." While his friend, who was attractive (though not as attractive as he plainly thought he was), stood there looking bored, the older one spelled out the directions dryly and meticulously: "Take the next left up here" – he pointed – "then turn right onto Sonnenstraße."

"Sonnenstraße."

"Yes. After you pass Sendlinger Tor, make a right

onto Müllerstraße. On Müllerstraße there's a gay bar on almost every block."

"Thanks very much," Steve said.

"You're quite welcome," the German said. "Good luck." He gave Steve a half-smile – he wasn't unfriendly, after all – but his friend, who had been studying Steve as if he were an inanimate object, gave him nothing. And they continued on their way.

Steve followed the directions. About fifteen minutes later, after a brisk walk along crowded sidewalks on charming, lively little streets, he came across a bar on Müllerstraße called Bau, where an image of a rainbow was spread out across the tops of the three front windows. He opened the door and walked in.

The bar was small and dark, and there was only one customer – a meek-looking little guy who was sitting at the bar and busy with some activity involving a couple of books. Behind the bar, the bartender – a muscular, bald, bearded guy of thirty or so, in a black t-shirt and black leather pants – was rinsing beer glasses in the sink and setting them down in meticulous rows to dry on a black towel. He looked up at Steve with a welcoming smile that seemed terribly un-German.

"*Hallo!*" the bartender said, tilting his head with a hint of professional flirtation.

"*Hallo,*" said Steve. "*Ein Bier, bitte.*"

The bartender gave an economical little nod and started tapping a beer.

Steve sat down a couple of stools away from the

other customer, who hadn't even looked up at him. The books in front of the other customer, he saw, were hymnals. One of the hymnals looked very old, the other brand-new. The guy was paging through both of the hymnals at the same time, looking back and forth between them and making meticulous notes in the new one.

The bartender, who had finished tapping Steve's beer, wiped the glass delicately with a bar cloth and set the beer down in front of him. "*Vielen Dank*," Steve said, and handed him Joop's card. While the bartender ran the card through the machine, Steve noticed a small rack full of brochures at the end of the bar. He got up, walked over, took one of the brochures, and brought it back to his place at the bar, then opened it up to find a map showing every one of the gay establishments in the city. He began perusing it. *Where would Schrama go?* The map identified sixty-seven places in all. Sixty-seven! Most of them were bars and dance clubs, and about half of these were within three or four blocks of where Steve was now sitting. There were also restaurants, hotels, a bookstore, various clubs, and numerous organizations for gay Catholics, gay Protestants, and gay Social Democrats. Plus five bathhouses.

Steve scanned the list of establishments in hope of finding some name that sang out *Schrama*. But what did he really know about Schrama, or about Schrama's tastes? He knew that man was of a certain age, that he was richer than most people, that he had a Muslim boyfriend –

Die Hirtenflöte.

There it was, in black and white. A sauna. That's what it was: the name of a sauna. The biggest in Munich, it said, open all day and night every weekend, from Friday afternoon until late Sunday night.

And it was only a few blocks away.

Holy shit.

What was it Schrama had said about water?

Suddenly Joop's phone rang. Steve's whole body jumped. He scrambled to extricate the phone from his pocket. He didn't recognize the number on the screen.

"Hello?"

"Hi, it's me." Joop. Steve got up from the stool and walked as far as he could from the bar – and from the bartender.

"Where are you?" Steve asked.

"Are you in Munich?"

"Yes. In a bar. And you?"

"Relax. It's okay."

"What is this number? Where are you calling from?"

"Kalverstraat. I just bought a new cell phone."

"On Kalverstraat? What happened?"

"I got a call from the police. I was halfway out the door on my way to Arjan's."

"Oh, shit. And?"

"No, calm down. The cop called to say that a car rented in my name had turned up in Nuremberg. He said the German highway police had followed it because they could tell from the license plate that it was a Dutch rental, and there was something about the way the driver was driving that made them suspicious."

"Well, I didn't do a great job of shifting gears."

"That's it, probably. Or maybe they were just on the lookout for Dutch license plates on the Autobahn because car robberies now in Amsterdam are crazy high."

"Is that so?"

"That's what the cop told me. So the driver – you – parked the car in a place where you're not supposed to park except for loading and unloading. You went into the hotel and then you disappeared. Very suspicious! Even before they called a tow truck, they called the Dutch cops, who traced the license and called the rental place and then phoned me right away, because they wanted to know if that was me who parked it in Nuremberg. I said no. I said I'd rented the car this morning and parked it on the street here and was going to use it this evening for a trip. I told him it had obviously been stolen. The cop seemed to buy my story."

"So what you're saying is – "

"What I'm saying is that they don't seem to know it was you driving the car. They don't seem to know there's a connection between the car and those guys getting killed on Bellamyplein. They didn't get a good look at you, did they?"

"No, now that I think of it, I guess not."

"Well, there you have it. Unless the police were playing some kind of game with me, they just think it's an ordinary stolen-car case."

"Thank God. So where are you going now?"

"I'm on my way home."

"And you're going to stay there?"

"I guess so. But from now on call me at this number."

"I will. Look, I just found out something. *Die Hirtenflöte?* You know what it is?"

"No."

"It's a gay sauna here in Munich."

"You're kidding."

"No."

"Shit. So you were right. It *is* about Munich."

"And about that sauna."

"And about somebody named Fabien."

"Who maybe has something to do with that sauna."

"So what are you going to do?"

"What else? Go to the sauna. And see if I can figure out why its name is on that piece of paper."

"Really?"

"Of course."

"Are you sure? Think about it. If there are people there who are hooked up with these guys from Bellamyplein – I mean, they'd definitely have seen your picture, and – "

"I know. But how can I not check it out?"

There was a long pause at Joop's end. "I know. Just be careful."

"I will be."

"And don't forget to eat something."

"You too. Thank you, Joop. For everything."

Steve hung up and put the phone back in his pocket. Then he walked backed to his stool, took a last sip of beer, and nodded goodbye to the bartender as he set the glass down.

"*Danke schön,*" the bartender said, swooping up the glass with another friendly smile.

"*Bitte schön,*" Steve replied, and walked out, the map folded in his hand in such a way as to give him an overview of the immediate neighborhood.

It was dark out now, and considerably colder than before, and the sidewalks were much less crowded. Steve turned from one quiet, narrow street lined with fine old buildings onto another, and then onto a cobbled, pedestrians-only thoroughfare. He skirted around a large baroque church and saw ahead of him a large, gray, grim, block-like, smooth-surfaced postmodern structure, standing off by itself, separated from everything around it by a flat, dreary expanse of concrete. Since he was in Germany, he knew immediately what it was. These things all had exactly the same look about them. He moved closer. Carved into the gray façade, like words on a gravestone, were statements, in various sizes and typefaces, mostly in German but a couple in English, about the evils of genocide.

He remembered the first time he'd seen a Holocaust memorial in Germany. It had been two full decades ago, on his first day ever in Europe. He'd been a college freshman, and as the Christmas break approached, his German friend Grete had not only invited but urged (indeed, all but ordered) him to accompany her when she traveled back home to spend the holidays with her family. "You're almost in your twenties," she'd said, "and you've never been to Europe! You of all people *have* to go to Europe! You *belong* in Europe! Besides, you've just finished a term of German – it would be great practice!"

And so he'd gone. On the first day of his visit, Grete's sturdy, stolid mother, bundled up in a heavy teal coat and wearing a matching dirndl hat, had driven him and Grete around their little hometown in Hesse, pointing out the sights as methodically, efficiently, and indifferently as if she'd done it a thousand times. At one point they reached the top of a hill and Grete's mother abruptly braked beside what appeared to be a long-untended vacant lot. In the middle of it, surrounded by high weeds, was something that looked like a very large gravestone. "A memorial. For the Jews that were killed!" Grete's mother had said briskly, in her strongly accented English. Whereupon the car had jerked into action again and they had driven on to the next point of interest.

That small-town memorial had been relatively modest. Usually these things were huge. The logic seemed to be that the larger they were, the sorrier the Germans must be. The ultimate example of this phenomenon, Steve reflected, was probably that dismal sea of stones near the Brandenburg Gate in Berlin. "Look how sorry we are!" it proclaimed. But who was sorry? "Look, we remember!" it shouted. But who remembered? Could it be that the conception and construction, over the decades, of all these mammoth, gloomy reminders of the urgency of memory were actually part of a desperate effort to finally earn the right to forget? Were these monuments formed out of regret and remorse, or out of resentment?

The Hirtenflöte Sauna, according to the brochure, was part of a hotel that also boasted a ground-floor restaurant. Steve found it in the middle of a charming block of upscale shops. The restaurant overlooked the street; it was dimly lit and very cozy-looking, with closely set tables, white tablecloths and candles. At the moment it was crowded, mostly with affluent-looking young people who were drinking beer or wine and looked as if they were having the time of their lives. The word *Gemütlichkeit* crossed his mind.

He entered the brightly lit, gilt-heavy hotel lobby. To his left, along a far wall, two young male clerks were chatting energetically behind the reception counter; closer to Steve, several middle-aged men and women were sitting on couches and chairs, holding hushed conversations or reading text-dense, solemn-looking German newspapers; at the bar, towards which he was walking, a half-dozen businessmen huddled together, clutching beers and watching a soccer game on TV. Nearby, along the back wall, was an inconspicuous red door beside which a small black plaque read, quite simply, "HIRTENFLÖTE SAUNA." Below the plaque was a button. Steve walked up to the door and tried it; it was locked. He pressed the button.

Immediately there was a buzzing sound, and when he tried the door again he was able to push it open.

He walked into a small, very dimly lit room with a high counter on the right. Behind it stood a heavyset middle-aged guy in a violet polo shirt bearing the name of the sauna and a silhouette of a shepherd playing a flute. He didn't greet Steve with either a word or a glance, but was already plunking down a white towel on the counter, along with a key on a ragged-looking wristband.

"Hallo," Steve said.

"Hallo," the man replied, his voice tired, as he looked down at a piece of paper.

"Wie viel?" Steve asked.

The man mumbled a reply that Steve couldn't make sense out of.

"Bitte?"

"You pay when you leave," the man grunted, in English, almost too weary, it seemed, to get the words out.

Just past the counter there was a small doorway, and beyond it the foot of a stairway headed upwards, the steps covered with an ancient olive-green carpet. He walked past the stairs and into a room, even darker than the counter area, containing two rows of white lockers facing each other. They were old and beat-up, and looked as if they'd been salvaged from a dumpster. Steve walked through the doorway, but it was so dark that he had to go back to the counter, where it was a bit lighter, to be able to read the tiny number stamped on his key. Fourteen. *Vierzehn. Viertien.*

He found the locker, turned the key in the lock, and pulled. But the door wouldn't yield. He yanked hard, and it opened with a squealing, scraping sound. This sure was one old, banged-up, junky set of lockers. But at least his own looked reasonably clean inside. Looking around to make sure no one else was present, he pulled the pistol out of his pocket and set it down in the locker. He then quickly pulled off his pants and threw them on top of the gun. He finished undressing, piled his clothes item by item in the locker, and finally, with difficulty, shut the locker door. Turning the key, he pulled it out, put the band around his wrist, and wrapped the towel around his waist, then walked through yet another doorway at the back of the locker room. It led into a somewhat better-lit passage-way lined with elegantly framed drawings – artistic male nudes, all of them – at the end of which he pushed through a door into a barroom that was lit as brightly as a soundstage and in which absolutely everything – the walls, the U-shaped bar, the stools – was a startlingly bright cherry red. Instantly Steve felt he recognized it. But why? Of course: it looked just like a set for one of the Disney kid shows.

At the bar, a couple of middle-aged customers were sitting in their towels, gripping the handles on their beer glasses, and looking blankly at a TV that was tuned to a German sitcom. Next to the TV was a digital clock; at one end of the bar was a neat stack of newspapers. Behind the bar, in a violet polo shirt and black slacks – apparently the establishment's employee uniform – was a skinny, bouncy little guy in his twenties who, with his dark, wavy hair and large brown eyes, looked more Latin than Teutonic. As Steve sat on a stool near the stack of papers, the bartender noticed him and rushed over with the urgency of an unusually alert ER nurse.

"*Bon soir!*" the bartender said with a big, toothy smile.

Steve was thrown by the French. "*Bon soir,*" he said. "*Vin blanc, si vous plait.*"

"*Tout de suite!*" the bartender said. He zipped over to a waist-high fridge, bent over, opened it, pulled out a wine bottle, closed the fridge, stood up on his tiptoes – he was petite – and slid a glass off an overhead rack. Holding the bottle at arm's length, he poured the wine with a flamboyant flip of the wrist that was right out of the overactor's handbook. Setting the bottle down, he picked up the glass, came over, and placed it in front of Steve with an over-the-top flourish, beside (not on) a coas-ter bearing the logo of Erdringer beer.

If there was one thing you could always count on in the Netherlands, it was bartenders putting glasses *on* coasters – never, ever next to them. But Steve wasn't in the Netherlands anymore.

"*Merci beaucoup,*" Steve said.

"*De rien!*" the bartender replied with another big smile. Steve showed him the number on his wristband. "*Quarante!*" the bartender said, his brown eyes twinkling, and zipped over to a keyboard where he quickly tapped in the number. He was a bundle of energy; watching him,

Steve feel old, lethargic, and scarcely up to the task he'd set himself.

He took a sip of the wine. It was sickeningly sweet. Riesling.

He looked around. There was a doorway and, beyond it, a set of corrugated metal stairs leading up to the next floor. Putting the Erdringer coaster on top of his beer, Steve got up, walked over to the stairs, and started climbing them. The heads of nails or screws poked out of the stairs and into the soles of his bare feet. It hurt. What idiot had designed this? Or was it some German S&M thing?

At the first landing – the stairs continued on for at least another flight – Steve pushed open a heavy metal door and was hit by a body slam of warm, steamy air. He walked into a room in which two guys were showering, one of them sixtyish, very tall, and exceedingly corpulent – a giant mass of salmon-pink flesh – the other a tanned, fit, well-proportioned guy of about thirty. Steve walked past them, up a couple of steps, and down a corridor lined with cheap white plastic lawn chairs, all unoccupied. Then, on the left, there was a jacuzzi in which three old guys, obviously regulars who'd been coming here since the world was young, were leaning back and having a leisurely chat; on the right was the wooden door of what appeared to be a steam room.

At the end of the corridor was a stairwell, with steps going up and down, that he recognized as the same olive-green carpeted stairs he'd passed in the locker room.

He climbed them up to the next floor, where, pushing through a door, he found himself in a very dimly lit, high-ceilinged space consisting of a maze of tiny cubicles. He walked up one narrow corridor and down another, inspecting them. Each cubicle contained a thin, ruby-red plastic mattress – a gym mat, really – on a knee-high wooden platform that was painted black. The mattresses looked as old and beat-up as the lockers downstairs. The walls on the cubicles were about six and a half feet high, with no ceilings on them: they were just like office cubicles, only with cheap mattresses in them instead of desks and chairs.

Steve checked the door on one of the cubicles. Yes, it locked from the inside. Good. Perhaps it would be best for him to spend the night here.

He walked down the metal stairs back to the bar, where he reclaimed his stool and his wine. The bartender gave him another of his big smiles. Steve smiled back and drank some of his Riesling. Yech.

The bartender, who apparently had a few free seconds, came over. "*Anglais?*"

"*Américain.*"

This seemed to thrill the bartender. *"De quelle ville?"*

"New York." This wasn't the right time to tell the truth.

"*Ooohh, tellement génial!*" The bartender was obviously flirtatious by nature, but now his flirtatiousness bumped up to a new level. Their eyes met and the bartender gave him a classic come-hither look. And then another customer called him over.

Steve got up, walked over to the pile of newspapers, and picked one of them up. It was today's *Süddeutsche Zeitung.*

He took it back to his stool and paged through it looking for any mention of what he'd already started thinking of, himself, as the "Bellamyplein killings." But there was nothing. Toward the back of the newspaper, however, an item in the list of forthcoming cultural events caught his eye. Tomorrow, Saturday, a celebrated "moderate Muslim" cleric, Usama Firat, was giving a lecture at Ludwig Maximilian University, right here in Munich. Educated at Al-Azhar University in Cairo, the flagship institution of Islamic theology, he was, according to the notice, a proponent of what he called "Western Islam." The lecture would be held in English.

Interesting.

And the most interesting part was that somebody had circled the announcement.

On the TV set, the sitcom ended. It was followed by several minutes of commercials. Then a news report came on. Steve steeled himself for a segment on the "Bellamyplein killings." But the program, which lasted a half hour, ended without any reference to them. As another sitcom began – this one an American relic from the 1980s with bad dubbing – he breathed a sigh of relief. Either the story hadn't gone international, or there were simply no new developments.

The evening wore on; the place filled up. Every couple of minutes, a new customer walked into the bar. Eventually it was packed, with all the stools taken and the walls lined with guys in towels holding beers or cocktails or glasses of wine. A couple of the men sitting at the bar ordered food, and soon the bartender, his energy not visibly diminished in the slightest, was spending much of his time dashing back and forth between the bar and kitchen, which the sauna apparently shared with the restaurant.

Steve finished his wine and ordered a white beer. He also asked to see a menu. After looking through it, he ordered the wiener schnitzel. A guy of fifty or so, who'd sat down beside him a few minutes earlier, said in British-accented English, "I can hear you're not German."

"No, I'm not."

The man was drinking what appeared to be a glass of whiskey. Looking into his eyes, Steve could see that it was far from his first drink of the day.

"American?" the man said.

"Yes."

"Where in America?" This wasn't exactly the direction Steve wanted this conversation to take.

"New York. And you?"

"Manchester. Here on business, are you?"

"Sort of. You?"

"Yes. I come here every month or so."

"Really? What do you do?"

The best way to avoid being asked unwelcome

questions, Steve had long since discovered, was to keep firing off questions yourself. Most people preferred to talk about themselves, anyway.

"I'm in sales."

"So you've spent a lot of time in Munich?"

"Yes."

"Do you like it?"

"Oh, it's a fine city."

"What, especially, do you like about it?"

"I take it you haven't been here before?"

"No."

The man took a sip of his drink. "Well, not to bring the mood down, but if you're here for any length of time you should of course go to Dachau."

Steve nodded. "Yes. Of course."

The man took a sip of his beer. The bartender served beers to a couple of other customers, then rushed into the kitchen.

"Not exactly a party," the man said.

"Excuse me?"

"Dachau. It's not exactly a party."

"No, I imagine not."

They sat there in silence for a couple of minutes. "So what's it like in Manchester?" Steve finally asked him.

"You ever read one of those Angry Young Man novels? Or kitchen-sink plays?"

"Yeah. Kingsley Amis, John Osborne."

"And all those grim old black-and-white movies starring Laurence Harvey and Dirk Bogarde?"

"Yeah. *Room at the Top*."

"Exactly. It's like that. Factories, council flats. Not a lot of sun. Plenty of rain. But not bad at all, really. In fact there's something lovely about it. Changing now, though."

"How so?"

The man looked torn – as if part of him wanted to speak and part of him thought it unwise.

"Well," he finally said, "there's been an awful lot of new people moving in during the last few years."

"And is that good or bad?"

"Oh, you know how it is. Everything under the sun is a mixed blessing, isn't it? The good with the bad?" He was silent for a moment as Steve stared at him, wanting more. Then the man looked quickly around at the faces within earshot. "One thing I ought to say is that it's nothing about race. In Manchester we've had people from the subcontinent among us for a long time, Hindus mostly, you know, and they've always been just splendid. Law-abiding, perfectly decent, upstanding citizens, many of them respected businessmen and professionals – doctors, solicitors. Never the slightest sense that they don't fit in or don't want to. But then there are the others." He didn't want to say the word.

"Muslims?"

A hesitation.

"Yes."

"And that's a problem."

"Well, let's say it's not always easy. Clash of

civilizations and all that. Very different values. An awful lot of violent crime."

"Does it make it tougher to be gay?"

An odd look came over his face. "You could say so. There's a good deal of – well, as I say, very different values. But it's not for us to judge, is it? After all, they're our natural allies, aren't they?"

"What do you mean?"

"What I mean is the obvious: we're an oppressed minority, and so are they."

"But do they see it that way?"

"Maybe not yet. But they will."

"How can you be sure of that?"

He gave Steve a *tut-tut* sound. "Because it's the truth. How can they not see the truth? They'll come around. They'll get it."

"I hope so."

They sat there drinking for a couple of minutes.

"In the long run," said the Englishman, "we'll be glad. We'll recognize it as a matter of cultural enrichment."

"Do you really believe that?"

"Look, I'm a good Labour voter. Labour stands for diversity. Do you know how that bloody Thatcher woman treated us inverts? Labour has turned that around so fast that it must make her head spin. So how can a member of the – " He chuckled. "A friend of mine used to call us the 'lavender fraternity.' How can one of us protest when Labour welcomes other groups in from the cold the way it's welcomed us? It's all about recognizing diversity as a strength, not a weakness."

Steve nodded.

They sat there and drank quietly for another minute or two. Then Steve said, "Kind of offbeat question."

The man's lips curled into a smile. He shook his drink. The ice clattered. "Yes?"

"I'm actually here checking things out for my boss," said Steve. "He's got weird tastes."

"Oh?"

"He likes water."

"Water?"

"Yes. Water. I know. Sounds funny, right?"

"Not necessarily."

"I thought he might like this place, but – well – his tastes are rather expensive."

"Well, then I don't think this is the place for him," said the man with a hoarse laugh. He sounded relieved by the change of topic. "I don't know what's more broken down, the place itself or the regulars. Myself included."

"Have you been coming here long? I mean to this sauna?"

"Twenty years or so, I suppose. And I always see the same faces. We hardly know each other – at least not from the waist up, and certainly not from the neck up – but in a sense we've grown old together." He took a big sip of his Scotch.

"But you still come here. Broken down though it is."

"Oh, it's partly habit. At this point, I think I actually enjoy the familiarity, the sameness. Even the grottiness. It's been many years since I came here for a wild time. I used to be something of a randy adventurer, I suppose, but it feels like centuries ago. These days, I just want to relax and enjoy a couple of drinks. And look at the pretty boys." He nodded toward the bartender. "And the food, believe it or not, is actually top-notch."

"Really? Here?"

"Yes. You'd never guess it, would you?" He laughed again and sipped some Scotch.

"No."

"But in answer to your question, I'm afraid I'm not the best person to ask." He was about to take another sip of his drink when he said, "No, wait a minute, I tell a lie. There *is* a place I've heard about. It opened just a few months ago. It's – what do they call it? – a thermal bath complex. It's supposed to be the largest place of its kind in the world."

"Thermal bath complex? What's that?"

"Excellent question. Now that you ask, I can't say I'm entirely sure. But somehow those words have stuck in my head. 'Thermal bath complex.' Perhaps I've remembered them precisely because they sound so odd. 'Thermal bath complex.' Anyway, you might want to look into that. It's supposed to be somewhere out of town." He waved his hand vaguely. His fingers, Steve noticed, were thick and gnarled, his nails yellow. "I'm sure you can easily find out where it is."

"Thank you."

"You're very welcome."

At that moment the bartender emerged from the kitchen with a plate and set it in front of Steve with one of his patented flourishes. *"Voilà,"* he said. On the plate, in addition to the wiener schnitzel, were three small boiled potatoes garnished with chives and small white ceramic cups of horseradish and cranberry sauce. It certainly *looked* good.

"Merci," Steve said.

"De rien," the bartender smiled, crinkling his nose. *"Bon appétit!"*

Steve cut into the veal and tasted it. *"Delicieux,"* he said. The bartender clapped with delight at his verdict. Steve turned to the man beside him. "You're right," Steve said to him. "The food here *is* great."

The man nodded and gestured to the bartender with his now-empty glass. The bartender nodded, took down a bottle of Scotch, poured him another drink, and brought it over.

"Merci, merci," the Englishman said. *"Encore une chose, mon cher,"* he added, his voice thicker than it had been just a couple of minutes earlier, his French accent as deliberately bad as that of every other Englishman Steve had ever heard speaking the language. *"Mon ami ici est curieux sur...sur? Au? De?"*

"Curieux about what?" the bartender asked.

"About that new thermal complex outside of town. Do you have any idea what I'm talking about?"

"*Mais oui,*" the bartender said. He turned to look at Steve. "You can get there on the S2. Very easy!"

"Have you been there?" the Englishman asked him.

The young man's face lit up. "*Oui, c'est très géniale!*"

"Oh!" said Steve. "Well, that sounds promising. Thank you!"

"Yes," said the Englishman. "*Merci,* Fabien."

Fabien!

Steve looked at the bartender with new eyes. What did this bouncy little French guy have to do with those monsters on Bellamyplein?

Fabien turned away, and a fat man at the other end of the bar waved him over.

So this was Fabien. What was going on here?

Steve started to pick at his wiener schnitzel, but didn't take his eyes off Fabien. For a while Steve just sat there eating and studying Fabien at the same time. At nine o'clock, the lights went down a bit, the TV was turned off, and dance music began playing. The music was too loud to allow for easy conversation – which wasn't an issue at this point, since Steve's English chum was now three sheets to the wind and thoroughly preoccupied with his drink. At one point Fabien came over, shot a sidelong look at the Brit, and leaned in close to Steve. "*C'est ivre,*" he said in a loud whisper, right into Steve's ear. Steve could feel his breath. And he could smell it, too – it was minty fresh. The boy pulled his head slightly back, and his dark eyes, which stared straight into Steve's from mere inches away, exuded sensuality. The moment could hardly have been more intimate.

"*Bien sûr,*" Steve whispered back.

Fabien turned to look up at the clock. It was 9:17. "My shift ends at ten," he said, not taking his eyes off Steve's. "Do you want to meet upstairs? In one of the *cabines?*"

Steve responded with the tiniest of nods.

"Ten after ten. *D'accord?*"

"*D'accord.*"

In the minutes that followed, Steve finished his meal and ordered another glass of wine, this time specifying a pinot noir. When he started to show Fabien his wristband to pay for the wine, Fabien shook his head and said something Steve couldn't hear over the music. Steve cupped his hand to his ear. "On the house," Fabien shouted.

While Steve sipped his wine, his English seatmate seemed almost to be falling asleep. Finally the man yawned, stood up unsteadily, and slapped Steve on the back. "Well, mate," he said, speaking loudly to be heard over the music, "it's time for me to turn in. Have a good time in Munich."

"Thanks," Steve said. "Good talking to you."

The man headed for the locker room. Steve finished his wine. The bar was now packed with patrons, virtually all of them in their twenties and thirties, and Fabien was extremely busy; but every so often, in the middle of making somebody a drink, he looked up and glanced over at Steve coquettishly. At a few minutes to ten, another bartender came out of the kitchen – a musclebound blond, a German from Central Casting. He greeted Fabien with a macho nod, pulled out his phone, and made a call while leaning against the bar. Apparently he was taking the next shift.

At ten, Steve got up and headed for the corrugated metal stairway, catching Fabien's eye just as he started climbing the steps. He went up to the next floor, walked past the showers, which were crowded now, and along the corridor. Up here the music was deafening, even louder than in the bar. Three or four dozen towels, some apparently dry and some dripping wet, were now drooping from hangers outside the door to the steam room. Steve took one of the dry ones and continued quickly to the end of the corridor, then hurried down the carpeted stairs to the locker room. It was empty.

He pulled off his wristband, unlocked his locker, took a quick look around to make sure he was alone, then reached in, pulling the gun out from under his clothing and wrapping it in the towel. He closed and locked the locker, then walked back up the carpeted stairs, the towel under his arm. On the stairs he passed a couple of young guys, and on the third floor he passed a few more. They were all cruising around, on the prowl for a few moments of physical contact with a stranger. Steve noticed that the doors of several of the third-floor cubicles were shut.

Inside, he knew, bodies were heaving, voices almost certainly groaning; but the music was so loud that none of it was audible. After a brief search he found an empty cubicle – or *cabine,* as Fabien had put it – with an open door. He stepped inside, put the gun on the floor in the corner of the *cabine* and the towel on top of it, then sat down on the thin ruby-red plastic mattress, facing the door.

The minutes went by. Guys walked past, almost in a steady stream. He didn't have a watch, but after a while he figured that it must be at least 10:10. Could it be that Fabien had changed his mind?

But no, suddenly there he was, not in uniform but, like Steve, naked except for a peach-colored towel wrapped around his waist. He looked even tinier now than he had in his uniform – hairless and rail-thin, his calves no thicker than Steve's upper arms.

Steve stood up and took a step outside the door of the *cabine.*

"Oh, there you are!" shouted Fabien. "I've looked for you all over! It's so busy tonight."

Fabien walked up to him, put his hands on Steve's shoulders, stood on tiptoe, and kissed him on the lips. The kiss was immensely sensuous. Steve put his hands on Fabien's bony little waist.

"You're so tall," Fabien shouted over the music. In fact Steve wasn't particularly tall; Fabien was tiny. But clearly he was practiced at such blandishments.

Steve smiled and stepped back into the little

room, pulling Fabien with him. Fabien removed his hands from Steve's shoulders and ran them down his chest, then put his mouth to Steve's ear. "Your chest is so muscular," he shouted.

Taking his hands off of Fabien's waist, Steve pulled the door of the *cabine* shut and locked it. They kissed again. Fabien put his arms around Steve's waist; Steve held Fabien's head in his left hand and put his right hand on Fabien's upper back. He began to move that hand down Fabien's spine, but Fabien removed his own left hand from Steve's waist and moved his arm back to block Steve's right hand from going any lower. Fabien pulled his head a couple of inches back and fixed his eyes on Steve's.

"Not yet," Fabien said. "*Doucement.* Slowly." Fabien kissed him again.

Now it was Steve who pulled back from the kiss. He put his lips to Fabien's ear.

"I have a question."

"*Oui?*"

"Why was your name on a piece of paper found on one of the Bellamyplein corpses in Amsterdam?"

Fabien jerked away from Steve, his dancing eyes suddenly abaze with rage, and in the same motion flicked off his towel to reveal and click loose a black leather belt, yanking off the buckle, which wasn't just a buckle but a handle to a four-inch knife. Fabien thrust the blade toward Steve, who stepped back, kicked Fabien so that he slammed against the wall of the *cabine,* and reached under the towel for the gun, with which he shot Fabien in the thigh just as the little bartender was coming at him again with the knife.

The sound of the gunshot was explosive. But the thumping bass of the dance music was so loud that the gunshot sounded like part of the song. Fabien crumbled to the floor, his face writhing in pain, his leg bleeding. Steve wrenched the knife away from him with his free hand and tossed it to the far end of the mattress. Then he picked up Fabien's towel with the same free hand and clumsily tried to wrap the towel around the boy's leg, in hopes of stanching the flow of blood. As he did so, Fabien clawed at Steve's face.

Finished with the leg, Steve used both his free and and the hand clutching the gun to hold Fabien down by the shoulders. "Why?" Steve shouted, leaning in close toward Fabien's face. "How could a gay French guy like you – "

"*Je ne suis pas français! Je suis algerien!*"

"Algerian? You're Algerian?"

"*Oui!*"

"From where? Which city?"

"What?"

"Where are you from in Algeria? Algiers?"

"I've never been to Algeria."

"What are you talking about?"

"I grew up in Paris."

"Then you're French."

"I spit on the French!"

"Do you even speak Arabic?"

"No."

"Then you're French! How can you call yourself anything else?"

"You don't get it! You could never get it! Don't you understand what the French did to Algeria?"

"Yes, I do. But I also know what these people you're working with think of gays! Don't *you* know?"

"Of course I do! It's because I'm gay that I have to do this! Allah would send me to hell for what I've done in these *cabines,* but he'll send me to heaven for what I'm doing for him now!"

"What *are* you doing for him? Tell me!"

"No!" With sudden, surprising strength, Fabien broke free of Steve's hands and tried with both of his own hands to grab the gun.

"Please, Fabien!" Steve said. "Don't!" A second later the gun went off, the bullet piercing Fabien's neck.

The blood gushed. Fabien fell back, his head hitting the floor hard. Steve dropped the gun, pulled off his own towel, and tried to use it to stop the bleeding. Fabien's eyes were open, and full of terror. His lips moved. Steve leaned in, putting his ear right up against the boy's mouth.

"*Allahu akbar,*" Fabien said, and died.

VII

THE MAIN BUILDING OF LUDWIG MAXIMILIANS University is a handsome, imposing nineteenth-century structure, three stories high, that fills a very large block of central Munich.

It was late morning, and even though it was a Saturday, there were plenty of people, mostly young, streaming in and out of the doors that opened out onto Amelienstraße. Among those entering the building with Steve were several hijab-clad women and robed, long-bearded, Mediterranean-looking men. Steve assumed they were here for the same reason he was.

Together, they all made their way upstairs to the university's Grosse Aula, or Great Hall. It was an impressive space – a distinctively European, distinctively German space – that combined grandeur with simplicity. Twenty or so rows of ordinary wooden chairs, divided by a central aisle, faced a stage on which there stood a single plain lectern. Above was a wraparound balcony featuring high arches and high windows that let in the bright midday sunshine.

Filling the wall behind the stage was a gilt-edged mural that drew on imagery from the ancient European world. At its center stood a man in a chariot that was being drawn by four horses, two of which seeming to be pulling him in one direction, two in the other. Flanking the charioteer and his horses were images of four robed classical figures.

Steve tried to figure out what he was looking at. Was it an illustration of Apollo and some of his fellow deities? Or was it, perhaps, a reference to the chariot allegory from the *Phaedrus?* He quashed the second thought almost instantly: in Plato, of course, there were only two horses, and they had wings; these horses were of the earthly, non-winged variety.

Both levels of the auditorium were crowded with people. Some were almost unmistakably students or professors; others, the long-bearded men and the woman in hijab, were plainly believers who might or might not have some connection to the university. Some were seated, some looking for seats or seeking out friends, others standing and talking in groups along the walls. The noise level seemed unusually high.

Since it appeared as if most of the seats were already taken, Steve grabbed one quickly, near the back and a couple of seats in from the center aisle, next to a couple of middle-aged women, presumably Germans, who weren't wearing hijab. Almost at once, a bearded young man appeared in the center aisle from out of nowhere and beckoned Steve with his index finger.

Steve looked at him quizzically and pointed to himself: *Me?* The bearded young man nodded. Steve stood up and walked over to him. The young man said something to Steve in strongly accented German. Steve made out the word *Frauensitzplätzen.* That was enough for him to get the idea: he had taken a seat in the women's section. The young man led him to a seat on the other side of the aisle. Steve hadn't even noticed that the auditorium was divided by sex. Now that he took another look, he couldn't believe that he hadn't realized it immediately.

Then again, who would expect that a German university in the year 2001 would allow an audience to be segregated by sex?

His new seat placed him next to a group of young men, apparently Muslims, some with beards, some without. They were talking eagerly among themselves in a language he didn't know. He strained to listen. After a moment he had the strong feeling that it was the same language he and Joop had heard through Niek's floor.

Plopping his shoulder bag on his lap, he thought about the copy of Schama's book that was inside, but he knew better than to take it out and read it while waiting for the program to begin. Instead he studied the faces around him. Most of them were young and eager.

Who had circled this event in the newspaper? It *had* to have been Fabien, right? Had he planned to meet someone here? Or had he just wanted to hear the lecture?

Fabien. Steve thought about him. After killing him, Steve had climbed over the *cabine* wall, leaving the body inside the locked compartment. He'd then made his way to the Englischer Garten and found a place to sleep on the grass amid a cluster of trees. He hadn't seen the TV news this morning, so he didn't know whether the body had been found. The sauna was supposed to be open all night and into the morning, so it was conceivable that Fabien's body was still lying there undiscovered.

Steve looked up at the stage again, and perused the mural more closely. He thought about the two winged horses in Plato's allegory. One of them, which seeks to draw the chariot upward, symbolizes man's immortal soul, his yearning toward truth, beauty, reason, wisdom, goodness; the other, which seeks to pull the chariot downward, represents man's mortal part – his baser, more irrational, and merely physical attractions and appetites. The task facing man, according to Plato, is to try to attain as long and steady as possible a contact with the Higher Things while at the same time keeping the horses in balance. Those who tackle this difficult challenge most successfully, said Plato, will become "philosophers and lovers"; at the lowest end of the spectrum, beneath the politicians and landowners, the businessmen and physicians, the artists and farmers, were Plato's two most despised groups: the demagogues and tyrants.

After another ten minutes or so, a heavyset young woman in a dark brown hijab walked up to the lectern. In German, she asked everyone to please have a seat and quiet down. When the audience had done so, she switched into English. "I am deeply honored to welcome our distinguished guest. He is the head imam of the al-Qasim mosque in London, and he will be speaking to us today in English. Brothers and sisters, Usama Firat."

To thunderous applause, a trim, smallish man in a nicely cut pinstriped suit briskly mounted the steps to the stage and walked over to the lectern. He nodded at the young woman, but didn't shake her hand. She gave him a small bow and walked offstage. He grasped the sides of the lectern. At least from where Steve was sitting, he looked surprisingly young – not yet forty. He had a small, scraggly beard and mustache and wore wire-rimmed glasses and a cylindrical white hat. He exuded self-confidence; clearly, he was used to this kind of reception.

It took a full minute for the applause to die down. "Thank you, my brothers and sisters," Firat said. "Thank you to the Muslim students of this university for inviting me here. And thanks to all of you for coming. There is nothing that makes me more hopeful for the future of Islam on this continent than the spectacle of auditoriums like this filled with devout and engaged young believers such as yourselves." He spoke impeccable Oxbridge English.

"Let me begin by saying that it has never been a more exciting time to be a Muslim, and especially to be a Muslim in Europe. Our prophet, peace be upon him, told us himself that Islam would ultimately conquer Rome. What he was saying was that Europe will ultimately become a part of the *ummah*, the House of Islam. Indeed, if you look around this city, or for that matter this very room, you will see that we are already well along on the path to that magnificent consummation."

Hearty applause. Steve glanced over at the guys sitting next to him. They were clapping eagerly, plainly mesmerized.

"Now," Firat continued, "let me underscore that this conquest will not necessarily take place through war.

In fact, as the history of this world unfolds before my eyes day by day, it seems increasingly probable to me that the annexation will be a peaceful one. We are, after all, a peaceful people with a peaceful faith. We say to the unbeliever: fear not, for as long as you do not resist the truth that we possess, the truth vouchsafed to us by the prophet, peace be upon him, we will remain people of peace. We do not even compel the unbelievers to join the faith. We ask only that those who do not revert to Islam accept its authority and its ascendancy. But at the same time we do trust in the inevitability of the ultimate conquest of these infidel lands, most likely, as I say, not with swords or bullets, but rather with the truth and beauty of our faith, which, as we know, are powerful enough weapons to win the submission of even the most recalcitrant hearts and minds."

More applause.

"We are, then, all of us – every Muslim in this room – part of a great historical movement. And a great historical moment. We are, quite simply, the people who will Islamize Europe. And in doing so, we will be doing a service not only to Allah but to Europe itself. For this continent is in profound need of what Islam has to offer. This continent is infected, polluted, poisoned by sin. The word *islam* is the most beautiful word in any language because it denotes submission: the surrender of one's self-seeking, of one's selfish dreams, of one's foolish illusion of self-determination, and the subordination of oneself to the only God, the only truth, the only path. There is no salvation but through Islam, and Europe desperately needs to be saved – saved from materialism, saved from selfishness, saved from individuality. And saved from all of the other evils that beset this godless continent!"

Applause.

"And we all know what those evils are. I have been criticized for giving them their proper name. But when I speak of them, I am only quoting the Holy Quran itself. It is the Holy Quran, after all, that tells us that the sons of Zion are the most dastardly of creatures, filthy and impure – "

At this, the crowd broke not just into applause but into cheers. The guys next to Steve started whooping.

" – the brothers of apes and pigs – "

More cheering.

" – the spreaders of corruption, the slayers of prophets, the wellspring of all killing and destruction, all adultery and prostitution." The cheering was so loud that Firat stretched out both hands and gestured for the audience to quiet down. "The Jews," he went on, "have been the cause of all anarchy, all wars. They control the world, and they exercise their control by reducing the rest of humanity to depravity with greed and sex, alcohol and drugs. As we advance toward the creation of an Islamic Europe, let us remember the words of Adolf Hitler, who wrote of the Jews in *Mein Kampf,* 'they corrupt the German youth, and I need the German youth to turn into real men so I can take over the world.' As Allah has said to us about these subhuman creatures: separate their heads from their bodies, and the blood will pour out."

At this point, scattered members of the audience leapt to their feet cheering. Again, Firat gestured for silence. Obediently, they sat.

"And then there are the others who corrupt our youth. Remember how Allah punished the people of Sodom. Remember how Lut's people were addicted to this foul and unnatural depravity. And remember what Lut said to them: 'What! Of all creatures, do you approach males and leave the spouses whom your Lord has created for you? Indeed, you are people transgressing all limits!'"

More cheers.

"Now, the scholars of Islam do not all concur on the proper punishment for the sodomite. This disagreement, far from being some kind of weakness, only underscores the important fact that Islam, contrary to what our ignorant enemies routinely claim, is not mindlessly monolithic. We do have different schools of thought, and we welcome intelligent and informed scholarly debate about this and other theological questions. What all of us do agree upon, however, is that sodomy is not a mild offense and that the punishment for it should therefore not be gentle. After all, Allah did not just discipline the tribe of Lut with mere burning. No, brothers and sisters, what did he do? He turned the city upside down and rained upon it brimstones as hard as clay!"

Again, people rose to their feet – this time fully

half of the audience. Firat let them cheer for thirty seconds or so, then gestured again. They resumed their seats.

"Allah, peace be upon him, knows no yesterday, today, or tomorrow," Firat said. "The words of the Holy Quran are as true now as on the day they were dictated to the Prophet, peace be upon him, and they always will be. Therefore, for all those who commit sodomy, the penalty should be as severe in our time as it was in the time of Lut. Some say that the sodomites should be beheaded with a sword, then placed in a coffin and set afire. Others say that they should be taken to the summit of the highest available mountain and rolled down the slope until they are dead. Still others say that they should be burned to a crisp. For my part, I adhere to the teaching that prescribes stoning unto death. And when it comes to this offense, there is one point that is too infrequently emphasized by some of my fellow scholars – namely, that even those who have not committed sodomy, but who exhibit attributes of homosexuality, and who plainly have homosexuality in their minds and hearts, should be scourged. Because the very thought of engaging in such vile acts is itself a threat to the purity of the *ummah*. Some would argue, of course, that these tendencies are innate, and that persons who manage to keep these tendencies under control should not be punished. But Allah has taught us that a perversion cannot be innate, and that the mere sight, the mere sign, of homosexual tendencies, whether or not acted upon, is a poison to society and must be eradicated. Again, yes, once again, as the one and only god, Allah, has said, *separate their heads from their bodies and the blood will pour out!*"

By this point, Firat's voice had reached a crescendo. And when he finished this last sentence, almost everyone in the audience stood up. The crowd was at a fever pitch. Steve was stunned, and shaken, by the artistry with which Firat had transformed them from a couple of hundred quiet individuals who had walked into a university auditorium on a Saturday afternoon into a single passionate organism with murder in its heart.

Steve looked up at the guy next to him, who was almost jumping up and down with excitement. At the same moment, the guy glanced down at Steve and registered the fact that he was still sitting. The guy elbowed his friend on his other side, and the two of them looked down at Steve, their eyes blazing and lips curled into twin snarls. Steve suddenly felt distinctly unsafe. Then Firat gestured once more, and within seconds everyone was again silent and seated.

Now, Firat spoke so softly – nearly in a whisper – that Steve almost had to strain to hear him.

"We, the Muslims of Europe, have a sacred obligation," Firat said. "We are under great pressure to adapt, to accommodate, to assimilate. But to do this, my brothers and sisters, would be to abandon our faith, to forsake our Holy Quran, to betray our beloved prophet, peace be upon him. It would be to turn our backs on the things of God and to embrace corruption and sin. Never forget: in the face of this relentless pressure, we must all

245

stand firm for the enduring and immutable truth of Islam. Always remember: we are not German or English, we are not Austrian or Swiss, we are not French or Dutch. We are Muslims, Muslims, *Muslims* – "

With each word, his voice seemed to grow louder and more urgent – and the crowd increasingly agitated. As he spoke, more and more members of the audience rose to their feet and made noises. Not just cheers, but...*noises.*

Savage ones.

"Muslims!" Firat proclaimed. "Muslims – who are destined for eternal life in Paradise, while *they* are destined for an eternity of torture in a fiery Hell. It is not for us to adapt to them, but for them to adapt to us. We are here not to change ourselves in order to gain acceptance, but to change the society around us so that it accepts, bows down, submits itself to the true faith. So do not be tempted by the things of this world! To the sisters in this audience, I say: Do not be tempted by the lies of the infidel to stray from the modesty that Allah has decreed as your lot in life. Be the servants of your fathers and uncles, brothers and male cousins, husbands and sons, as you were created to be, and you will be lifted up in the hereafter! And to the brothers who are here today, I say this: The infidel women who are willing to give themselves to you are harlots! If you want the company of a beautiful woman, dedicate yourself to Holy Jihad and win a place in heaven, where you will spend eternity with seventy-two black-eyed virgins!"

By now the decibel level exceeded anything Steve had ever experienced at a rock concert. He couldn't see anybody who was still sitting, except for himself. The guys next to him were hysterical, but their adoration of the imam didn't keep them from also looking over at Steve. They were staring straight into his eyes now, and shooting him daggers. As Steve glanced around, he saw that others nearby, on both sides of the aisle, had also noticed that he was still sitting – and were also visibly disgruntled about it. Steve shuddered to think what they'd do if they knew what he'd been up to during the last four days.

Maybe it wasn't the best idea, he thought, to have come here this morning. The last thing he needed right now was to draw this kind of attention to himself. So he stood up, turned, headed up the aisle as fast as he could without running, and pushed through the door at the back of the auditorium.

He was already hurrying down the stairs when a male voice behind him shouted: "Hey!" Reaching the landing halfway down to the ground floor, he looked up to see two young Muslim guys in jeans and polo shirts – not the ones who'd been sitting next to him – at the top of the stairs. "You! Stop!" one of them shouted. He pointed at Steve. Steve started rushing down the stairs at top speed. They came charging after him. "We saw you!" the guy yelled. "On Al-Jazeera. Murderer!"

Leaping to the foot of the stairs from almost halfway up to the landing, Steve turned right onto a corridor, racing as fast as he could. He pushed through the first door on his right into an empty, half-darkened lecture hall and threw himself into the space between two rows of seats, where he stretched out flat. Lying there, he heard the guys thunder down the corridor past the lecture-hall door. He waited a few seconds, then got back up, went to the door, and looked out the little window at face level.

The coast looked clear. He was about to open the door when somebody pushed it open from the other side. His two pursuers piled into the room, their bodies smacking up against his. Instantly they began throwing fists at his head. He reached into his pocket, pulled out the gun, shoved the barrel into the belly of one of them, and pulled the trigger.

The explosion sounded even louder than it had on Bellamyplein. The guy he'd shot jolted backward and doubled over, clutching his stomach, while his friend, the rage on his face replaced by a look of panic, fled out the doorway and down the corridor. Without pausing for a second, Steve pocketed his gun and rushed down the corridor in the other direction. He passed a few students, all of whom were standing stock still, holding their books and papers, looking terrified; they'd all obviously heard the gunshot, but they were also plainly paralyzed with fear and confusion.

Steve reached the main entrance, pushed through the doors, ran past a fountain, hooked a right, sprinted to the university U-Bahn station a few yards away, and raced down the stairs. At the platform, a few people were boarding a train; he scampered into the first open door and then kept moving, making his way quickly toward the front of the train. Not until the doors closed did he turn around to see if anybody was behind him.

Nope.

The train pulled out of the station; he got off at the first stop, Marienplatz. Walking along the platform, he phoned Joop, who answered after one ring.

"Visser," Joop said. His last name. He sounded tired.

"Did I wake you?" Steve asked.

"No, no. I'm having trouble sleeping. You sound out of breath."

"I just had a close call." Steve, who'd already told him last night about Fabien, brought him up to date as he followed the signs to the S-Bahn.

"Al-Jazeera," Joop said. "I didn't think about that."

"Me neither."

"Of course your face must've been all over Al-Jazeera."

"Yep."

"Are you okay?"

"I'm fine."

"Do you think you killed him?"

"It's a stomach wound. He'll probably survive if they get him to a doctor in time."

"Either way, between this and Fabien, the Munich police will definitely know you're in town now."

"Well, I don't know if they'll connect Fabien to me – "

"They will if they can find some customer of that dump who can identify you."

"Yeah, and who's willing to admit publicly that he was there. A lot of those guys look like husbands on the down low."

"Did you get any sleep last night?"

"I went to the Englischer Garten and found a little clearing. I slept on the grass for three or four hours."

"Just like a real *Hirt*. It wasn't too cold?"

"No, it was fine."

"Good."

"So how are things going there?"

"Nothing new," Joop said. "We didn't even make the TV news last evening or this morning."

"Nothing about Fabien?"

"No."

"Good."

"Have you done any more thinking about Fabien?"

"Yes. But I can't come up with anything. Who knows what role he was playing in all this?"

"Well, you said he was very cute and an expert coquette and an obvious bottom. I should think somebody like him would come in pretty handy to a bunch of murderers whose target is a middle-aged gay man who's obviously a top. With, I might add, a taste for younger Muslim guys."

"You're right. That makes perfect sense. It's obvious, in fact. How come I couldn't figure that out?"

"Maybe because you've been through sheer craziness for the last couple of days? And slept last night on damp grass in a park?"

"No, let's face it, I have no business being here. I have no idea what I'm doing. I've seen too many fucking action movies. I should've stayed put in Amsterdam. Or maybe gone to Granada. My Spanish is better than my German." Steve stepped onto an escalator heading up to the S-Bahn.

"Don't second-guess yourself," Joop said. "And don't feel bad about having done what you needed to do to protect yourself. Just do what you can."

"Okay. Thanks."

"Call."

"I will."

"Conserve the phone battery."

"Right."

They hung up. Reaching the S-Bahn platform, which was almost empty, Steve looked at the departure boards. Apparently six S lines, including the S2, stopped here. In one direction, the S2 terminus was Erding. In the other, it was Dachau.

Yes, Dachau.

The Erling-bound S2 pulled in almost at once, and Steve stepped aboard. Like the platform, it was nearly empty. He took a seat near the door.

A couple of minutes later the train slowed and

came to a stop at a place called Riem. An attractive blonde woman stepped aboard with a little blond boy who was about six or seven years old. They sat on the other side of the door, and on the opposite side of the aisle from Steve, facing him. The doors closed and the train started to move again.

The little boy was lively, jabbering gaily at his mother. She was wearing a pastel-patterned housedress and a white button-up sweater, which she'd left unbuttoned. Her hair was in a pony tail. Steve studied her face as her son yammered on. She looked exhausted, as if she hadn't gotten any sleep. He wondered: where are they going on this Sunday morning? Where's the boy's father?

The train rolled through suburbs and countryside, stopping at places called Heimstetten, Grub, Poing. Steve looked out the window at the fields and trees. When the little boy let out a shriek, Steve looked back at him and his mother. It was nothing; the child was just overexcited. The mother's eyes met Steve's apologetically. Steve smiled and tried to communicate, with a shrug and a shake of the head, that it was fine.

He thought about the little boy. How many times, he wondered, had the boy been a passenger on this train line, whose western terminus was a place called Dachau? How many years did you wait, if you were his mother, before you explained to him that that word, Dachau, which had always been an innocuous part of his life, possessed a not at all innocuous significance for the world beyond Munich? Or did you just wait for him to learn

252

about it in school? When his teacher took him on that grisly but obligatory class trip, did you talk about it with him beforehand? If so, what the hell did you say?

The mother and child got off at a stop called Ottenhofen. A couple of minutes later, the train pulled into Altenerding. This wasn't suburbia any more; it was exurbia. Steve got off the train, and noticed that three other passengers had also deboarded – a young straight couple and an elderly woman. They walked over to cars parked alongside the tracks. Steve noticed a small cobalt-blue sign that pointed the way down the road that crossed the rail line. *Therme Erding,* it read.

Steve followed it, and after walking a hundred yards or so past a few little wooden buildings on his right side – a gas station, a couple of shops – and a thicket of trees on the left, he reached a crossroad at which a sign, pointing to the right, read *Anne Frank Schule.*

Steve had never really thought about it, but of course there had to be tons of schools in Germany (and maybe in the Netherlands too?) named after Anne Frank. How many? he wondered. How many Anne Frank Schools did it take to make everything all right, to make the past go away?

Distracted, Steve inadvertently stepped off the sidewalk into the bike lane. A few seconds later, a middle-aged woman pedaled by and yelled at him. Instantly, as if by instinct, Steve jumped back up onto the sidewalk.

Walking along, Steve thought of what his Polish Catholic grandmother used to say to him – passionately, out of the blue, clutching his hand, staring into his eyes: "Always remember, the Jews are the best people in the world!" Steve had never understood what that was about. His grandmother had fled Europe during the First World War, sailing in steerage from Rotterdam to New York at the age of fifteen, and had spent the rest of her life in Chicago. What had happened to her, what had she experienced or observed, at that tender age, that made her feel such a pressing need to repeat that statement to her grandson, over and over again, with such urgency? To Steve, it had always been part of the mystery of Europe, the heaviness of Europe, which throughout his childhood had seemed a world – and then some – apart from the safe, easy Disneyland that was America.

Steve kept walking down the road. A few dozen steps from the train tracks and then there were no more trees on his left – just farmland on both sides. Up ahead, in the distance, at eleven o'clock, he could see a bizarre structure, or conglomeration of structures, composed of a mishmash of elements that bore no stylistic resemblance whatsoever to one another. There was a path leading to it, and another *Therme Erding* sign directing him up the path.

He turned and walked toward it. It was the weirdest-looking thing, gigantic in scale, and almost otherworldly, rising up out of the fallow fields like the Emerald City.

As he got closer, he could see that these architectural elements were in fact all connected, forming one strange, sprawling building. Part of the conglomeration was a massive parking structure, several stories high. After another minute or two he got close enough to see that cars were pouring into the parking structure, and that people were pouring out of it and toward a set of glass doors leading into this enormous complex.

When he reached the doors, he went in too. The space he entered was huge, bright, high-ceilinged, lined on three sides with shops – no walls or doors dividing them from one another or from the center of the space, just elaborate displays and signs and sales counters. The signs advertised various brands of soaps and perfumes, towels and swimsuits, floats and rafts. He walked over to some shelves packed with towels of different colors. He grabbed one – it was blue – and used Joop's credit card to buy it from an alert young man in a black t-shirt and black trousers.

Along one wall of this large space were two enormous archways, under each of which was a row of eight or nine ticket counters, like so many supermarket checkouts. At each of them, a dozen or so patrons were queued up to buy tickets. Demographically, they were all over the place – young, middle-aged, old; mostly straight couples, although there was also a group of six or seven women in their thirties who were laughing it up together, and another group of college-age guys who looked half-awake; Steve guessed that they'd been out all night drinking and had come here to sweat it out.

255

Steve got on one of the lines and within a couple of minutes reached the counter. The pretty, wide-eyed young woman behind it, who was wearing the same black uniform as the guy who'd sold him his towel, gave him a big smile. Steve ran Joop's credit card through a machine, and, just like the clerk at Die Hirtenflöte, she handed him a wristband with a key on it.

But this place was nothing like that cramped little sauna, with its crummy old lockers and smelly mattresses. Some yards beyond the ticket counter was a fifteen-foot-high partition on which, about ten feet up, there were large numbers in bright gold next to arrows pointing to the left and right. Steve checked the number on his wristband – 2983 – and, after consulting the sign, headed to the right, as did several other customers. Behind the partition was another high-ceilinged area, this one about the size of a football field. It was an immense locker room, by far the biggest he'd ever seen, full of endless rows of seven-foot-high lockers, all of them shiny and brown and marmoreal. The space was as well-lit and as spick-and-span as the locker room at Die Hirtenflöte had been dark and grungy. At the end of each row of lockers were four-digit numbers alongside arrows pointing this way and that. Following the numbers, Steve and several other people made their way past dozens of rows of lockers, and then alongside one of the rows and through a doorway into – to his astonishment – another massive locker room, every bit as large as the first one. He followed the numbers until he was finally close to his destination. 2985.

2984. 2983. Several of the people who'd bought tickets just before him were already standing at nearby lockers, stripping down, and several of those who'd bought their tickets just after him were stopping at other nearby lockers.

He opened locker number 2983. This time he didn't take the pistol out of his pocket – he just took his pants off carefully and folded them neatly, taking special care not to let the gun fall to the floor. He finished undressing, and stuffed everything into the locker except his towel. He shut the locker, wrapped the towel around his waist, and started fiddling with the plastic wristband, which, unlike the frayed rubber band that had passed for a wristband at Die Hirtenflöte, was a cleverly conceived, and rather challenging, invention: it took Steve a moment to figure out how, after pulling it tight, to lock it into place.

Looking around, Steve suddenly realized what this arsenal of elegant, faux-marble lockers reminded him of: a columbarium. A gigantic columbarium, containing the ashes of thousands upon thousands of souls. Then an ever darker thought occurred to him: at both ends of the S2 line were sprawling installations, both of them utterly different, except for the fact that one of them had used to, and the other one still did, process people by the hundreds, strip them naked, and give them numbers.

An arrow pointed the way out. Steve followed it through a men's shower room into...Oz. It was a world unto itself, huge beyond description.

Disney World, only nude.

He followed the crowd through a low passageway into an area called the Palazzo Veneziano, where the architecture did indeed look like something you might find in a Venetian palace. There was a large blue-tiled pool and, alongside it, tables at which men and women in towels were eating pasta and drinking wine. A sign advertised standard Italian dishes, in addition to a forty-Deutschmark wiener schnitzel special.

Steve continued on through a high, wide passageway. He passed a counter, on his right, at which several patrons, also in towels, were in line to buy ice cream. Beyond the counter was a circular bar, surrounded by stools, at which men and women in towels sipped large colorful cocktails decorated with little umbrellas, maraschino cherries, and wedges of lime, lemon, and orange. Some distance ahead, Steve saw enough palm trees to fill a small island in the South Pacific.

He proceeded, and found himself in a glass-walled, glass-roofed space that was as big as any airport terminal area he'd ever set foot in. The centerpiece was a huge, amoeba-shaped body of water, which a sign identified as the "Champagne Pool." It was ringed by the trees, their palms spreading out high above the water, and by a profusion of tropical plants, some of them bearing flowers in a range of brilliant colors. At the pool's far end was a small flap-covered opening in the glass wall through which the inside pool flowed into what appears to be an equally large heated outdoor pool. It was early in the afternoon on a cool, gray spring day, and even from where

Steve was standing, about forty or fifty yards away, he could see steam rising up off the surface of the water outside.

On the side of the pool closest to him were several rows of white reclining beach chairs, about half of them occupied by men or women who were either lying naked or sitting in their towels reading or sipping a drink. Just beyond them were two sweeping grand stairways with white balustrades. One of the stairways curved up, the other down – leading to what, he didn't yet know. A bit further away, overlooking the pool from a mezzanine level, was a Vietnamese restaurant. In the pool itself were dozens of people, some swimming around, some standing in the water chatting with friends, others standing in front of nozzles from which powerful jets of water sprayed on their back. Still others were sitting around a clover-shaped bar that jutted out into the pool, the bartenders fully dressed in their black uniforms and standing on a dry floor while the customers, on the other side of the bar, sat naked on stools enjoying their drinks, the water coming up to somewhere around belly-button level. Next to a set of stairs leading down into the pool were several racks covered with pegs on which the people in the pool had hung their towels – hundreds of them. Steve walked past the pool and through a high, columned archway facing it. At the far end of a colonnade was a grotto-like space where a few naked men and women stood under a bouquet of giant *faux* callalillies while warm water rained down upon them. Soft music was playing. A sign on the wall identified this as the "Calla Kaskaden," or callalilly cascade. The walls, Steve read, were covered in quartzite, the ceiling made of something called "Pedras Salgadas" slate.

On two sides of the grotto were glass doors leading to four small saunas, in each of which a number of people were sitting. Each sauna was different: one had stone walls and a burning fireplace; another was crowded with small trees and plants and lit by green lights hidden among the vegetation; a third was identified by a sign as the *"Aromasauna,"* the fourth as the *"Citrussauna."* Each also had a different temperature – forty degrees celsius, fifty, sixty, eighty.

Steve stepped into the Citrussauna for a moment. There was gentle music – not the same music that was playing in the grotto – and the air smelled, naturally, of oranges. He walked back out, and headed down a corridor past several more saunas. One, tiny and filled almost entirely by a rectangular wooden table and two benches, was called the "Zirbelstube," the Zirbel being a kind of tree, if he remembered correctly, and *Stube* meaning room. It was occupied only by men, who were crammed together as on a rush-hour subway, and was indeed marked *"Nur Männer"* – men only. Another sauna was labeled "Laconium" and featured the scent of *"frischer Lavendelblütenessenzen"* – the essence of fresh lavender. At the center of yet another sauna was a cylindrical white object, like a giant boiler. A sign identified it as an infrared sauna. Further along, larger than any of the others, was a sauna in which three rows of benches, arranged in steps, surrounded a fountain from which a gush of water surged so powerfully that it soaked the ceiling. Just beyond it was a "waterfall shower." And then there was a rectangular room, the size of a four-car garage, that looked exactly like something out of an ancient Roman bath – white columns and trimming, and a blue pool that looked identical to the one in which Laurence Olivier had tried to seduce Tony Curtis in *Spartacus.*

As Steve moved from one space to another, he was agape at the sheer scale of this place – sauna upon sauna upon sauna, pool upon pool upon pool, each with its own distinctive look and feel and theme and atmosphere and temperature, as if to satisfy every possible whim of the most demanding of souls. He was agape at the immaculateness of it all – there wasn't a trace of trash or speck of dirt anywhere. And he was agape at the brilliance with which the people who imagined this place into being had managed to create an illusion of a timeless world of utter luxury, out here on the edge of a small German town. It was as if they'd performed a thorough, expert study of the history of extravagant pleasure, and brought all their findings together in this one remarkable place. It was like something set up as a private pleasure palace by the richest and most imaginative of despots.

For a while, he just kept walking. All around him, going in and out of the saunas, or, like him, just walking around, were men and women, some naked, some wrapped in towels. The whole thing, he thought, should seem terribly decadent, hedonistic. But it didn't, not at all. The place was far more sanitary even than Disneyland – and somehow felt every bit as wholesome. No, more wholesome. Disney wholesomeness was fake wholesomeness – kids dressed up as Mickey and Snow White. This was real.

In fact, it was more than real. It was heaven. Paradoxically, the heavenliness of it undercut the effect of the adrenaline that he'd been running on since Bellamyplein, and caused him to feel suddenly, cripplingly overwhelmed by everything that had happened in the last couple of days. He knew he needed to stay focused on his task, but he also knew he wouldn't be able to do that unless he allowed himself a few minutes to breathe – and to have a beer.

Returning to the "Champagne Pool," he hung his towel up on one of the racks, stepped down into the water, and waded over to the bar, to a space between two women who were sitting there enjoying their beers.

"*Weissbier, bitte,*" he told the bartender, a young brunette, and pushed his wristband to her across the bar.

"*Weissbier,*" she said with a bright red lipstick smile as she snapped up the band. She was probably no more than twenty years old, and very pretty. She turned, took a couple of steps, and tapped the beer with one hand while running the band across a scanner with the other.

"*Danke schön,*" Steve said as she set down the tall glass and wristband.

"*Bitte schön,*" she replied distractedly, already casting a look around to see who else needed a refill.

Steve was one of about three dozen customers clustered around the clover-shaped bar, some sitting, some standing, all naked. Pretty much everybody except him seemed to be with somebody. He put the band back on his wrist and fumbled with the fastener, then grabbed his beer and walked slowly through the warm, chest-high water toward the middle of the pool.

Looking around him, he thought of the men in the "community center" on Bellamyplein. What would they make of this? Could anything be more alien to their sensibility? Wasn't this exactly what they were at war with? And he thought of Hitler. How could the same country that had produced Dachau also produce this? How to make sense of it? Yes, the Nazis had fetishized the perfect Aryan body, celebrating robust health and exterminating the handicapped. But Steve also distinctly remembered reading somewhere that the Nazis had been deeply suspicious of the German naturist movement – which predated their own movement by decades – because of its implicit enthusiasm for social diversity and harmony. Steve remembered something else, too: that so many Nazis had been devoted to naturism that Hitler, who hadn't compromised on much else, had felt compelled to tacitly accept it.

Steve took a sip of his beer, then made his way over to a spot at the edge of the pool. He sat on a ledge about a foot below the water's surface and right next to one of the sets of steps that led into the pool. As he sat drinking his beer, naked men and women walked up out of the water or down into it. They ranged in age from sixteen (the minimum age for entry) to ancient, and were of every shape and size imaginable, although almost everybody was white and presumably German. Some of the bodies were beautiful; some were almost skeletal, and some morbidly obese. Steve noticed that almost everybody's pubes were shaved – male and female alike. Did they always shave them, he wondered, or did they just do it when they knew they were coming here? One striking fact was that nobody seemed self-conscious about being naked, although now and then a very young guy would look around nervously before giving his dick a quick tug.

What most impressed itself upon Steve, however, was the sense of common, vulnerable humanity – of pure freedom from aggression. Absolutely everybody here seemed to be having a good time. At the bar, some lively conversations were underway, but there were no raised voices – no friction, no hint of tension. Nobody was acting up or doing anything inappropriate. Yes, some of the young straight couples were standing shoulder to shoulder, cozy together, off to themselves, looking affectionately into each other's eyes, but nothing overtly erotic was going on. That wasn't what this place was about. Every so often a group of straight boys in their late teens or early twenties would scamper down the stairs into this huge bath of naked women, and not even among them, these kids presumably at the height of their horniness, did Steve observe the slightest hint of arousal.

While he was sipping his beer, taking in the sight of the people walking alongside the pool, Steve noticed someone who was actually not German-looking – a short, slim Mediterranean male, about thirty years old, and wrapped in a towel whose elaborate design, in shades of dark red, brought to mind a Persian carpet. Steve's gaydar went off.

The guy hung his towel on one of the racks, stepped down into the pool, and waded past Steve to the bar. After purchasing a beer, he looked around for somewhere to sit. He found a place on the other side of the steps from Steve. A couple of minutes later, when Steve finished his beer, he went to the bar to buy another one. After he'd paid for it, and turned around, he saw that an elderly man and woman had taken his spot. He noticed that there was room next to the Mediterranean-looking guy. He waded over.

"*Ist der Platz noch frei?*" Steve asked, indicating the space beside the guy.

"*Ja.*" A friendly nod.

Steve sat down and drank some of his beer. Two or three minutes went by. Then the guy said something in German that Steve didn't catch.

"Sorry," Steve said in English, "my German is a bit rusty."

The guy wasn't fazed. "British?" he asked.

"American. You?"

"I was born in Turkey," he said. "But I've lived in Germany since I was a kid." He spoke a kind of mid-Atlantic English, neither identifiably American nor assertively British.

"In Munich?"

"Yes. Now, anyway."

"Do you like it?"

"Yes."

"But you didn't grow up here?"

"No. I grew up in Berlin. And I went to university in Heidelberg, and then Oxford."

"Oh, really? What did you study?"

"Medicine. I'm a doctor."

"An M.D.?"

"Yes. And you?"

"I'm a writer," Steve said. To keep from turning the focus on himself, he quickly added, "Your parents must be proud of you."

The doctor gave a little laugh. "Not exactly."

"What do you mean?"

The doctor shook his head almost imperceptibly, and was silent for a moment. Then he sipped his beer and looked around. "Isn't this place something?" he asked, in a tone of genuine wonderment.

"Yes."

"It's like a vision of utopia," he said. Steve could hear a touch of Oxford in his voice. "A future world, or an alternate reality. Sensible and...serene. No? Wouldn't you say?"

266

"Yes. Serene. Definitely."

"A world like the one John Lennon sang about. No religion. A heaven right here on earth."

"No hell below us," Steve said. "Above us only sky."

The doctor smiled. "Most Americans are quite religious," he said. "Isn't that so?"

"In one way or another, yes."

"Are you?"

"No," Steve said, with a firm shake of the head.

"Your parents?"

"Not really."

The doctor nodded. They sat there and drank beer in silence. "Actually," the doctor said after a while, "Christianity is not so bad. In some cases anyway. The idea of it is beautiful, of course. Love thy neighbor."

"Yes. The gospel message. Some Christians actually live by it. But some of them seem never to have heard of it."

"Yes."

"And they fuck it up. And turn it into the opposite of what it's supposed to be."

"Yes. Exactly. They fuck it up."

"I guess you weren't brought up Christian, though."

"No."

"Muslim, I guess?"

"Yes."

"So what would you say about Islam?"

"What do you mean?"

"Do Muslims fuck up Islam? Do they turn it into the opposite of what it was supposed to be?"

"Well, you might say that some of them do. Only in a very different way than Christians do with Christianity."

"Meaning what?"

"That the original idea of it is frankly nothing less than monstrous. The only really good Muslim is a Muslim who *isn't* a good Muslim, if you know what I mean."

"I'm not sure I do."

"Millions of Muslims are good people. Wonderful people. The best people you'd ever want to meet. They don't care if you're a Muslim, a Christian, a Hindu, a Buddhist, an atheist, whatever. They don't care if you're a man or a woman, gay or straight. They're good people. They only wish you the best. But by being that way, they're betraying their religion, which tells them to have nothing but contempt for the infidel. To see the woman as inferior. To see the gay person as an abomination deserving of death."

"You don't think you're exaggerating just a bit?"

"Not at all. Islam was fucked up from the beginning. Islam is fucked up at its core."

"But how can a religion with so many adherents – "

"I don't care how many adherents it has. Or supposedly has. Mao claimed to rule over a billion

Communists. Stalin over God knows how many hundreds of millions more. How many of them were really Communists in their hearts, I don't know. All I know is that the sheer numbers didn't make Communism right, or good, or desirable."

"Good point."

For a few moments they sat and drank their beers in silence.

"You know," the doctor finally said, waving his arm to indicate the spectacle around them, "I actually think Jesus would like this. In fact I think this is probably not very far from what he had in mind. But Muhammed? What do you think he'd make of it?"

"I don't know."

"I'll tell you. He'd be outraged. He'd start by chopping off all these women's heads. That one. And that oen. And that one. All those beautiful women." He pointed to different women around them, young and old, all smiling and happy. "Think of it. All decapitated. Every last one of them. For dishonoring their families."

"I take it you've left the faith," Steve said.

The doctor chuckled. "Yes," he said after a pause. "You could put it that way." He drank some beer. "I had a simple choice."

"A choice?"

"Yes."

"And what was that?"

"But then of course, more often than not, life really does come down to simple choices, if we're honest with ourselves. Not simple in terms of weighing the perils or summoning up the necessary courage, but simple in the sense that it's clear what the options are and what consequences will follow."

"And your choice was?"

"It was Islam – or life."

"Life? Is that what you said?"

"Yes, life."

"What do you mean?"

"When I was at university I went home one weekend and – stupidly – told my parents I was gay. We were having dinner. My father ordered my mother and sisters out of the room and then they beat me."

"Who beat you?"

"All the men. My father, my uncle, my brother. I was at Oxford, and on the verge of becoming a doctor, and they beat me like an old, dusty rug. And when I was lying on the floor aching and bleeding, my father put a Koran in my hand and held a knife to my neck and told me to repent. So I repented. Or said I did. And then I went back to Oxford and never talked to any of them again. When they tried to contact me, I moved. I changed my phone number, and I legally changed my name. I even got a – what's it called? A court document saying they couldn't come near me."

"A restraining order."

"Yes. Not that such documents mean anything to them. They have no fear of the authorities here in Europe."

"And then?"

"And then, as soon as I graduated from university, I moved here, to Munich, the other side of the country from them."

"What a family."

"It's not the family. It's the religion. In fact it would be a wonderful family if not for the religion. That's what's so tragic about it all. These are good and loving people twisted by a mental illness – a mass psychosis, disguised as a faith – into monsters capable of killing their loved ones."

"But why did they move to Europe in the first place?"

"The same reason hundreds of thousands of others did."

"And what's that?"

"Free stuff."

"Simple as that?"

"I guess you don't value free stuff the way some people do."

"So they didn't know about European democracy and diversity and all that before they came?"

"Well, yes. But they didn't think anybody would expect or force them to embrace European democracy and diversity. And they were right. Nobody *did* expect or force them to do so. On the contrary. They were congratulated for clinging to their primitive values and beliefs. They were viewed as authentic, as exotic. The fools here in this country acted as if the most dangerous thing that people like my parents were bringing with them was food that was too heavily spiced. It's as if they didn't realize that people from a different culture have different assumptions, thoughts, prejudices, that are as deeply rooted as – as – what are those big trees you have in California?"

"Sequoias."

"That's it. As deeply rooted as a sequoia."

"It sounds as if the native Europeans had a pretty condescending attitude toward newcomers like your parents."

"Yes. It was nothing *but* condescension. And sheer ignorance. People like my parents came to Europe viewing native Europeans as mere infidels, a lower class of humans than themselves. *Haram:* unclean. Other people might call European women strong and independent; people like my father saw them as whores who didn't know their place. And saw their fathers and husbands as weaklings incapable of taming them. As for European freedom, all they could see when they looked at it was heresy – a violation of the proper Islamic order. And the welfare state, of which they took full advantage? As far as they were concerned, it was nothing but the creation of suckers – idiots begging to be exploited."

"And you're not just talking about your parents? This was –"

"This was almost everybody we knew."

"That sounds pretty hostile. Pretty extreme."

"Extreme? I haven't even gotten around to what

was extreme about it. Have you heard of forced marriages?"

"I've heard of arranged marriages."

"Same thing. In the community I grew up in, you didn't pick your own spouse. You married somebody your father or your grandfather or your uncles or some other old man picked out for you. Usually the spouse was your cousin, somebody you'd never met, somebody from back in the old village who was probably illiterate and totally ignorant about the West and who was also being forced into the deal."

"But what if you said no?"

"Ah, that brings us to honor killing. Usually girls, but often also boys, murdered by their families for just such offenses. But not just for saying no to a forced marriage. Was your daughter found alone in a room with a male from another family? Kill her."

"But why?"

"It's right there in the name of the crime. Honor killing. Every female in the family is a pillar of the family's own virtue. The slightest deviation from absolute purity, and – *zzzkkk!*" The doctor ran his finger across his neck.

Steve thought suddenly of the man whose throat Joop had cut with the broken wine bottle.

"In Islam," the doctor said, "there are plenty of capital offenses. And plenty of families ready and willing to play the part of judge, jury, and executioner. Leave the faith? *Zzzkkk!*"

He ran his finger across his neck again.

273

"What ever happened to live and let live?"

"That's not an Islamic concept. Islam teaches that your role as a Muslim is to conquer the world in the name of your faith. And when people like my family came to Europe, they found a continent that, in their eyes, was all but begging to be conquered. Germany didn't just encourage them to retain their culture, practice their religion, and preach their values. It *subsidized* all of this generously, paying for exclusively Muslim schools, where children, to put it plainly, were taught, at the expense of German taxpayers, to hate every one of those German taxpayers."

"Well, that's crazy. On the part of Germany, I mean."

"Of course it is. It's suicidal. Think of it. A whole generation of European leaders invited Muslims into their countries by the hundreds of thousands – all the while refusing to face up to the very nature of Islam itself. The brutality, the violence. The evil."

"It's obvious this has a lot of personal meaning for you."

Silence. Steve looked at the doctor. He was staring into the distance – into the steam rising up from the surface of the outside part of the pool they were sitting in. "When I was younger," the doctor said, his tone softening, "we used to go back to Turkey every summer."

"Oh?"

"Yes."

"Where? Your home village?"

274

"Yes. I looked forward to it. Not because I wanted to see my family. But because I had a...a friend there."

"Oh."

"My first boyfriend. I loved him. He loved me. His family found out."

Silence. Steve looked into his dark eyes. "No," Steve said.

"Yes."

"No."

"Yes. They killed him."

"No."

"Yes. That's honor killing too, you know."

"It's not just girls, then?"

"No. Usually, yes. Girls."

"But not always?"

"No."

"Boys aren't exempt."

"No. Especially if they're..."

"Gay."

"Yes."

"What happened to his family? Were they arrested?"

"Of course not. In Muslim countries, the police routinely turn their back. Everybody does. The neighbors, the courts. Naturally, some people have their private misgivings, but – "

"They don't dare speak up."

"No."

"But why not?"

"Because they know that the Koran says it's legitimate to kill people for such reasons. So if they spoke up against it, what would they be doing?"

"They'd be speaking against Islam itself."

"Exactly. And thus identifying themselves as apostates."

"And deserving of death themselves."

"Precisely. I have a cousin here in Germany. A *kusine* – a girl cousin. She was a very good student and wanted to be an engineer. Instead they made her marry one of our other cousins, this one a big cretinous bully from our grandparents' old village in Turkey. She resisted them. Or tried to. She was terrified of him. He's a total barbarian. A cretin, totally unworthy of her. But they beat her unconscious, and threatened to kill her, and she finally gave in. Now they have five kids. And he beats her constantly. She's been sent to hospital I don't know how many times. Her life is hell. Here in Germany, in the same country where you have this."

Again he gestured to take in the pool and their fellow patrons.

"There should be laws against that."

"There are laws. But the authorities are scared to do anything. They claim to care about women and gays and individual dignity and all that, but they don't want to be called anti-Muslim bigots. Somehow that's become the worst thing of all."

"So they don't get involved."

"No. Instead of seeing us as individuals, like them,

they see us as part of a group. A group that operates by its own rules. And they have this disgusting idea that those barbaric rules have to be respected more than the people who are suffering because of those rules."

"And that's the worst bigotry of all."

The doctor looked at Steve with something that appeared to be real respect. "Yes, it is," he said.

For a moment they sat there drinking in silence. Then the doctor asked: "Did you ever hear of Henriette Becker?"

"No."

"Anthropologist. University of Tübingen. She's considered an expert on the Islamic world, and she's on TV here all the time. The other day she wrote an article in *Der Spiegel* – that's a newspaper here – "

"I know."

" – saying that if Muslims rape German women, the men aren't responsible."

"What?"

"Yes. Because of what their religion and culture tell them about women."

"But that's – how can she – "

"Simple. As she sees it, the women are responsible, because of the way they act and dress. It sends the men the wrong signals, you see."

"They're asking for it."

"Yes."

"But how can *Der Spiegel* publish such nonsense?"

"Because that's how everybody in the German

establishment thinks about these things. As they see it, this is now a multicultural society, where some people live by the tenets of Islam, and all the rest need to change their ways accordingly, or face the consequences."

"And how does that make you feel?"

"Furious. There are people who move here from the Islamic world precisely because they want to escape the tyranny of Islam and live in freedom. But those people – people like me – the authorities ignore. Instead they cater to the ones who come here wanting to make this a *part* of the Islamic world, to impose Islamic law and shut down freedom."

"But how can they do that? The authorities, I mean?"

"Because they just don't get Islam. They treat it like – like some kind of tender flower that's so easily offended. But it's not a flower. It's the exact opposite. It's a – a *Panzer*, a tank, ready to roll over everything and crush everybody. Including them and their good intentions. They think Islam is just like Christianity, only with different superficial details – a beard, a veil."

"Christianity with curry."

The doctor laughed. "Indeed. They don't get jihad. They don't get sharia. They've never believed in anything themselves, so they're constitutionally incapable of understanding just how radical Islam is at its heart, how seriously its adherents take it, how it governs absolutely everything they think and do, how it imprisons their minds like the severest jailer ever."

"So how did you manage to break out of that jail?"

"Good question. One thing was studying medicine. I came to understand that Islam operates very much like an addiction. It causes good and smart people to do bad and stupid things. Things against their own best interests. After all, Islam's worst victims are Muslims themselves. In a free country like this, the idea should be to help such people to liberate themselves from it – as with any addiction. Not to be enablers. Or to praise them for their addiction."

"That's an interesting way of looking at it."

"It also helped that I read a lot of history. Since World War II, Western Europe has been peaceful and prosperous. Its people act as if history is over. History is never over. We're living in history, amid changes that are visible, even obvious, to a few of us but invisible to most of us. Changes that we can affect by choosing to take action – or by choosing to turn away and do nothing."

The doctor glanced at the beer glass in his hand. It was empty. Another gulp, and Steve's was empty too.

"I'm afraid I have to visit the men's room," the doctor said.

"Me too. Do you know where it is?"

"I'm a regular here. I know where everything is. Come on."

Setting their glasses down on the edge of the pool, they waded over to the steps, climbed out, and wrapped their towels around their waists. "This way," the doctor said, and led him toward the grand white stairway that curved upwards from the main level to a sort of mezzanine. The part of the mezzanine that overlooked the pool appeared to be pretty much just a place to stand and chat and enjoy a drink, as a few people were doing. Passing through this area, Steve and the doctor walked into, and through, a section in which immensely large, bone-colored linen sheets hung from a very high ceiling, forming linen-walled rooms, as it were, containing plush snow-white couches and leafy plants in white planters. It took a while for Steve to realize that music was playing – very, very softly. Bach. Just beyond this area, on the left, was a men's room. Steve and the doctor went in together, and after they came out, the doctor said, "Have you been up here before? On this level?"

"No," Steve said. "It's my first time here. And this place is like the Louvre or the British Museum or the Metropolitan Museum of Art. Too much for just one visit."

"You can say that again. But just come look at this." The doctor led Steve through a decorative archway and down a corridor. They passed yet more small saunas, although these ones, up here on the mezzanine level, wee less heavily trafficked than the ones downstairs. Once the saunas were behind them, the corridor widened into a very large, rotunda-like space, in the center of which was a massive wine-red tent out of *Lawrence of Arabia.* They entered the tent through an open flap. Inside, two concentric circles of snow-white cots, about thirty in all, surrounded a blazing fire. It was warm; soft Arabic music was playing; on the far side of the tent, a middle-aged man and woman in white robes sat on adjoining cots, being served tall drinks from a silver tray by a slim young man in a black uniform and fez. Otherwise not a single soul was here, aside from Steve and the doctor. As Steve looked around, taking in what might well, he reflected, be the ultimate example of sheer self-indugence, he noticed the sign just inside the entrance. It was small and black, and looked as if it was made of lacquer, and had just one word written on it, in elegant gold calligraphy.

    Alhambra.

VIII

STEVE HAD TAKEN SPANISH for six years, from seventh to twelfth grade. His teachers, he remembered, had not only loaded him and his fellow pupils up with vocabulary words and drilled into their heads the conjugations of every irregular verb in the language; they'd also taught them about history and culture. Steve had learned about the Aztecs, Incas, and Mayans, about Simón Bolívar and Pancho Villa, about the Islamic conquest of Spain, the Christian reconquest, and the Spanish Empire in the New World.

And he'd learned about the Alhambra – that elaborate complex of palaces in Granada, in southern Spain, a mere sixty kilometers or so from the Mediterranean, that was as spectacular as any structure of its time. Miss Yrisarry, an eager teacher who had visited the Alhambra in person, showed Steve's class the beautiful slides she had taken of it, in all its magnificence – the grand archways and arabesques, the courtyards and colonnades and canopies, the designs and decorations, all of them detailed beyond imagination. Miss Yrisarry explained to them that the Alhambra, dramatically situated on a lordly mountaintop in Andalucia, looking down upon the mazes of simple stone houses that made up the city of Granada, had been the epicenter of Islamic Spain. But somehow Steve, at least, had never acquired the big picture of Islamic power in Europe – not in Spanish class, and not, so far as he could remember, in any middle-school or high-school or college history class. As far as he could remember, no teacher or professor had ever explained to any class he was in that the Moorish incursion into Spain had been only a part of a violent and relentless centuries-long effort to Islamize Europe in much the same way that the Prophet and his followers had Islamized the formerly Christian regions of the Maghreb and the Levant.

Steve didn't remember ever learning about the Battle of Tours, in the year 732, in northern France, at which Frankish troops under Charles Martel turned back a Muslim army that had come up through Iberia – and that might otherwise have conquered all of Europe from the west and thereby, of course, thoroughly altered the course of Western history. Nor did he remember learning about the 1529 siege of Vienna, where the relentless expansion into Europe – this time from the east – of the Ottoman Empire under Suleiman the Magnificent had finally been halted and begun to be rolled back. Yes, Steve had learned about the Crusades, but his teachers had never sufficiently emphasized the fact that these often derided military expeditions had been attempts by Europeans to recover lands that had been Christian for centuries until they'd been brought, by brutal force, into the *ummah,* the Nation of Islam.

Steve would not, in fact, become properly educated on any of these matters until quite a while after this particular chapter of his life was over.

"What's wrong?" the doctor asked.

Steve was standing motionless, looking at the sign that said *Alhambra.*

"I need to make a phone call," Steve said, his mouth so dry that he could barely speak.

"Are you all right?"

"I need to go to my locker."

"Meet you at the pool bar afterward?"

"I don't know. I may have to leave."

"Well, in that case, mind if I come with you to your locker?"

"Not at all."

They walked back through the maze of linen sheets, down the big curved stairway to the champagne pool, past the Palazzo Veneziano, and through the men's showers into the cavernous locker area. Steve found his way to his locker and opened it. Digging into his pants pocket, he took out his wallet and Joop's phone, and pulled out of the wallet the slip of paper with Daniel's phone number on it.

"I'll give you some privacy," the doctor said, and withdrew to a space a few yards away – a clearing in the jungle of lockers, where there were several beautiful white chairs at white tables, each equipped with a large mirror, hair dryer, and box of tissues. He sat down. Mean-while Steve dialed Daniel. He answered after one ring.

"What are you doing in Germany?" Daniel said. He wasn't happy. He sounded reproachful, like a parent talking to a small child who'd gone off the block without permission.

"How can you tell I'm in Germany?"

"Don't be stupid. What are you doing in Germany?"

"I figured it out."

"Figured what out?"

"The Alhambra."

"What do you mean?"

"Remember? What the guys said downstairs on Bellamyplein? They mentioned the – "

"Yes, I remember."

"Well, they weren't talking about the real Alhambra. They were talking about this big tent here. I'm at – "

"I know exactly where you are. And this call confirms it."

"Confirms what?"

"That it *was* you who killed that guy in the gay sauna last night. And who injured the guy at the university today."

"Well, you're obviously keeping up with the news."

"Do you mind telling me what the hell you're doing?"

As quickly as he could, Steve told Daniel about the piece of paper that had led him to Die Hirtenflöte, and to Fabien. And about the circled newspaper announcement that had alerted him to the university lecture.

"So how many more people do you plan on killing before you're through?" Daniel asked.

"Daniel, it was kill or be killed. I'm not going to argue with you about that. I called to tell you about the Alhambra."

"Okay, tell me."

"There's a big tent at this place. Kind of off the beaten path. I was just there. It was almost empty. It's called – are you ready? – the Alhambra."

"I see."

Daniel didn't sound impressed. At all.

"You see what I'm getting at? This is where they're planning to take Schrama out."

"I understand."

For a moment Steve didn't say anything. "Why do you sound like that?" he asked.

"What do you mean?"

"You sound almost...indifferent."

"What, did you expect me to burst into song?"

"Look, I know you're a professional, but still – "

"Congratulations. I think you've done a good job. But I told you not to leave Amsterdam."

"I couldn't help myself."

"I trust you're going to go back to Amsterdam now?"

"Daniel, I'm wanted by the police there. My face has been all over the news."

"If you haven't noticed, it's all over the news in Munich now, too."

"Okay, but – "

"Why couldn't you have just listened to me? I told

you to lay low. None of this would've happened if you'd just stayed put and kept your head down."

"Lie low."

"What?"

"The expression is lie low, not lay low. Dr. Andrus."

"You know, it's not too smart of you to test my good will like this."

"Same back at you."

"Look. Go back to Amsterdam. If you get arrested, we'll take care of it."

"What about this? Are you gonna take care of this?"

"Take care of what?"

"The Alhambra. Are you going to do whatever you have to do to keep these people from killing Jeroen Schrama?"

This time it was Daniel's turn to sit in silence for a few seconds.

"I told you," he finally said. "Just go back to Amsterdam."

"No."

"That's not a request."

"You mean you're giving me an order? As if I worked for you?"

"Let me put it this way. If you get arrested and want us to intervene on your behalf, you're going to have to do what we say. And you're going to have to stop shooting people. If you keep committing murders, sooner or later people are gonna start getting upset."

"Answer me. Are you going to stop this murder or not?"

"I'm not in a position to answer that."

"What does that mean?"

"What that means is that just as you don't work for me, I don't work for you either."

"But you do work for me. I'm an American citizen. And if you don't act to protect Jeroen Schrama, I'll go to the media and tell them you knew about these people's plans and didn't do anything to stop them."

There was a pause. "You don't want to make threats like that," Daniel said.

"Is *that* a threat, Daniel?"

Another pause. This time a long one.

"Let me explain something to you," Daniel finally said. "And if you ever quote this in public, I'll deny it and you'll never again have an opportunity to say anything to anybody. Jeroen Schrama is a destabilizing influence in the Netherlands and potentially in all of Europe."

"Destabilizing? What the hell is that supposed to mean?"

"It means that he profoundly alienates half his country's population, including the entire business establishment, and the major media, and every single Muslim in the country. The more political power this guy accumulates, the more you're going to inflict instability on what is now a very stable member of the Western alliance. And if he were to get elected prime minister, forget it. It would outrage Muslims not only in the Netherlands but around the world. There'd be disorder, riots, acts of terrorism. It would turn Europe upside down."

"You mean you're just gonna sit there and let him be murdered?"

Daniel sighed. Actually sighed.

"Answer me!" Steve said.

"Why don't you spend two minutes thinking about what I just said before you get all crazy?"

"Why don't *you* think about this? The long term. *Without* Schrama. Europe gets more and more Islamized. And freedom gets more and more undermined. How does that add up to stability?"

"We're betting that Muslims in Europe will gradually assimilate."

"You do a lot of betting, don't you? Well, I think you're betting wrong on this one."

"You don't really know anything about it."

"Well, aren't we lofty."

"You remember Robert Frost? 'The Road Not Taken'?"

"Yeah, what about it?"

"'Two roads diverged in a yellow wood.' That's you and me."

"Your point being?"

"My point being, go back to L.A. and make another infantile movie. Or some more insipid TV shows for children. Leave this stuff to the grownups."

"Leave what stuff? Allowing a man to be murdered?" Steve was all but shouting.

"Please. I'm trying to be a friend here. You don't want to get involved in this."

"I already *am* involved."

"Listen to me. Jeroen Schrama is a silly hysterical fag. And right now you're sounding very much like one yourself."

"*You're* calling *me* a fag? You fucking closet case."

Again, a pause. "You'll be sorry you said that," Daniel said softly.

"Fuck you."

"No, fuck you," Daniel said, and hung up.

Steve stood there for a moment in something very close to shock. But then his mind snapped into focus, and he realized he had to get out of this place pronto. Not only were the Dutch and German police out to arrest him and a Muslim terrorist group out to kill him; the CIA might well be ordering a hit on him.

The doctor was still hovering a few yards away. Steve caught his eye and waved him over. "Sorry about that," Steve said.

"No problem. Do you want to go back to the champagne pool?"

"Actually, I have to go."

"Leave?"

"Yes."

"That's a shame. You have an appointment? A date?"

"Not exactly."

"You mean no."

"Yes. I mean no, I don't."

"So you don't have to be anywhere."

"No. But I have to – I know it may sound strange, but I have to leave this place. Now."

The doctor looked into Steve's eyes. "That *does* sound strange. Could it be that all the nudity is getting to you? As an American?"

Steve half-smiled. "God, no. It's not that."

"Because you can't imagine how far afield this is from the culture in which I grew up. All the women of the extended family sitting around drinking tea all day. None of them allowed to go across the street unless she covered herself properly and was accompanied by a male member of the family. They'd never be able to imagine – "

"No, it's nothing like that. It's – well, I don't want to be dramatic, but it might be dangerous for me to stay here."

The doctor's eyes widened. "Do you want to tell me about this?"

"You'll think I'm crazy. In fact you probably already suspect I'm crazy."

"I told you I'm a doctor but I didn't say what kind. In fact I'm a psychiatrist. I've been studying you ever since we began speaking. I can tell that you're terribly anxious about something, but I don't think you're crazy."

"Thanks. I appreciate that. In fact, at the moment that counts as a helpful reality check."

"Look," the doctor said. "I'm ready to leave too. If you wanted to have dinner and talk...?"

Their eyes met. Steve asked himself: *Do I dare bring him into this?* After a moment he answered, "I'd like that."

"Good. I'll meet you at the checkout, okay?"

"Great."

The doctor walked away. It occurred to Steve that he should give Joop a quick update. He dialed him. Joop picked up at once. "Visser." He sounded uneasy.

"It's me, Joop. Everything okay there?"

"Yes, and with you?"

Steve told him, very quickly, about the Alhambra. Even more quickly, he summed up his conversation with Daniel.

"Holy shit," Joop said.

"Precisely."

"What do we do now?"

"I don't know. Let me get out of here. I'll call you back. Maybe one of us will have come up with something by then."

When Steve arrived at the checkout, the doctor was waiting for him, already paid up and ready to go. They left together. "Where's your car?" the doctor asked.

"I took the train."

"Good, you can drive with me and we can talk in the car." He led Steve to the parking structure, where they rode an elevator up three flights. The elevator was large; they were the only passengers.

The doctor's car was small, sunshine yellow, unpretentious, and as clean inside and out as an operating room. "It's about a forty-minute drive," he said to Steve as the car turned onto the highway. He was a fast, confident driver. "Is that enough time for you to fill me in on your situation?"

"Probably just the right amount," Steve said. As they raced down the Autobahn, Steve told him about the flat in Bellamyplein and the voices from downstairs. About the gun. And about the killing. The doctor didn't seem terribly fazed.

"Well," the doctor said, "it was wise of you to fetch the gun from that fellow's flat."

"I still have it."

"You mean you have it on you right now?"

"Yes."

Steve began to reach for it, but the doctor shook his head. "No, I don't need to see it. I know what a gun looks like. Let's hear the rest of your story."

Steve told him the rest. About what the men in the "community center" had said. About Schrama. And about their puzzling mention of the Alhambra.

The doctor's eyes, responsibly, had been on the road, but now he looked at Steve, comprehending.

"Oh, my," he said.

Steve continued. He told him about Fabien. And about what had happened at the university. And he filled him in about Daniel, concluding with the phone call they'd just had.

"Now I see why you wanted to get out of there," the doctor said.

"Yes. After that conversation, I feel safer if he doesn't know where I am."

"Not to mention the police," the doctor said. "Your face must be all over the TV news by now."

"I know. But I figured if there was one place where people wouldn't have seen the news in the last couple of hours, it'd be the place we just left."

"I guess that makes sense. But why not just go to the police and explain the situation?"

"Because I'm not sure they'd take me seriously. About the plot to kill Schrama. And even if they did take me seriously, I'm starting to wonder whether they'd respond to the information in a useful way. Frankly, in the last few days I've stopped trusting pretty much anybody in authority, at least when it comes to these issues. Do they understand just how evil and dangerous these people are? That's an easy one: no. Do they care about Schrama's life as much as I do? Or is he a problem to them – a guy they'd never kill themselves, but whom they wouldn't mind seeing removed from the picture? So you tell me, am I crazy?"

"On the contrary. That may be one of the sanest rants I've heard in quite a while. Where are you staying?"

"I don't know. Last night I slept in the Englischer Garten."

"Well, you can't do that tonight."

"No, I guess not."

"Tonight you stay at my place."

"Are you sure?"

"Of course. Unless I change my mind and decide that you're crazy after all."

The drive back into Munich seemed a lot faster to Steve than the train ride out. He was surprised to discover that the doctor's home was near the university. He found a parking space on a narrow side street and they walked half a block to the tasteful four-story building in which the doctor lived. "I'm on the third floor," he said. They took the elevator up. "By the way," said the doctor, "my name is Muhammed Demirkan."

"I'm Steve Disch."

Muhammed did a double-take. "Not the Steve Disch who made *Sentimental Education.*"

"That's me."

"*Heiliger Bimbam!*" Muhammed said, plainly more astonished by this than by anything Steve had told him in the car.

"*Heiliger* what?"

Muhammed laughed. "It's just a silly German expression. Let me translate: Holy shit! Roughly speaking."

He unlocked his apartment door and waved Steve in. The flat was small and simply furnished – a couch, dinner table, chairs, lamps, and bookshelves, almost all of it straight out of the IKEA catalogue. A bachelor pad. There was also a large fake-wood file cabinet. While Muhammed made drinks in the kitchen, Steve checked out the shelves. Medical textbooks and volumes on psychiatry, from Freud to the latest DSMV. Classic literature – Goethe, Hölderlin, Rilke, Tolstoy, Wilde, Conrad, Gide, a hardcover Shakespeare, all of Proust, several volumes apiece by Dickens, Trollope, Flaubert, and Balzac, and matching sets of Heinrich Böll, Günter Grass, and Thomas Mann. Plus a few raggedy paperback volumes of gay nonfiction. Not a single item on the shelves betrayed Muhammed's cultural background; there wasn't even an old, dog-eared copy of the Koran. The same went for the pictures on the wall. There were prints of Klee and Matisse, but nothing even vaguely Turkish or Islamic. Nor were there family photos.

Muhammed came out of the kitchen with two identical brown drinks in heavy tumblers. He handed one to Steve. He sniffed it. Scotch. "Cheers," Muhammed said solemnly, clinking his glass to Steve's. They drank. "Too strong?" Muhammed asked.

"No, perfect."

Muhammed gestured toward the couch. They sat.

"When we were talking in the pool," Muhammed says, "I knew something was very wrong, and I was prepared to help you if I could do so in some way. After you told me what you told me in the car, I was even more determined to help, because it speaks to everything I am and have been through, everything I believe in and stand for. But when you told me your name – now I feel moved to declare myself entirely at your disposal, because your film played a fundamental role in helping me to embrace who I am and what I believe in and stand for."

"Well, golly," Steve said. "Thank you."

"So tell me, what *can* I do? Have you come up with anything?"

"I think so. I need to make a phone call, and need you to talk to them."

"Done." Muhammed reached for his phone.

"No, we'll use this one," Steve said, pulling Joop's phone out of his pants pocket. "I don't want the call to be traceable to you."

"Very well. What do you want me to say?"

Steve explained in detail. "Got it?" Muhammed nodded. Steve dialed Schrama's office and handed Muhammed the phone.

It rang a few times before someone answered. "Hello?" Muhammed said. "Is this Jeroen Schrama's office? No? Oh, I see." As Steve expected, the call had bounced to the Tweede Kamer switchboard. "I'm sorry, I know it's after hours, but I'm a good friend of Jeroen's and I'm planning to come to The Hague tomorrow from Berlin and I'd like to – oh? Is that so? I see. No number at all? You can't even contact him and ask him...? Are you sure? I see. I see. All right, very well. What a shame. Thank you anyway. Goodbye."

Muhammed hung up and looked at Steve. "He's out of town. He's taking a couple of days off and doesn't want to be bothered, so he hasn't left a forwarding number."

"Maybe he's already here."

"Or on his way."

"Thanks for doing that."

"My pleasure."

"I have another idea," Steve said. He held out his palm; Muhammed placed the phone in it. "Sorry about this," Steve said as he phoned Joop.

"Not at all."

Joop picked up at once. "Me again," Steve said.

"Any ideas?"

"Yes. My new friend here just phoned the Tweede Kamer. Schrama's out of town."

"Your new friend?"

"A guy I met at that place today. Terrific guy." Steve was very aware of Muhammed sitting next to him, hearing every word. "I'm staying in his apartment tonight."

"Really? Are you sure you can trust him?"

"Absolutely."

"Okay. If you say so. So Schrama has left town? Do you think maybe he's there already?"

"Could be."

"Then what do we do? What's your idea?"

"That guy," Steve said. "The guy who works in Schrama's office. He's always at April at happy hour on Saturdays. Always."

"Let me guess. You want me to go to April?"

"Do you mind?"

"There are worse assignments."

"Find him. Explain the situation. Ask him where Schrama is."

298

"Will do. But first you have to tell me what he looks like."

"Early twenties. Tall, almost your height. Very slim. Cute. Great bone structure. Dark hair."

"That describes about half the guys who come to April on a Saturday night."

"He always wears one large hoop earring. And a sleeveless black t-shirt and black jeans."

"Okay, that's better. In fact I'm pretty sure I know who you're talking about."

"Good. Be careful."

"You too. By the way, what's your friend's name?"

"Muhammed."

"Muhammed?"

"Muhammed."

"As in...Muhammed?"

"You got it."

"Are you kidding?"

"No."

"Are you crazy?"

"At this point, I can't rule out that possibility. But he says I'm not."

"Huh?"

"He's a psychiatrist. And he says I'm not crazy. Although he may have changed his mind by now." Steve looked at Muhammed. Muhammed shook his head. "No, he says he still thinks I'm sane. Then again, maybe *he's* crazy."

"This is getting weirder and weirder."

"I know."

"Talk later."

"Yes."

Steve hung up. "He was surprised by my name, wasn't he?" said Muhammed.

"A bit."

Muhammed laughed. "I can't blame him. Come on, let's go eat."

I T WAS A SMALL NEIGHBORHOOD RESTAURANT, clean and cozy. Only two of the dozen-odd tables were occupied. A slight Chinese waiter of about thirty came over to their table with a big friendly smile and greeted Muhammed in slightly halting German. Muhammed introduced Steve to the waiter, whose name was Chen. They shook hands. Chen, who was wearing a clean, freshly ironed white dress shirt and scarlet apron, led them to a table by the window and came back almost immediately with a couple of large scarlet menus.

"Shall we order a bottle of wine?" Muhammed asked.

"Sounds good."

"Red or white?"

"Your choice."

"Do you like it dry or sweet?"

"Dry, please."

Muhammed ordered a bottle of sauvignon blanc. Chen nodded and walked away. Steve and Muhammed looked at their menus. They were only in German, but Steve was able to make out most of it.

"Do you want an appetizer?" Muhammed asked.

"If you have one."

"Spring rolls?"

Steve nodded.

"Very good."

A skinny, earnest-looking little Chinese girl, maybe ten years old, walked out of the kitchen with a school textbook and notebook under one arm. She had long hair and was wearing a mauve t-shirt and jeans. "Hilde!" said Muhammed.

Her face breaking into a grin, she came over to the table and gave Muhammed a hug with her free arm. He asked her, in German, how school was going. She answered in what sounded to Steve, anyway, like perfect German, telling Muhammed that she loved history and science. Indicating her books, he said that it looked as if she had a lot of work to do. She nodded solemnly and explained that she had to go over to another table and do her homework. He told her to go ahead. She walked to a table for two beside the kitchen door, sat down, opened the textbook, and began reading, the look on her face as serious as that of a Talmudic scholar.

"You see," Muhammed said to Steve, watching the little girl with admiration, "the problem isn't immigration."

"Her name is Hilde? A German name?"

"Yes. They come from one of the great ancient

cultures of the world. But they want her to grow up as a part of this society. Can you hear how perfectly she speaks German?"

"Yes."

"Her grandmother works here too. She can just barely string together a few menu words in German. She brought Chen here when he was a teenager – his German is just fine. But Hilde's is perfect. She can speak Chinese too, but they speak to her almost entirely in German. Even the grandmother tries her best to do that."

"That's nice."

"Yes, that's the way to do it."

Chen came out of the kitchen with the bottle of wine and a bucket of ice. He set down the bucket, showed Muhammed the label, then took a corkscrew out of an apron pocket and opened the bottle. He poured a bit of wine into Muhammed's glass. Muhammed tasted it and nodded with a smile. Chen filled both of their glasses and put the bottle in the bucket, then wrapped a white cloth towel around it. *"Würden Sie bestellen?"* he asked.

Muhammed turned to Steve. "Are you ready?" Steve nodded. Muhammed told Chen that they would both have the *Frühlingsrollen*. Chen then looked at Steve. *"Hühnerbrustfilet mit Gemüse und Cashewnüssen, bitte,"* Steve said, closing his menu. Chen looked at Muhammed. *"Schweinefleisch süß sauer für mich,"* he said.

Chen nodded, smiled, took their menus, and headed back toward the kitchen. Just before reaching the door, he stopped and said something in German to Hilde,

302

who'd been writing diligently in her notebook. His voice was gentle. She looked up at him, smiled, and nodded.

Chen went into the kitchen. Hilde returned to her homework.

"*Schweinefleisch*," Steve said.

"What's that?" Muhammed asked.

"You eat pork."

"And I drink wine, too," he said, lifting his glass. "*Prost!*"

"*Prost!*"

They sipped their wine.

"Does your family know you eat pork?"

"They know I suck dick. Next to that, eating pork is nothing."

"It's a shame you have to be estranged from them."

"Better estranged than dead," Muhammed said briskly.

They had some more wine. Steve looked over at Hilde. She caught him looking at her and gave him a big smile. He smiled back. She returned to her work.

Steve put down his wineglass. "Would you prefer not to talk about them?" he asked Muhammed.

"Oh, I don't mind. What do you want to know? My father and his brothers own a successful trading company based in Istanbul, with offices in Berlin, Frankfurt, and Hamburg. That's why I chose Munich – they haven't expanded here. Not yet, anyway. Aside from me, every male member of the family works for the company – my father, uncles, brothers, cousins. A hundred-headed creature. My father and uncles are smart cookies, my father especially. In fact, I think it's fair to call him a business genius, a line in which I have no talent whatsoever. In any event, they had a long-term plan. They wanted to live in the West, raise and educate their kids in the West, enjoy all the advantages of the West. But at the same time they didn't want their kids to become Westernized. It's totally irrational thinking, of course. You might almost say schizophrenic, if you wanted to throw around psychiatric terms a bit too loosely. But it's perfectly typical of many Muslims who move to the West."

Chen came out with two small plates. On each of them were two spring rolls. He set them down on the table with a smile, then left.

"*Bon appétit,*" said Muhammed.

"*Bon appétit.*" The spring roll was very tasty, with a nice crunchy coating and a rich burst of flavor from inside.

"Think of it," Muhammed said after a swallow. "My parents sent me to universities where I read Freud and Jung, where I learned everything about genome sequencing and the theory of special relativity and so on. And yet they expected me to keep believing that the Earth was flat, that it was the center of the universe, that Allah had dictated the Koran personally to the Prophet, and that a woman should be punished by death for being raped.

Insane! And when the time came, they wanted me to marry a cousin of mine from our ancestral village. I'd never met her before. All I knew was that she was ugly – I'm sorry, but it's true – and illiterate. I mean, literally illiterate. And she was no more interested in marrying me than I was in marrying her. She was thick as a brick, but she was smart enough to tell at first glance that I wasn't into the ladies."

"So what happened to her?"

"Oh, she's doing fine. She married my brother."

"Do they love each other?"

Muhammed drank some wine. "Did Watson love Crick? Did Rodgers love Hammerstein? Did Mozart love Schikaneder? It's an arrangement. They both understand and accept it. It's a game. Play by the rules, or you're out. In her case, saying no would probably mean signing her own death warrant. Besides, Islam doesn't want men and women to love each other all that much. You're supposed to reserve your greatest love for Allah. Love meaning fear, of course. And submission. Islam isn't big on real love. Human love."

"That's quite an indictment."

"But the sexual impulse is something else again. Islam recognizes it as natural – for men, that is. Men aren't expected or required to be able to control their own libidos. That's why they're allowed multiple wives. A woman can't say no if her husband wants sex – and if she does say no, her husband can rape her. A woman has to sequester herself at home, and cover herself in public, to avoid tempting men – but if a man gets tempted anyway, it's still her fault. And she can pay for his horniness with her life."

"You can tell the whole thing was invented by a man."

"Exactly. A straight man. With one hell of a sex drive. Islam all but regards a man's sexual impulses as sacred – and a woman's as evil. It's why they're given clitoridectomies when they're little girls." Steve looked over at Hilde, busy doing her homework.

Chen came out with their entrees and set them down on the table. He asked them how they'd liked the spring rolls. Muhammed assured him that they were excellent. Chen smiled and took the appetizer plates back to the kitchen.

"Looks good," Steve said.

"Everything's good here." They dug in.

Across the room, little Hilda scribbled away in her notebook.

A N HOUR LATER, STEVE AND MUHAMMED were back in Muhammed's apartment sipping cognac. "So have you read all those books?" Steve asked, nodding toward the shelves.

"Yes."

"Including every Shakespeare play?"

Muhammed nodded. "And every sonnet."

"My favorite is 151."

"That's a relatively obscure one."

"'Love is too young to know what conscience is.'"

"'Yet who knows not conscience is born of love?'"

Steve smiled. "I'm impressed."

"Don't be. I read them and they lodge themselves in my mind. It just happens."

"So what's in the file cabinet?"

"Patient files. On CD. And tapes of sessions."

"You mean audio tapes?"

"Yes. I put everything on tape. I've got a great little pocket tape recorder. I carry it everywhere."

Suddenly Joop's phone rang. "Excuse me," Steve said as he took it out of his pocket. "Hello?"

"He's not here."

"You're at April?"

"Yes. And he's not here. But I asked one of the bartenders. He pointed out a couple of friends of Mr. Hoop Earring. I went over to them and asked about him. I said I'd met him last week and that we'd agreed to meet again here tonight. They said – guess what?"

"What?"

"He's with Schrama. At the family castle. He and Schrama are apparently an item."

"Oh well, no surprise there. Did they say where the castle is?"

"They only know that it's somewhere in Bavaria."

"Bavaria is pretty big."

"One of them said he thinks he remembers Mr. Hoop Earring saying it's on the Isar. But he wasn't sure."

"By the way, what's Mr. Hoop Earring's name?"

"I thought you'd never ask. Wouter. Wouter Meijers."

"I have an idea."

"Forget it. I've already called information for his number. And I tried it. No answer. It's his home phone. They didn't have a cellphone listing for him."

"Shit."

"I also asked Wouter's friends where he's from. They said he's from Groningen. Not the city, the province. Some little town. They didn't know which one. I thought maybe if I could track his family down, they'd know how to reach him. But Meijers is a very common name, as you know. There must be hundreds of them in Groningen."

"What do we do now?"

"I don't know."

"Let me think. Let's talk later."

"Okay."

Steve hung up and returned the phone to his pants pocket. "Nothing?" Muhammed asked.

Steve explained about Schrama and Wouter – and the castle. Muhammed listened intently, staring into Steve's eyes, holding his cognac glass in both hands. When Steve had finished filling him in, Muhammed held his pose, thinking.

Finally Muhammed said, softly but clearly, "I have a patient."

"Yes?"

"He's rich. He lives here in Munich, of course. But like Schrama, he also has an old family castle. On the Isar."

"Really?"

"These people all know each other, don't they?" Muhammed said. "The old-family-castle set?"

"I don't know. I don't move in those circles myself. But I wouldn't be surprised."

"My turn to make a call." Muhammed took out his cell phone, scrolled through a list of numbers, clicked on one, and held the phone to his ear. He waited. His face fell. "No answer," he said, lowering the phone and clicking to cancel the call.

"Is that his home number? His number in Munich?"

"Yes. It's the only one I have for him."

"No cell phone?"

"Afraid not. He's seventy-something years old."

"And you don't have a number for the castle?"

"No," he said, shaking his head, staring down at his glass. "And it's not listed, either." Then Muhammed looked up at him. "But."

"But?"

"But I know where the castle is."

"Really?"

"Yes."

"May I ask how you know?"

"I would never violate doctor-patient confidentiality," Muhammed said. "But I will say that most people dream frequently about the houses they grew up in. And when they see their psychiatrists, they tell them about those dreams. And about the houses."

I T WAS AFTER NINE, AND THE AUTOBAHN was almost empty. Muhammed drove very fast and with perfect confidence. Steve couldn't help but be reminded of that cross-country trip with Daniel, all those years ago. The image of Daniel at the wheel, cocky, carefree, as seen from the shotgun seat, was burned in his mind forever.

"How does it feel to have killed?" Muhammed asked.

"To have killed?"

"Yes."

"Unreal."

"Mmm."

"Literally."

"Meaning what?"

"Meaning that I can remember doing it but..."

"Yes?"

"Somehow it doesn't seem real."

"Tell me about that."

"Those moments in the apartment on Bellamyplein. Those moments with Fabien. At the end. When I – "

"Yes?"

"When I killed him."

"Yes?"

"They're like things I saw in a movie."

"The mind is a remarkable thing."

"You can say that again."

"There's a reason why it feels unreal. It's for your own good. It's there to protect you."

"You don't need to tell me that. I know. I took Psych 101. I got a C, but still."

"I know you know. But a big part of my job is telling people things they already know. It *can* help."

"I'm sure you're right."

"I am."

Silence.

"One thing," Muhammed said.

"Yes?"

"You're doing terrifically."

"Thank you."

"But you're going to need to go through some serious therapy."

"Yes, if I make it through this alive. But one thing."

"Yes?"

"I've been telling you all about me. Can we talk about you?"

"Me? We've talked about me. I told you all about my family, my – "

"Not your family. You. What kind of personal life do you have?"

"Personal life? Me?"

"Yes. Do you have a rich and varied sexual life? Or is there one special person? Or are you one of these psychiatrists who do a wonderful job of fixing everybody else up, and then go home and watch TV alone until you fall asleep?"

"Not TV. I read."

"But you're all alone?"

"Yes."

"And you don't – well – you don't run out to the bars on the weekend and pick up guys?"

"No."

"Never?"

"Never."

"How can that be?"

"Now you're being the psychiatrist."

"But you're gay. What does it mean to be gay if you can't be with somebody? Whether it's the same person all the time or a different person every Saturday night? Don't you feel terribly alone?"

"I'm just fine."

"Is that why you became a psychiatrist? So you could interrogate other people, instead of letting them interrogate you?"

Muhammed smiled. "You're not as dumb as you look."

"But don't you want to be with someone? Don't you need it?"

"Yes, I do. But being a gay person from my background isn't the easiest fate. At this point in my life, I'm happy to be getting through my day and maybe helping other people get through theirs. My hope is that in time I'll be able to do more than that. But I need to give myself time."

"Time to do what?"

Silence. Then: "Time to dispel the rage and be able to love. To truly love."

"The rage?"

"The rage over everything I've told you about. Everything I grew up with. Everything that was imprinted on me, instilled in me, and that I've fought every moment of my life to expunge. Is that the right word, expunge?"

"It's a good word."

"To eradicate. To stamp out."

"But haven't you already gotten rid of it all?"

"Intellectually, yes. But it's still in there. And I fight against it constantly. The forced marriages. The honor killings. The disgusting anti-Semitism. And homophobia. And hatred for nonbelievers. It's all in me, like a poison. And yet these fools, these sociologists and anthropologists, these know-nothings like Henriette Becker – you know, that woman at Tübingen – they all claim that none of this has anything to do with Islam. All I can say is, read the damn book. Read the Koran. It's one long series of directives to kill – kill the Jews, kill the infidels, kill your mother or wife or sister or daughter for some objectively trivial action that the damn book tells you to regard as a capital offense. Kill, kill, kill. Orders to kill. Instructions on how to kill. Plus one assurance after another to the faithful that *they'll* end up in some cartoon heaven and that non-Muslims will spend eternity in a cartoon hell. Which the damn book describes, over and over again, with disgusting, pornographic glee."

They drove on in silence for a minute or two. Steve studied Muhammed's face. He was good-looking enough, but his intelligence and rectitude made him positively beautiful.

"But what about the Bible?" Steve said

"What about it?"

"There's some ugly stuff in there too, isn't there?"

"Oh, most assuredly. I've read it. But compared to the Koran, the Bible is amateur night. Besides, there's not a single Jew today who lives by, or thinks he *should* live by, every directive in the Old Testament. Even the most orthodox Jews have set the really nasty stuff aside. As for Christians, the message of love in the gospel is supposed to trump all the ugly injunctions in both testaments."

"It doesn't always work that way in practice, though."

"No, it doesn't. But even the very, very worst of Christians, for example the ones who belong to that famous little hate church in Nebraska, don't kill in the name of Jesus or call for killing in the name of Jesus. They say all kinds of incredibly monstrous things, but they don't kill."

"True."

"You know what's interesting about the Koran?"

"No, what?"

"It works the same way the Bible does – you

314

know, the gospel message trumping everything else. But with the Koran it works *the opposite way.*"

"What do you mean?"

"What I mean is that, yes, as Muslim apologists are always saying, there *are* positive statements in the Koran about loving one another and being kind to infidels. But these are that things Muhammed wrote when he was young, and according to every theologian, every Koranic scholar, who's taken seriously in the Muslim world, these passages are all trumped – the word the scholars use is abrogated – by passages that were written later. And that are uniformly wicked."

"I see."

"But if you want to understand Islam, reading and understanding the Koran is only step one."

"Step two?"

"Islamic history. Just look at it. Christianity was spread mostly by conversion. Islam was spread almost entirely through jihadist conquest. Oh, here's our turnoff. Let me concentrate on the road."

"Sure."

A sign read *St2085*. Steve saw an overpass up ahead. An exit lane materialized, and Muhammed moved into it, decelerating. At the crossroads they stopped. There were no other cars in sight. Muhammed took a left. For a couple of minutes they drove through farmlands. Then the road they were on ended at an intersection with another road marked *Erdinger Straße*. They made a right turn onto it, and after another couple of minutes it ended at yet another intersection. There were houses around them, lights. Muhammed turned left.

"I'm amazed you know your way around so well," Steve said.

"I've never been up here before. I just studied the map. The route is very straightforward." They clattered across a bridge. "Well, there it is," Muhammed said.

"What?"

"The Isar."

Suddenly they were in a city, or at least a town. "What's this?"

"Moosburg."

"Never heard of it." They passed a park, drove through a square. The city could not have been quieter. *"Dear God! the very houses seem asleep,"* Steve said.

"Good old Wordsworth," Muhammed said. He made one turn, then another almost immediately, then yet another. He never hesitated for an instant.

"It's hard to believe you've never been here before," Steve said.

"Memorizing a route on a map is nothing compared to getting through med school," Muhammed said.

They drove through the town, making turn after turn. It looked like a pleasant little place. Finally they found ourselves on a road marked St2085, which took them across the Amper, a tributary of the Isar. Back to farmland. After a few minutes Muhammed turned onto another road. "Almost there," he said.

"Is there a step three?" Steve asked.

"Step three? What do you mean?"

"Step one, the Koran. Step two, Islamic history."

"Oh yes. How could I have forgotten? Step three: the Enlightenment. The West experienced the Enlightenment. Christians learned to live and let live – well, at least they got better at it than before. They embraced secular government, the separation of church and state. They accepted the validity of the scientific method. They stopped viewing the Bible as the literal word of God and started reading it metaphorically, while simply ignoring the meanest and stupidest parts. Muslims still haven't done any of that with the Koran."

"But there *are* Biblical literalists. Fundamentalists."

"They call themselves literalists, but they aren't really. Not a hundred percent. If they were, they'd be – well, for one thing, they'd be killing every gay person who crosses their path."

There was a car about fifty yards ahead of them. Muhammed moved into the passing lane and zipped by it.

"Hmm," Muhammed said.

"What?"

"Let me correct myself there." He moved back into the right lane. "Millions of Muslims actually *have* put aside the meanest and stupidest parts of the Koran, in the privacy of their hearts and the privacy of their homes.

Otherwise they wouldn't be good people. They'd be monsters. But almost none of them dare to admit this in public. Because they know that if they were to talk about putting the Koran in perspective, about setting certain parts of it aside, about believing that even a single word of it wasn't divinely dictated, they'd be accused at once of deserting the faith, and they know very well that the penalty for that is death. About that fact, there's no ambiguity whatsoever. Every Islamic scholar agrees: anybody who walks away from Islam is condemned to death. And here we are."

"What?"

"We're here."

A crossroads, a cluster of houses. Muhammed made a right turn off the main road onto a narrow local road, not even two lanes wide. On both sides there was nothing but tall trees.

"Are you sure this is it?"

"At this moment, it's pretty much the only thing I *am* sure of," Muhammed said.

"What do you mean?"

"I mean that all this international cloak-and-dagger stuff is definitely out of my comfort zone. And I have a pretty good-sized comfort zone, if I say so myself. You've been at this for – how long?"

"Three days."

"Exactly. I've only been at it for a few hours. Compared to me, you're an old hand at this. A regular George Smiley. And I'm a greenhorn."

Steve grinned. "You could've fooled me. You seem unflappable."

"Doctors learn to seem unflappable. Psychiatrists especially. If our patients had any idea what we were thinking, they'd burst out of the room and never stop running."

Suddenly the trees fell away and the road opened up into a courtyard. The car crunched over what sounded like gravel. Ahead of them, illuminated only by the car's headlights, was a large white house. It wasn't beautiful, but it had a grandeur about it. There was a porte-cochère; Muhammed drove right up into it and parked. He turned off the ignition, and the car's inside lights and headlights went dark. They both turned to look at each other, but could hardly see anything. "Well," Muhammed said, "this is it. Either he can help us or he can't."

"Or he throws us out for waking him up at – what is it? Midnight?"

"Don't worry, he won't do that."

They got out of the car and walked up to the massive door. The only source of light, aside from the stars and moon, was the illuminated white bell button. Muhammed pushed it. There was the faint, shrill noise of a buzzer somewhere inside the house. They waited, and listened. After what felt like a full minute Steve heard a cough. He looked at Muhammed. He could barely make out Muhammed's silhouette.

"I'd know that cough anywhere," Muhammed said softly.

Suddenly there was light through the windows. Then footsteps, and the sound of heavy old locks in motion. The door creaked open, and they were face to face with a tall, corpulent senior citizen in an elegant but tattered silk maroon robe. He looked at Steve blankly, then turned to Muhammed, looking utterly baffled.

"*Doktor!*" he said, his voice as gravelly as his courtyard but far from grave. "*Habe Ich eine Verabredung nicht einhalten?*" Steve smiled. The man of the house had asked, jocularly, if he'd missed an appointment. Behind him Steve could see a crimson-carpeted staircase, a glowing chandelier, ornately framed portraits on the walls.

Muhammed laughed, then replied. Steve was able to make out the German well enough to understand that Muhammed was apologizing their late-hour disturbance and saying that they needed help with an urgent matter. Only then did Muhammed introduce Steve and his patient to each other. The man's name was Axel von Holzer. He gave Steve a slow, aristocratic nod and held out his hand. Steve shook it. Von Holzer's grip was surprisingly strong. He told Muhammed that of course he'd be glad to help in any way he could.

"All I need to know is this," Muhammed told him in German. "Do you know the Dutch politician Jeroen Schrama?"

"Yes, I do. He is a neighbor of mine."

"Is that so? Where is his *Schloss?*"

"It is only a short distance from here. I can draw you a map. Is he having a psychiatric emergency?"

WHILE MUHAMMED NAVIGATED THE CAR back up the tree-lined road, Steve called Joop and gave him a quick update. Hanging up, Steve turned to von Holzer's map. They were approaching the highway. "Okay, make a right here," he said. Muhammed did.

A few minutes passed. "Another right here," Steve said as a crossroads loomed ahead. Muhammed took the turn. The road curved past farms and farmhouses, crossed over the Autobahn, and passed through a village identified by a sign as Münchnerau. "One more right," Steve said.

"Here?"

"Yes."

It was another narrow road, leading back down to the river through farmland and then through trees.

"Are you nervous?" Muhammed asked.

"I've been nervous for a week," Steve replied. "Are you?"

"Hard to say. Adrenaline is an amazing thing."

"That's for sure. You know, maybe you shouldn't have told Axel my real name."

"Don't worry. He hasn't followed current events since Adenauer."

This time there was no spacious clearing. The road curved and suddenly the *Schloss* was right in front of them, surrounded by trees, their leaves brushing up against its upstairs windows. The house was exceedingly elegant – yellow with brown shutters and flower boxes outside every window. It was big, but not imposingly or intimidatingly so; in fact, despite its considerable size, it looked charming, homey – exactly the sort of place one would expect a tasteful, intelligent, and very rich gay man to live in. And the lights were on; in fact, it looked as if every light in the house was on. The house shone like a Christmas tree.

Muhammed pulled up to the front door. "Here we go again," he said as he turned off the ignition. They got out of the car, walked up to the door. "This time it's your turn to ring the bell," Muhammed said.

"Okay, but where is it?"

"I don't know. I don't see one either."

"I guess I should knock then."

"Yes. Knock."

Steve was about to knock when they heard footsteps inside.

"I guess they heard the car," Steve said.

The footsteps grew closer. The door opened. The person standing there wasn't Jeroen Schrama, and it wasn't Wouter either.

"How's tricks?" he asked, his tone supremely nonchalant. He was wearing a gray suit not unlike Cary Grant's in *North by Northwest*, and it looked just as spiffy on him as it did on Grant. Except for a sophisticated touch of gray at the temples, he looked as if he'd barely aged a day since college.

Steve was so stunned that he could barely get out his name. "Daniel," he said.

IX

D ANIEL WAVED THEM INTO THE VESTIBULE and shut the door. "This way," he said, leading them through a grand archway into a large, high-ceilinged room.

The first thing Steve noticed was the gleaming white marble floor; the second thing he noticed was the ceiling. It was covered with a breathtaking painting. Nudes. Birds and animals. Grass and water. And a myriad of otherworldly structures that vaguely, and variously, resembled a tepee, a Victorian lamp, a fairytale castle, a giant bubble.

"Bosch," Muhammed said.

"Only all-male."

"Heavens."

Indeed, it was an expertly executed variation on the central panel of the Hieronymus Bosch triptych *The Garden of Earthly Delights,* except that the naked people were all men – some of them standing alone, some splashing about delightedly in a pond, some frolicking with animals, others socializing pleasantly in pairs or groups. It hovered on the edge of the sensual, the erotic, but radiated a kind of innocence and peace. Steve had never seen anything quite like it.

His first thought was that it reminded him of the thermal baths. Dreams of paradise, he found himself thinking, never die.

Steve looked away from the ceiling to take in the

rest of the room. Along the walls were two elegant old glass-doored bookcases filled with thick, morocco-bound volumes; shelves crowded with blue-and-white Delft plates, dishes, and vases; and paintings by – if he wasn't mistaken – Vermeer, Frans Hals, and other seventeenth-century masters.

"My God, it's like the Rijksmuseum in here," Steve said.

"Do you think these are originals?" Muhammed asked.

"I strongly suspect they are," Steve said. "I don't think Schrama would settle for mere copies."

He looked through an archway that led into a formal dining room. On its walls were modern artworks: a Mondriaan, a DeKooning, others that Steve couldn't identify. From the dining room, a half-open doorway led into what appeared to be a kitchen.

"Have a seat," Daniel said.

The room contained several chairs and a couple of sofas, all of them upholstered in deep red or maroon. Daniel lowered himself into what looked like a Louis XIV chair. Steve and Muhammed sat facing him on a chaise longue next to a bar cart stocked with sparkling clear glasses and twenty or so bottles of mixers and hard liquor.

"Long time no see," Daniel said.

"You're looking good."

"Thank you."

Daniel didn't say whether Steve looked good or

not. Steve supposed that after the week he'd just been through, he didn't exactly look his best.

"Okay," Steve said. "Where's Jeroen Schrama?"

"I don't know. He was gone when I got here."

"No, he wasn't."

"Okay, so he wasn't."

"You didn't come here to protect him. You came here to intercept me. You probably parked somewhere out on the main road, and waited for him to drive off, and then you came here and broke in."

"Guilty. I knew you'd come here. After all, you've more or less run out of Muslims to shoot."

"Why are you talking to me this way?"

"Because your concern for others seems very selective. You're all worked up about Jeroen Schrama, but do you even care about the men you killed in Amsterdam? Or the young man you killed last night? Or the one you shot today?"

"You mean the jihadist fanatics who were fully prepared to kill me?"

"Yes. I'll have you know that the one you shot today is in the hospital."

"I wish he were in the morgue."

"Luckily for you, he's apparently going to be fine. Which just goes to show that you're not much of a shot."

"His body was pressed up against mine. I pulled out the gun and fired. I kept myself from being killed. I think that makes me a good enough shot under the circumstances. As for the guys in Amsterdam, I think they'd testify that I'm a pretty good shot, for an amateur. If, that is, they were alive to testify."

"You might want to know that your face is all over the news here today."

"Quelle surprise."

"You're not exactly Mr. Popularity. Germans aren't accustomed to having people at their universities being shot at. Bored to death, maybe. But not shot at."

"It's okay. I'm getting used to having whole countries angry at me. At this point I care more about staying alive than about winning popularity contests."

"So," interrupted Muhammed, who was looking directly at Daniel. "Why are you here?"

"I'm sorry, we haven't met."

"My name is Muhammed."

"I'm Daniel," said Daniel. "We're here – "

"We?" Steve said.

"Surely you don't think I'm alone? One of my colleagues is just outside the kitchen door, and the other, by now, should be right outside the front door. Anyway, Muhammed, in answer to your question, I'm here to take our friend back to Amsterdam. First of all, however," he said, looking at Steve. "I'm here to confiscate your weapon. I assume you're carrying."

"No thanks, I'll hang on to it for now."

"Well, just so you know, I have a gun too. As do my colleagues. And the difference between you and us is that we actually know how to use them."

"That's nice. Makes me feel good and safe."

Steve stared into Daniel's eyes, then looked at Muhammed.

"Did you notice?" Steve asked him.

"What?" Muhammed said.

"His eyes and mine. They're exactly the same color."

"Jesus Christ," Daniel said. "How pathetic. After all these years, you're still in love with me."

"And you're still in love with me, too."

"I was never in love with you."

"Bullshit. The only problem was that you were even more in love with the idea of being perceived as normal."

"Put it this way. I've made different decisions about my life than you did, because I always understood the world. And you didn't."

"What's that supposed to mean?"

"It means that you're still as naive as you were in college. You've made a great career for yourself – congratulations – but you never figured out just how serious the world is until a week ago."

"Ridiculous."

"I grew up being told every day of my childhood about the reality of Communism, in every last horrible detail. What it had done to my family back in Russia. How my parents had to flee like mice from the Soviets. How my

327

father, a respected scholar, was reduced to a beggar. I was more grown up at the age of ten than you are now."

"Horseshit. You know damn well that I always hated Communism as much as you did."

"Not enough to get your priorities straight. Yes, I could've decided to live an openly gay life, as you did. But if I'd done so I wouldn't have been able to do all the things I've done for the cause of freedom. Things about which you have absolutely no idea."

"I'm sure you've done very important work."

"Damn right I have. Within weeks after the Berlin Wall fell, I was flying back and forth between Budapest and Bucharest and Warsaw and Prague and Sofia, helping politicians and business people make the transition to democracy and capitalism. I was right there in the middle of all that while you were in L.A. writing crap for Disney and blowing guys you picked up in West Hollywood."

"Well, you *have* kept up with my career."

"People all over Eastern Europe respect me like you wouldn't believe. If I were openly gay, many of them wouldn't even give me the time of day. Some of them would probably want to beat me to death with a lead pipe."

"Nice people you've been helping."

"Everything isn't black and white. It's not a world of perfect good versus perfect evil. That's precisely what you don't get."

"Of course I get that," Steve said. "And I've never put down what you've done. But let's get one thing straight. I've done my part for the cause of freedom too. Freedom for gay people. Freedom for them to pursue happiness, freedom for them to live their lives without being tormented and harassed, freedom for them to be true to who they are."

"And he's made a difference too," added Muhammed.

"What are you two, a tag team?" Daniel sneered.

"I'm one of the many people in whose life he has made a remarkable difference," Muhammed said. "I don't know you, but I know that thanks to him, and people like him, things have changed so much for gay people in the Western world that I suspect you might have made a different decision about your life if you were starting your career now, in the world he's helped change, than you made twenty years ago, when he and you were students together."

"I'm sorry," Daniel said, "but the world is about a lot more than just gay rights. It's about freedom."

"And how is gay rights *not* about freedom?" Steve asked. "Only for people like your dad is freedom such a beautiful word and gay rights such an ugly one."

"Shut up about my dad."

"You think of him as this big anti-Communist hero. And, yes, he was a fierce enemy of the Soviets – which is understandable, given everything they took from him, stealing his ancestral home and robbing him of his privilege and all that. But has he ever really been all that crazy about freedom? Real freedom? It doesn't look like it to me."

"What do you know about it?"

"I know this much. I met him, and I've actually read some of what he's written. And what I see is a man who for all his fulminating against Communism is really fond of severe authority of the good old-fashioned pre-Soviet type. He loves the Czars. He loves the Popes, the ones who were Popes back when Popes had armies. I remember your telling me that he was in Vilnius or Riga or someplace like that during the Nazi occupation. How did he feel about them? The Nazis, I mean. I haven't run across anything in his writings about them."

Daniel leapt up out of his chair, his eyes blazing with fury. "Don't you dare talk about my father like that!" He hovered over Steve threateningly.

"I'll talk about your father," Steve said, looking up into Daniel's eyes. "Your father fucked you up. You want to talk about freedom? He singlehandedly kept you from ever being really free."

"You motherfucker. You see everything through your fucking gay prism."

"No, you're the one who seems to be doing that. I'm not just talking about your being gay. I'm talking about your being your own person. In college you let me see glimpses of the man you might have been if you hadn't been entirely under your father's thumb. But even then you were already doing your best to quash your real self so you could be, or to seem to be, exactly what he wanted you to be. And yes, that does include your being honest with yourself about being gay."

"Everything's not about sex."

"Okay, go ahead and tell yourself that this is all about being gay – and that being gay is all about sex. Whatever you have to do to get through the day. To maintain the charade. To keep the mask from falling off. But somewhere deep down inside, you know better."

"Blow jobs. Hand jobs."

"Personal integrity. Wholeness. Love."

Daniel snorted contemptuously. "Love! What part has love played in *your* life all these years?"

"Okay," Steve said. "You've got me there. I've avoided love. But I've known what love is. I remember." He stood up. Their eyes were inches apart. "I remember what you and I had, all those years ago."

"Fuck you. We never touched each other."

"Exactly. Nothing remotely sexual ever happened between us. But we were helplessly in love with each other. You know that, whether you're willing to admit it or not, even to yourself."

"Okay, fine. You want me to say it? I'll say it." Daniel turned away from him, walked across the room. Steve looked at Muhammed. His eyes met Steve's. Plainly, he hadn't counted on all this. "Yes, I loved you," Daniel said, his back to Steve. "But that was a long time ago. And I was very young. Now I'm a man. I've put childish things behind me."

"Yeah, that's a good idea. Quote Saint Paul. Terrific. Your father really did a number on you."

Daniel turned around. "I'm a man," he repeated in a louder voice. "I have a wife and a daughter. And I can't imagine my life without them. And I've never regretted for a second having made the choice I made."

"I'm not asking you to reget or apologize for the choice you made. I just want to hear you speak the truth."

"The truth! You know what, that's exactly it. That's exactly what makes you so childish. Truth! You sound like a four-year-old. Let me explain something to you: living in the adult world isn't about telling everybody the truth about everything. It's about looking around you and understanding what kind of world you're living in and figuring out the best way you can make a positive difference in it. We live in a world dripping with evil, and life is about siding with whoever or whatever is the least evil, and fighting for it, and, yes, even lying for it. Because the people on the other side, the really evil people, the tyrants, lie about absolutely everything, and there's no way you can beat them without lying through your teeth yourself. So when you're in there fighting, really fighting, you have to put the truth aside. You just have to. And I'm not saying it's easy. It takes an amazing amount of strength. Sometimes you can hardly remember yourself what's true and what isn't, what's right and what's wrong, and why you're doing what you're doing – why this, why now, why here. But you hang in there and you fight with everything you have to do the right thing." He paused and looked into Steve's eyes. "But you wouldn't know that. Because it all looks so easy when you're just sitting there alone in your room putting words on paper."

"Excuse me," Muhammed interjected, looking at Daniel. His voice was soft, his tone polite. "If you're such an expert on fighting evil, why can't you see the evil in Islam?"

"Islam? You mean all of Islam? You're talking about a religion of one point – "

"Yes, one point five billion people," Muhammed said. "Or point six. Or whatever. So what? Why are people always citing that figure as if it proved anything? An evil ideology is an evil ideology. During the Cold War, well over a billion people in the Soviet Union, Eastern Europe, China, Mongolia, Cuba, North Korea, and North Vietnam were nominally Communists. How many of them really were Communists, deep in their hearts? And how many were prisoners of tyranny, like members of your own family in Russia, I'm sure, who played along with the system to avoid the Gulag or firing squad? It's the same with Islam. One point five billion people live under its yoke. That doesn't mean that all of them support jihad and the sharia – although my own experience suggests that fully a third or a half of them actually do. In any event, that number alone, one point five billion, scarcely makes Islam virtuous. Because what we're talking about, when you come down to it, isn't the one point five billion people. What we're talking about is the contents of a single book that you can read in a few hours. Islam is that book, and that book is Islam. Period. And no person could ever come away from reading it and say honestly that the message of the Koran is in any way benign."

"Benign or not," Daniel said, "what do you expect us to do? Make war on a religion? A religion that counts some of our major strategic allies among its adherents?"

"You mean allies like Saudi Arabia? Which executes gays and apostates, and funds madrasses and mosques all over the Western world that serve as jihadist training camps? You've called our friend here naive – what could be more naive than your attitude toward Islamic jihad? How can you talk about not wanting to make war on a religion when that religion is already making war on you?"

"Listen, Muhammed," Daniel said. "I don't know what personal frustrations have entered into your geopolitical analysis, but the fact is that Islamic terrorists – such as those guys whom our friend here bumped off in Amsterdam – have hijacked Islam."

"No, they haven't," Muhammed said. "I know that's the official line of every foreign ministry in the Western world, but it's either an expression of ignorance or an outright lie. The terrorists are doing exactly what the Koran tells them to do."

"Look – "

"Let me ask you: have you ever read the Koran? All the way through?"

"No, but I – "

"All right, that's all I need to know. Because

countless Muslims *have* read it. Every word. Many of them know the whole thing by heart. And that, aside from fear, is the main reason why so few of them dare to stand up to Islamic terrorism. Because they know that in the eyes of the religion in which they were brought up, in the eyes of the book that they were taught from the cradle to regard as the word of God, these monsters who kill in cold blood are the very best Muslims of all. And that very fact, my friend, is what makes Islam the epitome of evil."

For a moment, Daniel seemed incapable of a snappy response. Shaking his head, he walked back over to Steve and Muhammed. He looked uncomfortable, pained.

"Look," he said, his voice somehow more human than before, "I take your point. But I didn't come here for a debate. I came here to pick you up – " He pointed at Steve – "and put *you* in a car back to Amsterdam."

"Can't we even have a drink first?" Muhammed asked, nodding at the drinks cart.

To Steve's surprise, Daniel didn't dismiss the suggestion. "Have a drink if you want a drink," he said, the stridency gone from his voice.

Muhammed stood up, went to the cart. "Well, I'm having some Scotch. What about you two?"

"That sounds fine," Daniel said. He was looking down at the floor, apparently lost in thought.

"Me too," Steve said.

"Okay, sit down," said Muhammed. "Both of you." Steve and Daniel obeyed.

335

Muhammed set out three whiskey glasses, picked up a half-filled bottle of Glenlivet, and started pouring drinks.

"How old is your daughter?" Muhammed asked Daniel.

"What?"

"Your daughter. You mentioned that you have a daughter."

Daniel looked up at him. "Eight."

"What's her name?"

"Nora."

"That's a beautiful name," Muhammed said. He handed Steve and Daniel their drinks, then picked up his own.

"You think so?" Daniel asked.

"Oh yes." Muhammed sat down beside Steve again.

"Yes, it's a beautiful name," Steve said.

"It's the name of the heroine of *A Doll's House*," Muhammed said. "Are you familiar with the play?"

"Vaguely," Daniel said. "Not really. That's not why we picked the name."

"Cheers," Muhammed said, raising his glass.

"Cheers," Steve said. Daniel gulped some of his Scotch.

"In *A Doll's House*," Muhammed said, "Nora tells her husband that when she was young and living in her father's home, he told her his opinions about everything, and so she had the same opinions, or so she told him,

336

because she didn't want to make trouble. And then when she married her husband, Torvald, she took on his opinions, or pretended to. She's not even sure which. You get that? She's not even sure whether she really agreed with him or was just pretending. Isn't that something?"

Muhammed looked at Daniel, awaiting a response.

"I guess," Daniel said, looking down into his Scotch.

"Well, today that kind of subservience is pretty much history in the Western world. Thanks in large part to people like Ibsen. But in the Muslim world, it's still the story of ninety-nine out of a hundred families. Women like my mother, my sisters, my aunts and sisters-in-law, still live like that. Except that it's much worse for them than it was for Ibsen's Nora. Most of them couldn't even imagine having as much freedom as Nora had. Because at least Nora was allowed to go outside the house by herself. She could meet her friends without supervision. It would never have occurred to Torvald to beat her if she cooked a bad meal, or if she told him she didn't feel like having sex. Ibsen thought of Nora as a prisoner, and he was right. But compared to the overwhelming majority of women in the Muslim world today, Nora was amazingly free."

There was a silence. Not a comfortable one.

"I take your point," Daniel finally said, still studying his Scotch.

"But?"

"But we can't change the world."

"We being who?"

"America. The West."

"The Free World."

"Yes, the Free World."

"Okay then. We can't change the world. But by the same token we can't let the rest of the world change the Free World in which we live. I know what the Muslim part of the world is – and I know the dreams it lives by. And my one nightmare is to experience that part of the world transforming this part of the world into a copy of itself."

"That's absurd," Daniel said. "It'll never happen."

"Why?"

"Well, for one thing, Muslims are a ridiculously tiny percentage of the population of Europe."

Daniel's glass was almost empty. Muhammed stood up, took it from him, and went to the bar cart to freshen it. "You know," Muhammed said, "too many people who study subjects like history and international studies never take even the most basic courses in math. As a result, they don't realize that a tiny percentage in one generation can turn into a substantial percentage in the next, and a huge percentage in the generation after that. Especially if we're talking about a host population that reproduces at far below the replacement rate, and an immigrant population that reproduces – "

"Now that's just racist," Daniel said.

"I'm talking about my own family," Muhammed said, handing him his drink. "Am I racist against them?"

"You're a self-hating Muslim."

"No, that's exactly what I'm not. I'm what Islam despises and fears most of all. I'm a self-respecting Muslim. Or, rather, ex-Muslim. They tell us to respect the religion. To revere it. To fear it. I choose to respect myself. Can you honestly argue with that?" He looked at Daniel. "Honestly. Would you want Nora to grow up in a Muslim country?"

"Don't bring my daughter into this," Daniel said.

"But she's precisely what this is about," Muhammed said. "This is about Nora. And all the other Noras in America, in Europe, and around the world. As a father, you should care about these things a thousand times more than I do, or than Steve does. Because as a loving father you shouldn't ever want to risk her growing up in a society that views her as a second-class citizen. A society that counts her testimony as being worth only half that of a man. A society that teaches its young men that because she's a nonbeliever who doesn't walk around in a veil, she's fair game – "

"That's enough," said Daniel sharply.

"I'm sorry," Muhammed said. "But it's the truth. I'm sincerely trying to keep you from ever having to experience in your family the same things I've experienced in my own family. Okay?"

"Okay," Daniel said.

"That being said, I need to add that I've never been a father, so I'm sorry if the way in which I talk about these things cuts a little too close to the bone."

Daniel sipped some of his drink. "That's all right," he said.

There was a lull, a silence, that felt almost comfortable, almost relaxed.

"So," Muhammed finally asked Daniel, his tone calm and conversational, "why do you want to take him back to Amsterdam?" He gestured toward Steve.

"Because it's been decided. It's not up to me."

"What do you mean? What's been decided?"

"That if these people are planning to kill Schrama, it's best not to interfere."

"You mean, best not to stop them."

"Yes."

Muhammed looked at Steve. So did Daniel. They sat there in silence for a moment.

"Why not just turn him in to the German police?" Muhammed asked, his voice still low and calm.

Before Daniel could answer, Steve jumped in. "Because," Steve said, "he's worried about the off chance that they'll actually believe me when I tell them about the plot to kill Schrama, and that they'll do something to stop it."

Muhammed looked at Daniel. Daniel shrugged and nodded.

"Well," Muhammed said resignedly, "all I can do is repeat myself. With all due respect, I think you're seriously – and dangerously – misreading the world situation."

Daniel shot a sullen look at him, but when he

spoke his tone was less angry than curious. "Who the hell are you, anyway?"

"Somebody," Muhammed said simply, "who knows more about Islam than you or your colleagues do."

"Also," Steve added, "he's the only person in the room, Doctor Andrus, who's actually a real doctor."

"Good for you," Daniel said to Muhammed, not unkindly. He then pulled a pistol out of his jacket pocket and pointed it at Steve. "Now give me your gun."

Quickly and smoothly, Muhammed pulled Joop's gun out of his pocket and leveled it at Daniel. "No, you give him your gun."

Daniel looked genuinely stunned.

"No," Daniel said.

"Let me break this down for you," Muhammed said in a composed, firm voice. "You're not going to shoot him. And he'd never shoot you. But at this moment, given your willingness to let a group of terrorists assassinate a politician, I'd have no trouble whatsoever putting a bullet in you. Not in your head or your heart, but in your arm or shoulder. So please hand over your gun and spare all three of us any unpleasantness. And don't turn and aim it toward me, because the instant I see you make that move I'll pull the trigger."

"No."

"All right then. Here's something you might want to take into consideration." Muhammed nodded toward Steve. Steve reached into his pocket, took out Muhammed's tape recorder. Steve clicked *stop,* then *rewind,* then *play.* Daniel's voice came out of it, crisp and clear.

" – *decided. It's not up to me.*"

Then Muhammed's voice: *"What's been decided?"*

Then Daniel again: *"That if these people are planning to kill Schrama, it's best – "*

Steve clicked *stop* and put the tape recorder back in his pocket. Meanwhile he studied Daniel's face. Steve had once been able to be able to read Daniel like a book. At this moment, his expression almost looked like one of disappointment.

In Steve.

Daniel felt betrayed.

For a moment, the three of them just sat there in silence. Then Daniel shrugged and handed Steve his gun. Steve pointed it at him. "What a fool you are," Daniel said to Steve in a defeated tone. "I came here to help you. And this is what I get."

"We should tie him up or something, no?" Muhammed said to Steve.

"Remember, there are two other men here with me," Daniel said. "You guys won't make it out the door."

"Yes," Steve said to Muhammed. "Let's tie him up. Why don't you see what you can find in the kitchen?"

"Will do." Muhammed went into the dining room and through to the kitchen. Steve heard him opening and shutting drawers and cabinets. But Steve's eyes didn't leave Daniel. And Daniel's eyes were fixed on him.

Suddenly Daniel leapt at him – sprang at him like a cheetah. He slammed Steve back onto the bar cart, which skidded away, sending bottles and glasses crashing to the marble floor. As Steve hit the floor, on his back, he heard glass shattering, smelled a heady mixture of alcohol – vodka, gin, brandy, sweet liqueurs – and felt his clothes and hair being soaked. Daniel was kneeling on top of him, holding him down by the shoulders, his face a portrait of rage. Steve clutched the gun tightly in his left hand. Muhammed, he realized, had been right; he couldn't bring himself to shoot Daniel. But he could hurt him.

Fortunately, Daniel was just as thin and physically unintimidating as he'd been when they were students together. Resisting his pressure, Steve lifted his left arm and, as hard as he could, smacked Steve in the skull with the gun frame. Daniel's eyes closed, his head slumped, his body fell on Steve's, his cheek touching Steve's lips. Meanwhile Muhammed, hearing the commotion, had come running in. He pulled Daniel off Steve and rolled him onto his back.

"Is he all right?" Steve asked.

Muhammed felt for Daniel's pulse, pried open an eyelid.

"He'll be fine. Are you okay?"

"Sure."

"Good. I'll be right back. I found some duct tape. Don't take any chances. Keep your gun trained on him."

Steve scrambled to his feet and stood there, sticky, soaked, smelling of booze, and looked down at

Daniel. Lying there unconscious, Daniel reminded Steve of all those times when they'd spent a night in the same room, even in the same bed. Invariably Daniel would fall asleep first, after which Steve would lie there awake and study his face. He looked exactly the same now. He looked vulnerable – the very opposite of his waking, arrogant self.

Steve got down on his knees, leant over Daniel's face, and gently kissed his lips.

"Oh my," Muhammed said. He'd come in a roll of duct tape in one hand and Rob's gun in the other.

"I guess that was inappropriate," Steve said, getting to his feet.

"Well, I suppose that if you've already knocked a man unconscious, giving him a kiss is more or less a footnote."

"So what do we do?" Steve asked.

"Let's tape him to that," Muhammed said, pointing toward a particularly heavy-looking upholstered chair along one wall.

"Okay."

"You take his arms and I'll take his legs?"

"No, I can handle this. I've carried him before. He's light as a bird." Steve set Daniel's gun down on a chair, then, kneeling down, put his arms under Daniel's back and knees. He lifted. Yep: in all these years, Daniel had never put on a pound.

"You've carried him before?"

"We got drunk one night," Steve explained as he

carried Daniel over to the chair. "It had been raining heavily for hours, and there were puddles everywhere, and he was wearing a pair of nice new leather shoes, while I was just wearing some ratty old sneakers. So when we left the campus bar to go back to the dorm, we came to one of these puddles and he told me to carry him across." Steve set Daniel down gently in the chair. Muhammed knelt down, put Ron's gun on the floor, and started taping Daniel to the chair.

"He *told* you to carry him across a puddle?"

"Yes. Ordered me."

"He wanted so desperately to touch you."

"Yes."

Muhammed shook his head. "Poor fellow," he said, as he gently taped Daniel's left arm to the left arm of the chair. "So – do you really think there are two men waiting for us outside?"

"I don't know. What do you think?"

"Not two. Maybe one. Wait a second." Muhammed paused in his taping to check Daniel's jacket pockets. He found a cell phone. "Here," he said, tossing it to Steve, who got on his knees, put the phone in his pocket, and helped Muhammed tape Daniel to the chair.

"You know," said Muhammed, "I think I can do this myself. Why don't you take a quick shower?"

"Shower? Are you kidding?"

"And find some fresh clothes. You're soaking wet and smell like a distillery."

"But – "

"Do it. You'll thank me later."

Steve shrugged, pulled his wallet out of his pants pocked and tossed it on the floor, then turned, ran into the vestibule, and climbed the stairs two at a time. Upstairs was a wide, white-walled corridor lined with framed etchings. Vases of fresh tulips stood on two small, handsome, highly polished dark-wood tables. There were a dozen doors, high and wide, up and down the corridor, all of them closed except for one, to his left, which was half-open. He went to the half-open door and pushed it all the way open. Behind it was a large bedroom with a king-size canopied bed and a sumptuous white silk comforter, sheets, and pillows. The bed was flanked by small tables on each of which stood an elegant lamp with a white lampshade; facing the bed was a doorless closet that took up the whole length of the room. The bed was unmade. Steve raced past it to an open door that – yes – led to a bathroom. He walked in. The white-tiled floor was wet, and three soaking-wet white towels lay crumpled on it, beside a glass shower that was large enough to hold an entire boy band. Steve kicked off his shoes, stripped off his liquor-drenched clothes, and stepped into it, turned on and adjusted the water, smeared himelf with soap he got from a glass dispenser attached to the wall, and rinsed himself off as quickly as possible. Stepping out of the shower, he grabbed a clean towel from a shelf beside the door, then dried himself off as he walked back across the bedroom to the closet. Dozens of elegant-looking suits and tuxedoes and pairs of trousers hung there, above rows of

346

drawers. He opened one drawer: socks, all black. He grabbed a pair and pulled them on. In other drawers he found black underwear, neatly pressed jeans, a professionally folded lilac polo shirt. He dressed himself as fast as he could. Schrama was taller than him but had approximately the same build, so the only problem was that the jeans were a bit too long. He rolled up the cuffs, went back to the bathroom, put his shoes back on, and hurried back downstairs.

Muhammed was still on his knees, taping up Daniel.

"Cool duds," he said, looking up at Steve.

"Thanks." Steve picked up his wallet from the floor, then, pocketing it, went over and snapped up Daniel's gun from the chair he'd set it down on.

Muhammed picked up Rob's gun, then stood up and looked down at Daniel. "I can see why you love him," he said.

"Loved, not love."

"He's very handsome. And there's something touching about him. Something tender and vulnerable. That he's trying so hard to cover up."

"So you can see it too."

"Of course. Oh."

"What?"

"He's coming to."

Steve looked at Daniel. His eyelids were fluttering. His head jerked. After a moment, his eyes opened and darted from one of them to the other. Then he looked down and took in the tape. At once he began wrenching his body this way and that, trying to wriggle his way out.

But the tape held.

"Good tape job," Steve said to Muhammed.

"Let me loose!" Daniel screamed at the top of his voice.

"Quiet," Muhammed said, "or we'll tape over your mouth too."

"Are there really two men waiting for us outside?" Steve asked.

"Yes."

"What's their phone number?"

"Why should I tell you?"

"So you can call them off."

"Why would I do that?"

"Do it for Nora," said Muhammed gently.

Daniel's eyes met Muhammed's. "No," he said firmly.

Steve tapped Muhammed's arm. Muhammed turned to him, and Steve jerked his head toward the gun in Muhammed's hand. "His leg," Steve said. Muhammed nodded and aimed the gun at Daniel's leg. "Do it," Steve said, "so that Nora doesn't have to grow up helping her daddy in and out of a wheelchair." Steve picked up the phone and held it in front of Daniel's face, ready to punch in a number.

Daniel looked at Steve as if he were someone he'd never seen before. He turned to Muhammed, and then back to Steve. Then he shook his head, muttered

348

something, cleared his throat, and rattled off a phone number. Steve punched it in and held the phone up to Daniel's ear. One ring, two. "Chuck?" Daniel said. Steve could just barely hear the voice on the other end. "Yes," Daniel said. "Everything's fine. Take the car up to the main road, turn right, go another kilometer, park, and wait for my call." Another pause. "No time now. I'll explain later." Steve took the phone away from Daniel's mouth and hung up, then pocketed the phone.

"What about the other guy?" Steve asked.

"There's only one," Daniel said.

Steve and Muhammed exchanged a look.

"Thank you, Daniel," Steve said.

From outside came the sound of a car starting. Steve and Muhammed stood up and went to the window to see a forest-green Audi driving away.

"We'd better be going," Muhammed said.

"Yes." Steve turned around. "Bye, Daniel," Steve said. "I hope we meet again under more pleasant circumstances."

Daniel shot him a look of pure rage. "Fuck you!"

"WELL," SAID MUHAMMED. They were driving up toward to the main road; there was no sign yet of Daniel's colleague. "You certainly have good taste in your objects of affection. 'Fuck you,' indeed!"

"I was very young," Steve replied. "Besides, you yourself said you could understand why I fell in love with him."

"Yes, I said it while his mouth was shut. Like many handsome men, he looks much handsomer when his mouth is shut. And also, much smarter."

"Okay, here comes the intersection. Cut the headlights."

Muhammed did so. Instantly, they were plunged into almost total darkness, although there were lights on the main road.

"I'm turning left," Muhammed said. "You look right."

At the crossroads, Steve did so. There was no traffic. Far off, in the darkness, he saw a tiny pair of headlights. Not moving. A car parked by the side of the road.

Chuck.

"See him?" Muhammed asked as they took the turn.

"Yes."

Muhammed sped up. "Keep your eyes on him as long as you can," he said.

"Okay. He's not moving."

"Good. Let me know when he's out of sight."

The road curved. Trees blocked Steve's view of Chuck.

"OK. Out of sight."

Muhammed switched the headlights back on. Steve looked at him and exhaled in relief.

"Are you sorry yet," Steve asked him, "that you went to the thermal baths today?"

"No," Muhammed said. "Not yet."

"Don't you have appointments tomorrow?"

"Just a couple. But I've already sent a text message to my secretary asking her to cancel them."

"I'm sorry."

"Do you always apologize so much?"

"Yes."

"Don't."

"Okay."

"So. Here's the situation. Schrama and Wouter came here from Amsterdam and arrived at his palatial residence only to leave earlier this evening. Why? Where did they go?"

"I don't know. An emergency?"

"Let's not think emergency, because that would leave us without a second step. What if there was no emergency? Where would they be then?"

"Maybe some neighbor invited them over?"

"Do you think Schrama, when he's come all this way with Wouter, would want to spend a few precious hours on a Saturday night at some other old guy's castle? Would that be Wouter's cup of tea?"

"No, I guess not."

"You guess not?"

"I know not."

"Where are they, then?"

"Munich?"

"Okay. Let's go with Munich. But where, exactly? And why?"

"I don't know."

"Think about it. There are two of them. Let's start with Wouter. What do you know about him?"

"Nothing, really."

"That's not true. You've been in his presence several times. You've made observations."

"Well, I know he's gay. He works for Schrama, and is apparently involved with him."

"What else?"

"I don't know."

"Yes, you do."

"Well...he's tall and very skinny and cute."

"And?"

"And every time I've seen him at April he's been wearing the exact same outfit, black jeans and black t-shirt and a big hoop earring."

"What else?"

"Well, of course, there's the fact that he's always at April on Saturday nights."

"Right. And what kind of place is April?"

"Young crowd. Loud music. It's the busiest gay bar in all of Amsterdam."

"There you go, then."

"What do you mean?"

"Wouter's a creature of habit. Every Saturday the same bar, the same clothes, the same hoop earring. In other words, he likes going out to places like April on Saturday nights. Busy, fun, noisy gay places. Do you remember what day today is?"

"It's Saturday."

"Right! And we're looking for someone who can't get through a Saturday night without going to a busy gay bar."

"So you're saying Wouter got bored?"

"He's young. He's cute. He's restless. He's this famous politician's current boy toy, but if he's typical of the species he doesn't want to spend a whole Saturday night alone with his sugar daddy in some stuffy old castle. So he nags him into going into the city."

"That makes sense. But would a man like Jeroen Schrama actually let some boy toy dictate his actions like that?"

"I can see that you haven't known very many sugar daddies."

"No, I haven't."

"Of course there's another possible scenario," Muhammed said. "Maybe it was Schrama himself who got bored. Remember *The Great Gatsby*?"

"You mean the book? Yes. What about it?"

"These decadent characters are all lounging around in a fabulous mansion on the North Shore of Long Island, listening to music and having drinks on a beautiful summer day. It's delightful, the ultimate in leisure. They have everything they could possibly want and then some. But they all have the chronic affliction of the rich. Which is?"

"I don't know."

"Yes, you do. Think."

"Boredom."

"Of course. They're bored by their own privilege. So what do they do? Do you remember?"

"Yes. They drive into Manhattan."

"And?"

"And get a room at the Plaza Hotel and sit around *there* for a while."

"Exactly."

"So you think – ?"

"I'm thinking it's possible that Schrama himself just wasn't in the mood to hang at his magnificent castle."

"And decided instead to check into some fancy hotel in Munich?"

"Bingo. So let's sum up. At this moment they could either be at the hottest gay bar in Munich. Or at the city's fanciest hotel."

"Or perhaps Wouter is at the bar, and Schrama's at the hotel waiting for him."

"Could be."

"So what's the Munich equivalent of what the Plaza Hotel was in New York City in 1925?"

"That's an easy one. The Vier Jahreszeiten."

"The Four Seasons."

"Yes."

"You sure?"

"No question. It's been there since the 1950s. Queen Elizabeth stayed there. Churchill. Liz Taylor. A guy like Schrama would never stay anywhere else."

"And what's the hottest gay bar?"

"That's also an easy one. It's a place called New York."

"New York?"

"Yes, New York."

"Funny."

"What's funny?"

"Wherever you go, there are bars named after other cities."

"The grass is always greener."

"So where do we go first? The hotel or the bar?"

"I don't know. Let's think this through. *Scheiße.*"

"What?"

A pause, a bit too long. "Headlights."

"What?"

Muhammed's voice had shifted. "There are headlights behind us."

A shiver ran through Steve. He turned around. "It can't be them. He told Chuck to stay put. And we tied him up tight. And we've been driving very, very fast. Chuck would've had to drive back to the house, cut Daniel loose – "

"Unless Daniel somehow got loose himself. And called him on the house phone."

"What do we do?"

"Never mind."

"What?"

"The car's turning."

"Oh, good."

They both caught their breath.

"Moosburg up ahead."

They drove through the town. It was as quiet as before. Steve looked at his watch. It was close to midnight.

"So how late would that bar be open on a Saturday?"

"Till five or so."

"Okay."

"Don't worry. It's probably not even getting started yet."

"And here I thought Bavarians were conservative."

For a few minutes, they drove in silence through the town. Then there was a buzzing sound in Steve's pants. He and Muhammed looked at each other. It wasn't Muhammed's phone, and it wasn't Joop's.

"What do I do?" Steve asked as he dug the cell phone out of his pocket.

"Well, if you don't answer, he'll assume the worst and drive back to the house."

Steve saw the name *Chuck* on the phone. He clicked to take the call and held it up to his ear.

"Hey," Steve said.

"Danny?"

"Yeah?"

"What's going on?"

"Just stay there, I can't talk now."

Dead air. Then: "You're not Danny."

Click.

Steve looked at Muhammed as he set the phone down on the seat beside him. "Well," he said, "I didn't get away with that for long."

"No problem. We're far enough away from there. Look, here's the *Autobahn*." Muhammed pulled onto it and sped up even faster.

"He said 'Danny,'" Steve told Muhammed.

"What?"

"He was never a 'Danny.' Or a 'Dan.' It never occurred to me to call him by a nickname. And if I had, he'd've put the kibosh on it."

"I would never say this to a patient of mine," said Muhammed. "But you're not a patient of mine. So I'll say it to you. Snap out of it."

"I thought I had. Years ago."

"You know what I think?"

"No, what?"

"I think you're in love."

"I'm not in love with him. I mean it."

"I didn't say you were in love with Daniel. You're not. You're in love with Joop. That's as clear as day. But you're still so scarred by what happened with Daniel all those years ago, and so used to what I assume has been a lifestyle of meaningless hookups with all kinds of superficial idiots, that you can't bring yourself to trust entirely in your love for Joop and in his love for you. And so what do you do? You obsess over Daniel, this figure from your past, with whom you're not in love at all, and with whom, besides, you know very well you could never have an honest, authentic, mutually respectful relationship."

Steve looked at Muhammed in awe. Muhammed shrugged and offered Steve the tiniest smile. "Sorry," he said.

"Your fees," Steve said, "must be sky-high."

Muhammed shook his head. "You're much more of an open book than you realize."

They drove along for a couple of minutes. "Of course," Steve said, "the logical thing would be for me to be in love with you."

Steve looked at him. Muhammed's eyes stayed on the road, and his expression didn't change. "I mean," Steve went on, "we've read the same books. We know the same poems by heart. Joop doesn't read. I don't mean he's illiterate. He's smart. But he's not very interested in books. Everybody thinks the Dutch are voracious readers, and many of them are, but he's not one of them. He didn't even know that Vondelpark in Amsterdam was named after a great Dutch poet until I told him. When I first asked him about Jeroen Schrama, he couldn't place the name right away."

A good minute went by before Muhammed spoke. "Love isn't logical," he said.

"No."

Silence. A minute; two.

"A thought," Muhammed finally said in a low voice.

"Yes?"

"These guys in Amsterdam. The ones who are planning to murder Schrama."

"Yes?"

"The Alhambra. How do they know he'll go there?"

The question threw Steve. It was the most obvious question of all, but in the madness of the last few hours, it hadn't occurred to him.

"I don't know," he said.

"Another thought."

"Yes?"

"Is it possible that they have some way of ensuring that he *will* go there?"

"Like what?"

"Think about it."

Steve did so. After a couple of minutes, a thought entered his mind – and froze his blood. "Wouter?"

"Yes."

"Are you suggesting – ?"

"He wouldn't be the first native European to serve the cause."

"But – why? Why would he?"

"Two possible reasons. One, a big payday. Two, he's a believer."

"A believer?"

"No one's as zealous as a convert."

"But he can't be a devout Muslim! He's a barfly. A party boy."

"Take it from me, that doesn't disqualify him in

the slightest. You wouldn't believe the level of self-deception and self-contradiction these terrorist types are capable of."

"You really think that's possible?"

"Of course it's possible. The question is whether it's the case."

"But Wouter! That – I mean – "

"Think about it: how else would these people be able to place Schrama in a certain spot, at a certain time, so that they could kill him? Either they enlisted the services of this sexy young thing who already had Schrama in his thrall. Or knowing he was Schrama's type, they hired him to *get* Schrama in his thrall. So much in his thrall that he could pretty much demand that they go to a certain place at a certain time, and make the whole thing happen."

"But Wouter? Earring boy? Really?"

"What's the problem? Is it so hard for you to believe that somebody who looks like this Wouter could be as capable of this – of embracing Islam and committing an act of terrorism – as somebody who looks like me?"

Steve was saturated with guilt. He realized that that was exactly what he had been thinking, however unconsciously.

"I'm sorry," he said. "You're right."

"I told you," Muhammed said. "Stop apologizing."

"Okay."

"Now, let's go back to our earlier question: what

do you know about Wouter? One thing you know is that he's not just involved with Schrama; he *works* for him. Now, did he work for him first, and then get involved with him, or was he involved with him, and then Schrama gave him a job?"

"Does it matter?"

"I don't know. Maybe not. But somehow it seems more likely to me that he was working for Schrama, and then got involved with him, rather than the other way around."

"I agree."

"Why do you agree?"

Steve thought for a moment.

"It may sound silly, but I don't think Schrama would give a job to somebody he was involved with. I think he has that much principle. I think he'd be more likely to get involved with somebody who was working in his office."

"Which is also a question of principle."

"True. But – I don't know how to put it – "

"Don't worry, I follow you."

"Good."

"So that brings us to our next question. Did these people, these would-be murderers, recruit Wouter after he was already working for Schrama? Or it is possible that they placed him in Schrama's office? That they have somebody on the inside, in the Dutch Parliament, or somewhere in the Dutch government's hiring apparatus, who was able to arrange for him to get that job?"

"Are you kidding? That doesn't sound far-fetched to you?"

"Far-fetched? Are you really asking me that question after what you've been through during the last week?"

"Question withdrawn."

"So what do you think?"

"I don't know."

"Well, if they placed him in Schrama's office, that would suggest he's a convert. If they got to him after he was already working there, that might indicate that –"

"That's he's in it for the money."

"Exactly."

"Well, if I had to guess, just on the basis of my casual obsevations of Wouter, I would say that..."

"What?"

"That he's more likely to be in it for the money. I just don't see him as a believer in anything."

"Okay. Now, another question about him. When you've seen him at April, has he been alone or with friends?"

"Always with friends."

"Does he come in with them, or meet them there?"

"He usually meets them there. There's a bunch of them."

"Describe them."

"Describe them? They're all more or less exactly like him. Young, cool, whatever."

"Nobody who looks, um, Muslim?"

"Never. All ethnic Dutch guys. Wait a second."

"What?"

"I remember that when I first started seeing him at April, he would always come in with another guy."

"An older guy?"

"Yes."

"And what was that like?"

"What do you mean?"

"Did they look like a couple?"

"Yes."

"Tell me more."

"I don't remember much more. I didn't study them. As far as I can recall, they'd just hang out with Wouter's friends, the same ones he hangs out with now." Steve scoured his memory. "The older guy would usually hang back, just stand or sit there with his drink. They would all be drinking beer, and he would always have a cocktail. And he – well, he would sometimes hover there, just behind or beside Wouter, looking possessive. You know how older guys act when they're in bars with their boy toys?"

"Yes. And this guy was somebody like Schrama? A man of substance? A professional, a businessman?"

"Yes. Definitely. Nice suit. Sometimes he would actually come in with a file folder and put on his glasses and read through some papers and make marks on them."

"And, of course, he was ethnic Dutch?"

363

"Yes."

"See? And you said you didn't remember all that much."

"I didn't think I did. I'd forgotten all about him until just now. It's been a while."

"How long? When was the last time you saw him and Wouter together?"

"Just a few weeks."

"And we don't know, do we, just how long Wouter has been working for Schrama?"

"No."

"Do you think Joop is still at April?"

"There's one way to find out. Shall I?"

"Why not?"

Steve dug into his pocket, took out Joop's phone. He punched in Joop's number. It rang. Then, suddenly, there was a cacophony of music and voices and clinking glassware – a wall of noise.

"One second," Steve heard Joop shout into the phone.

"Okay."

After a few seconds, the music faded. Steve heard a door slam.

"I had to step outside. It's crazy in there," Joop said. "What's going on?"

"Everything's okay here. I'll fill you in later. Are Wouter's friends still there?"

"Yes. They went out, I guess to a couple of other bars, and they just came back a little while ago."

"Can you ask them something?"

"What's that?"

"Ask them how long Wouter's been with Schrama. And when he started working for him. We're curious to know which came first: the relationship or the job."

"'We'?"

"Yes. Muhammed and I."

"Oh."

"Also, if any of them knows anything about how he got the job with Schrama, that would be great."

"Okay. I'll see what I can do. Of course they've all had a few drinks by now. So I don't know what I'll be able to get accomplished."

"Do what you can."

"Okay. I'll call you back."

Steve hung up. He looked at Muhammed. "The city," Muhammed said.

"What?"

Muhammed nodded toward the windshield. Steve looked. The buildings of Munich loomed up ahead.

"Wow. That was quick."

"When he calls back," Muhammed said, "why don't you tell him how you feel about him?"

"Huh?"

"He thinks he's lost you to me."

"What do you mean?"

"Just a couple of days ago it was the two of you against the world. And now it's 'Muhammed this,' 'Muhammed that,' 'Muhammed and I.' He was okay with being dragged into a nightmare situation with terrorists, taking part in a double killing, hiding from the police. But he was only okay with it because you were there with him. Because the two of you were in it together. But now you're here with me. And he worries that he's lost you. That you've given your heart to somebody else."

"He's not like that. He's Dutch."

"Don't be silly. He's in love with you."

"How can you know that? You've never even met him."

"How did his voice sound when you said 'Muhammed and I'?"

Steve looked at him. "Maybe you're right."

"Has he said that he loves you?"

A pause. "Yes."

"Quite a while ago, right?"

Another pause. "Yes."

"And you're in love with him. You've been unable to say so before now. You had issues with it. But after all that you've been through in the last few days – with *him* – those issues must seem pretty minor. No?"

"Yes."

"You love him. So why don't you tell him so?"

"What, now?"

"When he calls back. Tell him. Who knows how all this will turn out? You may be sorry if you don't."

"You mean, say 'I love you' to Joop?"

"Yes. Now where do we go? The hotel, or the bar?"

"My pick?"

"Yes."

"I don't know. The hotel?"

"Good choice."

"Why?"

"No reason. It's just a little closer."

They drove on for a while in silence.

They changed highways at a cloverleaf, passed an IKEA, the four huge yellow letters blazing in the dark. Then they were on the streets of Munich: Schenkendorfstraße, Ungererstraße, Leopoldstraße. The traffic was as heavy as in any major city on a Saturday night.

Muhammed made a turn at almost every corner, then pulled into the entrance to a parking garage.

"Are we at the hotel?"

"It's a couple of blocks away."

"So we have to walk? What if somebody recognizes me from the news?"

Muhammed wove among the parked cars, slid into a space, shifted to park, turned off the ignition. Then he reached across Steve's lap and opened his glove compartment. "See those?" There was a pair of dark glasses on top of a black scarf and a pair of black leather gloves.

"Yes."

"Put them on."

Steve did so. "You think this'll do it?"

"Yes."

"But won't I attract attention wearing dark glasses at this hour? Won't I look like an idiot?"

"Not in this neighborhood. You have your gun?"

"Yes, do you have Daniel's?"

"Yes."

They got out of the car and walked out onto the street. It was a beautiful night, with a bit of a breeze. The sidewalks were crowded with attractive, well-dressed people, all of whom looked as if they'd had a lovely evening and were headed from one night spot to another, or back home, or to a hotel. Steve and Muhammed walked past the Munich branches of Prada, Louis Vuitton, Dolce & Gabbana. This was obviously the very spiffiest part of town. Nobody paid Steve the slightest notice. He relaxed a bit. "So you like living in Munich?" he asked Muhammed.

Muhammed smiled in a funny way.

"What?"

"That's the very first thing you asked me," Muhammed said.

"What do you mean?"

"Today. In the champagne pool."

"I did?"

"Yes."

"And what did you say?"

"I said, yes, I do like it."

They continued walking along.

"Gosh," Steve said.

"What?"

"It's hard to believe that that was just today. It

seems so long ago already. I mean, I feel as if I've known you..." Steve didn't complete the sentence.

Muhammed touched his arm. At first Steve thought it was an affectionate gesture. Then he looked up and saw that they were at the entrance to a hotel – an indisputably grand hotel. He heard cloth whipping in the wind and looked up. Four huge flags were flying proudly above them: the German *Bundesflagge*, the Union Jack, the French *tricoleur,* and the Stars and Stripes.

"We're here," Muhammed said.

X.

SOME OF US OUTLIVE OTHERS. It's the way of the world. It's the first fact. The final fact. And the toughest one to live with.

Years later – which is to say, years after the traumatic days recounted here – Steve would actually stay at the Vier Jahreszeiten, while in Munich for a conference on Islam in Europe. By that point he would have made two documentaries on the subject and become, at least in the eyes of certain people, something of an expert on it.

One bright morning, before participating in a panel discussion about the danger that Islam poses to Western civilization, Steve would stand at the window of his high-ceilinged suite at the Vier Jahreszeiten, would look out at the city of Munich, and would think back on that most unreal – and at the same time most intensely real – week of his life. He would remember every moment of it, and would turn over in his mind again and again the things he had said and done that had turned out to be turning points.

HE FOLLOWED MUHAMMED INTO the hotel lobby. It was large and elegant, dimly lit, with sofas and tables and lamps and a stained-glass ceiling. Muhammed led Steve to the front desk, where Muhammed addressed the glamorous young female clerk in perfect German, his voice oozing with charm. Yes, she said, her smile perfect, her eyes glistening, Herr Schrama was registered; he'd just checked in this evening. At Muhammed's request, she phoned up to the room. No answer. Muhammed asked her the number of the room. She told him: 304. He thanked her, and turned to Steve.

"I'll stay here at the hotel," Muhammed said.

"What?"

"In case they come back. Or one of them comes back."

"Do you know what Schrama looks like?"

"No, but that doesn't matter. I'll go upstairs and wait outside their room. Meanwhile, you go to the New York Club."

"How do I get there?"

Muhammed was already walking him back out onto the sidewalk. "Take a cab. It's on Sonnenstraße."

There was a line of cabs at the curb. Muhammed opened the back door to the first one. Steve climbed in. Muhammed leaned in and was about to speak to the driver when he got a look at him – a broad-shouldered, Mediterranean-looking man with a small scraggly beard. Muhammed's pause lasted only a half second, but it registered with Steve – and, clearly, with the driver. "*Sonnenstraße fünfundzwanzig*," Muhammed said loudly.

The driver, meeting Muhammed's eyes, asked him something in another language.

Steve recognized it. From Bellamyplein.

Muhammed replied in the same language. There was a palpable tension between them. Muhammed turned

371

to Steve and, lowering his voice, said in English, "Maybe you should take another cab."

"No," Steve said softly. "It's okay."

Muhammed looked again at the driver, who had turned away from him, and then again at Steve. "Okay," he said, uncertainly, keeping his voice down. "Maybe I'm overreacting. Look, I'll call you if they show up here. And you call me if they're there."

Steve nodded. He swallowed, touched his upper lip with his tongue. Muhammed seemed about to say something else, but didn't. His eyes fixed on Steve's, he slammed the door shut. The driver pulled away. Steve looked around to see Muhammed watching as the cab drove off.

"American?" grunted the driver in a strong accent as he raced down the street.

"Yes. You?"

"You know where I am from."

"Turkey?"

"Yes."

"Like your friend."

"Yes."

"Where you from in America?"

"Los Angeles."

"Two of my brothers live in New York."

"Your brothers? Really?"

"Yes. I have eight brothers. New York, Marseille, London, Rotterdam, and here." He looked at Steve in the rear-view mirror. "Why you wear glasses?" he asked.

Taken aback by the change of subject, Steve was speechless for a second. "Why do you ask?"

"Dark outside. Why glasses? Are you blind?"

"No. I was, um, in a very bright room in the hotel."

"You were in hotel less than one minute. I saw you go in."

Steve didn't know what to say. The driver stared at him in the mirror.

"Take off glasses," the driver said. It wasn't a suggestion; it was an order.

Steve took them off. The driver kept looking back and forth between the road ahead and at Steve's face in the rear-view mirror. But the driver said nothing. His eyes were ice-cold. He drove a few blocks, speeding up. Soon the car was moving dangerously fast, but Steve said nothing. As it approached an intersection, the driver took his right hand off the steering wheel and pulled a cell phone out of his shirt pocket. He tapped in a number; after a moment he barked a couple of sentences into the phone. Steve couldn't understand what he was saying, partly because he was speaking heavily accented and broken German. But he was able to make out two words.

Amerikaner. And *Amsterdam.*

The cab reached a square. In what felt almost like an act of violence, the driver made a sharp and sudden left, barely decelerating at all, and Steve was thrown against the door. Looking ahead, he saw that the street they were on was about to split in two, a tree-filled divider

373

opening up in the middle. But the driver made a right just before reaching the divider. Now they were on a narrow one-lane road, with a building pressing up against them on the left and a high stone wall on the right. They rushed through an intersection on a green light, and in the middle of the next block the driver slammed on the brakes. Swiftly, Steve looked around. There was no sign of anything remotely resembling a bar or nightclub – just a stone-walled building on the right that looked as if it might be a church and, on the left, an iron fence about twenty feet high. Behind it was a severe-looking five-story building that seemed to fill the entire block.

Before Steve could figure out what to do or say, the driver opened his door and stepped out. Standing up, he was even taller than Steve would have guessed, and massively built. He walked around the front of the car.

Suddenly understanding exactly what was going on, Steve grasped the door handle, swung the door open, stepped out, and tried to make a run for it. But the driver was on him immediately, grabbing him from behind, pinning his arms at his side, and lifting him several inches off the ground. Steve couldn't even reach the gun in his pants pocket.

"No!" Steve screamed. "Let me go! Let me go!" He struggled to break free, but the driver was ridiculously strong. He carried Steve around the back of the car and toward the fence, where there was an open gate. As they approached it, Steve saw three young police officers running in their direction from the building.

One of them shouted out, *"Ist dies der Amerikaner?"*

"Jawohl, jawohl," the driver shouted, his deep, gravelly voice ringing in Steve's ear.

They reached the gate; the cops surrounded them; the cabbie set Steve down. At which point, without giving the situation any thought, Steve took off, running down the sidewalk as fast as he could.

The cops shouted; Steve could hear at least one or more of them racing after him. After just a few seconds he entered a pedestrians-only square that seemed unusually crowded, given the late hour. Steve zigzagged through the crowd, hoping to lose his pursuers, then plunged into a very narrow, uncrowded street. Running down it, he looked behind him to see all three cops turning the corner and barreling toward him. Without slowing down, Steve pulled out the gun, stretched his arm behind him, and fired a shot – not at them, but at the surface of the street a few yards behind him.

After running for another second or two he looked around again: no sign of them. Had they retreated? Re-pocketing the gun, he reached an intersection, took a right. Another narrow street. By now he was breathing heavily, starting to tire. He was a terrific sprinter, he knew, but no marathon man.

At the next corner, he reached a tiny square – a stamp of grass, a couple of trees. He kept running, crossing the square and plunging into the narrow street beyond. Then he hit a broad, busy avenue with a tram line running down the middle of it. He recognized it at once. He'd been here last night. It was Sonnenstraße.

He stopped for a second. To his right was a store with mannequins in the window, wearing wedding dresses. On a small blue plaque high up on the corner of the building he read the house number: 17. Okay, so which way? It was a coin toss. He turned left, ran up the sidewalk.

Storefronts. A furniture store. Then – aha! – a big number 25 over a grungy-looking passageway. He dove into it. A tacky sign for a travel agency. Another for a beauty parlor. Then a big garish sign with two words on it: *New York.*

He opened the door and went in.

The place was dark and packed; dance music was blaring. The people were young, stylish. Steve scanned the faces. No immediate sign of Schrama and Wouter, both of whom were tall enough to be easily picked out if they were present. But, he reflected, they might be sitting at the bar, which, he discerned, was on the far side of the room, below a sprawling Manhattan skyline in purple neon. Beyond an archway was at least one other room. He pressed his way into the throng and moved toward the bar, wondering if he was mad to be here. The cabdriver had known he was going to Sonnenstraße 25; it was only a matter of time before the cops burst in. But he could think of only one thing. He had to find Schrama.

He reached the bar and looked in both directions. There were five guys working behind it, all of them in skin-tight white t-shirts and all of them busy. There were no stools. One of the bartenders, a tallish blond, came over to him, asked if he wanted anything. "I'm looking for a couple of friends," Steve said in English. "Two Dutch guys? Both tall?" He raised his hand and held it, palm down, way above his own head. "One older, and one young and very skinny, all in black, with a big hoop earring?" He held his thumb and index finger to his earlobe to mimic a hoop earring.

The bartender nodded. "They were here a little while ago. I think maybe they went back there." He jerked his head toward the archway. "Do you want anything?"

"Not right now, thanks."

Before Steve had finished saying the word *thanks,* the bartender had abandoned him for a paying customer further down the bar. Steve moved away from the bar and toward the archway. Pushing his way through the crowd and under the arch, he found himself in a more intimate, somewhat quieter room with a smaller bar – this one square, surrounded by stools, all of them occupied, with two t-shirted bartenders in the middle, rapidly filling orders. Sitting on two of the stools facing Steve were Schrama, who was tossing back a blue cocktail, and Wouter, who, sitting on Schrama's right, was looking at him thoughtfully. Beyond them was a steel door with a green neon sign over it reading *Ausgang.*

It was Wouter who noticed Steve first. Their eyes met just as Steve, having pushed his way through the crowd, reached the side of the bar facing where Wouter and Steve were sitting. As Steve squeezed past one seated customer after another, headed closer and closer to Schrama and Wouter, the look in Wouter's eyes was easy to read: he was panicked.

Steve reached them before Wouter could figure out what to say or do. Steve touched Schrama's shoulder. Schrama turned, his drink still in his hand. He recognized Steve at once. "I need to talk to you," Steve said.

"No!" Wouter shouted angrily. He pulled out a cell phone. Steve took a step, grabbed it from him, tossed it into the crowd behind him. One of the bartenders, noticing, moved toward him. He was about to speak when Schrama asked, his tone unexpectedly civil, "What is this about?"

As if on cue, Wouter pulled out something else: a gun.

Steve and the bartender were the only ones to see it. As Wouter raised it, it was unclear to Steve whether he was about to point it at Steve or at Schrama. Before that question could be answered, Steve heard a loud noise from behind him; he turned to see several police officers burst through the back door, their guns drawn and aimed. One of them, looking straight at the gun-wielding Wouter, pulled off a shot. Steve turned back to see the bullet hit Wouter right between the eyes.

The gun fell from Wouter's hand, and Wouter himself collapsed to the floor.

In the ensuing hysteria and confusion, Steve rushed out the same back door through which the cops had stormed into the place. Running up a narrow back street, he took out his phone and called Muhammed. No answer. At a cross street, he saw a cab approaching with its light on. He hailed it. After glancing at the driver – nope, different guy; this one looked German – Steve asked to be taken to the Vier Jahreszeiten.

Getting there took only a couple of minutes. Approaching the hotel, the cab passed a double-parked police car, its red roof light blinking, then another, and another. There were cops up and down the sidewalk, some conferring with one another, some talking on cell phones.

"You can let me off here," Steve told the driver. The hotel was still a block or so away. Paying the driver, he clambered out of the cab and crossed to the other side of the street, facing the hotel. People on the sidewalk had stopped to gawk at the spectacle of all these police cars; Steve moved through them to get closer to the hotel. When he reached a spot directly opposite it, he stopped and took it all in.

There were several police cars parked in front of the hotel, plus an ambulance and an unmarked black panel truck. Policemen were everywhere, outside the hotel and, he could see, inside the lobby. A couple of them were blocking the hotel entrance, prohibiting people from going in or out.

A female voice beside Steve asked, "*Was ist geschehen?*" Steve turned. A pretty young woman was standing next to him with a handsome young guy. They were stylishly dressed, affluent-looking. "*Ich weiß nicht,*"

Steve said, hearing the hollowness in his own voice as he looked back at the hotel.

He stood there for a minute or so, not knowing what to think, what to do. Should he run? What was happening? Then several policemen who had been standing on the sidewalk went into the hotel. A moment later, they came back out, this time escorting two of their colleagues who were carrying a black body bag. They took it to the black panel truck.

As Steve watched these events unfold, his cell phone rang. He answered it.

"Did you ever see *The Godfather?*"

It was Daniel.

"*The Godfather?*"

"Yes. The movie. *The Godfather.*"

"Uh-huh."

"Remember how McCloskey had to let the precinct know where they'd be able to reach him? And how the Corleones had a contact in the precinct who told them the name of the restaurant, and were able to plant the gun so that Michael could kill him and Sollozzo?"

"Yes."

"Well, same thing here. Ten minutes after Schrama booked the room, we knew about it. Because he had to tell his office where he was."

"Daniel, who's in that body bag?"

A pause.

"I'm sorry," Daniel said, and sounded as if he meant it. "But it's Muhammed."

"No. No! Why? Why did you – "

"I didn't. Chuck did. He went up to Schrama's floor and – "

"Oh God."

"Muhammed pulled out his gun. Correction: *my* gun. Chuck took him out with one shot. He died instantly. I'm sure it was painless."

"But why – "

"Look, I don't know who Muhammed thought Chuck was, but when Muhammed pulled out that gun – "

"Oh God."

" – Chuck assumed he was a Muslim terrorist out to get Schrama."

"I thought you wanted to let the terrorists take Schrama out."

"Yes, we were. But Chuck wasn't about to let a terrorist take *him* out."

"Oh God."

"Look, Steve. I'm sorry. I really am. No hard feelings, okay?"

"'No hard feelings'?"

"Steve – "

"Are you kidding? 'No hard feelings'?"

"Again, I'm sorry. Really. I don't know what else to say."

"Chuck *killed* him?"

"Muhammed pulled a gun. It was either kill or be killed."

"But Muhammed wouldn't have killed Chuck!"

"You know that. I know that. But Chuck didn't."

"But it wasn't *supposed* to be him! *I* should've died!"

"I know how you feel, but life doesn't work that way."

Steve stood there, numb, for what felt like an eternity. Finally Daniel said: "Are you there, Steve?"

"Where are you?" Steve asked.

"Huh?"

"Where are you? Right now? Geographically?"

"I'm right across the street from you."

"What?"

"At the hotel."

"Are you kidding?"

"No. I'm at a window on the fourth floor. At this very moment I'm looking at you out there on the sidewalk."

"You can see me?"

"Yes."

Steve looked up and scanned the fourth-floor windows. "I can't see you."

"Of course you can't. The lights are out. The room's dark. In any case, I won't be here long. And you shouldn't hang around either."

"But what about – "

"It's over, Steve. Wouter's dead. And just a few minutes ago, the Dutch AIVD moved in on the terrorist cell in Amsterdam, including the guys you overheard on Bellamyplein. And the Germans have nabbed the people they was working with here in Munich. In the next few hours we'll probably be finding out a lot about Fabien. Oh, and not so incidentally, you can stop worrying about being picked up by the cops, because you're entirely in the clear."

"How'd you manage that?"

"Easy. We told our Dutch and German friends that you're one of us."

"One of you?"

"Yes. CIA. Oh, and your bank accounts have been unfrozen. And if anybody dares to try to ask you any questions, refer them directly to me. And be obnoxious about it. And the same goes for Joop. Oops, I mean Bart."

"How long have you known his real name?"

"Never mind. Give him my best, by the way."

"But what about – "

"Enough," Daniel said. "Don't you see? It's over. You don't need to keep your neurons spinning like this. You can relax."

"But I can't. I can't relax. Not after this. Not after what I did to Muhammed."

"You didn't do anything to him."

"Didn't do anything to him? What are you talking about? I killed him."

"You didn't kill him. Chuck killed him. If you killed anybody tonight, it was Wouter. You brought the cops right to him, and they finished him off just in the nick of time. And good riddance."

"But Muhammed – "

"Stop it. Muhammed was a grown man, acting on his own convictions. And he acted courageously."

"But I can't believe it. He was too – too alive to die. Too smart. Too good."

"I was only in the same room with him for a few minutes," said Daniel, "but I could see he was a special person."

"He was."

"And he was something else. And please listen to me when I say this. He was the last person in the world who would ever have let himself be persuaded by you or anybody else to do something that he didn't want to do, and that he didn't believe in completely. You know I'm right about that, don't you?"

"Yes."

"Good."

"I only knew him for a day," Steve said, "and I knew I had a friend for life. A friend who was also a truly great person. The kind of person who can really save this continent."

"Please, take my advice. There'll be plenty of time later for recriminations, however undeserved. And plenty of time for mourning. For now just try to calm your mind and put yourself back together. Take a good deep breath. Have a drink. Have ten. It's over."

"Okay."

There was a brief pause. "By the way," Daniel said, "just one tiny little detail. Officially, the person killed here tonight was a Romanian gypsy who had a long rap sheet, was in the country illegally, and was shot when he broke into a hotel room and pulled a knife on smebody. Muhammed died tonight of a heart attack at the Großhadern clinic at Ludwig Maximilians University. All right?"

"Sure," Steve sighed. "What's the difference at this point?"

"One more thing," Daniel said. "I knew you were desperately in need of sleep, and didn't have any place to lay your head tonight, so I took the liberty of reserving a room for you here. I hope you don't mind."

"Here? You mean at the Vier Jahreszeit?"

"Yes. Just identify yourself at the front desk."

"Are you kidding?"

"Don't worry," Daniel said, "it's already paid for."

"By the Company?"

"No, by me. With my personal credit card." A pause. "Feel free to raid the minibar."

"Thank you," Steve said. "I will."

"Look," Daniel said. "I wish I could talk more right now, but I can't. I have to go. As you may imagine, I have a few things to see to. But I *would* like to..."

"Yes?"

"Well, what I mean is, maybe you and I can talk again before too long. Maybe even in person. Someplace between Amsterdam and Prague. Preferably without guns or duct tape."

"Would you really want to do that?" Steve asked.

"Yes. I would. Would you?"

"Yes."

"Good. Then we'll be in touch."

"Okay."

Without another word, Daniel hung up.

Across the street, two cops slammed shut the back doors of the black van. One of them signaled to the driver. The van's engine started up, and it drove off.

The ambulance cleared out, too. One by one, over the next few minutes, so did the police cars. Pedestrians stopped staring and resumed their late-night activities, ambling up and down the sidewalk.

Steve, for his part, found it hard to move. Eventually, however, he went down to the corner, waited for the light to change, then crossed. He entered the hotel lobby and walked to the front desk. Two minutes later he was in a top-floor suite. He found the minibar, made himself a gin-and-tonic, then sat down with it at a table by the window. He picked up the phone and dialed a number. Two rings. An answer.

"Met Joop."

"It's me," Steve said.

"Oh, thank God," Joop said, his anxiety palpable. "Are you all right?"

"Joop," Steve said, "I love you."

H E WAS STIRRED AWAKE BY THE hotel phone. The bedside clock read 10:05. He lifted the receiver after four rings. "Hello?"

"In Bavaria," said a familiar voice, "almost everything is closed on Sundays. That's what good Christians they are! But fortunately this doesn't extend to most of the first-rate restaurants and bars. So I hope you will be able to join me today for a late brunch?"

"It would be an honor, Herr Schrama. May I bring a friend?"

"Absolutely."

Steve showered, then order coffee from room service. Shortly after eleven, he was sipping his second cup, wearing a fluffy white hotel robe, when a knock came at the door.

"It's me."

Steve got up, ran to the door, flung it open. Joop stood there, holding a carry-on. "Some clean clothes for you," he said, holding it out. Steve took it, dropped it to the floor, threw his arms around Joop.

"Oh good," Joop said, sniffing the air, when they were finally through with their embrace. "Coffee."

L ATE THAT NIGHT, A LIMOUSINE from the Dutch consulate pulled up at the main entrance to the thermal baths, escorted by four police cars, a dozen police officers on motorcycles, and several other vehicles. The uniformed officer in the limo's shotgun seat got out and opened the back right door. Jeroen Schrama stepped out, briskly, none the worse for wear after an afternoon and evening of vigorous drinking; Steve and Joop, ditto, got out on the left. With a couple of dozen

Dutch and German officials in front of and behind them – some in police or military uniforms, some, the politicians and diplomats, in civilian garb – they walked to the door, where another dozen or so police officers were waiting, along with seven or eight men and women, executives of the company that owned the baths, and another couple of dozen young people in black t-shirts and trousers, all of them workers at the baths. The suited officials who had come with Steve, Joop, and Schrama exchanged a few words with the waiting executives and police officers; then, at a nod from one of the executives, four of the young people in t-shirts opened the two pairs of doors wide, and the executives and several of the police officers led Steve, Joop, and Schrama through the empty, half-darkened lobby into the first and then the second mammoth locker room, both of which were also empty and half-darkened now, and then out into the massive baths area itself, all of it eerily unoccupied, eerily quiet, the lights low, as on the set of a film that had stopped shooting for the night.

They passed the Palazzo Venezio and walked to the Champagne Pool – empty, empty, empty. They were all wearing hard shoes, and their steps resounded in what seemed an unnatural, unnerving way on the hard floors. And then they climbed the stairs – slowly, formally, funereally – and made their way through the area of plush white couches and leafy plants, and past the series of small saunas, and down the ensuing corridor as it widened into the large space outside the enormous wine-red tent.

As if following a script, the diplomats and politicians, police and military officers, executives and t-shirted day workers all parted to allow Steve, Joop, and Schrama to enter the tent alone. Once they were inside, Schrama and Joop stood and scanned the space. Steve watched them as they did so. And then they both looked at Steve.

"Well," Steve said. "This is it."

THE MUNICH WALDENFRIEDHOF DIDN'T LOOK like a cemetery, but rather like a forest with gravestones here and there. It was a warm, breezy morning, and while one of Muhammed's colleagues, a bearded man in his sixties, stood at the gravesite celebrating Muhammed's life and work in appropriately secular terms, Steve and Joop hovered at the back of the crowd.

A couple of hundred people had shown up. Steve scanned the faces; most of the other mourners were middle-aged men and women in dark formal dress, presumably fellow psychiatrists. There wasn't one person who looked as if he or she might be a member of Muhammed's family.

"Was it worth it?" Steve asked Joop, without taking his eyes off the man with the beard.

"What do you mean?"

"The trade-off. Muhammed's life for Schrama's. Is any man's life worth another's?"

"That's not the right question."

"Why not?"

"You know why not. Muhammed may have been a great guy, but Schrama can save Europe. It's not just about his life. It's about what he can do with his life."

When the brief ceremony was over, a tall, elderly man approached Steve and Joop. He was wearing an elegant suit and sporting a row of medals on his chest. For a moment Steve didn't recognize him; then he realized that it was Alex von Holzer. His eyes, Steve saw, were moist.

"Herr Holzer," Steve said, extending his hand. Holzer took it and squeezed it tightly. Steve introduced Joop, and they shook hands.

"A horrible thing," von Holzer said in English, his voice trembling but strong, and his English surprisingly unaccented.

"Yes."

"At my age, and with my state of health, I should be in that grave. Not him. Such a brilliant, vibrant man. What an irrational world."

"Yes."

Holzer shook his head slowly, then looked around. "Quite a place, no?"

"It's a beautiful cemetery."

Holzer pointed. "Over there," he said. "Do you know what is beyond those trees? The grave of Leni Riefenstahl. You know who she was, I presume? The director of films glorifying Hitler and the Third Reich?"

"Yes," Steve said. "*Olympia.* And *Triumph of the Will.* I've seen them."

Holzer looked at Joop. "And you?"

Joop nodded. "I've seen them, too."

"And up that way?" Holzer pointed in another direction. "Do you know who is buried there? Emmy Göring. The widow of Hermann Göring. The First Lady of the Third Reich, they called her, because she acted as Hitler's hostess at parties. Two famous women, Riefenstahl and Göring. And then, down this path?" He nodded toward a pretty little path that led to a cluster of trees and then disappeared behind them. "Someone whose name the world will never know. My first love, the love of my life, who died fighting with the Resistance against the whole lot of them, against Hitler and Göring and Riefenstahl. A mere boy."

Holzer looked over at Muhammed's grave. "The evil and the good. All together in death. And in the years and decades and centuries to come, how many people who wander among these stones will know the difference? What can you tell from a name on a grave marker? A horrible thing."

"Yes. Horrible."

"It can seem senseless. And yet we must always fight back against the evil in the world, even though it seems to come towards us in endless waves, like the sea striking tirelessly against the shore, and even though the fight takes the lives of our very best and bravest and most beautiful, and even though when it is all done the heroes end up buried alongside the villains, their graves tended with the same care and respect. You are an American, yes?"

"Yes."

"Well, then, perhaps you understand all of this already. I happen to be a great admirer of your country. America gets a lot of little things wrong, but it has tended to get the big things right. I hope you appreciate that. Many Americans don't seem to. They take their country's greatness for granted."

"You're right," Steve said. "They do."

For a moment the three of them stood there in silence.

"Well," von Holzer finally said, "despite our terrible loss, it has at least been good to speak to the two of you. Good day to you both. Take care of yourselves."

"You too, sir," Steve said.

"Good day," Joop said.

Von Holzer nodded again, and turned, and slowly walked away.

As the old man headed toward a parked limousine, Steve saw a solitary figure, in the distance, standing next to a tree. Daniel, in a dark suit and tie. Daniel noticed Steve noticing him.

Steve nodded almost imperceptibly. Daniel nodded back.

O N THE PLANE THAT AFTERNOON, Joop asked Steve, "So...how do you feel about going back to Amsterdam now?"

"Well," Steve said, "I look forward to living with you."

"I do too. But Amsterdam itself? How do you feel about it now?"

"I don't know. Hard to say. Maybe a little bit gypped."

"Gypped?"

"Deceived. You know. The city was just so – I don't know..."

"So cute."

"Funny. I never thought of it that way. I would have said glorious. Majestic. I thought Amsterdam was a place that somebody should write a symphony about. Or an immortal poem. But I guess that's what it all came down to. As you say, it was cute. Like living in Disneyland. All façades. All fake."

"Well," Joop said, "I wouldn't say fake. Amsterdam has always been totally real to me. But then I never saw it as a Fantasyland to begin with. It's just a place, like any other. Prettier than most, but just a place. It's where I live. It's as real to me as – as Los Angeles is to you."

"Well, that makes sense."

"Of course it does. Do you know how many Europeans are taken in by the mystique of Hollywood? Or New York, the Big Apple? If you can make it there, you can make it anywhere? Have you read about the Japanese tourists who collapse when they visit Paris, because it's not everything they expected? Well, you did the same thing with Amsterdam. You got sucked in. And you never imagined there could be a – a serpent in your Paradise."

"No, I guess not," Steve said.

"Do you want another drink?" Joop asked.

Steve nodded. Joop buzzed the flight attendant. She came. He asked for two more vodkas with orange juice. She nodded and went back up the aisle.

"By the way," Steve said. "Speaking of New York. Schrama has invited us to go there with him."

"Really? When?"

"Late this summer. He's giving a talk about Islam in Europe. He's going to spend a week there, doing media interviews, meeting other politicians – that sort of thing. He says he'll put us up, all expenses paid. Big fancy hotel. You want to go?"

"When is it?"

"In September. His talk is on the Tuesday. I think the date is the eleventh."

"Why not?"

"Good. I'll let him know. I only – "

"What?"

"I only wish Muhammed could be there with us."

Joop took Steve's hand in his. "I do too," he said.

Steve looked at him with a pensive smile. And they leaned back in their seats as the plane took them home.

Made in the USA
San Bernardino, CA
13 August 2018